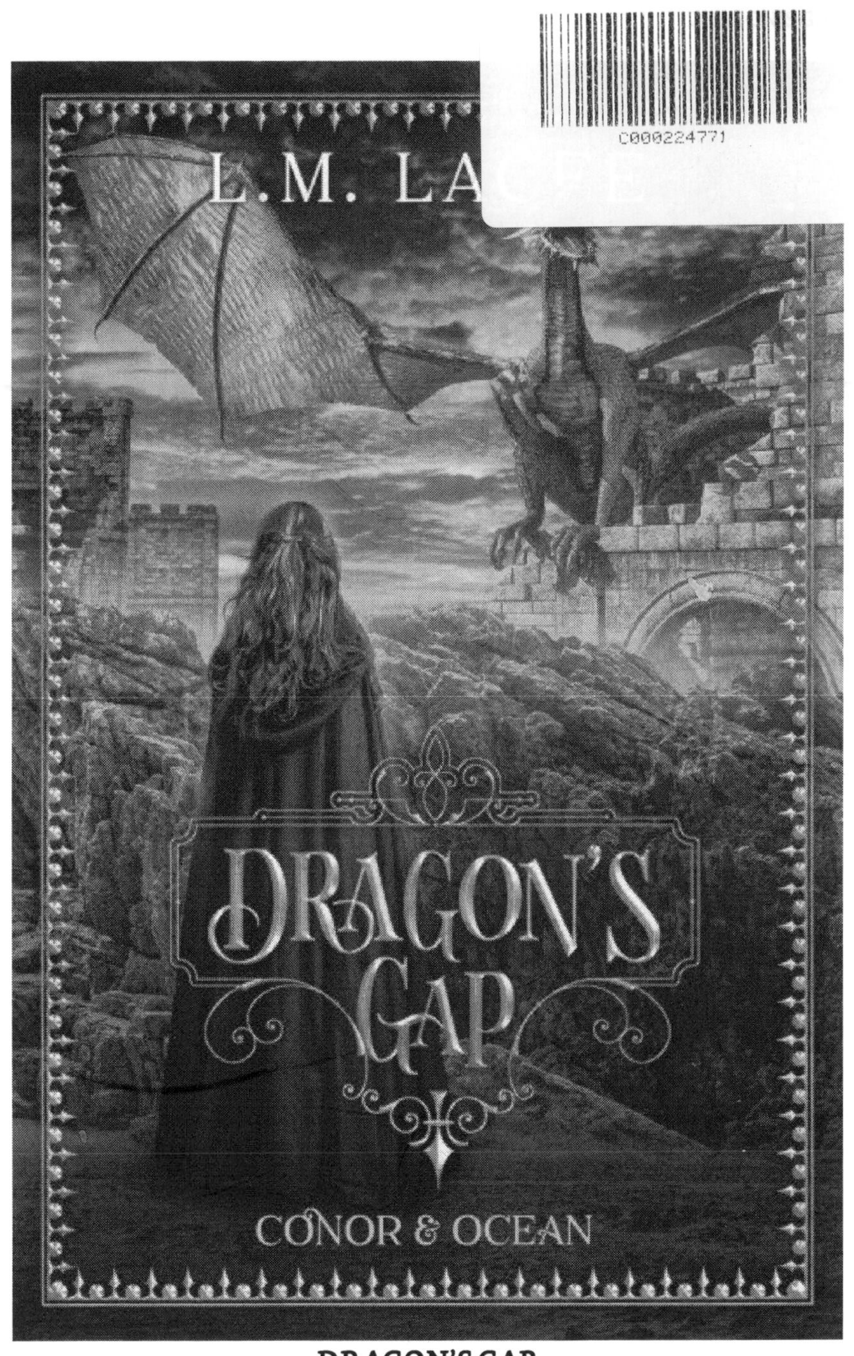

DRAGON'S GAP
Conor and Ocean's Story.

By L. M. Lacee

OTHER BOOKS IN THE DRAGON'S GAP SERIES

Reighn & Sage's Story
Sharm &Edith
Love's Catalyst
Storm & Charlie
Ash & Olinda
Ace & Harper
Conor & Ocean

Visit my website at LMLacee.com for information and updates.

COPYRIGHT

Dragon's Gap Book 7

Published by PrivotelConcepts

DRAGON'S GAP SERIES

I strive along with my editor to produce error-free books. If you discover a mistake, please contact me at leonieauthor@gmail.com so I may correct it. Thank you.

ACKNOWLEDGMENTS

DEDICATION FOR DRAGON'S GAP

This is dedicated to all of you who have come to know and enjoy the many characters I had so much fun creating in my epic saga Dragon's Gap.

I thank you and hope you enjoyed these adventures as much as I enjoyed writing them.

L.M. Lacee

CONOR & OCEAN

TABLE OF CONTENTS

PROLOGUE:

Twenty years earlier!

The tall, impossibly beautiful man, dressed in clothes that cost more than she or her mother earned in a year. Walked into Sancia Kathan's shop. Instinctively, she knew she was in the presence of someone who was not from this world.

Fear held her tongue for a moment as she wondered who and what he was. Her gifts told her he was no shape shifter, nor was he a witch. All she did know was she needed to be careful?

Raw power washed over her, causing excitement to tingle over her skin and raising goose bumps along her arms. When he spoke, her eyes nearly rolled back in her head. Never, in her twenty-one years of life, had she ever met or heard someone like him. "Your shop is delightful." He told her in his musical voice.

Sancia blushed. "Thank you, but it was my mother's shop. I just took over last week."

"Your mother is not here?" He asked as he strolled around, looking at the sparkling shelves with their magical ornaments, and bunches of herbs hanging from every available space.

Sancia shook her head then realizing he was not looking at her, hurriedly explained. "No, my mother passed away two weeks ago."

He walked back to where she stood behind the old scarred wooden counter, her fingers clutching at the edge to stop them trying to touch the silver-haired male. He smiled at her, making her blush deepen, as she worried he may know how attracted to him she was. His bright blue eyes shone like the sparkling crystals her mother used to collect when they washed up on the shore. Those eyes and that smile combined to make her knees weaken as he sorrowfully told her. "I am sorry for your loss."

Sancia shrugged, she and her mother seldom agreed on anything. Mainly because as Sancia knew she was a better, more powerful witch than her mother, Maria Kathan had ever been or could have ever have been.

For years Sancia had been casting spells and making potions for people her mother turned away. By the time she turned twenty-one. She was tired of her mother's constant lectures about witches doing no wrong, or that Sancia's pride in her powers would be her downfall. So far her mother had been wrong on both counts. As she looked at the beautiful male standing on the other side of the counter from her, she knew her mother was wrong again. Beauty was not just within a body; it could shine from the surface as well.

Breathlessly, she asked. "What is it you need?"

"You are the only herb witch in this town?"

Sancia laughed lightly. "I am the only witch in this state."

"I need a potion that can fell a dragon."

Sancia stopped laughing and looked the handsome male over again as she shook her head. Her mother had drummed into her from the time she could understand. That one; dragons were real and two: no one should be foolish enough to go against the dragons.

Sancia, although she did not know why, heeded her mother's warning now. "I am sorry, I cannot help you."

The male smiled again. "I am willing to pay twenty thousand dollars."

Sancia almost swallowed her tongue, thinking he must be desperate to offer that much money. For a heartbeat, she wanted to agree. Automatically her mind started cataloging the ingredients for such a potion and how long it would take to age for potency. Then she sighed inwardly and casually stated as she drew an imaginary symbol on the wooden counter.

"That is a lot of money, but I decline."

"Fifty thousand."

Sancia felt her heart speed up again and heard her mother's warning voice in her mind. But dear Goddess, how could she refuse? That was a lot of money, she refused to look at him directly. From under her lashes, she watched him as a frown marred his forehead. Then he leaned in a little closer making her dizzy a little from his scent, she delicately sniffed but could not make out what it was. Sandalwood and something else, something sweet. Then all thought flew from her mind as he whispered. "Seventy-five thousand dollars in cash."

The amount succeeded in banishing her mother's voice from her mind. She steeled her resolve and placed her hands palms down on the wooden counter to hold herself in place as she breathed out. "One hundred thousand dollars cash only."

Then she prayed with all her might that he would say yes. "Agreed."

He smiled as Sancia remained motionless from shock at his easy acceptance. It did flirt through her mind to wonder if she could have asked for more. But with another look into those beautiful, watchful eyes, she trembled, knowing it would not be a wise move. Instead, she nodded and said. "Up front?"

"Half now and half on completion. Do we have a deal?"

Sancia sealed her fate and blocked the wails of despair from her mother and the long line of witches that came before her.

"Deal, it will be ready in five months."

CHAPTER ONE:

Present day:

Sancia walked back into her home as much as she had loved her month long vacation overseas. It was with relief she let herself into her home, she could not wait to sleep in her own bed. She had never been so tired, the trip home had taken her three long tiring days; she did not even stop to unpack, just dumped her bags in the lounge of her house and grabbed a quick shower then dropped onto her nice comfortable bed. She was asleep just as the sun began to set.

Sancia woke as her feet touched the wet grass of her backyard and found herself in her nightgown, bathed in moonlight. A voice filled the moonlit backyard and covered Sancia in fear, causing her heart to pound and her body to break out in sweat.

Little witch, do you know what day it is?

Sancia closed her eyes and dropped her head on to her chest. Of course she did, it was twenty years to the day that she had given the beautiful stranger, the small brown bottle of potion. Over the years she had almost convinced herself it had all been a dream. The male, the potion, the dragons.

She raised her head as she felt someone arrive in front of her and found herself looking up at a tall hooded male and into the face of her demise. Sancia knew her mother's warnings were finally coming true, in truth her fate had been sealed the minute she had accepted the commission to make the potion.

She looked into the eyes of the male standing before her and saw swirling universes and knew she saw them because the being before her allowed it.

Little witch, why did you make the potion to fell the dragon?

Who are you?

Oh little witch, you know who I am.

An Elemental?

Little witch, why did you make the potion to kill the dragon?

It was a lot of money, more than I had ever seen before.

So you went against your teachings and forfeited your life... for money?

Weeping Sancia nodded. *I did. I was young and stupid. I am sorry.*

Are you? What have you done to repent since then?

I have spent the last twenty years helping people, following my mothers and her mother's teachings. I give away as much as I earn.

The Elemental nodded, and the voice was softer than before when he asked. *I see, and you think this makes up for the poisoning of a chosen one?*

Sancia sighed and shook her head. She had learned a lot about the dragons over the last twenty years and knew they were chosen by the Goddess. *No... no... nothing will. I am sorry... did the dragon die?*

No, he survived by the will of his ancestors.

Oh, thank the Goddess. Sancia clasped her hands to her chest as she breathed out. Her biggest fear was the dragons would trace the potion to her, if the dragon died.

You are relieved, and yet you should not be. The potion or a variation of your potion has been used many times to try to take the lives of others.

I did not know that. I am so very sorry.

Do you know why I am here?

To take my life?

Little witch, what would that teach you?

Sancia shrugged. *I suppose not much, really.*

No. I have a better solution. So let us make a deal, your life for servitude.

Oh... oh, I never thought of that?

I am sure you did not.

With her heart screaming in pain for what she was about to commit to, Sancia whispered. *What must I do?*

Serve the people and shifted of your world until we feel you have atoned for your crimes.

What if I do not?

The voice became sharp and hard. *Little witch, does your life mean so very little to you?*

No... no, it does not. Sancia asked again in a small, timid voice. *What must I do?*

A notebook appeared in her hands. *Fill this and when it is completed your debt is repaid.*

She flipped the book open as her heart sank when she saw all the pages. But relief in having her life made her lift her head and say. *Thank you, Elemental.*

Go in peace. We will talk again, little witch.

As she turned to walk back into the house, she heard her mother's voice telling her. *My daughter, be thankful for your life. Your pride is what caused you to become beholden to the Elementals.*

I know mother... I know!

CHAPTER TWO:

The girl whispered. "Are you sure we are doing the right thing?"

The boy whispered back. "I don't want it, do you?"

She frantically shook her head. "No, I don't, my dad will kill me. What about yours?"

"I don't have a dad remember, but my mom would kill you and me."

She softly cried, making sure not to raise her voice as she moaned. "Shit, I just want this to all go away."

The boy sighed and nodded. "Me too. Okay, so I'm gonna wrap it up in the blanket and get rid of it." He grimaced at the smell as he began wrapping the bundle up.

The girl whimpered. "Yeah, okay. Hurry so I don't have to look at it."

Standing he said. "Alright, did you take the medicine the witch gave you?"

"No... I am scared, what is in it, what did she say again?"

He sighed dramatically as only a teenage boy can. "Damn Trudy, you are a pain, just take the medicine, she said if you do, it will be like it never happened."

"Are you sure?"

"Shit Trudy, why do you have to make a big deal over everything?"

Pouting like the teenage girl she was, she whined. "Like this is my fault, you asshole, if you..."

"Aww, shut the hell up and drink the stupid medicine. I am gonna dump this and then I am going home."

"What about me, Robbie? Come on, Robbie. I am sorry." Trudy cried as tears ran down her face and splashed on to her hand that was holding the small brown bottle of clear liquid.

Robbie turned and walked away, the bundle in his hands. Trudy was scared to drink the contents of the small bottle, the other medicine the witch had given her yesterday had tasted funny and made her feel all light-headed, and her body had felt strange all night. But thinking of her father and his anger, if he should ever find out what she and Robbie had done and who Robbie was… he would go ballistic if he found out her sweet Robbie was a shifter. In the end, it amounted to her fear of her father being far greater than her fear of what was in the small bottle and the weird taste of the witches' medicine.

When Robbie didn't turn back around, she gulped the liquid in the bottle and seconds later felt a soft warmth steal over her.

Robbie walked around the corner, he held the bundle in arms that trembled with fear but he knew he was doing the right thing. It was the only thing he could do, no matter how wrong it was. Trudy was human, and he was a lion, his mother and her father would not care they were in love. Pure blood lines were all that his mother cared about now, she said they were safe from the sentence handed down by the Goddess. He was not so sure she was right. His friend Micky who was a wolf left yesterday for some place far away because his father said they were not safe from the sentence. Robbie was too young to disobey his mother and run away with Trudy. So he never questioned her belief, she said they were safe, so he had no choice but to believe her.

He shook at the thought of what she would do if she found out he and Trudy had been together. And as for Trudy's father, his heart beat a quick tattoo, and his body shook harder with renewed fear at the thought of the ex-marine. He may be human, but he was scary and he hated shifters. Trudy told him he often said that a good shifter was a dead shifter.

Trudy lay back as the warmth invaded every layer of her skin, she swore she could feel bubbles in her blood. They tickled causing her to giggle but then the warmth started heading toward hot and then it zoomed right through to burning. Fire licked along the inside of her skin, centering on the lower portions of her body and zapped the scream from her throat. She curled into a ball of pain and wished Robbie would just come back, shoving her face into his sweater, hoping to smother the screams that wanted to escape, fear of who might hear made her whimpers and groans almost silent. The pain was way worse than what she had just been through she sobbed into the sweater as her sweat drenched body convulsed several times. Just when she thought she couldn't take anymore and was sure the witch had killed her for what she and Robbie had done. The heat left and finally after what felt like hours of torture, the pain subsided. She lay panting, but with each breath the evidence in her body was removed and memory started to fade.

The witch stood behind a tree, watching the teenagers, the day before, the boy had come to her, asking for a cure, something to make a terrible mistake go away. Not an uncommon request as the only resident witch in the territory, she got plenty of customers. Usually, this problem was handled very early on but for some reason they had left it until now, making the solution harder. As she told the boy, there would be no way for her to dissolve their mistake, they had waited too long, but she could make it as though it never happened. She had given him three bottles filled with three different potions. So far it looked like he had followed her directions exactly. It remained to be seen if they would follow through on them all.

Which is why she found herself standing at ten o'clock on a dark moonless night, behind a bar in the middle of nowhere, watching two stupid teenagers fix a problem. The witch flicked her fingers at the boy, taking control of his body. She veered him from the dumpster he was heading toward, to a gun metal gray four door pickup. Another flick of her fingers and the back door of the truck opened, he placed his burden on the floor and then slammed the door closed.

She gave him back control of his body and mind as he walked

toward the girl on the ground. He slipped another small bottle of clear liquid from his pocket and swallowed the contents throwing the bottle into the dumpster, not noticing the small flare of flame as it disintegrated just like the small bottle lying next to the girl named Trudy's out stretched hand disappeared. Quickly the teenage boy helped the girl up and drunkenly they staggered from behind the building.

To any observer, it would look like they had done a spot of underage drinking. By morning neither of them would remember the events of the night, and there would be no physical reminders for either of them. Magic was a wonderful tool. Her father and his mother would be unable to detect what had taken place this evening.

Sancia watched their progress, she had done all she could to ensure a positive outcome. She pulled out a small notebook, opened it to a page and placed a tick beside the sentence written there. It had been three months since that fateful night she had made the deal with the Elemental, and she had only filled three pages.

Sighing, she had to admit she may not have filled many of the pages in her notebook, but she did enjoy the added boost to her natural powers the Elementals had graced her with, even knowing they came at a price. She flipped the pages and placed a cross beside the teenager's names. They only received this kind of help once. She would not give them the same kind of assistance again. Smiling, she now had another mark in the good column of her notebook. She hoped she would be able to remove the stain from her soul. Just to make absolutely sure nothing went wrong, she stayed guarding the vehicle with its precious cargo until fifteen minutes later a woman stepped out from the bar.

She was five-foot-five with shoulder length hair, which was a deep plum color with blue highlights. The witch bet they were as natural as the color of her silver flecked lavender eyes. She had a small straight nose and bow shaped mouth, in a round face that matched her curvy body, or at least that was the image. Sancia had seen in her vision the night before.

The woman stretched her arms high into the air and rotated her body from side to side as she reached her vehicle. Only when she heard the doors unlock did Sancia breathe a sigh of relief. With a boom that sounded like thunder in the night sky, she disappeared, returning to her home to await the next time she was needed.

CHAPTER THREE:

Having consumed a great steak dinner, washed down with a strong cup of coffee. Ocean Walker felt full, happy, and most of all thrilled to be getting back on the road again. She had only stopped because she had needed gas, food, coffee and the restroom.

Now she had resolved all of those issues she was once again ready to roll. She had been thankful her navigation system had shown her there was a small rest area just off the highway. Usually, she would never enter a bar, but necessity ruled and as drunk as the patrons had been, they had still given her a wide berth. She had only been forced to growl at two or three of the men when they tried to come on to her.

She may be only half a shifter but people, drunk or sober recognized a predator in their midst. Even if she was short, and a little overweight. Being a half-shifter of some undetermined species still tended to make people wary of her. She was always careful of where she ate and slept, one never knew who and what was around.

Especially these days, when life for full and half- shifters was precarious. Ocean knew her mother had been human, but as she had never been forthcoming to who or what her father was, she knew nothing about him. Other than he was a shifter, and she was fairly sure her mother only told her that because she was forced to by law.

Ocean always suspected she was a product of a one-night stand, and her mother had been embarrassed and ashamed. Evidenced by how little she spoke about him, and now she was gone, too late to ask her who and what he was. She only had the location of where she was conceived. That was all her mother told her when she had pressed her hard at the age of sixteen for some information about her father. Hence the name Ocean.

At twenty-nine, it no longer worried her, the angst of having a father or not having a father was for the younger her. The older version realized it made no difference to her life, if she knew who he was or not. She had inherited gifts from his shifter blood that benefited her life, and for that she was grateful.

Like most shifters, Ocean had the natural aversion to smells and loud noises. So as she climbed back into her truck, and at five- foot- five it was a climb, she lowered the front windows hoping to rid her nose of the smell of fried foods and alcohol. Her ears were still ringing five miles down the road from the bars country band.

Eventually, as the miles passed under her wheels, her ears quietened and the fresh air did its job and her nose was more or less back to normal. The night was mild, so she left the windows down because the wind felt good against her warmed skin. A few more miles and the silence of the darkened highway started to play on her nerves. Her shoulder blades twitched as though something was making them itch, and she could swear she was hearing snuffling noises.

Ocean reached over to turn the radio on but her nose caught a smell, one she was familiar with, coppery with a slight tang to it. Slamming on the brakes, she skidded to the side of the road, she was now fifty miles north of the bar. Reaching into the door pocket, she took out her gun, slipped off the safety and threw herself from the vehicle.

With no small amount of trepidation and adrenaline pumping into her system she wrenched open the back door and felt her bottom jaw drop and hit the road. As her eyes widened, almost popping from their sockets. First; with disbelief and then plain out denial.

Ocean put the safety on the gun and returned it to its hiding place. Then, like any rational woman on a darkened highway, she proceeded to pace back and forth in front of the open doors. Desperately mumbling over and over. “No… no… no… No way in hell… why me?” She demanded to the heavens at the top of her voice, while she scowled up at the darkened skies, hoping and praying for an answer. When the minutes ticked by and no answer arrived. She sighed as her shoulders slumped in resignation, and she let her eyes once more drift to the bundle on the floor of her truck.

Until a small cry sounded from the blanket, making her realize there was more than just her feelings of helplessness to consider. Sending up another useless prayer, hoping she was wrong and knowing she was not. She scooped up the bundle and folded back a corner of the bloody blanket, only to find exactly what she hoped she would not. A baby!

Ocean felt the air leave her body as she stared into a very small wrinkled face of an obviously just delivered baby. The infant was covered in dried blood and other stuff; she really did not want to think about. A baby, what the hell did she know about babies?

At this point she didn’t even care what sex it was. She looked back down the darkened highway, retracing her steps and coming to the inevitable conclusion. The baby had been placed in her vehicle at the bar while she had been having a meal. Someone probably a frightened young girl had obviously given birth and then dumped… No not dumped, Ocean thought carefully wrapped and placed the baby in her vehicle hoping, she guessed that she would care for the infant. As she looked into the tiny scrunched-up face with its shock of gold fuzzy hair, Ocean hung her head in defeat, there was no going back. This baby was now her responsibility until she handed him or her off to someone who knew a hell of a lot more about babies than she did. But until then she needed to step up and give the infant a shot at making it through the night, and for that she needed help.

Wrapping the blanket more securely around the small body, she tucked the baby closer to her own body as she stepped inside her truck. Back in the driver’s seat, she closed the door, laid the baby on her lap and pulled onto the highway. Turning the heater on to keep the cab warm. She asked her navigator for the address of an all-night pharmacy and hotel. A quick glance at the baby assured her it had settled and seemed to be asleep. She really had to find out what gender he or she was, but not now.

Ocean hoped the warmth from the heater and the contact with her would keep the baby from waking. She had things to accomplish. Once she had the coordinates, she drove with fast precision for an hour until she spied the bright lights in the darkness. Pulling off the highway, she made her way to the center of the small town where the pharmacy was. She placed the baby, who thankfully was still asleep, on the floor of the cab and hopped out.

The lights of the pharmacy drew her in and with a quick look at the store map she snagged a cart and so armed headed to the baby section. Bewildered Ocean stood at the entrance to her private hell, the aisle stretched before her, every conceivable product for a baby was there. They glared at her, demanding attention, demanding she make a choice, demanding she move and purchase something. Ocean felt icy fingers of sweat slide down her spine. How and who she wondered knew what to buy.

An almost silent step behind her alerted her to the arrival of help. When a quiet voice said. "I know it is daunting, but if you like, I could help?"

Ocean turned her head and looked up into the eyes of an older woman. "Do you work here?"

Which showed, she thought, how frazzled she really was. The woman obviously did as she had on the stores green uniform. Smiling, she answered. "I sure do, sadly tonight is my last night. They are downsizing. Last on, first off." She sounded cheerful about it, and Ocean could detect no underlying sadness or worry, so she asked. "Do you have kids?"

"I sure do a boy and a girl, older now in high school their daddy works construction. I just do this for the extra money."

Feeling the time slipping away. Ocean took a breath. "Okay, I need everything for a new born from diapers to clothes to blankets. It needs to last a few days to a week."

The woman eyed her, and the desperation in Ocean's eyes must have been in her voice because her tone became soothing as she said. "That is not a problem. You would not believe how many times over the years that the unexpected has happened. So the owner has put together an early or preemie baby kit."

Ocean just nodded, like she knew what the woman was talking about, preemie. She vowed to look up the term later.

"It has everything you could want and need. The supplies will last a week, so it will give you or the new mom time to decide what is needed and what is not. There are a few extra things you will have to buy separately..."

Ocean cut her off, saying apologetically. "That sounds exactly what I need, I hate to be rude but unfortunately I am on a really tight timeline. I will take the kit and everything else you think I will need."

Smiling, the woman walked down the aisle. "Sure thing, just follow me." Then she started pulling stuff from the shelves, placing them in the cart Ocean pushed slowly behind her. She stopped looking at what the woman put in and just hummed.

Have to hurry... Have to hurry. Under her breath as the woman made her way down the aisle, ending finally with a baby bath wrapped in cellophane, she asked. "Do you care what color?"

"Um... No. The cream one will do." It was hard for Ocean to keep the edge of worry from her voice, but she didn't want to answer any more damn questions.

As nice as the woman was, it was obviously a slow night, normally she would have stayed and chattered for a while, but tonight that was not possible. The woman pulled the pale cream bath off the shelf, Ocean could see it was jammed filled with baby things, like towels, cloths and lots of bottles and jars. Ocean was sure she saw something that looked like moisturizer in among the other bottles. *Why did a baby need moisturizer?*

Eyeing it dubiously she opened her mouth to ask but a quick look at the large clock on the wall halted her tongue. Time was ticking by, the woman asked. "Do you have a car seat?"

Ocean just stared at her, she grinned. "I'll take that as a no."

Then she hurried around the corner of the aisle, picking one up, saying over her shoulder. "That should do it. We are done. If you come this way, I will ring you up?"

As they walked to the counter, Ocean spied a Moses basket. She knew what one was, she had seen a documentary, days ago about the making of them. Flipping it into the cart, she thought it would make a better bed than the baby bath, warmer too. Especially as it was complete with sheets and blankets. In minutes she had paid, loaded up the cart, thanked the woman profusely, and almost ran from the store.

Dumping everything into her back seat, she rushed around and jumped in. Taking a breath, she reached over and gently put the baby back on her lap just as he or she stirred a little. Starting the engine, she slowly backed out and drove to the motel that the navigator said was only ten minutes away.

Driving into the well-lit car park, she was glad to see it was one of the better chains, getting a room was easy. The night manager, a young man with opened text books scattered around, said he was a student and was working his way through college. He seemed nice and was very helpful, she gave him a good tip. It was late which meant he could have made her renting a room harder as she experienced in the past, and when she explained she had a baby, he offered a downstairs room and extra towels and even a crib. Which she declined, he was quick to assure her the adjacent diner opened at 6.00 am.

She placed a wake-up call for seven in the morning, hoping she would need it; and the baby would not keep her awake. She parked right outside her room taking the baby in first, she placed it in the middle of the bed, then unloaded the car of all the baby gear and one bag for her.

It was now edging toward midnight, and she still had heaps to do. First thing she did was grab her tablet and search for what to do with a newborn baby and how to bathe said baby.

Following the directions from the nurse on her tablet. She placed the baby bath on the table and filled it half full with warm water. Luckily, there was a waste bin in the room she could use. Then she read the instructions on feeding and bathing a new born and made up a small bottle of formula, warming it in the electric kettle.

Ocean got everything that the nurse said she would need ready and then turned her attention to the quiet baby. She unwrapped the blanket and found out the baby was a girl. A very tiny girl, but she had all her fingers and toes, which the nurse assured her was a good thing. Shrugging, Ocean held the baby like the nurse on the screen showed and proceeded to give her, her first bath. When she was finished, she wrapped the now slightly chilled baby in the towel and the baby promptly peed.

"Oh dear." Ocean scowled at the screen and then down at the baby. "She never said anything about you peeing. I wonder if you are meant to do that."

The baby just blinked, then opened her small mouth and made mewing noises. The longer Ocean stood there doing nothing, the louder they got. "Shit… shit!"

Ignoring the nurse on the screen. She quickly dunked the baby's bottom half into the water and washed her again. This time she dried her quickly and as she had already placed the clothes like the nurse advised on the bed, diapering and dressing her only took a minute or two. With a quick tutorial from her tablet on how to wrap a baby. It took only three tries until she got it right, and by this time the baby girl was starting to go from mewing noises to an almost cry.

Grabbing the bottle and testing it like the nurse had shown earlier, she popped the nipple in the baby's mouth when she opened her mouth to cry again, and the sucking commenced. Relief almost made her dizzy, she fed the baby as the nurse instructed, burping her half way through, and then trying to get her to have some more even though she had fallen asleep. When finally she and the baby gave up altogether, she placed the baby in the Moses basket.

It took only minutes to clean up her mess and even though the shower looked inviting, Ocean ignored it and fell into bed fully dressed. One hand on the basket, sleep swept her under in seconds.

CHAPTER FOUR:

Ocean had been awake for an hour she had showered and packed her car. After two extra bottles for the baby throughout what had been left of the night and diaper changes. She felt she had a good handle on the whole baby feeding thing, helped along by the nurse on her tablet.

Now sitting in the diner at seven thirty in the morning; with the place slowly filling up, and the sleeping baby in her pretty little Moses basket next to her. She sipped her third cup of coffee, while making inroads on the huge breakfast she had ordered, while she listened unashamedly to the whispered conversation from the booth in front of her.

"It's not like that Kadee, we have to stay. You know it is too dangerous for us to go back."

"It might not be as bad as you think Paige?"

"Yeah, Kadee it is, you know it is. You heard grandpa he never lies. He told us what to do."

"I know... I know it is just..."

Ocean could hear sniffling noises; one of the girls was crying and trying not to. The other girl was trying to be brave, but Ocean could hear and feel the fear and stunned bewilderment in her voice.

"Kadee, grandpa told us to come here. So that is what we did. Remember what else he said?"

The one named Kadee had blown her nose before she answered, her voice although still watery was stronger. "Yeah." He said. "Go to this diner and wait for the lady with the purple hair and a baby. She will take you somewhere safe."

Ocean groaned inwardly and looked up at the ceiling as though she could see the heavens. *Seriously!* She asked the universe. For the last eight months Ocean had been on the road. First she had traveled from Hawaii where she had been living for the last year and a half until her mother passed away from a heart attack.

Her mother had been forty years old when Ocean made her surprise entrance into the famous Helena Walker's reclusive life. Helena had managed with the child in her way, giving as much attention as needed to her daughter, when she remembered she had one. From the time Ocean had been old enough to understand she had known she came second if not third to her mother's art. By the time she was five, she started caring for herself, with the help from the internet and a few neighbors. By the age of ten she had discovered photography, and with a camera her mother unknowingly purchased for her. She scoured her home town capturing life in its rawest form. When she left home at seventeen, she had already decided what she wanted to do with her life. She was going to become a wild life photographer.

Sadly that never eventuated, instead she became what she termed a humanity photographer. Basically, she would tell people, she took photos of people, shifters, anyone of interest doing or not doing something interesting. By the age of twenty-four, she was successful and her photos had graced the covers of several prestigious magazines. By twenty-seven she had three worldwide showings of her work to acclaim.

In the middle of her last world photo shoot, her mother was struck down with a stroke. She and her mother over the years stayed in infrequent contact and that was usually only when Ocean reached out to Helena. On hearing of her mother's stroke Ocean immediately cancelled her tour and flew to her mother's side. Tragically it was not a happy reunion, in truth it had been an arduous and thankless time of her life, looking after a woman who resented her and wishing it had been different for them both. In the two years she nursed her mother Ocean watched her wither away. Although Helena could talk, she sadly never recovered her ability to paint, or to lift a brush or pencil to sketch. It was heart-breaking for not only Helena but Ocean.

Unfortunately, being the woman she was, Helena took the failure of her body out on Ocean. Her life was her art, and she made sure Ocean knew that without her art, there was nothing left of value to her. She cursed her constantly as she cared for her, and when she was not doing that, she would tell Ocean on an almost hourly basis that she failed her miserably, that she would never be enough to hold her to the world. She made her aware her art was her only point to existence, the only reason she had existed, nothing or no one else mattered, least of all her untalented daughter.

Helena Walker could not abide the thought of never being able to create again, she willed her life to end on a daily basis almost as often as she begged Ocean to end her life for her. And when she refused, Helena would condemn Ocean to hours of verbal abuse, screaming and cussing, demanding she leave her alone. Then screaming if she followed her orders.

One night, almost two years after she had taken over the care of her mother. Ocean looked at the frail body of the woman who barely resembled the person she had grown up with. Tired and dispirited after days of little sleep she was unable to bear the bitter, angry woman her mother was and as she dressed Helena in her favorite nightwear, she kissed the wrinkled cheek and stared into the cold bitter eyes and told her to leave.

"Mother you should just let go. The afterlife may give you what you cannot get here. What I cannot give you, go... why linger, it cannot be for yourself or to just torment me?"

Helena snarled and lifted her lip at her daughter. Ocean straightened her blankets ignoring the sneer on her mother's face and shrugged as she stood looking down at her.

"Consider me tormented. I know I am less than what you wanted, staying to remind me of the failure you say I am, hurts you far more than me." She looked into the eyes filled with hate and smiled, whispering. "Because one day very soon, I will walk out that door and leave for good, and you will still be here consumed with hate and bitterness. So think about that, while you decide why you are still here. Because I don't care what you think about me." At Helena's look of disbelief, she shrugged again. "Believe me or not, I really don't give a damn."

Helena said nothing as Ocean turned from her and walked from the room. However she could not stop the tears falling as she left the only woman she had known as a mother alone, to decide if the life she had now, was better than the afterlife she always spoke of.

Minutes later sitting in a rocking chair on her mother's small deck attached to her home, as she had done from the time she was little. Ocean hoped Helena found peace somewhere other than in her hatred of her. In the early hours of the next morning, two years to the day of her first stroke, Helena Walker passed from this world. Never once telling her daughter she loved her or was proud of the person she had become.

Days after the large well-attended funeral, while dealing with her mother's possessions Ocean found in among Helena's correspondence a letter addressed to her. It was dated several years in the past as she turned it over, she saw it had been opened and resealed. Inside was an invitation to learn who she was and to find out about her parentage. It offered her a safe place to live, to work in freedom for all shifters and others not completely human, a place called Dragon's Gap.

It had taken Ocean days to come to terms with her mother's further betrayal and her anger and resentment of that betrayal. She had thrown her first and only temper tantrum it lasted days. She had stormed around Helena's home and let the tears of loss and anger flow as she ranted and raged at a dead woman. Finally accepting for the first time, that no matter what she had done with her life, she was never going to be loved by Helena Walker.

Overwhelmed by her hurt and anger as well as the implications of the letter. Ocean cleaned her mother's home from top to bottom. Anger drove her need until her body was unable to cope with the demands of her pain anymore. Finally Ocean's mind and body switched off, causing her to fall into a deep healing sleep which lasted for days. When she finally woke, she spent time working through her feelings now the first flush of anger and hurt were gone. Over the following days she found some hard won balance and finished what she needed to do for a woman who she never really knew and sadly loved deeply. Then she made plans to travel to this place that called to her soul.

After she had finished wrapping up her mother's life. She left Hawaii and decided to travel across America, visiting as many of the places she had read about or flown over as she could. She photographed people and places she never realized were in her world and enjoyed meeting and listening to people's life stories. Some were better than hers, some worse. Every one of them their own and precious for it.

As she traveled, she found it was just as well she had obtained a gun and became proficient in its use. As a photographer and a female, she had thought it would be safer if she learned to shoot properly, and unfortunately she had been forced to use her gun on occasion. Passing through small towns and driving along back highways not well travelled, was not always safe, as she found out on more than one occasion.

She had many hours to think on her journey to Dragon's Gap, and one of her realizations was she had never accepted she was different because her mother never accepted that part of her? It was never talked about or acknowledged that she was a shifter of some kind. Over the months, she discovered it was not shameful to be proud of that fact. She also acknowledged the deep well of anger that was as much a part of her as her otherness was. Now eight months later, she knew she was close to her objective Dragon's Gap, and it looked like she was to gain more than just a baby to travel with her. Life was full of surprises, or at least hers was.

Coming back to the here and now. She looked first at the sleeping baby, and then the two girls who had entered the diner, and taken the booth directly in front of hers. They both went silent except for the sound of their growling bellies.

Ocean ate two more bites of her food before the one called Kadee spoke again. She seemed resigned to their fate now.

"Okay Paige. I know you are right. I just wish, you weren't."

"Like I don't?" They both grinned at each other and then the one called Kadee looked up and noticed Ocean staring at her as she chewed her food. Shakily the girl asked. "Can I help you?"

Ocean realized the girl with her back to her was her sister and was a little older when she turned around and glared at her.

Ocean smiled and raised an eyebrow. "Couldn't help but overhear."

"Because you have no manners. Listening to other people's conversations is rude." Said the glaring Paige with a slight snarl in her voice.

Ocean grinned to herself, it appeared neither girl was a coward, they seemed tough, or at least trying to be. She knew she was going to like these two. She took another sip of her coffee, and as she placed the cup down she shrugged her shoulders. "Just thought I could tell you of a place for our kind that is safe and guarded but I see I was mistaken. Sorry didn't mean to butt in."

She placed another fork full of food in her mouth and while her eyes twinkled at them, she chewed. The two girls looked at each other and as sisters were wont to do, had a non-verbal conversation. By the time Ocean had chewed and swallowed her mouthful, they had silently gathered their bags and stood, at a nod from her; they slid into the seat opposite her and the baby.

Now looking at them, it was obvious they were sisters. They both had the tanned, Californian teenage look going on, with medium length golden hair tied in ponytails. They had the rounded faces of youth with clear skin and blue eyes that looked at her with suspicion. Over the past months with help from various shifters who had taught her how to use some of her senses in a shifter would. She knew it was possible to learn what kind of shifter was in your vicinity just by scenting the surrounding air. For Ocean it was an exercise that was more miss than hit, but she tried now and was fairly sure the girls scented as lions. She thought perhaps they were not full-bloods but for her it was hard to tell she was still not sure what markers she was meant to scent for.

While she had been looking them over, it appeared as though they had done a quick inventory of her. She saw them sniff and wrinkle their noses a little, perhaps they were as inexperienced as she was or maybe they were trying to figure out what kind of shifter she was. *Good luck!* She thought, *after all this time if I can't figure out what I am. I doubt you can.*

She did not say anything instead; she held out her hand and introduced herself. "Ocean Walker."

She shook each hand that was offered. Paige, the older one, made the introductions. "I am Paige Corrin and this is my sister Kadee."

Ocean asked. "You hungry?"

At their nods she motioned the waitress over and told them. "Order what you want."

The younger one kept a frown on her face as she said. "Are you sure, we can eat a lot?"

"Aren't you adorable? Yeah, I am sure, we metabolize food fast, so order plenty. We have a long drive ahead of us."

Both girls looked slightly puzzled as she spoke. Paige opened her mouth to ask a question, but Ocean made a negative move with her finger as the waitress rolled on up to their table. She was a worn woman in her mid-fifties who concealed a good heart behind the gruff exterior she showed the world. Which she proved when she eyed Ocean and the girls suspiciously and asked. "You girls alright?"

The older of the two girls answered for them both. "Yes, thank you, we were a little concerned when we first got here, but not now."

The waitress turned her hard eyes onto Ocean. "You know these girls?"

Ocean smiled. "Not really, but they are going in the same direction as me and the least I can do is make sure they arrive at their destination safely."

The waitress said nothing. Connie had seen many people,

some good, and some bad pass through the diner in her thirty years of being a waitress here at her brother's place. She could spot a bad person as soon as they sat down, they had a sense about them. This one with the baby she was a good one, not a fool. If these girls were thinking to put one over on her, they would be in for a surprise, and if she said she was going to look after them, she meant it. She kept her thoughts to herself and pulled her pencil from behind her ear asking. "What are you having?"

The girls with one swift look at Ocean, who gave them a small nod, ordered enough food to feed at least four teenaged boys. Ocean had to give it to the waitress she never batted an eyelash at the amount of food they asked for. She just asked Ocean if she wanted a refill on her coffee and stepped away.

The girls fell silent, hands gripped each other under the table. Kadee wasn't sure if it was her or Paige who was shaking so much. She had been really afraid all night and this morning but less now after meeting this woman. She hoped she could do what she said but she was so small and round. She wasn't old like grandpa, and he hadn't been able to keep them safe. Well, that was what he had said. *I can't keep you safe girls. You must leave.*

He had helped them pack a large backpack each, with clothes and shoes and as many momentous and photos as they could jam in. Then he had driven them to the bus depot in the next town and told them to stay on the bus until morning. They would come to this small town called Paxton Point, then they were to get off the bus and go into the diner at the motel. Kadee was tired, hungry and sad, she tried not to be, but every time she closed her eyes she saw her grandpa watching the bus leave with tears rolling down his face. She wanted to scream and cry, but she couldn't because Paige was being so brave, and she had to be as well, but it wasn't fair. It just wasn't fair!

She looked into the calm lavender eyes of the woman with the cool name Ocean and the even cooler hair. *Who named their kid that, she wondered and why did she have that color hair.* Something inside her said that she and Paige were going to be okay.

Paige wasn't having the same thoughts, even though she was older than Kadee she was not brave. She was really scared and knew things Kadee didn't, about the reason they had to leave in the middle of the night. And every time she remembered her grandpa's whispered words, she broke out in a sweat. Fear had eaten at her insides all through the long bus ride. Ever since she had kissed him goodbye, she knew she was never going to see him again. No matter what he told Kadee, their grandpa was gone, and they were alone. She looked at the short woman and wondered, were they really alone now? The woman had a weird name and weirder hair. *She would not admit she liked either.* Her eyes clashed with Oceans and knew she could see the suspicion and fear in her eyes. What she read in Oceans was calmness and acceptance. It baffled Paige, *what did she have to accept?*

As the silence went on Ocean was reluctant to break it in the diner. So while they waited for their food, Ocean finished her meal and sipped at the remaining coffee in her cup.

Finally, Paige asked. "Should we tell you why we are here?"

Ocean shrugged. "You can if you like, but I would rather you waited until we are in the car." She leaned a little over the table and whispered. "Too many ears here."

With a look around the diner to emphasize her point, at least three people were taking covert looks at their table. The girls looked where she did and sort of shimmied down in their seats. The scent of fear wafted across the table, making Ocean realize they were younger than she had first thought. She had assumed because they were by themselves they were at least in their late teens, but now as she went back over the conversation she had overheard she realized her mistake. Plus the fearful looks they kept throwing toward the men at the counter who had being eyeing them since they had entered the diner sort of confirmed it.

Soothingly she asked Paige. "How old are you and Kadee?"

Paige mumbled, but it was clear to Ocean's ears. "I'm thirteen almost fourteen and Kadee is twelve. Why?"

Ocean made a flicking movement again with her finger as the

waitress came over with a large tray of food and drinks. Once she had deposited the plates and refilled Ocean's coffee, she tucked the tray expertly under one arm and braced the other on her hip. "Look I know it is not any of my business but you should know those four over there." She nodded her head back to the men at the counter. Ocean looked to where she indicated and then back at the waitress with a raised eyebrow and smiled as the waitress said. "One of them is the Fire Chief, and he's got a bee buzzing about these young ones."

Ocean had been nodding before she stopped speaking. The girls were eating as though they had never seen food before, their eyes wide with apprehension.

"Oh not a problem, if you would like. I will talk to him and Connie?"

"Yeah."

Ocean rose from her seat saying to the girls. "Finish your food but seriously slow down, you will get sore stomachs at the rate you are shoveling it in. We have time I swear. So Connie, what I was saying was thanks for looking out for the girls. If you have a minute, could you warm this up for me?"

She handed her a baby bottle, her girl was going to wake soon. So apart from getting ahead of the crying, she also elevated her standing in the eyes of Connie, who smiled. Her suspicion that the woman was one of the good ones was confirmed, working on the belief that no one with a baby was a bad person. Connie had a spring in her step as she accepted the bottle and walked over to the men at the counter who had frowns on their faces. Ocean slowly drifted toward the men and stopped close to the man with the heavy frown, deciding he would be the Fire Chief. He was the oldest one there and just had the look of command about him.

"So gentlemen, I was just telling Connie here, that I was mighty pleased, there were still people in the world, who cared about a couple of young girls. She told me of your concern but as I told her. I am going to make sure they get to where their grandpa wanted them to go. I will be sure to tell him how you were undertaking to look out for his girls."

By the time she had finished talking, all the frowns were now smoothed off their faces. It was the mention of the grandfather that turned the tide in her favor she knew. This was not Ocean's first experience with honest, hardworking country folk. When she was sure they had relaxed, she changed the subject. "Connie says you are all fine men." And didn't all their chests puff out a little at that, even the Chiefs. "She said you were Firemen?"

At their affirmative nods she asked. "Well, it seems I have a need. I was told by the lady at the store that I needed to have one of you gentlemen install the carrier I just brought for my baby girl. Apparently it has to be done right and believe me, I looked at it. I cannot make head nor tail on how it is meant to be done."

The Chief nodded to the young man at the end of the four stools. "Jerry there, will get that installed for you, iffen you'd like to go with him. He is the best at carriers and baby seats for youngins."

The young man turned a shade redder than he had been at the praise from his chief. He puffed his chest out a little more and stood quickly from his stool. Ocean smiled kindly at him.

"Well, that would be wonderful. Now if I could prevail on you gentlemen to keep an eye on my girls there, while I show Jerry the car."

"You go on Misses; we will make sure your youngins isn't bothered." The Chief told her as the other men nodded their agreement with the statement. Ocean had no problems about leaving the diner with a quick word to the girls, she swiftly left with Jerry and was charmed when he opened the door for her.

When she showed him her truck and the carrier he gave her a quick lesson on how to place the baby in it. Then urged her to go inside out of the cold wind, promising to have it completed in a few minutes. She left him to it and raced back inside slipping back into her seat with a small wave to the men.

Just as Connie brought the warmed bottle over, the baby started to stir. When Connie made to move off, Ocean halted her with. "Girls please tell Connie what flavored milk shakes you like?" Then she said to Connie. "Could you please make them large and to go, also could I have a large coffee to go as well?

The girls politely gave their preferences all the while watching Ocean remove the tiny bundle from the basket. She moved the blanket from the baby's face and looked up to find three sets of eyes on her and the baby.

Connie drew in a sharp breath as she said. "That babe is only hours old and you Missy, don't look like you just gave birth?" At her tone the girls stopped eating the last of their food. Their eyes swinging from Connie's to Ocean, finally stopping on the baby.

Ocean smiled and answered. "I did not. Nevertheless, she is mine. Her Mama could not take care of her. I guess that is what happens when you are a child yourself." She raised her eyebrows at the glowering woman before her and watched as her expression morphed into sad acceptance.

"I suppose it is, babies having babies, what is the world coming too?"

Ocean hummed as she shook her head in agreement her eyes sad too. Connie nodded her head, thinking her assumption that this woman was a good one was proved again without a doubt. Not many would take on an infant that was not theirs. She turned and wandered behind the counter refilling cups as she went. Both girls stared opened mouthed at Ocean. Paige said. "Wow, I thought she was going to call the police."

Kadee nodded. "Me too, that was scary shit."

"Language." Ocean murmured. "I had it handled. Now, I don't want to nag. Especially as I said we had time but now as the little one here has woken, we have two maybe three hours before she wakes again. I don't know about you two but I think we have spent enough time here."

Just as they both agreed. Jerry came back in and said. "It is all finished Ma'am."

"How much do I owe you, Jerry?"

The young man gulped as he looked at the two girls who were staring at him as he slowly went redder than he had been when he had approached her. "Oh no, Ma'am, no charge it was my pleasure."

"Why thank you Jerry, my daughter and I really appreciate it. I know I will feel good knowing she is safe in her carrier now."

He really was a sweet boy Ocean thought as he nodded a few times and backed away, words had finally deserted him it seemed. The girls ducked their heads as soft giggles escaped from them both. Ocean's voice was stern and filled with a warning as she scolded. "Laugh, and I will be very angry. That young man did me a very big favor, and you will not belittle him or me with your childish behavior." She heard their audible swallows and could scent the trace of fear at her words and tone, their yes Ma'am, was respectful. Quietly they finished their drinks shooting worried glances toward her as she fed the baby.

Ocean let them stew for a few minutes and then in a completely different tone of voice, which radiated happiness, she said with her eyes on the baby as she drank her bottle.

"When we are finished here, we will be going. So if you guys need to use the restroom, do so now, because we aren't stopping for another two hours."

The girls giggled in relief at her relaxed tone and scampered from the booth toward the restroom. Ocean looked at her baby and shook her head mumbling under her breath. "That's right Ocean, whether you want one or not, you have yourself a family. Two almost teenagers and a baby, not even a full day old." Sighing she continued on her quiet rant. "Yeah cause giving this baby up would be so easy and getting rid of those sweet wounded girls would be a joy. Face it Ocean, it isn't happening, you are a mom, accept it and move on."

She almost giggled herself, at her thoughts, although her next ones wiped the smile from her mind. *I guess I can say goodbye to finding a husband. Not that I had much luck in that, anyway. Men do not like short, chunky women, especially when they have anger issues.*

As she looked down at the baby, there was no denying the feelings she had for the babe in her arms, she whispered. "Sorry little one, no daddy. I will just have to be enough for you and your new sisters."

The baby blinked at her twice, which Ocean was coming to realize was all she would commit to as far as talking went. She placed the baby on her shoulder and rubbed her back as she grinned and whispered out the side of her mouth, "Smart girl!"

By the time the girls were back, Ocean had finished feeding the baby and done a quick diaper change. While the girls retrieved their backpacks, she lifted the basket and diaper bag walked over to the checkout, nodded to the men and left two, one hundred-dollar bills by the till, asking a stunned Connie. "This should cover ours and the men's breakfast, yes?"

At her nod she continued. "Please keep the change and thank you for your help."

With that, she indicated the girls to follow her and was pleased to hear them politely thank Connie for her service, as they grabbed up their shakes and her coffee. Then they both threw Jerry a smile as they left and kindly looked away before his face caught fire again. She was proud of them as if they were her own, and when they glanced her way, she let them see she was. Their smiles grew wider, they may be wary of her but they sought her approval. It was a start.

The air was chilly, snow was on the horizon, Jerry had said earlier. Ocean believed him as she hurried to her truck unlocking it by remote before she got there. She saw the newly installed baby carrier, and placed the baby inside and did up the straps, according to the instructions Jerry had given her. She snuggled the baby with a blanket and closed the door shutting out the cold. The girls stood shivering in their jeans and teeshirts. "Do you girls have anything warmer?"

"We could have. Grandpa packed most of this for us." Kadee told her.

Paige answered. "We haven't looked yet?"

Ocean nodded a story for later, right now she needed to get on the road. Clothes they could do later, the heater in her truck was good enough.

“Okay.” She said as she opened the tail gate and placed the basket in. “Girls put your bags in here until later, and then figure who goes where and jump in, it’s cold.”

Shivering and goose bumped they shoved their bags in the bed of the truck. Paige opened the passenger door and scowled at Kadee when she complained. A hurried conversation in whispers that Ocean plainly heard, these girls had not mixed with shifters enough or at all, so did not know shifters, even half shifters had hearing as good as bats. Ocean decided to keep that gem under her hat for now as she listened to the quick fire exchange and frowned.

“I want to sit in front.” Kadee grumbled.

Paige hissed. “No, listen we don’t know anything about her. So I will sit in front and you be ready to jump if we have too, okay?”

“But I like her.”

“Yeah, well me too, but she is still a stranger, we have to be on guard.”

“Are you going to tell her about grandpa and what he told us? Because she has a baby and a strange name and purple hair.”

Paige didn’t answer her; Kadee grabbed her sister’s arm and shook it. “And the letter Paige you have to give her the letter.” Their grandpa had slipped the letter in the pocket of Paige’s jeans telling her to give it to the woman with the baby and the unusual name. He told them she would have purple hair, and she would be at the diner but Paige was hesitant to do it. What if Ocean was the wrong lady, what then? Paige said nothing just stared ahead at the open door. Kadee unhappily started to walk around to the back door as she passed Paige she said. “You better give it to her Paige.”

Paige jumped into the truck. “Yeah… Yeah.”

With both girls in, Ocean shut the tail gate and leaned on the metal, Interesting!

Life took many turns and here was another one. Paige and Kadee were young, too young to be on their own, making adult decisions that was what Ocean was for. Trust would come in time but if it had not developed before they reached their destination she would force the issue. She hoped she wouldn't have to. Wind whipped around her, reminding her she had no time to waste. Moving swiftly she jumped in her seat and turned the key. The heater blazed before they had even driven from the car park. It was eight thirty in the morning. They still had a long way to go before nightfall. As well as baby breaks and food stops to contend with. Road trips Ocean decided were never what you expected.

Out the corner of her eye, she watched the sisters ignore each other. She would give them until the next baby stop, then they would have words. She grimaced inwardly, *fun times.*

Paige stared out the side window. They had been driving for about an hour already, she looked back at Kadee and saw she had fallen asleep, she cleared her throat and blurted out.

"Our grandpa, he said we had to go to that town and wait for a lady with a weird name and purple hair and she would have a baby. He said she would look after us. Is that you?"

Ocean smiled. "Well let's see I was in a small town, and I have a weird name. I like to call my hair color plum not purple and I have a baby. So I am guessing your grandpa was physic or something, because it sure sounds like me."

"He wasn't physic, he was really afraid, and he said he had a vision, the Goddess told him to get us out of town."

"Yeah, I have heard of that happening." She looked over at the young girl. "He wasn't crazy you know. There are Goddesses and they are real, they are for our kind apparently, shifters and half shifters."

"Have you met one?"

"Nope, but I have met people who have."

Paige said softly. "So grandpa was right, we are shifters?"

"Well, I think you are half shifters."

"What kind?" She asked eagerly.

Ocean could see she was intrigued with the idea. "I would guess, but I am not very good at knowing things like that. I would say lion."

"Oh, yeah, that makes sense."

"Paige sweetie, your grandfather was scared and I am guessing he knew he couldn't protect you or Kadee. He was a really brave man, to love you so much, to trust you as he did. He let you go hoping you would stay safe until I arrived. A very special man just like his granddaughters."

Paige sniffed. "Yeah, he was. I loved him heaps. I will miss him." She started crying, soft sounds of heartache filled the car; Ocean let her have the time to get the tears out knowing there would be more. After a few minutes Paige sniffed and wiped her face on the tissues Ocean handed her. "Thanks."

"No problem. Tell me what your grandfather told you about why you had to leave?"

"He said we were shifters and that our dad was a lion and our mom was a half lion. Our grandmother was a full lion and that some bad people were coming to get us for their breeding program. He gave me a letter for you, telling you all about them and he hoped you would stop them. Can you?"

Ocean shook her head. "I cannot by myself, but I hope where we are going there may be people who will know who can do so. Or will be able to themselves. Should we look for your grandfather?"

Paige said sadly. "No."

Ocean was sure she heard the girl's heart breaking as she said. "No, our granddad, said once we were gone he would go to join grandma. She died a long time ago same as our momma and daddy and he missed her. He said he had waited to deliver us, as he promised the Goddess he would. Now it was his turn to find grandma." She paused for a minute then asked softly. "Do you think he will find her?"

Ocean sighed. "I do... I really do, he was a good honest man. Who raised you alone and did a good job. He kept his promises. I would think a Goddess would reward a person like that."

"Yeah." Said a small voice from the back, Kadee whispered. "I am going to believe he is with grandma and momma and daddy, because I don't want to think of him all alone. Is that okay

Paige?"

"Yeah Kadee, it is. We will believe that."

"I like that idea too." Ocean told them both.

Kadee murmured. "I am going to miss grandpa. I loved him a lot." Paige pushed her hand back, and the girls held hands as Kadee cried her own tears. Ocean drove and said nothing, letting them grieve for a very special man they had loved. A few miles were traveled in silence apart from sniffles and quiet words between the two girls. Eventually, Paige passed Kadee her milkshake and turned back around. The first round of grief was finished, there would be more Ocean knew but for now they seemed to have taken the edge off.

Paige asked Ocean. "You are a shifter too, what are you?"

"Good question, I don't know, I have never met my father, my mother would not allow me to mix with shifters or talk about what I was. So I grew up fairly ignorant, but I have known for years I was not a full human." She asked the girls. "So why did you end up living with your grandfather?"

Paige said sadly. "Our parents died in a car accident with our grandmother when we were real little. I was eight I think, and Kadee was smaller."

Ocean sighed as she said. "I am really sorry to hear that."

Now she knew why they had not known they were lions, it would seem their parents probably thought they had time to tell them, sadly they were wrong. Poor granddad, so much grief, so much pain. Ocean felt for the man, two little girls to raise all by himself and just marking time until he could go join his mate. She shook her head. He had so many hard decisions to make, tell or not tell until sadly time ran out, and he had no choice. He had to let them go and hoped they would be safe.

Ocean hoped someone out there would tell him they were safe, that she had them. That his girls were going where the Goddess had told him they needed to be. Neither of the girls spoke again and when Ocean saw a sign for a gas station and rest stop ahead, she turned off the highway and drove to it.

Pulling up at the gas pump she and the girls got out.

While the girls searched for sweaters in their backpacks, Ocean stretched the kinks out of her body as she scanned the area. Everything looked okay, several cars sat in the parking lot adjacent to the gas station, which appeared empty. Once dressed the girls came to her, and she sent them inside the station's café to purchase gas and food. She knew they were hungry again, so she gave them instructions to get food and coffee for her.

She handed the money over to Paige saying. "I need the letter Paige. I need to make sure your grandfather's information reaches the right people."

As her hand automatically sort for the letter in her back pocket, she asked with a trace of fear in her young voice. "How do you know who the right people are?"

"I just know. Where we are going, I believe there will be people, who stop people like the ones that wanted you and Kadee."

Paige bit her bottom lip and sighed. "Maybe he was wrong, maybe he sent us away for no reason. He was old."

Ocean smiled. "He was old and loved you and Kadee, and he believed the Goddess when she told him to send you away. He was not wrong."

Paige hung her head, and Ocean let her think on it. Finally, she withdrew the letter and handed it to her with tears in her eyes. "It is all I have of him."

Ocean took the letter and cupped the young girl's cheek. "No sweet girl, you and Kadee, have much more than this one bit of paper. You have all the love and memories in your heart and soul of him. He loved you and taught you to love, that is a fine legacy to leave behind." She kissed her forehead and hugged the teenager as the other flung her arms around them both saying. "Yeah Paige, he loved us heaps."

Ocean hugged them both then released them. "Now think about this, with this piece of paper. You and your grandfather will stop any more young girls, having to leave their homes, in the middle of the night. You are all heroes. So girls what do we do now?"

At their puzzled looks she said. "I am guessing you and Kadee want to stay with me?"

The girls sniffled back their tears and grinned, Paige said. "Yeah, can we? Grandpa wanted this, said you were the one for us."

"And maybe." Kadee said. "You could maybe, teach us about shifters and lions, maybe?"

Ocean grinned. "Yeah, I can do that or at least find someone who will. So go get food and coffee and I will feed little miss here, while you are gone."

Paige asked. "Does she not have a name?"

"Not yet."

Kadee asked. "Is there a reason for that?"

"Yep, I haven't found one for her yet."

Kadee asked. "Oh okay, will you tell us how you got her?"

"Yep, when we get rolling again."

They turned to walk away, lighter in their steps, Ocean said. "Stick together and go to the bathroom, no more stops for a while."

Both girls turned around and walked backward, calling out. "Yes Ma'am." Then turned and raced into the gas shop. A few minutes later a young woman emerged and came over to her.

"The girls said you needed gas?"

"Yes please, fill her up." Ocean requested as she picked up the baby and took her to the passenger seat and started her on her bottle. "Cute baby."

"Thank you."

A woman came nearer and Ocean could scent some type of cat. She hoped she was right; it would mean she was getting better. *Huh practice!*

"Morning, how are you?" The woman asked, she was older than Ocean, maybe forty, forty-five years old. A few more lines on her face, work-roughened hands, she had a nice face to photograph. "Fine thank you and you?"

"Good, those your girls in there?" She pointed toward where the girls had gone. Careful now, Ocean kept one eye on the baby and the other on the woman who was leaning against her car in a semi-relaxed pose. "Yes, are they alright?"

"Yes, flirting with my boys, seem to be enjoying themselves."

The young woman finished and Ocean thanked her before she walked back into the shop. When she was out of sight the woman straightened and asked Ocean in a voice laced with tension. "Are you going to Dragon's Gap?"

Ocean smiled as she raised the baby to her shoulder. "We are. You?"

The woman stuck her hand out. Ocean took the offered hand and shook. "Yes, we are, my name is Ruth."

"Hi, I am Ocean."

Ruth said. "My boys and I are Jaguar and we are with a few others, we got here but we sort of ran out of luck. It almost seems like we were waiting and then you and your girls showed up, and it just feels right somehow."

Ocean said. "Seems like this is the day for strange and exotic things to be happening."

The woman called Ruth gave her a confused look, Ocean grinned. "Don't mind me. Strange things have been happening to me lately, so I will put this down as another one. I know where to go from here. Would you like to follow us?"

Ruth sighed her relief. "That sounds great, we have three cars all together."

Ocean smiled and finished up feeding the baby. "It is still a drive, unfortunately, I have to stop for this one, but if we time it right, one of those stops could be for lunch. We should still get there by late afternoon. Not to be rude but do you all have money for food and gas?"

Ruth grinned. "Oh sure, more than enough."

"Oh good. So Ruth how did you know?"

Ruth seemed to understand what she was asking and smiled as she asked. "New to this?"

Ocean shrugged. "In a roundabout way, still learning what a shifter can do. So short answer. Yes."

Ruth laughed. "Well your girls scent lion."

"See, I thought that too."

"You scent like something I have never come across before."

"Yeah, I get that a lot. Where are you from?"

"We all come from New Orleans. You?"

"Hawaii!"

"Well, you are a long way from home?"

Ocean nodded. "Aren't we all?"

Ruth sighed as she watched her sons leave the shop, when they saw her they waved and went to the car. "Yes, we are."

"Alright then, it seems the girls are finished flirting with your boys, so when they make their way here, we will be on the road."

They smiled at each other. "We will be ready to go." Ruth waved her thanks as she returned to her car. She pointed to the three vehicles that had been empty but were now jammed packed with kids and belongings, one of them even towed a large covered trailer. Ocean bet it was filled with household items.

She looked at their cars and then hers and realized she was grossly under-prepared for this adventure, just as well she had money. Sighing she watched the girls come out from the shop carrying drinks and bags of food. Paige said as she passed Ocean her coffee. "I paid for the gas as well, is that okay?"

She grinned. "Thanks Paige."

When they had taken their places in the car, she told them about the woman Ruth and the cars that were following them. Kadee said. "Yeah, we were talking to her sons, they said they had been here since last night waiting. You think they were waiting for us?"

"Yeah, as weird as that seems, it is what I think. So if you are all buckled up, let's hit the road."

"Yeah, because that is the only weird thing about this whole adventure." Paige muttered as she slipped her belt on.

Ocean grinned. "That's the spirit. Call it like you see it, adventure sounds good."

Both girls grinned. Ocean put the pickup in gear and headed out onto the highway for the next stage to their new home.

Dragon's Gap.

CHAPTER FIVE:

Some hours later, Ocean and the trio of cars who were following her drove down the dusty road. They came to an intersection where a young teenage girl stood by the side of the road. Ocean pulled her pickup to a stop and lowered her window.

The teenagers smile widened as she asked. "Hey, how you all doing?"

"We are fine."

"So do you have young?"

"I am guessing you mean a baby?"

"Oh sorry, yes a baby?"

Ocean smiled. "We do, she is a day old."

"Wow! She is really young. Okay, so you go left under the trees, then follow the signs."

"Thank you."

"Hi." She said to the girls who grinned in return. Kadee said. "Hi, I am Kadee and she is my sister Paige." She pointed to Paige in the front seat.

The teenager nodded, then told them. "My name is Joy, see you around."

"See yah!" The girls called back.

Ocean eased her foot back on the gas and steered the truck to the left. In her review mirror, she watched the other cars slow to a stop and talk to Joy. Then the first car rolled on, taking the left-hand road behind her.

"She was nice. I hope everyone is as nice as her." Kadee said as she looked out the windows.

"I am sure they are." Ocean murmured.

"Do you think they have schools here?" Asked a worried Paige.

"Oh sure, it is a real town with shops and everything." Ocean said and crossed her fingers she was right.

"Oh, my goodness look Kadee, it is a tunnel of trees." Paige squealed in awe.

Kadee asked, just as awed. "Oh wow, how do you think they made them do that?"

"Maybe it's magic!" Paige giggled.

Ocean was trying to keep her concentration as they passed through a barrier of some sort. It was like fingers running over her entire body, making her want to scream and laugh at the same time. She would have liked to say it hurt, but before she could decide if it was painful, they were through and she breathed out in relief.

"Are you okay?" Paige asked as she looked at Ocean and saw her hands clamped to the steering wheel.

"Yep, just the barrier was tricky."

"What barrier?"

"Oh... Oh, okay, never mind sweetie, must have been my imagination." Ocean frowned, now why had she felt a barrier and they had not.

That was something to think about later, right now her attention was on where she was driving. They drove through, or to be accurate, around a town and along a cobblestone street toward a building that looked like an old town hall. She assumed this was where they were meant to be, as several cars were lined up in front of her she noticed when she stopped the other cars were no longer following her.

A female stepped out from between the cars and Ocean heard both girls draw in their breaths as Kadee whispered in awe. "Oh Paige look, she has pink hair."

"With pink and red wings." Paige whispered back as she turned to Kadee, and both girls laughed with glee and they said together. "Wings!"

Ocean smiled when the female with wings made hand gestures indicating Ocean should take her car around behind the building. As she parked, the female floated up to their car. Ocean lowered the window but not as fast as Kadee apparently.

"Hi, what are you? Am I being rude asking? Oh my goodness you are beautiful and have really beautiful wings too."

The female smiled and answered her. It seemed a teenager was not something new for her. "No, it is not rude, depending on how you ask. I am a faerie, and it is nice to meet you and thank you. I think my wings are beautiful too. My name is Birdy and if you go through the glass doors, you will be in the center." Just then the baby murmured. Birdy looked in the window. "Oh, you have a little one. Do you need a healer?"

Ocean said they did as she got out. Birdy smiled and said. "Well go through the doors turn right, then third door on the left."

"Thank you, Birdy." Ocean said. "I am Ocean Walker these delightful girls are Paige and Kadee."

"Welcome to Dragon's Gap." The faerie greeted them as she turned to go, Ocean asked her. "Is there a hotel in town?"

"Yes, I can book you a room or two."

"Thank you, we only need one with two beds. Are you sure? I can do so myself."

Birdy smiled. "I am sure, your phones will not work here. We have our own network. The hotel is down off the main street, turn left and two streets over. It is called, The Welcome."

"Cool name." Paige said as she and Kadee got out.

Birdy smiled. "I agree. I will leave you now, if you get lost, just ask someone, they will guide you to the hotel. Oh, what name do I book it under?"

Ocean was reaching in for the carrier. "Walker, three people and a baby."

"Done, again welcome to Dragon's Gap family Walker."

"Thank you." Ocean replied. The girls waved and called out. "Goodbye."

Ocean carrier in hand smiled as she closed the door. The

faerie flew off, and the girls stood wide-eyed, looking after her. Then they looked over and saw several lions stop and stare at them, the girls moved back against the car. Ocean moved slightly in front of them and stared at the lions in return.

The lions let out several roars and ran off, the girls let out the breaths they had been holding. "Well, that was scary." Kadee said shakily.

Ocean turned to her. "Do not show them fear, even if you feel it, keep your faces calm and as still as you can, and if they move toward you, scream loudly and keep on screaming."

Paige asked. "What good will that do, they are lions?"

Ocean smiled and pointed up as several shadows were seen above them. Both girl's jaws dropped open. Paige squeaked. "Are they..."

Ocean almost giggled at their looks. "Yes dragons, they will hear and come to help you. Come on girls lets go." She moved, and they stumbled after her as they went through the glass doors, their eyes still skywards.

Ocean stood outside the wooden door and knocked. The girls stood at either side of her, she could feel them trembling.

"Girls, I swear it is okay, we are safe here. I know it is hard for you, but you have to trust me on this."

"We do trust you." Paige told her. "It is just that there are Dragons here."

"Dragons." Kadee agreed with a tinge of awe and fear in her voice.

"Why are you so surprised? It is called Dragon's Gap. You are lions. We saw a faerie and other lions and you both scented wolves when we got out of the car."

Both girls shrugged and looked at her like she had two heads. "Yeah, but that's sort of normal, kinda." Paige explained.

"But dragons are not normal." Kadee and Paige said together.

"It would depend on whose point of view you were taking." A deep voice said from above them. They both looked up and up some more. A male stood in the open doorway, he was tall, real tall and big. Both girls scrambled behind Ocean with a startled.

"Eeek!"

Ocean just kept herself from laughing as both girls, with huge eyes, stared at the giant of a male that had opened the door, while they had been questioning her.

Ocean grinned at the male. "Hello, I am looking for a healer."

Sharm grinned down at the trio. "Ahh, well, that would be me. I am Sharm Kingsley, healer and doctor. Please come in?" He opened the door wider, and Ocean and the girls walked in.

Ocean with confidence, the girls hesitantly, making sure to stay behind her. "I am Ocean Walker; these are my girls, Paige is thirteen and Kadee is twelve and this is my baby, she is almost a day old."

Sharm smiled and let a little of his energy flow from him and watched as a calmness settled over the small party of females. As they walked deeper into the medical ward, he said with a smile. "Well, that makes it all perfectly clear."

Ocean grinned. "As clear as mud, I know. So if you could look at the baby, I will explain?"

"No problem." He showed her where to place the baby and as Ocean did, a tall, beautiful, white-haired female entered the room with two little bear cubs following behind her.

"Sharm darling, Tayla and Ivan's little ones are going back to their parents, they wanted to say goodbye." She looked up from her phone, realized they were not alone, and blinked several times. Then Edith smiled and said. "Hello."

She looked at Sharm as he mind-sent to her. *My love, it seems Andre`s other daughter has arrived.*

Oh, she looks just like Ciana. So similar.

Twins are like that.

Was there tone?

Sharm bent over the carrier, a smile in his eyes for his shadows question. He unstrapped the baby, not wanting to look at Edith, knowing he would laugh out loud. Ocean and the girls both returned her greeting, then Sharm introduced her.

"This is my shadow or what you may know as mate, her name is Edith."

The two bear cubs came scrambling to the girls who had promptly sat on the floor exclaiming. "Oh my goodness, you are the cutest cubs ever." Then proceeded to have their arms filled by bear cubs who climbed all over them and made small bear noises filled with happiness, the girls were smitten.

Ocean grinned as the girls fears and suspicions melted away. She found her hand gripped in Edith's and felt her bear looking at her. "Hello, you are?"

"I am Ocean Walker. I have been traveling to Dragon's Gap for a few months now. I finally made it." She laughed gently as she looked at the girls.

Sharm said. "With a few extras it would seem."

"Destiny." Edith intoned. "Is a strange Goddess, I have learned."

"There is truth in that." Ocean agreed as the girls were occupied with the cubs, she quickly explained to Sharm and Edith how she came to be the guardian of the three girls. Once that was told, they turned their attention to the baby who lay asleep in her carrier. Sharm gently lifted her out and placed her on the examination bed. Edith placed her hand over the baby's chest. Ocean gave her a questioningly look, absently Edith answered. "I found I can tell age and species of any given person. It is a unique gift."

"I am sure it is. When you are done with her, can I ask you to tell me what I am?"

Stunned, Sharm and Edith stared at her, Sharm asked. "You do not know?"

"No, my mother was less than forth coming, don't look so appalled. I have come to terms with it. Being here has stirred the want to know up again, if you know what I mean."

"Yes, I do, this place does that. I believe it is in the air or the magic that is all over the place." Edith said cryptically.

Sharm said. "Ocean you are half dragon, your father is here as well."

"He is?" Stunned, she said nothing more, only looked at him for a few minutes then she seemed to shake herself and say. "You know, in all my imagining, I never considered either of those two things. That I could be a dragon and my father would be alive and I would meet him, here of all places. I think I am in shock."

Sharm held her hand. "Dear one, that means we are related, your father is my father's brother, we are cousins."

"Oh, now, see that is just ridiculous." She said softly. Her eyes held confusion and hope.

Edith said with a laugh. "It gets better, just wait." She would say no more but changed the subject. "I can tell you that this little girl is not quite twenty-four hours old and is a full lion."

Ocean sucked in her bottom lip. "Well, that could cause problems. Lions don't give their cubs up lightly."

Edith sighed. "Not that any shifter does, but if they knew about her, I would assume you would have seen them on your way here?"

Ocean thought on it. "Yeah, I agree. So I think that this little cub is the product of someone's bad judgment and my good fortune. She is mine now. Is there a way for that to be recorded or something? And the girls as well, who I think are also lions. I originally thought they were half, but I think I was wrong."

Both girls came to where Ocean and Edith were, Edith held her hand over each of the girls and said. "They are more lion than not, there is a little human in the mix, but remote like a generation back."

"I am guessing their grandfather." Ocean said thinking of what the girls told her of their family.

Paige agreed. "Yeah, that makes sense."

Ocean asked. "So do you think they will shift?"

Sharm asked both girls. "Have either of you shifted yet?"

Kadee shook her head. "Never, are we meant too?"

"Paige?" Ocean asked, noticing she was frowning.

"No, I haven't either."

"Why are you frowning, is something wrong? It means nothing if you have not shifted. It is okay." Ocean told her, hoping to dispel any concerns she had.

"No, it is not that, I just... Well, I am wondering if the medicine grandpa gave us to take..."

"What medicine?" Ocean asked, concerned now.

Paige took out a bottle of tablets from her pocket and passed them to Sharm, who had his hand out. He looked at the clear bottle, which had no label. He shook one out onto his palm.

Paige told him. "We have to take one every day."

He sighed. "A witch's potion. Your grandfather knew some powerful people. I have not seen this for many years."

Ocean demanded to know. "Okay, so what does it do?"

"It has the ability to stop the shift happening." He asked the girls. "Have you been taking these for many years?"

Paige nodded. "Yep, since we each turned eight."

He said. "Well, okay, so we have a choice. We can wean them off the medicine slowly over the next few months or stop them all at once."

Ocean asked. "Why the two options?"

He smiled, and Ocean was amused to see both girls flutter their eyelashes at the handsome male, although it seemed he did not notice. However, Edith did, and she rolled her eyes, making Ocean smile.

Sharm oblivious to the byplay said. "Option one; just as I said will be a slow withdrawal over weeks but they are both in their puberty years, so we have to take that into consideration. Option two; we stop the medicine and they shift within days to a week."

Ocean looked at both girls. She wanted to say stop the medicine now, but they had nowhere to live. Things were a little uncertain, the information that she had a parent alive and here at Dragons gap, sort of threw her through a loop. She needed to think about how that impacted her life as well as the girls. This was not the right time to cope with two girls shifting to their lion when she had no idea about shifting herself. She needed to get them settled, so she said. "I see, well we will decide after we have a place to live. Alright girls?"

"Yes Ocean whatever you decide." Paige agreed as Kadee nodded her agreement.

"Good." She smiled at the girls. "Thank you."

They could have made this so much harder. Edith said. "I think that is for the best. You are safe here, this is the ideal place to shift for the first time."

Sharm bent over the baby examining her and said. "My soul, call Reighn. Have him come and declare the family citizens of Dragon's Gap. That will ensure there is no way they can be claimed by anyone else."

He turned to look at Ocean and then asked the girls. "Is that what you wish? To stay here and be a family?"

Ocean held her breath. She had already accepted that the girls were hers, but to actually ask the girls was something she was going to deal with in the future. It was such a big decision for them. Kadee and Paige held each of Ocean's hands as Kadee asked. "Does that mean we get to stay with Ocean and the baby and be a family?"

Sharm nodded and said. "Yes, that is exactly what it means, but if you wish. I can and will find you another family. Plenty of couples here would love to see if you are a fit with them."

Both girls shook their heads and said together. "No thank you."

Paige explained. "We are happy, our grandfather said Ocean was the one for us, we would be safe with her and she would become our guardian."

Ocean laughed a little. "You never told me that Paige?"

She ducked her head as did Kadee. "I know, me and Kadee decided to see if you wanted us first. Grandpa said the Goddess told him to send us to you, and you would be our new mom. We wanted to make sure."

Kadee said hesitantly. "If you don't want us, we can go somewhere else."

Ocean pulled both girls into a hug. "Nope, not happening, you are mine and I am yours, we will become a family like your grandpa hoped we would. I already knew when I saw you at the diner you were mine."

Paige stared at Ocean. *So that was the reason for that look in her eyes. She already knew we were hers.* She grinned as a feeling of rightness flowed over and around her. The worry each of the girls had carried in their hearts left with a rush. Ocean was positive she could see it coming off of them in waves. Kadee said. "Do we get to call you mama, mother, mom, old lady or what?"

"Cheeky, Ocean or mom will do. You are too old to be calling me mama, and I am too young to be called mother or old lady."

They grinned, then Paige said. "Okay, can we have your last name?"

Ocean felt happy and sad at the question and asked. "What of your parents?"

Paige said. "We really don't remember them. Grandpa brought us up, but we are starting a whole new life, Kadee and I talked and we have our photos and memories, but we want to be a family to belong to you and the baby. So, can we?"

"I want nothing else, to have you as mine fills my heart with happiness. Just promise me you will always remember your parents and your grandparents. They were special people to have raised you both to be who you are. So I do not want you to forget them, ever."

"We won't, we swear." Promised both girls.

Sharm said. "Hold on, that may be premature. Ocean may want to change her last name to her fathers?"

Paige gave her a concerned look. "Oh yeah, will you?"

Ocean smiled. "I have lived this long with the name I have. So probably not. Let us just go with what we have now and figure the other stuff out later."

The girls nodded as Ocean refused to acknowledge Sharm and his shadow's concerned look. To change the subject, she asked the girls. "Now what was your grandfather's name?"

Kadee answered. "Parker, his name was Parker Collins."

"Why?" Paige asked quietly.

Ocean grinned as she gave each of the girls a final hug. Then she reached out and accepted the dressed baby from Sharm, looking down into the small angelic face with a head of golden fuzz, she said. "Because, I would like you both to meet your sister. Parker Colleen Walker."

They both clung to her, and she heard Kadee say. "Yeah, that is so cool."

Paige murmured. "He would have liked that."

Edith said with a tear in her eye. "That is so lovely, Sharm is the baby well?"

"Yes, Ocean your daughter is in good health, she is exactly how she should be for an almost day old baby cub."

Ocean grinned. "Thank goodness for that. I have no clue what I am doing, everything I know I learned from my tablet."

Edith gasped. "Ocean, that is terrible. Sharm, Reighn and Sage will be here in a moment. I will take these monsters to their parents, and we will meet up..."

Just then, Reighn and Sage entered. "Did I hear someone mention my name?" A deep male voice asked as a huge male walked in with a small woman next to him.

"Eeep!" Squealed the girls as they dived behind Ocean, then they both yelled. "Ocean!"

The cubs shifted into two naked little boys and started squealing as well. The baby came awake and proceeded to cry, or at least mew like a newborn. Sharm laughed when Ocean asked. "Does that happen a lot around him?"

Reighn held his daughter Molly in his arms, whose bottom lip started to tremble, as the younger girl the woman carried, watched the people in the room. When she saw Edith, she squealed and reached for her, as Edith took her it was obvious to see the new woman was pregnant. The male tried to quieten the little girl in his arms by saying. "Molly, do not cry, my sweet one."

Reighn turned slightly to Sage and asked. "What did I do?"

Sage shrugged her shoulders. "Nothing my love. It is just your commanding presence that startles everyone."

Reighn huffed as he cuddled Molly and tried to cajole her into a happier frame of mind. "My daughter, if you stop crying for dada. I will take you flying later."

Molly looked up at her father, and Reighn was positive he saw a calculating gleam in her eyes for a second. Then, as he looked a little harder, he realized he must have been mistaken. His darling princess was as innocent as the pure snow.

"Kay Dada." She said and leaned her head on his chest.

Sage saw the small smile through the sniffles and huffed at him. "Seriously, you are wrapped around her fingers."

Reighn smiled as he felt the warm weight of his daughter in his arms. He probably was, but no more than his shadow had him wrapped around her fingers. He was a dragon in love, who loved and was happy. There was never a better time to be him. His dragon pranced in his mind, contented with his life.

Sharm and Edith drew the girls and Ocean toward the huge male and woman. Sharm said. "Reighn and Sage this is Ocean Walker, Andre`s daughter and her daughters Paige, Kadee and Parker. They have just arrived."

Reighn said. "Hello ladies, welcome to Dragon's Gap."

They all said hello back. Reighn told Ocean. "We need to talk Ocean. I feel there are things you should know."

Ocean dipped her head. "I should imagine there are many things I need to know. Right now however, I would like to get myself and the girls settled into our hotel and then get dinner."

Paige said. "Kadee and I can look after Parker if you need to go out tonight. It might be better without us asking questions and everything."

Ocean looked at the young girl who was trying to be so helpful and smiled. "Thank you, you are very sweet."

She looked at Reighn and Sage, recognizing the power of the couple. "If it is alright with everyone, may we do that? The sooner it is settled, the better."

Kadee asked Sharm. "You have TV here, right?"

He smiled as he assured her they did as well as cable.

Reighn said. "You are welcome to stay at the castle. We will make an apartment ready for you."

Ocean took a breath and declined. "Thank you, but I have made arrangements already. We will just follow through with them."

"I do not think Andre` will want that." Stated Reighn in his deep voice.

Ocean shrugged one shoulder. "Where is he to object?"

Reighn immediately looked uncomfortable, Ocean guessed the male who was supposed to be her father was not here. Which was proved when Reighn said? "Ahh! He is away at the moment."

"Oh, so he is out looking for Ocean. You should call him to say we are here." Kadee said innocently.

Ocean could have told her he was not, just by the uncomfortable looks on all the adult's faces, but she did not, anger reared its ugly head, causing the words to die on her tongue. Reighn cleared his throat and said again. "Ahh no! He was unable to hunt for Ocean."

Sage said. "It was a decision not of his choosing."

"So where is he then?" Paige asked, she could see they were hiding something.

Kadee eyed the four adults. "If he is Ocean's dad, why is he not here?"

"He could not be." Edith said soothingly. "It was not his fault. Something else took him away from Dragon's Gap for a few days."

"But what? He must have known she was coming. You all knew who she was. What could be more important than family?" Asked a frowning Paige.

Ocean decided to end the questioning. She could see the adults were uncomfortable and knew the girls were becoming belligerent on her behalf. She reiterated as she made to leave.

"Well, as I said I have made arrangements."

Reighn went to object once more when Sage placed her hand on his arm, saying. "Let us not disrupt Ocean's plans. I will send someone for you at around six o'clock. Will that be alright?"

Ocean's face was impassive as she said. "Yes, I will be ready by then." She looked at Sharm. "Thank you, Healer Sharm, for looking at Parker and for the information about the girls, you too

Edith for your help. Please have the recording of the girls as my family completed."

Sharm nodded. "It will be seen to right away."

"Thank you." She looked at the adults in the room who in one way or another may be related to her and said. "It was nice to have met you all. Come on girl's time to say goodbye."

Subdued the girls said their own goodbyes and followed Ocean from the room, both of them angry at the adults that had made Ocean upset. Sharm watched them get into their car from his window and said. "She is angry."

"She is furious!" Edith countered.

"Oh, was that why you told me to hush?" Reighn asked Sage.

"I never actually said hush."

"It was close." He grumbled as he put Molly down to play with the small boys who were now wearing clothes.

Sage said. "What are we going to tell her? I gather you never mentioned Ciana?"

"She had no idea she had a father, or he was here. So no and now I think about it, she never asked how we knew who she was." Edith replied. "Don't you find that strange?"

Sharm hugged her as he said. "Not really I think she was hit pretty hard with the information we gave her, she seemed stunned.'

Sage rubbed her forehead. "Shoot Edee, what do we do?"

Claire said from the doorway. "You tell her the truth."

"Claire, how are you?" Sage asked as Reighn hugged her. Then passed the small female to Sharm who hugged her as well. Claire over the months had become accustomed to the hugging. It was the holding her feet off the floor she had trouble with. "Down… down now!" She growled.

Sharm laughed as Edith said. "Really again."

Once she was back on her feet, Claire straightened her new shirt and asked. "How are you mummies to be?"

"We are fine." Edith told her. "Over morning sickness thanks to Ella."

Molly asked. *"Auntee Claire. Where Kammy?"*

"Oh sweetie she is with her Dada and Karl."

"Kay, me see soon."

"Tomorrow at story time." Claire promised.

Reighn asked. "Claire, you have seen Ocean."

Claire sighed and rubbed her heart. "I have seen angry thunderclouds and tempests around her. She has been ignored to one degree or another since birth. For her to take on those girls is her way of gathering a family."

"Sad." Sage murmured.

"So we know Ciana was brought up by loving grandparents and she and Andre` have bonded already." Sharm told them.

Sage sighed. "No matter what they say, she is never going to believe she is wanted or part of his family. She will see a unit with her excluded."

Edith looked out the window where Ocean's car had been. "Add to that, the fact he is not out looking for her. She will see it as another slight against her, another reason she is not really wanted."

"And he cannot be here tonight, this is not going to be easily made right." Reighn told them with a sigh.

"You could be right, or maybe the magic of Dragon's Gap and three girls in need will soften a shattered heart." Claire hoped. "Either way it is fraught with crossroads."

Sharm said. "I want to do something."

"What can we do?" Edith asked as she snuggled into his embrace feeling cold.

"Unfortunately nothing at the moment." Sage told them.

"What if I offer for her to live at the castle?" Reighn suggested.

Claire shook her head. "She will not accept, she will think it is because of Andre` and Ciana. Which it would be."

"That would not be all of it." He said defensively.

"We know that my love, she will not. So what can we offer her as an alternative?" Sage asked them all.

Edith said. "She has three lions to raise."

Claire smiled. "Oh Edee, of course. I can make a good case for an estate."

Reighn grinned. "My old estate, it is large and empty. It is not modern and will need work, so she will not see it as charity. You my dear Claire can sell it to her cheap."

They all looked at him. "What, I know how to be subtle."

"Yes of course you do dear." Sage agreed as the scowling male growled softly and Sharm snorted his disbelief, he did not miss the narrowed eyes of his brother.

"Okay, so can they move in right away or does it need work?" Edith asked Reighn, who nodded, then seemed to come to a stop. He remained still for several moments, just when they were starting to get concerned, he shook his head and said.

"It is ready, cleaned, with new mattresses and linen on the beds. Claire explain it is a packaged deal, furniture and household goods. Everything goes with it, lands and house."

"You are acting sneaky. What did you do?" Asked a suspicious Sage.

He grinned. "Let me just say; it will be hard to turn those two girls away from their bedrooms and the entertainment theater."

Claire and Edith grinned as Sage said. "Oh, sneaky dragon."

"I have my moments. Well, we will see what happens tonight."

"Andre ` cannot get back in time?" Edith asked worriedly.

Reighn shook his head. "No, they are still waiting for more clan members to arrive. He is hopeful they will be back the day after tomorrow."

"You will not recall him?" Sharm asked Reighn, who thought about it and looked at Claire. "Will it make a difference?"

"To Ocean, I suspect not. Let her mark her territory. She may be more receptive then."

"Well, we can only hope." Reighn said as he picked Molly up. "Let us also get home and prepare. Claire, will you come?"

"Yes, I will bring her, are you meeting in your conference room?"

"Yes. What about you Sharm and Edith?"

"We will attend." Sharm answered.

"Alright see you all at six."

CHAPTER SIX:

Claire rapped on the hotel door at ten minutes to six. The door was pulled open by a young girl.

"Hey."

"Say hello, please Kadee. Hey is not hello." Called out Ocean.

The girl, obviously Kadee, made a face then said politely. "Hello, my name is Kadee Walker. How may I help you?"

Claire could see how much she enjoyed saying her last name. Her whole body wiggled with delight when she did. Claire smiled, it was impossible not to in the face of her pleasure and said. "Very nicely done. I am Claire Axton. I have come to escort Ocean Walker to a meeting with the Dragon Lord."

Another girl just as tall with the same eyes and hair coloring. Although Claire could see she was a little older, came to the door and growled at her sister. "You are meant to invite her inside. Seriously Kadee, grandpa taught you better manners." To Claire, she said. "Would you please come in? I am Paige Walker, Kadee's sister."

Claire could see she shared the delight with her sister of saying her new last name. She stepped into the hotel room and took a quick look around, it was like every other hotel room she had been in, except it smelled clean and fresh. The bears that ran the hotel were sticklers for cleanliness, and it showed in the linens on the double beds. They had even provided a bassinet which stood on a stand between the beds.

"Thank you. Are you comfortable here?"

Paige said. "Yes, it is only until we find somewhere to live. We hope to be in a place by the end of the week."

Claire thought that sounded more like Ocean than her talking. She almost missed what she said next. "We want to start school next Monday." She thought a minute and then asked. "They do have a school here, right?"

"Oh yes, for all ages." Claire said without the laugh she suppressed. Both girls looked relieved.

Kadee eyed the small female with black and white hair. It was cool but not as cool as Oceans and she was wiry like a runner whereas Ocean was more what her grandpa would have called a bouncer. Claire looked nice though, like she could be trusted, like she had seen stuff and was not scared of things. Sometimes Kadee saw that same look in Paige's eyes.

She said. "So you are taking Ocean to see the Dragon Lord? We read all about him and his family from the guide book, we got at the center. It is very good, Paige and I made notes, Ocean said too. In case whoever wrote it, needs ideas of what else they should have in there."

"Ahh okay. Well the ladies who wrote it will be very pleased I am sure to receive any suggestions." Claire told them thinking about the hours Ciana, she, Frankie and Olinda had put into the guide book before Ciana left. Frankie would not be pleased to see someone had said they had missed things.

Kadee nodded as she said. "Knew it."

Ocean came out from what Claire assumed was the bathroom with a tiny baby held to her shoulder.

"Hello, I am Ocean Walker. You have met my girls, I see?"

Claire could not help but see the gleam of pride in the girl's eyes as Ocean called them her girls. "I have, they are charming."

Ocean eyed them both and smiled. "Yes, they are. So I will be ready in a minute."

"No hurry. How old is the baby?"

Kadee answered before Ocean could. "Her name is Parker, and she is only a day old. She is a lion like us."

Ocean said with a laugh as she wrapped the baby and placed her in the bassinet. "What she said. So Paige, she has had her bottle, and I changed her, she will sleep until I return, if you are worried, call the front desk…"

Claire handed Paige her phone. "Speed dial one, if you need your mom." To Ocean she said. "I will make sure you have everything you need tomorrow. The electronics you have will not work here, we have our own network and system."

Ocean turned to her and asked. "Why will you do that?"

"I am the liaison for Dragon's Gap; you fall under my umbrella. Think of me as your personal, girl Friday, anything and everything you need to know or want, I can probably advise you on how to get or get it for you."

"I see and for this you get what?"

"Hopefully a new friend. Can we really ever have enough friends?"

Ocean kicked up one side of her mouth. "No, not that I have found. In truth you do not seem the friend forever type."

"Oh really, I have been working on that too." She said without expression, making Ocean grin.

Claire said. "I always tell the truth, it can be hard for some to take."

Ocean nodded. "I prefer that to being kept in the dark. Ignorance hurts more in the long run."

"Got it." Claire nodded.

Kadee asked. "Are you two fighting?"

Ocean smiled. "No sweetie, just setting boundaries."

"So Lady Claire is our friend then?" Paige asked, proving she had studied the guide book. Ocean looked at the woman with black and white hair and nodded. "Yes." She then smiled at the confused girls. "So girls will you be alright?"

Paige nodded. "We have babysat a lot, and you know she will sleep until her next bottle. You have two or three hours. We will be fine."

"Okay, well, we are going. I will be no longer than an hour." She hugged both girls. "Stay inside. See you soon. Lock the door behind me." She and Claire left and waited until they heard the door lock. She shrugged at Claire's amused look.

"Nervous new mom."

"Hey, I know, I have two, a baby boy and Kammy she is three and a tiger she runs rings around me on most days."

"Oh, do not say that. They are all lions." Groaned Ocean.

Claire smiled. "Poor you. Listen, I am always... always available for coffee."

Ocean laughed. "Thank you."

"I thought if you didn't mind, we could walk. It is not far, and it is a beautiful night."

Ocean smiled and took a slow, deep breath of the fresh evening air. "Now that would be great. I have been in a car for days."

They walked along the cobbled streets in companionable silence for a while until Ocean said. "So, new friend what was it they did not tell me this afternoon?"

"Oh, you knew I was there?"

"Yes, I saw you as we left."

"I was only there toward the end. I do not want you to think I was spying on you."

"So why were you there, an accident?"

"No." Claire took a breath and said. "I am a Seer."

"Wow! Didn't see that one coming. So you saw me arriving?"

"Well yes, more than that, but basically yes."

"So what else?"

"I saw you surrounded by lions and other shifters and in a large estate."

"Well, that is interesting. Would you happen to know which estate?"

"Yes, as it happens, it became available today, and I already viewed it. I was hoping you would come and visit it tomorrow morning."

"That sounds good. We need a home, and I am thinking with lions, a large home with grounds sounds about right."

"Well, this one is huge and comes with a hundred acres or so, plus a ten bedroom country estate home, but I should warn you it needs updating."

"And they want to sell?"

"Yes. Oh, I should also tell you it comes partly furnished."

"I have no idea what to say, except yes, sign me up."

"Think about it and let me know?"

"I am serious, we will look at it but if it is what you say. I will buy it."

"Good around nine tomorrow morning."

Ocean smiled excited at the prospect she and her girls could be settled this time tomorrow. "Yep, sounds good."

They arrived at the castle, and Claire led her along the stone hallway. Ocean was impressed, it was a beautiful castle she asked Claire. "Do you think the girls could get a tour?"

Claire smiled. "Yes Frankie, Sage's PA, will gladly show them around, she knows everything there is to know about the castle from the ground up."

When Claire showed Ocean into the meeting room, she was unsurprised to see Reighn and Sage, who she now knew were the Dragon Lord and Lady. As well as Sharm and Edith, there was an older couple standing next to Reighn who inclined his head to Claire. "Thank you, Claire. Ocean Walker, I would like to introduce my parents, the former Dragon Lord and Lady. Rene` and Verity Kingsley. Papa is brother to Andre`."

Ocean bowed her head. "Hello."

"Hello." Verity replied.

"Good evening." Rene` said, and Ocean could see them taking in everything about her from her hair to her shoes.

Reighn said quietly. "Please before we sit, may we test your blood to determine that you are actually related to Andre`?"

"Of course."

A young male walked forward as Sharm held his hand out to her. "Your hand please."

Ocean placed her hand in his large one. He pricked her finger quickly and a bead of blood appeared. He dabbed it with a small square of cloth then handed it to the male who held it between his fingers, with another one, and then a minute later nodded. With a bow to Reighn and Sage, he left the room.

Ocean said. "I am guessing that was positive."

Sharm answered. "It was, the young male is able to sense DNA and compare it. He reunites families if needed."

"I see an admirable gift."

"We think so."

Reighn pulled a chair out for Sage as he said. "Let us sit."

After they had all taken their seats, Ocean asked of no one in particular. "So where is Andre`, I assumed incorrectly it would seem, he would be here?"

Reighn answered her. "Unfortunately, he was unable to be here. He is away and unable to return for two days or hopefully sooner. Before we go much further, I should tell you, he is with your twin sister Ciana and her daughters, which is how Sharm knew you were Andre`s daughter."

Ocean said nothing for a minute, then two, then five. She just sat looking at the wall opposite her. Everyone looked at each other. Claire watched Ocean and felt her heart ache for the sad, angry female sitting feet from her.

"My dear." Verity finally said softly.

Ocean turned her eyes toward her, then back to the wall again. Verity shivered in response to what she saw in that look, within her eyes she had seen Ocean's dragon and she was not a happy contented dragon. Not like the many female dragons Verity had encountered within the other females, or even her own over the last few months.

Verity said softly. "Please do not think he has no feelings for you or that he did not want to be here, he did, they did very much. He is torn between responsibilities. Ciana and her daughters needed him."

Still no response from her. Reighn said into the quiet. "He has seen a photo of Ciana's mother and does not recognize her. We were hoping you had a photo of your mother for him to see."

Finally, she spoke. "Why?"

Reighn explained about shadows, magic, Goddesses and Ciana and her daughters and how Andre` had been an unsuspecting victim in the conception of both girls. How until a few weeks ago, he had not even known she or Ciana were alive. Again, when he had finished speaking, she looked ahead of her at the wall. After a few minutes the silence got on Edith's nerves and she asked. "Ocean what are you thinking?"

Her voice was flat as she said. "Truthfully, that I am uninterested in meeting either one of them. It is just a waste of time. I have done what I set out to do. Come to Dragon's Gap and on my way I found three children that need me and that is all I want, all I need. So please tell him and her to not worry, I will be alright. I always have been. My girls and I add nothing to what the Goddesses wants for dragon kind or the world." She shrugged and returned to her silence.

"I don't think either of them see it like you do." Rene` said.

By consensus they had decided not to tell her of the key and lock situation preferring to let Andre` and Ciana handle that and now as he stared at her, Reighn was glad they had not.

Sage stated. "You are necessary to them, to us, to what may happen here. Why else were you drawn here?"

"I was not drawn. I found a letter after my mother's death that was an invitation to come here."

"May we see that?" Reighn asked shocked at her news, no one was sent a letter to come to Dragon's Gap.

"Sure." She drew it out of her back pocket and passed it to him. He read it then passed it to Rene` who hissed. "Where did this come from?"

"More importantly, who sent it?" Reighn asked as the letter was passed around to the others ending back with Ocean. They all stared at her as Reighn asked. "When did you receive this?"

Ocean shrugged. "Who knows, sometime in the last thirty years? As I said, I found it in my mother's things after she passed away."

Verity commiserated. "We are sorry for your loss."

Ocean shrugged. "Thank you, we were not close."

Verity looked at Edith when she heard the underlying angry tones in Ocean's voice and let Edith see the sympathy she felt for the female in her eyes. Edith returned the look, she too felt helpless in the face of so much anger.

Rene` said. "Andre` wants you here. Believe me when I tell

you this."

Ocean smiled and said. "But you do not know, do you? As he is not here, you cannot really know."

"I am his brother, I know."

Verity placed her hand on his arm, hearing the hurt under his words. Whether Ocean did, she could not tell as she just shrugged and said. "Maybe, it is a moot point though, as he is not here. So thank you all for the information. I will get you a photo Reighn. I must leave, I left the girls alone in a new place."

She stood, and Reighn stood as well. "Is there anything we can do for you?"

She turned blank violet eyes toward him and asked. "Why?"

Softly, he told her. "Because you are family."

"Oh, I suppose I am. No Dragon Lord, there is nothing I require from you or your family. Oh, wait." She passed him the letter Paige's grandfather had written. "This is a letter from the girl's grandfather, it explains why the girls had to leave and what is happening where they came from. I promised I would see if maybe someone could stop it."

Reighn took the letter. "I will make sure it is looked into and stopped."

"Thank you and good evening." Without waiting she walked from the room and took with her all the shock and anger she felt.

Sage blew a breath out. "Well, I can honestly say I have never seen anyone crushed so completely, as I just did."

"My heart hurts." Edith complained as Sharm hugged her.

Verity pressed her hand over her heart. "That poor sweet girl. I really am angry with the Goddesses. The mess they made of this, and now we have to help fix it and I am scared we will be unable too."

"Andre`, poor Andre` and Ciana. We will have to warn them." Cautioned Rene` his eyes on the door Ocean had walked out of. Why, he wondered, did he feel like she had closed the door on them all.

Claire nodded to Reighn and walked out after Ocean. Her

sympathy for her rode her hard, making her heart hurt and her soul cry out for her bonded. *My soul, I am here.* Lars called through their bond.

Lars, it is so sad.

Come home, dear.

I will… I will be there soon. I just need to make sure she gets home. I will meet you at the Welcome.

Okay.

Claire followed Ocean discreetly. Happier Lars was to meet her. She needed his arms around her. It was not fair what the Goddesses, in their single mindedness had done to these people and for the life of her she could not see how this ended.

Back in the conference room. Sharm said. “I feel very sorry for her and Uncle Andre`. She is so very angry.”

Edith agreed. “It is not going to be easy for Andre` or Ciana. They screwed this up by staying away.”

“We felt it would make no difference?” Said a saddened Reighn.

Sage stood as anger for Ocean bubbled up in her chest. “Well, we were all wrong, so very wrong. I do not care what you have to do Reighn, but make them come home.”

Reighn nodded. “I will try.”

Ocean found the gym on her walk home from the meeting, which had gone as she predicted it would. Well, not quite, but unfortunately close enough. Anger churned inside her as she slipped into the building, looking around she was happy to see it was almost empty. Either it was too early or too late for the citizens of Dragon’s Gap. Whichever it was, she was pleased. She did a quick survey, there was the usual gym equipment two males looked like they were doing a work out and amazingly enough a boxing ring toward the back. To the side were a group of people standing around treadmills and other machines. She knew there were two large people in the furthest corner from her.

She could not really tell if they were male or really large females as they were standing well into the dark corner. They looked to be engrossed in their conversation and took no notice of her, so she dismissed them as she did the others. She went to the desk and talked to the duty manager, who found her a pair of gloves. Normally she would wear her own, but she did not want to go back to the hotel and disturb the girls for them.

Conor Towers stood next to his half-brother Saul. They both scented the air as Ocean walked in and started talking to Mike, a member of their pride who ran the gym. Saul commented softly. "Trouble!"

Conor nodded as he watched the female walk toward the punching bag, she snapped the gloves into place as though she had done so many times before. *No novice.*

Then she stood in front of the punching bag and just stared at it. *She is heart hurting.* His beast told him.

Conor replied. *I can feel her pain just as you can, my friend.*

Saul grinned and asked Mike as he walked toward them. "Did you give her instructions?"

Mike shook his head and whispered. "She paid two hundred to use a pair of gloves and stand in front of the bag. Cute!"

Conor looked at them and knew they did not see what he did. How they could not see the anger and hurt coming off her or at least scent it in the surrounding air amazed him. It was as plain as daylight to him and his beast. She was getting ready to unleash her fury, he had seen many predators do the same over his lifetime, he himself had done so on many occasions. Usually on another predator or someone who thought they had the right to victimize others. Mike went to move toward her. Conor growled softly in warning and the young wolf froze.

"Leave her, watch and learn both of you."

He looked around as three more males and two females join them, like Mike, not everyone in his pride, was a lion. Some were strays, wolves, bears, cheetahs, tigers, unwanted rogues or just lonely. His pride had many shifters that he had collected, most of them as he and Saul had traveled to Dragon's Gap. They had followed him when he had promised them a safe home, not only within his pride but at Dragon's Gap.

More had joined once they arrived here, hoping to belong, some needed the structure of a pride, others had been brutalized by past alphas and required care and comfort that a large family like his pride gave them. That was not to say there were no problems within the pride or that everyone got on all the time. Which is why he had lieutenants or in the Gaps vernacular, deputies to his sheriff status? So far there was nothing he or his deputies could not handle and there was always the dragons as back up. On the whole life was sweet here.

They all stood around him and Saul and watched the female in silence because they wanted to see what she would do. Also because their leader, their Leo, watched, and they were his. Then several of them yipped or growled as Ocean screamed a primal scream of rage that seemed to reverberate through their bones and made the floor boards tremble. Then, as Conor predicted, she unleashed the fury he had scented within her.

Ocean hit the bag with everything she had for six long, hard punching minutes. They all could smell the blood as her knuckles split, then they heard the bones in her hands break as she continued punching in a one... two combination that did not vary or falter. She was relentless in her pursuit of whatever demon rode her.

Mike and Saul grimaced at each punch she landed on the bag and they were not alone. Several of the others whined in sympathy for her and her hands. Conor moved slightly and saw the small cougar standing in the shadows, just inside the doors of the gym. She looked over at him and very slightly nodded, as if he needed her to tell him and his beast they were watching his mate.

He turned back in time to see the female punch the bag so hard it split down the far side. Allowing the stuffing and sand to spill out and fall over the floor. He heard near silent gasps and shocked breaths being indrawn, and Saul's whispered. "Goddess."

The female stood completely still for three minutes with her head bowed. Her chest heaving from her exertions, arms hanging limply at her sides. Sweat covered her clothes and blood seeped from her wounds, making small puddles on the floor. Conor told his lion. *Bringing herself back from the killing edge. We have done the same and seen many others do so.*

His lion growled his agreement. *Many times.*

Without looking around, the female walked from the gym. Conor told his people who surrounded him.

"And now you know why she paid two hundred. Mike when she comes again and she may, make sure she has better gloves, and everyone knows not to charge her. Do you understand?"

"Yes, Leo."

Conor could hear all the others whispering as he moved from the dark corner they had stood in. He sniffed the air and found the trace of his mate. Never would she be hidden from him again. He smiled when he scented dragon, he would never have believed his mate to be a dragon. Then he shrugged, why not? Nothing in his life was normal, why should his mate be any different.

Mate is Mate. His lion stated and Conor grinned there was no arguing with his logic. He walked toward the cougar who waited on the steps.

Saul asked as he kept pace with him. "Is she the one?"

He, like all the pride, knew they were here at Dragon's Gap for safety and to meet their mates. If they were lucky enough to outlive the sentence. Conor grunted but did not reply. He stood on the step leading to the street and smiled. "Good evening, Lady Claire. You are out late."

"Good evening, Leo. I am following Lady Ocean. She is daughter to Andre ` Kingsley."

"Interesting, another daughter, the dragon must be very happy. To have no young and then to find out he has two."

Claire was unsurprised he knew about Ciana and Andre `, the male had a fabulous network, nothing happened anywhere at Dragon's Gap or the Castle without him finding out.

"Yes, he is. Sadly, she is not as happy."

"So we saw."

"She was hurt."

Conor nodded. "Yes, I do not think it was the first time. And I am sure you will have a healer with you when next you see her."

Claire laughed softly. Nothing got past the lion, he was an amazing male. Ocean and her girls could not do any better than to have him and his large pride to watch over them. She was tempted to tell him about the instant family he was to receive, but thought better of it. Some things are just too funny and for Claire this was one of those things. "I will, she is to have Reighn's old estate. I will show it to her in the morning."

He waited as his lion came to terms with the thought of his mate in the home of another male. Claire said casually. "It has been empty for over seven hundred years or so he told me today."

Conor smiled, the female really did know males. "Really, does she know?"

"Yes, I mention it tonight."

"That it was Reighn's?"

"Umm no, not that. I will tell her tomorrow, tonight as you saw was not the right time."

"I see." Was his only comment.

Claire tried not to be irritated at the enigmatic lion. It was not his fault he held his thoughts tight to his chest. It was what happened with leaders.

"Her name is Ocean Walker. She arrived today."

Saul voiced. "Been a busy day for her so far then."

Claire agreed. "It has."

Conor looked to where Ocean was slowly walking. "I will make sure she gets to where she needs to be. Allow Saul to escort you home, good night Seer."

"Good night sheriff Conor. I will take the offer up of an escort. Although I think that is my shadow coming."

With a nod Conor moved from the step and with his hands in the pockets of his jeans walked slowly after his mate. While Saul waited with Claire for Lars to arrive. "Not going to be easy for him." He stated more than asked.

Claire smiled. “You may be surprised, she has three lion cubs she has claimed.”

Saul grinned. “Well, I am an uncle. How about that? Thank you, Seer.”

She walked into Lars arms as he transformed from dragon and replied. “You are welcome Saul, the girls are delightful, more so I think when they shift.”

Lars saluted the lion in thanks for waiting with his shadow and then shifted to his dragon. Claire hopped on his back and he lifted off. Saul watched them fly into the dark sky, smiling at the news of his impending uncle status.

Ocean arrived minutes later at the hotel and let herself into the room. She was surprised to find both girls were asleep, it was not late she expected them to be awake, but obviously the extreme emotional roller coaster they had been on for the last few days with their grandfather. Then the long bus ride with no sleep had taken its toll on them. She was relieved at least now there would be no awkward explanation. She sighed as she watched them for minute snug under their blanket, snoring softly, she checked Parker to make sure she had time to shower before she woke. Then closed the bathroom door quietly and stripped off the bloody gloves from her split and swelling knuckles. She yanked her clothes off and stepped under the hot water and as she had done over the years she stuffed the wash cloth in her mouth and cried out her anguish.

When no more tears would come, she washed the blood from her hands and quickly finished her shower. Dry, she wrapped her hands in bandages she had ready in the med kit she always carried. This was not the first time she had beaten her hands bloody and broken.

Dressed in her long night shirt, she crept into bed and lay awake, going over the information she had received until Parker woke for her bottle. Then she slept until morning.

After following his mate to her room, Conor shifted into a large lion at least as big as a Kodiak bear and lay in front of her door. No one ever mistook him for any other lion as far as he knew he was the largest lion ever birthed. He was a First of a new changeling species that would evolve over time at Dragon's Gap.

When shifters were ready, he would know, and changelings would take their place in the world among the other magical entities. Conor had told no one other than Reighn who he was. He knew Sage, Edith and Claire knew it was hard to put anything past those ladies.

His pride just thought of him as the Leo, large, terrifying if he needed to be, and protector of them all. What he was, was magical, and that was something he kept to himself. He wondered what his mate would make of him and his lion and their abilities.

"Night Conor." Ken the bear who owned the hotel said as he walked pass the lion on his nightly patrol around twelve o'clock. "Your mate inside?"

Conor nodded. Ken grunted. "You sleep well now, you hear."

Conor grunted at him, Ken smiled as he moved off. He, like every other shifter or person in Dragon's Gap liked and admired Conor. He could not wait to tell his mate Lucy, about Conor's mate. She would be pleased everyone knew a Leo was more stable with a mate and young

CHAPTER SEVEN:

Next morning Ocean was in agony, her hands were more swollen than she could remember them ever being before. She lay with her eyes closed and tried to close her hands into fists; the pain made her suck in a breath and almost cry out. She must have broken more than one or two knuckles, it felt like she had broken every one of them. There was no way she could feed Parker or change her like this. She felt disappointed and mostly ashamed of herself, she had thought the days of self-indulgent punishment were over.

She silently berated herself, how responsible was she, there was more at stake now than just her. In her anger and hurt feelings, she had forgotten that fact, sitting up slowly she kept her eyes closed, and swung her legs to the side of the bed. Sighing again as she remembered that crying was not her friend, it left her swollen and red eyed. She pried her sore eyes opened and was instantly confronted by two sets of blue eyes. Paige demanded. "What happened?"

Ocean bowed her head, saying. "I am so sorry girls."

Kadee asked. "For what?"

"Who hurt you?" Paige demanded again.

Ocean shook her head. "No one honey... no one. I box. You know what that is."

"Sure you hit people." Kadee answered.

"Well yeah, I don't actually hit people. I hit a punching bag."

"And you did that last night?" Paige asked wide eyed.

"Yes."

"Your hands look bad." Kadee told her with lots of sympathy

in her voice. She was positive she could feel the pain coming from Ocean's hands.

"I wish I could say they do not hurt, but I cannot."

"I made you coffee, can you hold it?" Kadee asked as she held a cup in her hands. Ocean realized they must have been awake for a while. She had not heard a thing, either they were very quiet or she had fallen into a deeper sleep than she had planned. Another reason for her not to do this again.

She nodded. "Yes, I can, thank you Kadee."

She took the cup and not for a minute would she show them the pain that small action caused her. She sat and sipped as Paige asked. "Why do you do that to yourself?"

Ocean closed her eyes and said softy. "Anger, unresolved anger and hurt."

"Was it your family or the Dragon Lord, because I don't think it is wise to get that angry at dragons?" Kadee said with a frown of worry on her face.

"Yes and no. It was just stupid."

Paige motioned for Kadee to hush as she said. "We will see to Parker if you tell us what to do."

Ocean nodded as she sipped her coffee. Kadee and Paige bustled about looking after Parker, heating her bottle. Paige changed her and tried not to make a face as she did. Then she sat and started to feed the baby as Kadee changed into clothes in the bathroom. When she came out and was putting her shoes on when she said. "Ocean?"

"Yes Kadee."

"There was a huge, and I mean huge lion lying in front of the door this morning, when we woke up."

"Uhuh!" Ocean sipped her coffee as she looked at both girls. No, they were not scared. "Did he try to get in here?"

"No, it was a male. He had a huge mane and was beautiful for a male lion. He looked nice, right Paige?" Kadee looked at her sister. Paige nodded in agreement. "I thought so, he seemed real gentle."

"How do you come to that?" Asked a mystified Ocean.

Paige told her. "I think if he wanted to hurt us, he could have broken the door down and just walked in. He really was as big as a grizzly bear or an elephant."

"Wow! That is huge, are you sure?"

"Yep, real big." Kadee nodded. "He just got up and walked away when he heard us. Right Paige?"

"Yep." She concentrated on feeding the small baby. "Am I doing it right?"

"Yes perfectly." Ocean told her with a small smile.

Paige smiled at her praise, then asked. "Was it because of us?"

Ocean had no difficulty following her train of thought. "Oh, honey, no... No, it was just..." She shook her head. "Adult stuff."

"Oh!" Paige said in a small voice.

Ocean sighed, then remembered the estate. "So I have a home for us to look at."

"Really?" Kadee asked, and she could not hide her excitement at the thought. "What is it?"

"An estate, apparently it has over a hundred acres of land. It is a massive house which is meant to have ten bedrooms; it needs fixing up and is sort of furnished, we are going to see it around nine this morning. Claire is taking us; we will have to eat first." She looked at her hands when a knock sounded on the door. Ocean looked at the girls. "We are not expecting anyone, are we?"

Paige said. "Kadee open the door."

Claire and another female stood on the doorstep. Claire looked at Ocean. "The girls called, you need help."

Ocean sighed as she looked at both girls. "Of course they did, come in please." Then she told the girls. "Thank you for caring. I cannot remember a time when someone did."

The girls had been worried Ocean would have been angry. When they had woken and seen her swollen bloody hands, they had panicked and Paige had called Claire. She had reassured them she was coming with a healer and not to worry.

Claire looked at Ocean as she said. "I am sure we established last night; I am your friend."

Ocean sighed and sat again. "You did, and I thank you for coming. I assume the quiet lady with you is a healer."

Claire smiled. "She is, this is my friend Ella."

Claire took the baby from Paige and gently said. "Go and get dressed young one, and then we will go get breakfast."

Kadee asked Claire. "Are you taking us to see our new home?"

"Maybe, new home." Ocean cautioned as Ella walked to her and sat next to her on the bed. "Hello, I am Ella and may I?"

"Good morning, Ella. I am sorry to drag you out so early and yes please."

"Oh do not be. I am going on duty in half an hour, so it is no trouble." First she placed a hand over Oceans eyes, and instantly a cool wave of healing washed over her face. Ocean sighed her relief and mumbled. "Thank you, crying is not my friend."

Ella smiled and whispered. "I too have that problem." Next she started unwrapping Ocean's hands. Kadee watched her intently as Ella said. "I have a friend her name is Harper..."

Ocean interrupted her. "That wouldn't be Harper Easton, would it?"

Ella smiled. "Yes it is, of course her last name is Battle now. Do you know her?"

"We have met, what are the odds. So she is mated?"

"Bonded to a dragon. Ace Battle."

Kadee reminded her. "That means she is a shadow, remember Ocean."

"Yes, sweetie. I remember."

Claire raised her eyebrows, it sounded like there was bad blood between Harper and Ocean. Now she wondered what could have caused that, although with Harper anything was possible, she may have killed Oceans cat or something. Claire hid her grin and kept her thoughts to herself as she finished feeding the baby her bottle.

Ella said. "Anyway, she does this a lot or use too, thankfully not so much now." She finished unwrapping Ocean's hands and said softly. "Never this bad, you need to wear better gloves."

Ocean sighed. "Usually, I do. I was not in the right frame of mind last night. It will not happen again."

Ella smiled. "Harper says that as well."

She cupped her hands over Oceans and closed her eyes as Kadee said. "Oh wow, I can see that. It is amazing."

Kadee watched Ocean's skin knit back together, and the swelling go down as her bones mended. After several minutes, Ella opened her eyes. "Treat them with care for the next two days, no hitting anything." She admonished.

"Yes Healer Ella." Ocean smiled. "Thank you, Ella. I really appreciate it."

Ella gave her hand a pat as she took hers away. "I know you do, also you should know your daughter has the gift. She will need training."

They both looked at a wide eyed and flushed faced Kadee who burst out with. "That was the best thing; I have ever seen. It was amazing."

Ella laughed as she told Ocean. "You see, like calls to like."

"Yes, I have heard that. So who do we see about her training?"

Ella said. "If you like. I will organize someone to test her."

"Okay, but next week. This is our settling in week, the girls start school on Monday after we register and get clothes. Again, thank you, Ella."

"You are welcome. Now, I must go. I will see you all soon, bye girls, and Claire see you later." She left, closing the door behind her.

"She was nice, I liked her. Do you think I really can be a healer?" Kadee asked Ocean, who shrugged. "I do not know. We will get you tested and then you can decide, until then, we are looking at a home and school."

Paige said as she came from the bathroom where she had changed. "I will pack a bag for Parker."

Ocean nodded as she gathered clothes to change into for the day. Claire wrapped Parker, then placed her in the carrier. Within minutes Ocean was dressed, the room tidied, and they were walking out the door.

Breakfast was at a diner called Rockabillies. The girls loved the old style fifties booths and décor as well as the waitresses in bright authentic costumes who made them sigh with longing. Conor and Saul sat in a booth three across and back from Oceans. Saul glanced over at the table and back at Conor.

"So that is her then?"

Conor grunted in reply. Never the most talkative in the morning as a rule, today having slept in his lion skin, on a hard surface made him grumpy. Although the sight of his girls looking around starry-eyed made him think about smiling. Not so much his chirpy talkative brother who asked. "So you gonna introduce yourself?"

Another grunt as answer, almost made Saul laugh before he said. "Looks like her hands are okay, must have got them fixed."

Conor took his eyes from his mate and stared at his brother, golden eyebrows rose over amber eyes.

"What?" Saul grinned. "Everyone knows, if it was meant to be a secret, you went about it wrong."

Conor had no one to blame for Saul's reasoning. Not even the ones in the gym last night, who had heard him talking to Saul and Claire about Ocean. No, the fault was his, or at least his own beast's fault. He who had given the game away by lying across her threshold, guarding her door for the whole town to see. Ken had not been the only one to have seen him last night or this morning. It was enough for all the tongues of Dragon's Gap to start wagging.

Saul said with a grin. "Just saying."

"Don't!" Conor rumbled, suddenly he stiffened as did Saul when the diner door opened and several female lionesses walked in. At a quick count there were eight, and they were hunting. As Saul had pointed out, people knew that Ocean and her young were now Conor's, therefore untouchable. For Ocean to be challenged before he had claimed her as his mate was uncalled for.

Unfortunately, as Neila sauntered pass Conor and Saul with a smirk, she knew his hands were tied. If he stopped the challenge before it started, it would show everyone in the pride Ocean was weak. If he stepped in at any time, it would do the same. He had no option but to let this play out.

Claire saw the females enter and said hurriedly to Ocean. “Okay, so I know something, and I was going to ease into talking to you about it later today, while we looked at the house.”

Ocean’s eyebrows rose as she asked. “What would that have been my new friend?”

Claire grimaced as she hurriedly said. “The lion that slept outside your door...”

Ocean cut her off. “Is my mate, yes I know? Would that be the big intense guy with the amber eyes and golden hair?”

“Yes, he is the pride leader or Leo and...”

“The eight lionesses walking toward us are going to call me out.”

Claire grinned as she asked. “Shoot, what don’t you know?”

Ocean looked at the warmed jug of syrup. “If the maple syrup is natural?”

Claire laughed as Ocean looked at her wide- eyed daughters. “You heard that?”

“Yes.” Paige whispered as she held Kadee’s hand, who looked terrified.

“Now listen to me, the male over there seems to be my mate and your new daddy.” They both grinned at the face she made when she said the word daddy. “What is going to happen now is I am going to be challenged.”

“Why?” Asked a trembling Kadee as Paige shivered with worry. Ocean ran her finger down each of the girl’s cheeks in comfort. “Probably because he is the pride leader and they want to test his mate. To see what I am made of.”

“That is stupid.” Kadee said softly. “I don’t like it, there are eight of them.”

“I know and you are right, it may be stupid but it is the way of their species. They have issues we do not understand going back generations. Things like this will stop when people realize we are more than our base animals. Until then we go with what is happening.”

Paige asked softly. "Why does he not stop it? If he is the leader."

Claire said. "If he does, it will be worse for your mom. They will think she is weak and attack you or her later, they will assume she cannot defend you. They may say she cannot keep you as she cannot defend you. Do you see, he has to watch and wait like we do?"

"It is dumb." Kadee mumbled fearfully.

"We won't go." Paige told her bravely.

Ocean's eyebrows rose again. "Of course you will not go anywhere. You will sit there and listen and watch. This could be you one day, hopefully not, but if it ever happens, you will need to know how to handle it. But in saying that, if Claire or your new father orders you to do something, you will do it without question. Do I make myself clear?"

"Yes." Both girls answered tearfully.

Ocean shrugged. "You are young and believe me when I tell you, your new father, and our new friend Claire, will not allow a finger to touch you. Just watch, it will be okay."

Claire hurriedly whispered. "Not a finger, trust me."

Both girls nodded and Kadee whispered. "Should we tell them the Dragon Lord is our uncle?"

Claire smiled. "Not now, let's keep that in reserve; it's always good to have information that they don't have."

Paige whispered. "Yeah, like reinforcements."

Claire nodded with a smile as the eight lionesses finally arrived. A female stood and cocked out her hip in an insolent pose. She was obviously the leader, thin, big-breasted, big hair which again seemed to be the fashion. She wore tight, revealing clothes that left little to the imagination. Her eyes were blue with a ring of amber around the iris. Her face was long and narrow with high cheek bones. Ocean thought a lack of food shaped them rather than because she had naturally sharp cheek bones. At the moment, her bright red lips were in a pout.

She looked constipated, Paige thought as she and Kadee frowned at her. Paige's eyes hardened slightly as she looked at the other seven females. They were all young and there were two that were not much older than her and they all looked skinny. It was as though they were starving. Predators should not be hungry, Ocean told her and Kadee that predators like lions went crazy if they stayed hungry too long. These females looked hungry and slightly crazy. She wondered why, there was no need to be like that. The booklet they read last night said food was plentiful, and she doubted people would turn a hungry lioness away. They must know it was not good to have hungry predators around the town. Then she looked at their leader and saw why they were all like that. She was skinny, so they had to be like her. Paige bet she did not let them eat. She had seen that kind of girl at school. The bully usually was the leader; it was a pack or pride thing. It was just stupid if she was ever a pride leader she would never treat the pride like that, she would make sure they were always fed and happy, it would be her duty to do so. She looked over to the large male, and she bet he did not like what he was seeing.

Conor flicked his eyes toward the young female and smiled as she ducked her head, but not before he saw the spark of recognition in her eyes. Before he could dwell on what he saw Neila spoke.

The lead female looked over Ocean and the girls, she smirked at Claire. Her voice was as Ocean thought, whiny. It grated along her nerves. "Lady Claire, why are you here, eating at our diner, surely a step down for you?"

"I go where I want Neila. I do not answer to you, and you do not own this diner. You own nothing your Leo doesn't allow." Claire stated as she looked at her blandly.

Ocean knew she had her gun on her lap, as did the lionesses. A gun would not normally halt an attack unless she was an excellent shot, but they would let her think it did today. Tomorrow or the next day may be a different thing. Ocean was sure Claire was well aware of that fact and that she knew she had an enemy. So she would make that enemy go away, an enemy of my friend is an enemy of mine! Was a motto Ocean had lived by her entire life. Slowly Ocean stood and the eight lionesses shuffled back. "So Claire my friend, introduce me?"

Claire flipped her hand the lioness's way. "Ocean Walker meet Neila something or other, I never bothered to learn her last name and I don't know the others."

This made the lioness Neila snarl and again when Claire said. "She believes she is the Alpha female of Dragon's Gap."

Neila hissed. "Walking a thin line here liaison. The dragons are nowhere around now, are they?"

Claire smirked at her and placed her gun on the table top. "Try me, bitch, I've eaten bitches like you for breakfast, lunch and dinner."

Neila moved slightly, Ocean moved as well drawing her attention back to her, she looked Ocean up and down.

"What are you?"

Ocean sighed. "Tell me what you want. I have not eaten yet, and it makes me antsy."

Neila sneered. "Just wanted to see what kind of skank Conor has got himself hooked up too?"

The others with her laughed or twittered, some hesitantly, as though they laughed because it was expected, rather than they wanted to. Ocean thought, poor scared lionesses.

"Skank! Really me, I am not the one wearing slut lipstick. Now am I."

Before Neila could swing the fist she had readied, Ocean hit her with two short jabs to the chest and then as she bent over to get a breath. She grabbed her throat and took her to the ground, as she calmly said to the others when they moved closer.

"I will kill her, then you, so think really hard which way you want to go here?"

Claire stood in front of the table, a gun in each hand. Ocean grinned realizing Claire was a very good shot indeed.

With her hand around the gasping female's throat, Ocean said. "Now you listen to me, you made me tell a lie which I hate doing. I told my healer, I would not use my hands for two days, and you made me break my word. So guess who pays for that?"

The lioness wheezed a breath in and out as Ocean snarled. "So because of that, I am going to tell you how this is going to go down. I am a dragon. I will kill any who comes after mine, any of mine, so take this as a warning." She looked at the other seven lionesses and the people in the diner. Bypassing Conor's intent stare. "This is a warning for all of you here. I give only one." She released the female and stood.

Neila looked up at her and whimpered, then asked. "May I get up?"

"No, remain there." Ocean looked over the seven nearly emancipated females who had followed Neila and said.

"You who follow her may continue to do so, but not here. You will leave Dragon's Gap, do not let me see you after today. Now you may get up, Neila."

She slowly stood, her head bowed in submission as she whined. "May I stay?"

Ocean turned her back on her as she said. "No, I will not trust you. You had no right to challenge me until after my mating. You tried to shame or expose your Leo and me. You are contemptible, if you pull that knife Neila, my mate will kill you or my new friend will, unless I rip your throat out first."

Neila hurriedly took her hand from her pocket when she saw the hardened face of Conor as he and Saul walked over. Conor nodded to Ocean and Claire, he looked at Neila then the females with her and ordered. "Saul, see Neila and whoever is going with her out of the Gap. Make sure they are gone by noon. Talk to Johner about the ban."

"Yes Leo." Saul said, he, like several of the others, did not like Neila. They had suffered her because of her brother Migel. He was well liked. Saul asked Conor. "What of Migel?"

"Give him the choice."

Neila screamed at him. "You can't do this. We will die if we leave here!"

Conor's face became harder. "You should have thought of that. I am tired of your behavior. I warned you Neila, your brother warned you. The Matrons and Lady Grace warned you.

You were tolerated because of your brother, today challenging a female because you thought you had the right was a step too far."

"It was for us." She whined. "I know you want me. I am a pure lion, not like that, a dragon." She snarled, twisting her face into a sneer of disgust as she looked at Ocean with malice in her eyes. Conor's voice became icy as power bled into the tones.

"You and I were never together, here or anywhere. Your wishful thinking makes a fool of you Neila. Have some dignity and leave like the pure lion you say you are."

"You can't do this to me." She hissed. "I will kill you."

Saul said. "Repeat that again, so I can kill you and not worry about your ban."

Neila screamed loudly until Claire slapped her. "Shut the hell up."

Neila snapped her lips closed, and Claire nodded to Saul. "Drag her if you have too, just get her out of here." She looked at Neila and said. "You brought this on yourself. Now leave."

Neila growled out. "I did nothing wrong. It was my right to challenge."

Conor told her. "No, it was not, but you chose this action. Now you reap the rewards your foolish choice granted you, banished from Dragon's Gap as of noon today. Saul take her and any of the others that wish to go with her."

Saul and two other deputies who arrived grabbed an arm each and dragged Neila from the diner. Two of the females ducked their heads and left with them. Ocean looked at the remaining five females. "You five go and find a table and eat anything you want. Do you have money?"

They shook their heads no. Conor peeled off several bills for each of them. "Go and eat."

"Yes, Leo." They whispered.

Claire told them. "Come to my office at two today. I will find you a place to live and decide what to do with you."

"Yes, Liaison Claire." A young female with orange hair and a thin face with round brown eyes answered for them all. "Thank you."

She and the other four looked at Ocean. Three of them had tears running down their faces. Freedom did that, Ocean thought, feeling sympathy for them, they looked lost and alone.

Softly, she said. "I am Lady Ocean; these are my daughters. Paige, Kadee, and Parker. We are now part of Dragon's Gap pride, your pride if you want it, but you have to earn it. That means you have to add to the pride by doing what you can, if that is going to school or working, we will help you succeed in your endeavors. Be honest with Liaison Claire this afternoon, please."

"Yes Lady Ocean." Said the same female. They hurried to a table and quietly started looking at the menu.

Conor growled softly from his chest as he asked no one in particular. "How the hell did I let that happen?"

Kadee said. "Because you are busy, our grandpa had the same problem. You have to learn to delegate."

He looked down into her upturned face and smiled a slow smile. "You are very wise for one so young."

"I know, don't worry about it now, we are here to help you."

Conor grinned as he asked Ocean. "May I join you?"

"Of course." Ocean motioned to a seat. Her heart beat a fast tattoo against her ribs. Dear Goddess, the male was startlingly handsome, even with the light scar that ran along his jaw line. Conor took a seat next to Kadee, making her move closer to Paige. Ocean had quickly taken her seat beside Claire, leaving no room for Conor next to her. She turned to Claire and told her. "Let me know what they need?"

"Of course."

Conor cleared his throat and said. "I am sorry."

Startled, Ocean asked. "Why?"

"For all of this, it was not how I was hoping our first meeting would go."

She shrugged, trying for nonchalant and hoping she pulled it off. "Were you never going to introduce yourself or were you going to haunt us at night?"

He smiled at her. "No, I was working on it."

“Huh!” Paige laughed. “Working on it… mom you even scare lions.”

CHAPTER EIGHT:

They decided to visit the estate as soon as breakfast was over, it was a ten-minute drive from town. When they turned into the driveway, they came to a set of wrought-iron gates that were closed; the gates were shaped into the wings of a dragon.

Kadee tapped Paige on the shoulder. "Look." She pointed to the gates, both girls grinned, Kadee said. "That is so cool."

Claire and Paige hopped from the truck as Ocean grinned admiring the gates. "Now, that is what I call fate."

"Conor will be sad he is not on them. We should have a lion as well."

Ocean pulled on her bottom lip as she thought about what Kadee said. There probably were going to be lions living here. She was right, there should be a lion as well. "I will talk to Claire, if we decide to buy. She may know of someone who does iron work."

Kadee grinned as she huffed. "As if we won't, look at this place?"

Ocean shrugged. "The house could be a stone pile of rubble you don't know?"

"Nope, it is a castle, seriously a dragon that has gates like that would build a castle."

"You seem quite sure of that?"

"I am."

Her assurance made Ocean smile as Claire and Paige climbed back into the truck. They drove through the now opened gates. Ocean as well as the girls fell in love with the property as soon as they drove along the paved driveway. The lush rolling hills and groves of trees called to them. They were delighted to see an orchard and what looked like a stream and pond.

Ocean stopped at the girls insistence, causing Conor to pull up behind her in his pickup, as Kadee and Paige tumbled out of their vehicle in their excitement. He opened Ocean's door and grinned at her as Claire met them around the front of her pickup. "Well, they like it." Claire stated as they looked after the two girls who stood looking at the large brick wall that seemed to encircle the property.

"Look you guys." Paige pointed at the wall. "Do you think it goes around the whole place?"

Ocean shrugged. "Who knows?"

"Conor?" Kadee asked as she stared up at him. Conor quirked up one side of his mouth, figuring as this was the Dragon's Lords former residence it would be so. "I would say yes, but we could ask the Seer she knows everything."

Claire sniffed with disdain at his words. "I do not know everything, if I did I would know where my shadow hides his chocolate. Now that would be everything."

The girls as well as Ocean laughed at her pout. "Seriously, who owned this place? It is beautiful and are you positive they want to sell?" Ocean finally asked.

Claire nodded and bit the bullet, waiting for the explosion to come as she said. "Yes, they do, and it once belonged to the Dragon Lord, he lived here over seven hundred years ago. Which is why it needs some TLC?"

Kadee did a small dance and crowed. "Knew it... knew it had to be someone important."

Claire looked at Ocean, waiting for her anger, instead she received a shrug. "Glad he wants to sell it, from what I can see it looks ideal. Conor, what do you think?"

"It has possibilities." He agreed, surprised as well at her easy acceptance.

Claire smiled at her agreement. "The Dragon Lord walled in fifty acres, the rest is accessed through gates along the perimeter of the fifty acres."

Conor said. "This is a fine place for lion cubs to learn to run and be lions."

Paige looked up at him and asked in her soft way. "Will you teach us?"

Conor looked down into the blue eyes of his new daughter and knew he stared at a First. "Do you know who you are?"

Ocean moved closer but did not interfere. She felt Kadee shift closer to her and placed her arm around her shoulders. With those simple words Paige felt something shift within her mind and felt her lion, who slumbered under drugs, stretch. Her face paled as she nodded, her eyes brightened and a spark blossomed to life in the soul of her and her lion.

She whispered as her eyes turned amber. "I am like you."

Conor nodded. "Yes little one, you are."

She smiled, but a look of fear entered her eyes. He took her chin in his hand and lifted her face to his and in a voice that came from the gods he intoned. "We together will lead our people into the next era of changelings. Do not fear what is to come. You have been gifted parents and family that will make your burdens lighter." He kissed her forehead. "Remember my daughter, you are not alone."

She hugged him. "I was so scared to tell, I always felt different, like there was more to me but I could not find it." She shrugged. "I just felt weird all the time."

Conor smiled. "I know how that feels, but we will not allow you to be anything other than what you are. A young girl with potential who has a lion that is still sleeping within her. It is years until you will be called on to fulfil your destiny."

"What if she doesn't want to be a first?" Kadee asked.

He looked at her with sorrow in his eyes as he told her. "Sweet Kadee, Paige has no choice, destiny is destiny, like your mom and I. We are drawn to each other, even though we are not of the same species."

"Oh, so will she get as big as you?"

"Again that is destiny and genetics."

"Eww Paige, you could be a mammoth female lion." Kadee laughed as Paige pulled from Conor's arms and growled at her sister. "Shut up Kadee."

Which made her laugh harder and dance out of reach of her sister. Conor raised one eyebrow when he asked Kadee. "Are you saying I am a mammoth?"

Kadee stilled, then looked up into his smiling eyes and grinned cheekily. "Yep."

He growled deep in his chest and made a grab for her, letting her dance away as she screamed with laughter. Paige grabbed her hand, and they ran toward the house in the distance. "We will meet you at the house." She called back to Ocean, who called out. "Okay, wait for us there and don't go inside."

She looked at Conor she knew what a first of species was, there was a short explanation in the information packet Kadee read to her the previous night. "So, she is a First?"

"Yes. Do you know what a first is?"

"Yes, it was in the information packet we received."

Conor looked at Claire. "Really, I wonder how that found its way in there."

Claire smiled and shrugged. She would not tell him Reighn had said to slip a mention of it in with other details of the people from the Gap.

His eyes clouded over. "Her life will be very different from Kadee's and what I imagine she hoped it to be."

Ocean sighed. "I am thinking her life has been turned upside down in such a short space of time that this will just add another complexity to it. But she seems resilient, and well grounded. Plus she has you and me now."

He smiled as he nodded. "That she does as well as a family, loads of family."

That smile of his made her toes curl in her shoes, causing Ocean to feel heat prickle over her skin. She looked pass him and nodded as she asked. "Any idea who they are?"

As he turned with Claire, they saw Frankie and Joy bouncing their way onto the property. Claire laughed as she looked up at

Conor, who grinned.

"She even walks like her now." She explained to Ocean. "This is Frankie, Sage's PA and Joy."

"Oh, we met her yesterday." Ocean recalled, "Teenager... talkative?"

"Yep, that is Joy."

Frankie had started talking before she reached them. "Hi, we came when we heard you were here."

"Where is Johner?" Conor asked, expecting a horde of dragon's overhead any minute.

"Don't worry, Conor. Johner knows where we are. He dropped us off up the road, so he did not frighten the girls. Although now I see they are not here." She turned to Joy and grinned. "Yes, Joy you may go and find them, do not get into trouble your mom will kill me."

"Aww, Frankie what trouble can I get into?"

Frankie made a face that had Ocean worried until Claire whispered. "That is her thinking face."

"Really, it's disturbing." Ocean whispered back.

"Uhuh!" Was Claire's only comment.

Conor choked back a laugh at the conversation. Finally, Frankie said. "I can think of lots of things that I would get in trouble about, so my advice do none of them."

Joy nodded, smiled at the other adults and started to run off, only stopping long enough to hug Claire, then Conor and say. "Love you."

To which he replied. "You too sprite."

Making her giggle as she continued pass Ocean with a quick wave. She hooted with delight and ran to where she could see Kadee and Paige, who seemed to be waiting for her.

Conor, still smiling, told Ocean. "I train her as well as several others. She is a wolf and was abandoned. Joy is Ace and Harper Battle's claim. Do you know what that is?"

Ocean looked toward the running girl and nodded. "Yes, Kadee read the booklet. It was in there."

"Oh, did you?" Frankie shimmered as she moved closer to the

three adults, her eyes took in Ocean, knowing she was Ciana sister and Andre`s daughter. It was strange neither female looked like Andre` yet you knew he was their father, it was the feeling they had around them. Frankie worried the three would never form a family, and they needed to, not just for themselves but for the dragon nation, especially the females. If Ocean didn't open up her heart to Andre` and Ciana, then the gift from the Goddesses would falter and wither away. Ocean looked so much like Ciana it was scary because when Frankie looked into Ocean's lavender eyes, they were so unlike Ciana's calm, quiet eyes. Ocean's eyes were uncomfortable to look at.

"I helped write it." Frankie told her.

Claire told Frankie. "You did a good job although Kadee has ideas for some things you missed."

Frankie's whole body stilled. "She what?"

"Apparently we missed some things."

"Really, well I will talk to her." She stuck her hand out to Ocean. "Hi, I am Frankie Kingsley, shadow to Johner Kingsley. You just met my niece Joy?"

Ocean took her hand and felt the tingle of magic snake up her arm, she smiled as she replied. "I did, she is delightful."

Frankie's eyes widened, Ocean had not reacted to the tingle on her skin, and Frankie knew she felt it.

"You are not worried about what you feel?"

"No, should I be?"

"Yes, most people are."

"Well, I am not most people."

Frankie grinned as she said. "No, I can see that." She released Ocean's hand and wanted desperately to shake out her own hand. It was as though Ocean had left an imprint on her skin. It felt weird and nice at the same time. Now she sort of understood what other people felt when they first touched her. Before she could stop the words, she blurted out. "What are you?"

Ocean's lips smiled, but her eyes were watchful as she answered. "Dragon and human apparently."

Frankie nodded, but she doubted the female was telling the

whole truth or maybe like her she did not know. Either way, she needed to talk to someone.

Conor asked Frankie. "Although it is always a pleasure to see you, why are you here?"

"Oh... oh, well, Joy wanted to come. She has the rest of the week off school, due to some problems with the buildings. I think they have to be enlarged or something..."

"Frankie." Claire stopped the halt of words.

"Oh sorry." Frankie sheepishly said. "Joy sort of nagged to come see the girls, and I wanted to well..."

Claire cut in. "You wanted to see inside Reighn's old home?"

"Well yeah, I mean don't you want to know what kind of pad the male had as a teenager. Like is it a typical bachelor place?"

Claire laughed out loud. "Frankie, you know it won't be. It is seven hundred years since he lived here, and even then Lady Verity said he hardly stayed here. It was more an inheritance from his grand dam's side."

"Oh... so no pizza boxes or cans of opened beer with pool tables then?" She sounded so disappointed Ocean felt sorry for her as Conor said. "Never mind Frankie, shall we go find out, anyway?"

Frankie's face transformed from sad to happiness in seconds as she shimmied with pleasure. "Okay, can I ride with you, Conor?"

"Sure you can."

Ocean looked around and breathed deeply getting a small scent of Conor, Claire and Frankie but mostly she breathed in clean crisp air. "This is delightful. I think I love it." She looked up into the amber eyes of Conor and asked. "Do you like it?"

He smiled his toe curling smile. "What I see, I find pleasing to my eyes."

Ocean like Claire and Frankie knew the male was not talking of just the land. Flustered, she cleared her throat before she said. "Okay then, let's go."

The house when they pulled around the curved driveway was exactly as Kadee stated. A castle, granted not as large as the

Dragon's Gap castle but a castle all the same.

"Oh my!" Claire gasped, "I had no idea, I sort of only looked from the gates."

"What the hell." Ocean said at the same time. Eyes wide, Claire shook her head. "He never said it was a castle just that it was his place and you can buy it."

"Well." Ocean pointed to the three girls standing in awe looking up at the castles stone wall and turrets. "How much does he want for it?"

"So you are buying it?"

Ocean gave her a look of disbelief. "Can you honestly believe I can say no to them?"

They both looked to where the girls stood, their faces weathered in smiles, eyes shining in hope. So excited they almost vibrated with it. Kadee yelled. "Told you, a castle."

Claire laughed and agreed. "Okay, a dollar."

"I beg your pardon?" Ocean placed all her attention on Claire, who quietly said. "Your cousin wants to sell you and your family this castle and land for one dollar."

Ocean chewed her bottom lip and squinted up at the top of the castle, wondering if it was accessible. "Call him and tell him I cannot accept charity. I have some pride."

Claire was marshaling all her arguments when the next words from Ocean made her thoughts stall. "Tell him I will pay ten dollars."

Claire carefully clarified. "Ten dollars?"

"Yep, not a penny more."

"Okay." Stifling her laughter, Claire pulled her phone out and messaged Reighn, his reply was not long in coming, she read his text and told Ocean.

"He said deal."

Ocean smiled. "I thought he would. Ten dollars is ten dollars after all." She and Claire burst out laughing as they exited the truck. Conor looked over at Ocean and smiled, his mate was delicious especially when she laughed, he asked. "What is amusing you two?"

Frankie moved to stand with Claire. "Yeah, what is so funny?"

When the girls had joined them, Claire stated. "Ocean has brought the property. Girls you are home." They along with an excited Joy cheered and hugged everyone there.

Conor smiled. "Did the Dragon Lord drive a hard bargain?"

Ocean pulled her face into a frown when the girls stopped cheering and looked at her as she answered Conor.

"He did, but I told him ten and not a penny more. I was quite firm."

Claire mouthed. Ten dollars to Conor causing him to laugh and say. "Well good for you."

The girls not sure why they found this funny asked Frankie who smiling whispered what had happened. "Let's go inside before the girls break the door down." Ocean stated.

The girls whooped with delight and hurried to the door. Claire waited until Conor lifted out the carrier with Parker inside, as Ocean grabbed the baby bag. Then she handed him the key to the front door. He looked up at the two, fifteen foot tall, iron strapped wooden doors which would allow a fully grown dragon to pass through without bringing down the house.

"I would hazard a guess these are at least five inches thick if not more." Conor murmured.

"Why would they want them that solid?" Joy asked as she smoothed a hand over the golden wood.

"To stop marauders."

"What are they?"

Conor grinned at the inquisitive girls as he answered Paige's question. "Enemies, that wanted to get into the house."

"Like pirates?" Kadee asked. Conor smiled as he looked her over; she was a cute girl, she would be a beautiful lioness.

"Do you like pirates, Kadee?"

Before she could answer, Paige sighed as only a sister could when she told him. "She is crazy for them."

Kadee ducked her head as she toed the pebbles under her feet. Conor reached out and ran his hand over her hair. When she looked up at him, he told her. "You should talk to Andre` he was a pirate once upon a time."

Kadee's eyes widened as she asked in a hushed voice. "Really, a real-life pirate and Andre`... our grandfather Andre`?"

Conor cocked an eye at her. "Yep, with an eye patch and all. He commanded his own ship." Conor looked at Ocean and saw a relieved expression come and go. He reasoned she was probably pleased he did not belabor the point of who Andre` was.

"Oh wow!" Kadee almost swooned right then and there. She turned to Ocean and begged. "Mom, can you talk to him for me and ask some questions please?"

"We will see." Ocean told her trying not to be annoyed with Conor. It was not his fault he did not know how she felt about Andre`. Shoot, she did not know how she felt about the male that was supposed to be her father. Sighing, she said to take her mind off her thoughts about something she could do little about at the moment. "Getting old here, open up the door."

Conor grinned. "As you wish." Using the large iron key. He said. "We will change this."

"Just as well that will be hard to put in my jeans pocket." Ocean mumbled to Claire. Which seemed to be the funniest thing Joy and Kadee had heard for a while. They hooted with laughter as the three of them scrambled through the doorway. When Ocean went to pass Conor, he bent down and whispered. "Welcome home, mate."

She sighed and looked into his amber eyes and returned just as quietly. "You too mate."

She nipped in before him. Only to come to a halt in what was a very large imposing entryway, that was a delight to the senses. A large cathedral ceiling, reaching what Ocean thought was maybe thirty feet tall, greeted them. Hanging from the center was a huge elaborate chandelier; it was exquisite, each prong holding a bulb was molded in the shape of a dragon Ocean sighed. "Oh, I love it."

Paige asked. "You think it is electric?"

Kadee scowled at her. "Of course it is. Why would it not be?"

"This is a really old home. Maybe he never got around to doing it. He has not lived here for years."

"Seven hundred." Frankie muttered as she looked up at the beautiful wooden ceilings.

"See?" Paige told Kadee who opened her mouth to respond as Conor ended what he could see developing into an argument, when he turned the lights on. "We have electricity."

The girls all ahhh and oohed as the lights sparkled. Ocean looked around at the stone floors and the sweeping staircase that rose up to the next floor. The banister was a beautiful rose wood that was highly polished and gracefully guided the steps upward. The walls were covered in plaster board and needed new paint. "That seems sad." She indicted the covered stone walls, "We should take all that off and have the stone. What do you think?" She asked Conor who nodded and in his deep voice agreed. "It seems a shame to cover what has stood for years."

"Okay, so that all comes off." Like the others, Ocean noticed all the doors leading into rooms were in need of refinishing. The girls looked at her and Ocean smiled.

"Go... go look and find a bedroom each."

Claire yelled out as they started running up the stairs. "All the mattresses are new as are the linens so you can all move in today, plus there is meant to be an entertainment room somewhere."

With cheers of happiness, the girls continued up the stairs. "Really an entertainment room?" Ocean asked with raised eyebrows.

Claire nodded. "I think it was an enticement."

"Huh!" Was her only comment.

Conor looked around. "It needs updating."

"It does, do you know anyone?" Ocean asked as he grinned. "As a matter of fact, I do. Let's do a walk through and make a list of what needs doing, then we can see who we need to call."

Frankie pulled a tablet from her backpack. "Come on, let's go."

So the four of them walked around the ground floor as

Frankie tapped away on her tablet, making notes. While the other three pointed out work that would need to be done. They walked into the large great hall or lounge and stopped at the opulence that greeted them.

"Oh my!" Frankie gushed. "Isn't it great?"

"Well, that is one word for it." Ocean commented as she looked up at Conor. "Change it or leave it?"

Without hesitation, he rumbled out. "Change it and quickly."

Just then the girls arrived back. "So we found our rooms and an entertainment theatre for games and movies. Conor, it is fabulous." Kadee told him.

Conor grinned, "That is great."

But the three girls were not listening to him, they were taking in the whole golden room. "Wow! Someone liked gold, huh?" Joy nudged Paige.

The adults all agreed with Joy everything in the room was gold, other than the large stone fireplace that covered one full wall. Everything else, wooden floors, painted walls, furniture, there was not one fixture or wall that was not colored gold.

"This is definitely for change until then, let's not use this room." Ocean murmured.

"It will make a wonderful lounge for you all, though." Frankie sighed with pleasure. "Once it is decorated in normal colors."

They all agreed it would and moved on to the kitchen, which basically ran the length of the house, it was so large.

"This is like from the middle ages." Paige quipped as they entered, Ocean just stopped herself from grimacing in distaste.

Conor said as he looked around. "Well, this room will be the first to be remodeled."

"Although we can use the cooker, it is electric." Kadee mumbled doubtfully.

Shocked, Joy cried out. "There are no faucets. How did they get the water in here?"

Conor smiled at her stunned tone. "The kitchen boys or girls carried it in."

Horrified, the three girls looked up at him as Joy asked. "Like in buckets?"

Claire laughed at the expressions on all three of their faces. "Yes, they actually worked back then."

Paige asked. "But what about school?"

"There was no school."

Horrified all over again, Kadee squeaked. "What about books?"

"Nope, no books or computers, TV, nothing like that." Ocean told her.

"It was the dark ages." Paige cried as the other two girls nodded.

"Well yes, it was." Conor said. "That is why it is called, the dark ages."

"That is just wrong... so wrong we need faucets." Kadee stated. Ocean assured her there would be faucets and water. Kadee nodded and stated. "Good, because I am not hauling water. I go to school."

Which made the adults laugh. "You will not have too." Frankie said as she wrinkled her nose. "This is depressing, we need the dragons."

"Why, can they remodel fast?" Paige asked as she looked around at the dark, horrible room.

"Yes. If you can draw what you want, they will have it done in hours ready for the decorators to come in."

"Seriously?" Ocean asked Frankie and Claire, who both nodded.

"Yep." Claire told them. "They use dragon magic, which is how most of the Gap was developed so quickly."

"That is so cool." Kadee told Joy, who agreed.

Ocean agreed as well. "When can they come?"

Frankie shut her phone. "Two are on their way, draw what you would like and they will have it done in an hour or so, also George and Ivan are on their way."

"They are the decorators. They have their own company. We

are lucky they are free." Conor told Ocean.

She smiled and said. "Oh okay. So does anyone have paper?"

Within minutes Paige, Joy and Kadee were racing upstairs where they remembered seeing paper. Conor passed her a pen. She walked around the large empty room to the only piece of furniture there. A long scarred wooden table that had to be the original kitchen work bench. There were a few counters that remained against the wall, although they looked like they were ready to fall down. By the time the girls were back. She had a good idea of what she wanted and as they all surrounded her.

She bent over the paper and sketched her dream kitchen with a few ideas thrown in by the others. She drew a long kitchen island and butler's pantry, dish washers and an eight burner stove. Granite counters in black with a farmers sink, large walk-in cool rooms and a freezer.

At Conor's insistence she drew in the long table they were using as their kitchen dining table with at least twenty chairs around it. Placing it at the end of the kitchen, sitting in front of the new bay window that had window seating. The floors were to be stone, as were the walls, just cleaner, and she added a large window over the sinks. When she was finished, Conor and the girls along with Claire and Frankie were impressed.

"Wow, you can really draw, that is so life like." Frankie said.

Ocean smiled at the compliment. "Thank you, it is not a medium I do much of. This was fun."

Frankie asked. "What do you normally do?"

Ocean shrugged as she answered. "I take photos."

"Oh... oh my, you are that Ocean Walker, why did that not register before? I love your work. Absolutely love your work."

Ocean nodded. "Thank you that is kind of you to say."

"I missed your last showing. Will you show here?"

"There is a gallery?" Ocean asked, then inwardly cursed as she saw the bemused looks on her family's faces. "I am a little famous for my work."

Frankie snorted. "A little, your mom is really famous."

"Frankie please." Ocean flapped her hand around.

"What? They will find out."

"Yes, but later, today is about our home."

"Oh, okay, sure. Edith Kingsley owns the gallery; she will love to show your work." She looked at Claire as she sighed. "Just saying."

Which made the girls laugh. Stopping anymore of Frankie's observations, Ocean said. "Well, I will go visit her soon."

Claire said. "I am sure she would love that."

Frankie frowned because she had just remembered, Harper had a problem with Ocean Walker the photographer, what it was about she had no idea. She thought it had something to do with Ocean's mother but she was unsure. The dragons arrived bringing her back to what was happening, they were two older males. Ian and Adam.

Frankie had worked with them before, they were kind, patient and very fast. They took Ocean's sketch and smiled.

Ian congratulated her. "We are impressed, this design is outstanding, would you mind if we made some adjustments?"

Conor and Ocean shook their heads, Ocean said "Please do whatever you think would suit. I have never designed a kitchen before."

Conor asked. "Can you install a lift?"

The three males went with Conor and the girls to see where one could go, after they assured him that a lift was as easy as installing the kitchen. Frankie, Claire and Ocean took the baby in her carrier and went upstairs to tour the two remaining floors.

"This house is huge." Frankie stated sometime later as they came from what was obviously the entertainment room.

"It is, have you found your master bedroom yet?" Claire asked as she poked her head around a door to look into an empty room.

"No." Ocean called back as she came out of what would be a bathroom when upgraded.

Paige ran up the stairs. "It is on the next floor."

"What?" The three females asked her.

Paige grinned as she told them. "There is another whole

floor."

"You are not kidding are you?" Ocean asked her.

"No, we already looked." She showed them the staircase that led to double wooden iron banded doors like the ones at the entrance.

"How did we miss these stairs?" Ocean asked the other two females.

"Seems impossible." Claire agreed.

The door opened into a lounge that had doors leading off of it. A large stone fireplace covered one wall. It was magnificent. "You can see a couple of comfortable chairs and table here with a fire going, so romantic." Frankie sighed.

Ocean could also see it, just as she could see a very lifelike Conor and herself on a large mat in front of a blazing fire. She averted her eyes from the area not wanting to explain the blush she could feel creeping over her face.

They walked around the lounge and Frankie pulled open a door to a long closet. They could see no use for it, so closed the door and shrugged at each other. Then they found the bedroom with the biggest bed Ocean had ever seen and from the silence that descended on the group. It was the biggest they had ever seen as well.

"I forgot, I am meant to show Kadee and Joy." Paige called out as she ran from the room.

"Does she not walk anywhere?" Claire asked with a smile as she looked after the girl.

"Not that I have seen." Ocean replied absently as she tipped her head to the side while saying. "You know that is one huge bed right? It is not just my imagination."

Frankie agreed. "It's big alright."

Conor walked in saying. "Paige said the bed was... yes... she was not exaggerating that is really big."

He ended up next to Ocean staring at the bed. Ocean looked up at him as she said. "Your lion could lie on that, and there would still be room for us all."

He smiled slowly as he returned her look. "He likes that

idea."

"I bet he does." She mumbled as her body tingled from the heated look he gave her. "Did you see the fireplace?" She asked her voice a little higher than normal causing Conor to smile wider, knowing she was not indifferent to him, which made his beast stretch in anticipation.

"I did, I will have them all cleaned before we can safely use them. I have placed them on my list."

Claire called to her, and she gave him a vague smile as she hurried to see what she had found. Conor wandered from the room, he and his lion happy they had found their mate and she was receptive to him. Apparently his little mate did not care he was a huge male and an even larger lion. Maybe it is because she was dragon.

Claire and Frankie had indeed found another room which Claire told her was called a dressing room. Frankie told her there were two when Ocean asked why. Claire launched into a lecture about what dressing rooms were used for in the past. Frankie then told her about the revolving shoe rack which should be installed in her dressing room, they all sighed in delight and Ocean agreed she needed one.

They eventually left to look at what was behind the two other doors and found two small studies, in the second one Conor stood looking out the large window. "I like this room for a nursery for Parker. What do you think?" He asked the three as they entered.

Ocean smiled. "It's ideal, once we decorate it, she will be very happy in here."

Claire said. "Did you guys notice the French doors that go to the balcony?"

They walked back into the lounge to where she had pulled back the heavy drapes exposing several French doors as Ocean and Frankie went to open a door each. Conor stopped them.

"Ladies, I think it may be a good idea for us to find out how sound the deck is before you step out on it."

All three halted. "Ahh! Good idea." Ocean agreed.

They all took a step back and turned to him. "This is a massive master suite do you think we really need all this room?" Ocean asked him with a little worry in her voice because even though she broached the idea of a smaller room, she really loved the space and could visualize how it would look once a bathroom was added and it was decorated.

Conor nodded. "I do, we need a bolt hole from the pride when they descend on us. Also, one of those small rooms like the one we are using for Parker, is going to be where the lift will come too."

Ocean grinned as she said. "A private lift, how cool."

He winked at her. "I need fast access to the kitchen." They all laughed at his expression.

"You know?" Claire told them "You could put a little bar fridge in the nursery for snacks and drinks."

"Ohh, I love that, let's make that happen." Ocean agreed.

Conor nodded and said. "I will add it to my list."

Frankie asked. "Where are you going to put the bathroom?"

Conor said. "Come with me I will show you. I was thinking we could fit it between the dressing rooms we will take a little from both of them."

"We need a big one." Called Ocean as she trailed behind them, thinking Conor needed a huge shower and she loved a bath.

"Oh, it will be." They all went to where he opened the same narrow door they had earlier, that was between both dressing rooms. "This is where in the old days the manservant would stash all his cleaning equipment and clean or polish the masters' boots as well as press the masters' clothes."

"Oh!" Ocean and the other two said as understanding hit. It looked like a long four foot wide dark cupboard.

"What a horrible place to have to work in." Claire murmured.

"How do you know about all that?" Frankie asked Conor, who grinned as he replied. "I like history and especially I like to read about old homes."

"Oh okay."

He told Ocean who was standing back trying to visualise the

bathroom. "I will have Ian and Adam here after they finish the lift and the other bathrooms. By the time they are finished, it will be like it was always here."

She looked up at him and smiled to reassure him. "I bet it will, so where should we stay while we knock this place into shape?"

Conor looked around. "Here, we can eat out and the bedrooms are okay they all will have bathrooms within a week but Ian said he will complete one immediately and we can use that. I will have them do ours next. We can have the downstairs finished first."

Ocean shrugged. "Sounds good to me. We will need a bassinet for Parker actually several then she can come downstairs with us. We need to shop."

Conor nodded. "Good, so after we do lunch, you can shop and I will collect my stuff."

"Agreed." Ocean and Conor smiled at each other.

"Enough you two. Sheesh!" Frankie rolled her eyes at Claire.

Before Ocean could retort they all heard squealing and giggles. Claire and Frankie turned from Conor and Ocean and started toward the noise as Conor bent down and kissed Ocean, who wrapped her arms around his neck. He stood lifting her off her feet as the kiss became heated. Pulling away before he took her to the floor and showed her what a lion wanted from his mate. And truthfully when he finally made her his, he wanted a bed. He growled low in his throat as Ocean blinked to bring her thoughts back on line. "Oh... oh!" Was all she could think of to say?

"My thoughts exactly." He grumbled out. Conor grinned as his eyes heated with desire. "I cannot wait until we are alone."

Ocean blushed as he placed her back down on her feet and slowly let her go. Then he placed his hands in his pockets to keep from grabbing her again. He gave her a smile and swaggered to the bedroom leaving Ocean to fan her over heated cheeks. Claire stood just inside the door, she smiled when Ocean noticed her. "You two work well together, almost like you were made for each other."

"Well if you believe in stuff like that, we are." Ocean said as she walked toward her. "I really never thought I would have a mate. I figured my girls would be enough."

Frankie nodded as she said. "Oh me either, it is amazing, huh?"

"Yes, it really is." Just then Parker cried and Ocean said. "Time for a bottle let's go downstairs."

CHAPTER NINE:

As Ocean fed Parker, they discussed moving in. Conor agreed to have all the remaining items of Oceans and the girls at the hotel picked up. While he had his possession moved from his apartment. Saul walked in as he said that and was introduced to everyone.

"You are leaving now?" He asked Conor, who looked at his brother and said softly. "I am, this is my home now."

"Yeah, I guess." He sounded so sad, Ocean said. "No reason you cannot move in. There is plenty of room, and Conor could probably use the male company."

Saul's face lit up. "You mean that?"

Ocean said. "I usually mean what I say."

Paige said. "We could go look at the cabins out back. We saw them from upstairs. They may be liveable if you want to live there?"

Saul grinned. "It sounds good."

Conor told her. "Let's go look." With that he, Saul and the girls were gone.

Claire said. "That was nice, offering Saul a place here, he would be lost without Conor. They only connected a few months ago. His father is Conor's father when their dad died during a Pride war. I think Saul was only ten or so, his mother was scared for his life and she left, taking Saul with her."

Ocean looked after them as she asked. "She left Conor behind?"

Claire nodded. "She did, she was not his mother. Life was not easy for either of them. Conor survived to find Saul and together they led a pride of misfits here."

Ocean nodded as though she thought of something that made sense to her. "Family is family."

Frankie looked at her and asked. "Does that sentiment mean your sister and father as well?"

Claire looked at the suddenly serious Frankie, it was as though another being was superimposed over the normal care-free Frankie. Claire felt a shiver of apprehension as Ocean looked down at Parker's small face and sighed, "Frankie, you ask the hard questions."

"I know, but you are smart enough and wise enough to know it was not their fault as much as it was not yours. Others played god with your lives and now three people are hurting."

"That is true but..."

"Tell me Ocean what are you going to punish them for?" Claire asked softly.

Frankie said. "You can't really can you, it would be like punishing yourself. Because you didn't know about them either, just like they knew nothing about you. In fact the ones to be angry at are the Goddesses, and Andre` was really angry at her. Lord Rene` thought she was going to hurt him."

"When was this?" Ocean demanded as fear for the male she had not met came over her. Frankie looked out the corner of her eye at Ocean and seeing the concern casually said.

"When she came here to tell him about Ciana and her babies and you. Although she did not know a lot about you, he was so angry he told her she had to explain why she had done what she had. If you wanted her to, he said that you were so much more important than they knew and she was to stay out of his and his daughter's lives. He and his family would love you and fix the mess they had made." She looked at Ocean and asked. "You know what you are right?"

Ocean bypassed that question and asked one of her own instead. "How do you know all this, were you there?"

Frankie did the lips thing as she thought about that question, and then she shrugged. "Nope, I was not, I just know that's all."

Ocean said slowly as she realized this strange woman was so much more than the sweet woman she appeared to be.

Okay, so that gives me some things to think about."

Frankie nodded as she said. "Because I think it was as hard for them as it is for you to find out their daughter and sister was lost. And to take it out on them for something beyond all three of your control. That seems rather bitter and sad for the girls as well as you and them."

Claire told her as she tipped Ocean's face up to hers with two fingers under her chin. "You are so much better than that."

Ocean removed her face from those fingers and looked at her with sober eyes that held not anger only confusion.

Frankie chipped in. "You really are!"

With raised eyebrows, Ocean asked. "Am I?"

Claire smiled. "Yes, otherwise those three young girls and that male who has declared himself to be yours and his brother. Oh and let us not forget the five lionesses you will be taking on today are all wrong and you are a selfish, hard, bitter, nasty female!"

Ocean laughed. "Lay it out there my friend." She held her hand up. "No, I am not like that. I will not be like that and you are both right. My family, all my family deserves much more, so much more than an angry Ocean. They deserve aunties and uncles and grandparents."

"Oh, they will have heaps of them. But you are still angry, right?" Frankie asked hesitantly.

Ocean shrugged, feeling uncomfortable. "Yeah, I am, but I will deal with it, like I have been my entire life, it will fade."

"Good, so can I have a cuddle?" She held her hands out for the baby as Ocean grinned and passed Parker to her saying. "Thank you both."

Frankie smiled and said. "It is what we do, `cause we are family."

Ocean softly told her. "You need to find out who you are, sweet Frankie, time is running out. Soon it will not be possible for you to hide anymore."

Frankie looked a little awed as she said. “I was unaware I was hiding.”

“Which is why you are hiding.” Ocean told her just as softly.

Frankie stilled, as did Claire, who looked at Frankie and asked Ocean. “What do you see when you look at her?”

“Frankie surrounded by stars. Do you not see the same, Seer?”

Claire said quietly. “No, I never see anything around Frankie.”

“You need to see the seeker.” She advised Frankie.

“Oh… oh alright, I will do that.”

“Soon Frankie.” Ocean told her as she got up and left the room.

Frankie looked after her. “I did not know she was a Seer, did you?”

Claire shook her head. “Maybe she is, maybe she is not. She is a dragon with abilities just coming to light.”

“She sure is spookier than you all together.”

Claire cleared her throat. “Yes, she is. Will you do it?”

Frankie nodded. “I will go talk to Harper as soon as she returns.”

“Okay good.”

“Yeah good.” Frankie replied and to Claire’s ears she sounded scared.

CHAPTER TEN:

Later after a fabulous lunch at the hamburger place that the girls and Conor begged to go to.

Claire and Frankie knew Conor wanted to talk to Ocean alone, so they were going to take the girls to start on their shopping. Ocean handed Claire her credit card and smiling at Joy said. "Please buy all three of them something special to remember today by."

Joy beamed. "Really, me too?"

Ocean hugged the skinny teenage. "Definitely and if your dad says it is okay, you can spend the night. Only..." As she and Kadee started to squeal with delight. "If your dad says it is okay."

"That is so cool." Joy and Kadee said together.

"Great." Paige mumbled.

Ocean told her. "Buy a book you want to read or a movie."

Conor told her. "I will be bringing my games console. We can do that. I mean we have the theater after all, just waiting for us to use, right?"

"Seriously, I can play with you?"

He grinned at her eagerness. "Always, you have to be better than Saul?"

"Can I buy my own game?" She asked Ocean.

"Of course."

"Thanks, let's go." She ordered the two younger girls as Frankie slung an arm around her shoulders.

"So I like playing..." they were quickly down the street and Ocean missed what Frankie liked to play.

Claire grinned at the trio and Frankie. "You made them

happy, and I included Frankie in that."

Ocean shrugged. "That is my job. Maybe not so much with Frankie."

"That's what you think. So when I leave the girls to see the lionesses. I will give the card to Frankie, if you have not caught up with us."

"Okay and thanks Claire for everything." Ocean stood and hugged Claire, who returned the hug.

"You are welcome." With a wave to Conor, she left.

Sitting again, Ocean asked. "So Mr Towers, what do you need to discuss with me?"

Conor ordered more coffee and then told her in a quiet voice as he picked her hand up and held it. "I need to take Paige to the Dragon Lord."

Ocean replied in a voice just as quiet as his. "I see, would this have to do with her being a first, and I am guessing you do not need me there, as you said I instead of we?"

"Yes to both."

"Why does he have to know?"

"She is in his territory. He needs to know and keep her safe. She will be very important as she matures, as we mature and our race evolves into what we are to become."

"Why would she be unsafe? We are at the epicenter of dragon civilization, who would dare to hurt her?"

Conor grimaced as though his coffee tasted bad and told her about the attacks on the people of Dragon's Gap, the poisonings, the kidnapping attempts. When he was finished, she asked. "So this is where Andre ` and Ciana are now."

"Yes after the rescue, they left to bring Thorn's people here."

"Amazing elves, the girls are going to flip."

He grinned. "Speaking of the girls, have they shifted?"

Ocean explained about the pills, Conor sighed and swore softly. "Okay, we need them off them as soon as possible. Sharm needs to check them both over first, some of that stuff can change them at the DNA level."

"Oh my Goddess seriously?"

"Yes, it is okay, we will sort it out."

Ocean asked. "Can you manage two teenage lionesses, because you know I am going to be useless here? You, daddy will have your hands full."

Conor smiled widely as he heard her call him daddy, even though it was in jest it sounded great. "I will manage, and you should know they may not be teenage lionesses it depends on what the pills did to them."

"Okay, we will find out, I am sure. Now about Paige. Take her, in fact, take all three. Maybe you can persuade Frankie to give them a tour of the castle this afternoon and if Joy can stay over, they can come home with pizza for dinner?"

"You know?" He kissed her. "The pizza place only opened three weeks ago and already it is busy."

"I am shocked, no pizza how did you survive?"

Conor's face pulled into sorrow as his eyes laughed at her playful tone. "It was hard, so very hard."

"Funny lion, let's go before they break my credit card."

CHAPTER ELEVEN:

Conor sat in Reighn's office with a nervous Paige. "Why are you nervous, kitten? Reighn is your relation and one of the kindest males I have ever met."

Paige winced. "He may make me leave."

Startled, Conor asked. "Why would he do that?"

"Because I will bring trouble here?"

"Who told you that?"

Paige could hear his lion in his voice. She swallowed and whispered. "You kicked Neila out."

Conor nodded. "I did, but she was nothing like you. Neila was just wrong, wrong for the pride, wrong for Dragon's Gap. You saw that in the short time you were in her company. Can you honestly say you are anything like her?"

"No, she thought more of herself than she did the Pride or the Gap."

"Exactly, you my young kitten, are not wrong."

Paige looked at him with fear in her eyes and whispered. "How do you know, was that why those people wanted me and Kadee and why we had to leave?"

Conor pulled her gently onto his lap. "Sweetheart, your grandfather was a very intelligent, resourceful male who knew when he needed to protect his young. Which he did by sending them to Ocean and me. I believe those people did not know what or who you were, but I believe your grandfather and whoever was watching out for you did."

Paige laid her head on his chest as she said. "Like the Goddess, that is what Mom thinks."

"Yes, something like that." Conor rumbled. They were quiet for a minute or two, and then Paige asked. "Conor, can we call you dad? We don't remember our birth father very well. Kadee and I were really young when he died, and Parker's birth parents did not want her. There is no one to be upset if we do. It is just the three of us. I think Parker will grow up calling you dad, so Kadee and I want to as well. Then we will be a family."

Conor felt his heart expand as he cleared his throat. "We don't know each other really well. But as I am sticking around, I would really like it if you and Kadee considered me your dad."

"Because you and mom are mates?" He could hear the uncertainty in her young voice and hugged her to him. "Not just because of that, I would be proud to claim all of you as mine."

"So you can claim all three of us like mom did?"

"I will as soon as we see the Dragon Lord."

She heaved out a large sigh. "Good, we were worried you would not want us."

He tipped her face up to his. "Never ever worry about that. You are mine, all of you. Now, I have something serious to discuss with you."

Paige frowned. "What?"

"Your mom told me about the pills you take. I would like for you to stop taking them."

"Okay, they make us feel funny, so it will be good not to take them anymore. But then we will shift to our lion skin, right?"

"Yes, Sharm will have to check you both out to make sure you are okay. But if you stop taking the pills, it will not be long before you can shift."

"It will be fun, I think."

Just then Sage and Reighn walked into the office Conor felt Paige tremble. Slowly, as he did most things, he stood as Paige lowered her feet to the floor.

"Paige this is the Dragon Lord, Reighn Kingsley and his shadow Lady Sage."

"Welcome to Dragon's Gap again." Reighn said as he showed Sage to a seat. Paige looked up at Conor, who nodded for her to take her seat.

Sage also said. “Welcome Paige, it is very nice to meet you again.”

“I liked meeting you as well Lady Sage and Lord Reighn. I am sorry if I was rude to you yesterday and we love our home, thank you for selling it to us. It is fabulous.”

Sage said. “Paige honey, you were not rude. Standing up for your family is never wrong or rude.”

Paige let out a relieved breath. Reighn beamed a smile at her. “I am glad you like the home, did you find the entertainment theater?”

Paige almost bounced out of her chair as she replied. “Yes, dad and I are going to break it in later tonight, while Joy and Kadee have a sleep over.”

“A sleep over already?” Sage asked Conor, who smiling shrugged. “They are like-minded, apparently.”

Reighn asked. “What does Harper and Ace think?”

“I have no idea, now we are here because My Lord it has come to my attention that my Paige is a First.’ and we wished for you to know.”

Reighn looked at the scared teenager and softened his tone as he asked her. “Paige, do you know what that means?”

“Dad and I talked about it, he said we will have to have more talks later, he just wanted me to know.”

Sage asked. “You did not know before.”

Paige shook her head. “Not really I kinda always knew I was different, but I thought it was because we took the pills all the time, you know?”

“I do, yes.” Sage smiled at her, easing the tension in her shoulders immediately. “You know it is okay to be different. Everyone here is different, we are all weird in some way.”

Reighn snorted. “Sage, she did not say weird.”

Sage looked at Reighn. “She is a girl; she means weird.”

Paige tried not to laugh as the two exchanged words. Conor grinned at her. “Your cousins are slightly bent, but you will get used to it in time.”

Paige's eyes widened as a male and female entered. Reighn introduced Paige to the couple. "Paige, these are my parents Lord Rene` and Lady Verity, my father is your grandfather's brother."

"Oh hello." Paige tried not to be cool toward them, but it was really hard. She wanted to yell at them, that her mom was hurting and her mom's dad needed to be here to talk to her. But she did not because she was scared she would cry.

Verity sat beside her. "I am sorry you think we are your enemy."

Paige shrugged. "I don't, not really, it is just I think my mom is hurting and you don't care."

Verity took her hand in hers. "Now you know that is not true sweetheart, you are old enough to understand that adults have issues that are not easily fixed with a few words."

Paige looked at Conor's face, but he did not look angry or anything. He was staring at Lady Verity, then she looked at Lady Verity too and saw anger and fear and sadness in her eyes.

"I know that, but her dad is not even here. He should have been here to meet her, to hug her. She has an ache in her heart, and I think he is the only one to fix that."

Verity nodded. "Maybe you are right, maybe Andre` has the same ache and your mom is the only one that can fix that too."

"Oh, I never thought of that."

"No, I am sure you did not. Andre` could not be here because his other daughter, your mother's sister, needed him with her and her babies. But I will tell you something, he will be here by the morning. Now dear, I want you to help us..."

"No." Conor rumbled out, startling not only Verity but Paige as well. "We will not put that on her. She is only a child and as you said earlier, these are adult issues."

"Conor, I think..."

"Lady Verity, I admire and respect you very much. I count you, along with your family as my friends, but your fear is driving your decisions here."

Verity raised both eyebrows as she asked in a voice devoid of warmth. "I beg your pardon Conor?"

"Your fear of what may or may not happen with Ocean and what she may or not be to the females of dragon kind are asking you to go against your instincts. What I am sure are telling you that involving Paige in your quest to secure your future is wrong. She is a day away from arriving here, and you wish to burden her with dragon kind concerns?"

Verity looked at the calm male and the teenager sitting quietly beside her, who was pale and trembling her hand held securely in the Lions and shook her head. "Please forgive me. You are right. I am over wrought with worry, forgive me Conor, Paige." She stood abruptly and left by a side door.

Rene ` looked after her and sighed. "I too apologize, I should have never allowed her to come here. Paige, your grandfather is a good male. If you give him a chance, he will love you and your sisters and especially your mother with everything he has." With that, he too left, following his shadow.

Reighn stood. "Thank you my friend for being gentle with her."

Conor smiled slowly. "She is a delightful female who has been nothing but kindness to me and Dragon's Gap, how could I not."

Reighn leaned over and swept Paige into his large arms, causing her to squeak as he did. "You my lovely little cousin are adorable. Welcome to our large, ever growing family. We are very thankful you are here." He kissed her forehead as she smiled and wrapped her arms around his thick neck.

"Thank you, Uncle Reighn. I hope your mom is not too unhappy?"

"She will be for a while, but it is not your job to make her happy that is my fathers. Now when did I become Uncle Reighn?"

"Kadee and I have never had uncles and aunties before." She shyly told him. "Is it okay if we call you that?"

"Yes, little one, it is most appropriate. Now do you have any questions?"

"Yes, what did your mom mean?"

"As your dad said, it is dragon business; she should not have spoken about. I would like for you not to think on it for now. All will be clear when your grandfather and aunt arrive back. Can you do that?"

"I can and thanks, now what is my job?"

He placed her back on her feet and told her. "Your job is to grow, learn and enjoy being young and a lion, to love your parents and to be loved by them."

"But I am a first."

"Yes, and when that time comes for you to learn what that means. I, your father and anyone else we can find will help you with that until then be Paige. That is all you need to be."

She smiled as though a weight had been lifted from her shoulders. "Okay, dad has a question too."

They all looked at Conor, who nodded and said seriously. "I do. I would like it recorded that I have claimed Paige, Kadee and Parker Walker as mine."

Reighn grinned. "It will be so recorded."

Paige stepped from one foot to the other. "May I go, Frankie said she will take us on a tour of the castle... Oh!" Her eyes widened. "Our home is a castle too. It is so cool. We are going to name it."

Reighn grinned, "I am pleased you like it. Well, I am finished with you, so if your father does not mind, go find Frankie."

Paige turned to Conor. "Dad?"

"I am good, Frankie said, she will bring you home. Paige do not wander off without an adult." He told her seriously. "You have not been here long enough for people to recognize you. I would rather you were with an adult for a while until the Pride and the people of Dragon's Gap know who you both are and who you belong to. Your mother, I feel, will be terrifying if anything was to happen to you."

Paige nodded seriously as she said. "Yeah, I think she would rival you for fierceness. I swear we will not go anywhere without an adult."

"Thank you."

Sage closed her phone. "Frankie is on her way here now."

Paige smiled and said thank you, then slipped from the room just as Frankie and Kadee arrived, she asked, surprised to not see Joy. "Where is Joy?"

Kadee said. "Her dad wanted to talk to her, she has done the tour already."

"Oh okay, because we are having pizza for dinner."

Frankie sighed. "Yum pizza. I wonder if Johner will like that."

"You could have it with us." Paige shyly invited her. Frankie smiled and hugged the girl. "Thank you and then you would get to meet my shadow Johner. That is a great idea. I accept."

CHAPTER TWELVE:

While Conor was taking the girls to the castle, Ocean went back home, and entered an empty room on the second floor, where she decided to open a portal. Which, thanks to an inquisitive Kadee, who had read about portals and how the dragons used them to go from one place to another, had given her the idea.

The room she had decided on using was not big enough for more than a bed and side table. But it would be ideal to store all her mother's paintings. Once she retrieved them from her storage unit in Hawaii, where she had placed them for safekeeping, after her mother had passed away,

Of course, now she thought about it, she wondered how a person went about opening a portal. Never having done such a thing before she was a little intimidated, she frowned as she went through all the knowledge on magic she knew, which was pitifully little. Then, as if by thinking about magic, the information she needed just seemed to be there, waiting for her to find, almost like a memory.

She grinned as she stood hands on hips looking at the outside wall and wondered if it was her memory or her dragon's memory. Deciding to take a gamble she was not crazy, she asked her dragon she now knew lay within her. The silent, watching and waiting being that had resided alongside her for her entire life. *Well, which is it?*

She received no reply, but she knew she was there. She was positive she had felt her stir, more so since she had her session with the punching bag. *You may as well talk to me. I am not opening the portal until you do, and you know how stubborn I can be!*

Suddenly it was as if a door opened, and a light feminine voice answered. *You can be so very stubborn.*

Really, I am stubborn; you have been moving around and making suggestions for months now and not once have you said hello.

I was waiting.

I don't understand. For what?

An invitation. One would have been nice.

Oh, well, I am sorry, this is all new for me and you as well; I understand that so much is happening all at once. But that is no excuse I should have spoken to you earlier, I apologize. Ocean blew a breath out as she thought of the last few months and then the last few days.

Her dragon gushed in reply with what could only be a happy voice. *I too apologize, I am overwhelmed with all the new and exciting adventures we are having.*

Ocean grinned and said. *Adventures is a good term for what we are experiencing. So, okay, let's get this portal opened and bring all her work here.*

Because you want it to place on show or to annoy the female Harper Easton, or because you wish to have it for your own pleasure?

Her name is Harper Battle now.

You did not answer my question?

Ocean sighed and traced a design on the wall in front of her. She had not answered because she did not want to look at her motives. Now she was forced to examine the reason for her decision to bring her mother's works here. After a few minutes of introspection, she quietly said. *In all honesty for all the reasons, you stated but annoying Harper is a bonus.*

She is a very talented artist, or at least your mother thought she was.

I know she is. There is no denying that, but she does have a tendency to be judgemental and not always in a good way. A Miss Righteous.

You are jealous of her.

Maybe, Helena and Harper got on well. Helena enjoyed her. It was not the same with me; she had no time or love for me.

She was guilty, that is why.

Maybe you are right. Ocean agreed sadly as she opened the portal to her storage unit and started hauling the paintings into the room. Her mother had left a huge body of work behind, most of, if not all she had never shown. It took Ocean three quarters of an hour to swap it from the storage unit to the room. Once she was sure she had everything, she closed the portal and stood looking at all the work her mother had done. Then she opened another portal to her storage unit in New Orleans and removed all her own work to place in the room.

Tired, dusty and with muscles aching, Ocean knew she would have to go through every one of her mother's canvas's to see what was there. But not today, moving it here was enough for now. It was still early after she saw to Parker who thankfully had slept through the transfer of art. She showered in a bathroom which was newly finished and attached to what looked like Paige's room.

She decided to go look at some photos she had taken on her travels and see if any were viable to show. She and Conor had chosen an office each. His was very much the masculine one, while hers, she thought, may have been a secretary's. It was not decorated how she would like, but for now it would work.

Unfortunately, she had forgotten she had to transfer all her data from her laptop to her new computer, so instead of sorting through photos she spent time setting up her home computer and downloading and uploading her work. Finally, after two hours, she was finished and just in time as Parker wanted a bottle.

When she had seen to her needs, she walked around the house to see what miracles had been accomplished. Entering the kitchen, she was thrilled to see her design come to life; it was spectacular. Ocean could see years of love and laughter filling this room. The natural stone was still visible and the stone floor had been cleaned and re-grouted or cemented whichever it was. Ocean was glad to see the rather large holes in-between the stones were all gone. There were cupboards under counters, and an island made from black granite. The table Conor liked was refurbished and sat proudly in front of a sparkling clean bay window with a window seat. She turned around in delight and stopped when she saw a beautiful pink and red butterfly hovering outside the window in the sunlight.

She walked to the back door and noticed it was a huge stable door, how clever. Especially for little cubs. She opened it, allowing the butterfly to fly in. Landing on the floor, the butterfly which was no butterfly grew to become.

"Birdy, hello."

"Good afternoon, I was hoping to catch your attention."

"Oh, why, did you need something?" Ocean moved Parker higher on her shoulder as she rubbed her back, Parker snuffled then slept on. Birdy smiled at the picture they made.

"Yes, I was wondering if you were in need of a cook and housekeeper."

"Oh, I have not given it any thought."

At the resigned expression that crossed the faeries face, Ocean smiled and said. "Although now you mention it, I am seeing pitfalls if I take on a lion or lioness that may be seen as favoritism. The same applies if I take on a dragon they will think I do not like them." She sighed, "Either way it bodes ill for all of us."

Birdy nodded and said. "But if you take me on, no one can say anything. We faeries are everywhere and accepted, plus no favoritism."

Ocean led the way back to her office as she thought about what Birdy said. They stopped at the foot of the stairs as they heard creaking from above. Birdy stepped in front of Ocean and Parker and hissed softly. "Stay behind me and make for the door if you need to."

Ocean was going to say it was probably one of the workers but had no chance as Birdy produced a long blade. "Oh my." Ocean murmured as she looked up to where Birdy was staring.

When one of the male dragons came to the top of the stairs, noticing the faerie and blade, he nodded. "I apologize, we are installing bathrooms. I did not know you were employed. I will inform you when we are here from now on." He told Birdy, who inclined her head and made her sword disappear.

Ocean smiled up at him, she thought it was Ian. "Thank you, the kitchen is beautiful, just what I wanted and more. Birdy is our new chef and housekeeper."

He nodded with a smile. "That is good and thank you; we know your style now the bathrooms will reflect that."

Her smile grew. "You are amazing... absolutely amazing."

He saluted the two of them and moved off, Ocean still smiling told Birdy. "Got to love dragon magic."

"They do good work. So I am hired?"

"Please, anyone who will defend me and mine, like you just did earns a place in my home."

"I thank you."

They entered her office and took their seats, Ocean looked at the faerie and bit her lip before she asked. "Please don't take this the wrong way but will you be able to stand your ground against the lions and lionesses?"

Birdy replied with absolute honesty. "The Leo, never, unless he was half dead, in fact I am not sure anyone other than the Dragon Lord could." She shook her head at Ocean's raised eyebrows. "The other lions male and females, yes. I was a guard for the High Queen and recently joined Queen Scarlett's unit. I am professionally trained, I am intelligent and quick. Also, I am a damn good cook. I am also professionally trained for that position as well."

"Good, so we will have some lion and dragon staff, you will be our chef and head housekeeper. I work, Conor works. You would be responsible for running our home. I expect you to pick reliable people to come in daily to clean and tidy. It is a huge house, so we will need an army. The girls are old enough to look after themselves and their own rooms, this one." She nodded to Parker in her arms. "For a few more months is all mine and her fathers, after that, we will work something out."

Birdy smiled. "So when do I start?"

Ocean nodded. "When will your Queen let you go?"

"She already did."

"What if I had said no?"

Birdy shrugged. "I would have returned to another Grove."

"Tell me why us, why now?"

Birdy looked at Ocean "I am tired of killing, of always wondering if someone wants to kill me to get to someone else. I want to have a light." At Oceans confused frown, she said. "Light is mate for a faerie."

"Oh okay."

"I would like to one day have young. For once, I would like to do what I want. Cooking, caring for people who don't expect any more than good honest food and a clean environment to live in. This is what I want for now."

Ocean was moved at her impassioned speech and said softly. "Birdy, this is the right place for that, as you can see we are remodelling. Will you live in?"

"Yes, I can live at the Grove, but I wish to stay here. I should tell you my cousin Kai, if it is permissible will share a place with me. He is hoping to join the sheriff's department."

"Oh, okay." Ocean thought about that, "Is he a warrior?"

Birdy anxiously nodded. "He is trained. I should tell you he is the High Queen's brother, but he renounced his title. He wants to live here and hopefully find his light as well."

"I have no problem with that, but we will have to talk to Conor about him."

"I understand, Lions can be territorial."

"So I have heard, I would think it will not be a worry, if he is as nice as you."

Birdy grinned. "Kai is a gentleman and a deadly foe."

"Good, so extra security for the girls, I am thinking we can't have enough."

"Why do you think you would require that?"

"Again that is up to Conor to discuss with you and your cousin."

"Alright, so Lady Ocean, We are set?"

"Yes, except for pay. Unless you know how much you should receive?"

Birdy looked nonplussed. "No idea."

"Huh, well Conor and Claire may know."

She passed Parker to Birdy as she came around her desk and asked. "Wait one minute please."

Ocean went out and called. "IAN!"

"Yes Lady Ocean." He called back before he appeared again at the top of the stairs.

"Tomorrow can you come back and fix the cottages out back?"

"All five of them?"

"Yes please and can you make them two bedrooms each with en-suites and kitchens?"

"Of course, we will remodel them when we do the stables and swimming pool and tennis court."

Ocean blinked as she asked him, "We have all those?"

"You will tomorrow." He grinned as he returned to what he was doing, leaving Ocean laughing as she called out. "Thank you. Oh and Ian, there is pizza for dinner tonight, you are both welcomed to join us."

There was silence as Ocean thought maybe she had caught them both off guard. A happy and surprised voice floated back down to her. "We will, thank you."

She went back into the room. "So there will be a place for you tomorrow to call your own and pizza tonight if you would like to stay. You should invite Kai. Oh, what are your last names?"

Birdy hesitated for a minute, then shrugged. "It is Rainstree."

Not realizing Birdy was using the High Queens last name. Ocean grinned. "Okay, so great."

Birdy asked. "Ahh, you do not recognize my name."

"I have been here less than a day so sorry, no I do not."

"We are related to the High Queen and King."

"So you told me and I say, good for you, will it interfere with you working here?" Ocean asked, more to take the worried look from the faerie's eyes than she really cared about who she was.

"No... no, she knows we are both wanting to stay here."

"Good so..." Just then the two bears, George and Ivan arrived, Ocean asked. "That will be the painters, want to see the house?"

Birdy nodded. "Very much. They placed Parker in her bassinet the one Ocean had in her office and with the baby monitor in her pocket. She and Birdy greeted the bears and their workers, and together they all toured the house.

Just on dinner time, Conor and the girls as well as Frankie, and her shadow Johner, along with Kai, arrived. Followed a few minutes later by Claire and Lars, as well as Claire's Kammy and baby. Ocean looked around and could not keep the smile from her face. Her family was coming together and her home was filling with warmth.

When Ocean found out the two dragons, Ian and Adam lived alone, she offered them a cottage each to live in. With a look at Conor, who nodded, they agreed instantly.

Kai talked with Conor and was accepted to be his deputy as well as, funnily enough his second with Saul. Conor told her later it was not a matter of choice. It was as though he was a missing piece of the puzzle. Conor told her his lion felt connected instantly with the faerie. He liked the idea of Kai and Birdy living at the estate, as did the girls who were thrilled to learn she was going to live with them. Kadee especially, Ocean heard her asking a few times to see Birdy and Kai's wings, Birdy finally promised they would show her the following day.

Kadee was delirious with happiness; she had a new mom and dad. Her new best friend was having a sleep over and she had a tour of the castle and had gone shopping. They had brought heaps, and she and Paige had a new home and to make it all so much better Birdy who she liked a lot was going to come work and live in her home. She looked around and felt safe and happy. She had felt safe with Ocean but not happy, not since leaving her grandpa. Now though, it was like all the pieces of her heart had glued back together and life was getting better. Looking at Paige, who was being hugged again by Kammy, she could see the glow of happiness filling her up too.

The dinner morphed into a party when Saul delivered a stack of pizzas. He was pleased to be included as part of the family and was happy when Adam told him they were fixing the cottages, as he was to live in one.

Ocean looked around her kitchen with Conor by her side and Parker in his arms and was happy.

So happy. Murmured her dragon, content to be with her young and shadow. Conor's deep voice broke into her reverie as he whispered. "I can feel your happiness from here. You know I am staying the night?"

She coughed on the bite of pizza that became lodged in her throat. When she could breathe again she nodded and said.

"Yep, sure do."

"Nervous?"

She looked at him and grinned as her eyes twinkled. "Nervous, honey, I will rock your world."

Conor grinned and just stopped himself from whooping with delight, instead he told her. "I will keep you to that promise."

"Aww, honey that was not a promise... that was a warning."

Many hours later as Conor shut the bedroom door after settling Parker into her room. He stripped off his shirt as Ocean stood by the French doors brushing her hair. She wore a thin purple nightshirt made of silk. Conor nudged her hair away from her shoulder as he softly said. "This is nice."

Ocean frowned and cocked her head to the side. "You sound different, why?"

"I am worried." He confessed, as she turned and dropped the brush onto the floor when she saw his half-naked body, she slipped her hands up toward his neck. "Why, because you are big?"

Conor grimaced. "No, I had not thought of that."

"Oh, well is it because we don't know each other very well?"

"Not that either."

"Oh, well is it..."

"Ocean... it is because you are delightfully beautiful, and I feel under pressure."

"Oh!" She smiled as she nipped his chin with her teeth, making him bite back a groan of desire. "We could just cuddle."

Conor stilled, had he heard right, he looked down into her smiling eyes. "Excuse me?"

Softly, she whispered. "Cuddle, lions like to cuddle."

"Where did you learn that bit of information from?"

"Kadee, she read all about it and told me. She said I was to make sure I cuddled you a lot tonight, so you will not want to leave us."

"Cuddle!" Conor growled as he picked her up and walked to their enormous bed. "I will show you cuddle female." After he had placed her in the middle of the bed. He stripped off the rest of his clothes, much to Ocean's delight, and then laid down on his back and said. "Alright, rock my world."

Ocean, after one stunned moment, laughed and tackled him. Over the next few hours, she showed him how their world could rock together repeatedly.

While Conor and Ocean were cementing their mating. Reighn was standing pensively on his balcony, waiting for Sage to join him before they retired for the night, as had become their custom. "What has you so upset?" She asked him as she wiggled into her favorite chair with her small glass of watered down wine that Sharm allowed her.

"Someone opened a portal."

"That male, Definiao?"

"No, it was dragon magic."

"I thought you halted that."

Reighn turned to her and sipped his whiskey as he eyed her over his glass. She was looking beautiful, even more so with his hatchlings lying in her body.

"I did."

Sage's mouth fell open as she asked. "Someone opened a portal by overriding your magic, is that even possible?"

"It would seem it is possible. Yes, someone did bypass my magic to do so."

Sage sipped her wine, trying not to make a face at the

watered-down version, and worked at assimilating his information. "You are positive? It was not that male?"

"Most definitely."

"Who could do that then? You are the strongest dragon here."

"Exactly!" Reighn said, then took a swallow of his drink as Sage sipped hers. He looked out over the land and felt his dragons pride at what they had accomplished so far. And his relief in knowing his mother and all female dragons would soon know the thrill of flying. Sage asked, interrupting his thoughts, "Do you know who it was?"

"Yes." He turned and smiled at her slightly stunned face. "Why do you look puzzled my love?"

"I am sort of confused, you are not out there storming around throwing the person responsible in a cell."

"I do not storm anywhere. I regally walk."

"You really do storm my shadow. I am not the only one to have notice."

Reighn eyed her as she sipped her drink innocently. He would demand his brothers tell him who thinks he storms around tomorrow. "Regardless, I am the Dragon Lord. This is my territory. No portals are to be open without my authority. Ocean must learn this."

"Ocean opened it. Oh wow, she is amazing, what will you do?"

"Find out why she did it and ask her not to do so again."

"Well, that could be fun."

Reighn eyed her as he finished his drink and placed his glass down on the table. "You think I am sacred of her?"

Sage barely held her laughter in as she said coyly. "Well not scared so much as...." She did not finish as she saw the predatory look enter his eyes. She slipped from her chair and laughed as she raced into their bedroom with Reighn walking.

Not storming, he reminded his dragon after her.

CHAPTER THIRTEEN:

The next night following another full day of shopping and house renovations. Ocean and her family were just finishing dinner which Birdy, along with the girls had prepared in their brand-new kitchen and then they had eaten on their brand-new patio. When their home was invaded and once again there was a full house. Frankie and Johner arrived and introduced June and Fin to Ocean and the girls, who fell in love with June and Fin's babies, or their pink hair, which seemed to make the girls squeal with delight. The males did not understand it, the females just laughed indulgently at their antics.

Claire and Lars and their young ones arrived after the meal, bringing desserts with them. They sat around indulging in the sweet treats as well as tea and coffee, while the sun started setting. The girls showed Kammy how to catch fireflies, which were actual faeries, but no one thought to tell them as they were having so much fun. Birdy told the adults it was good training for the young faeries, and they enjoyed the delight on their young faces.

The following morning Conor had to go back to work and Claire, Frankie and Joy arrived to take the girl's school shopping. Ocean would join them later. She had some paintings of her mother's to sort out to take to Edith, who she had contacted the night before.

She was in the small room once more, sorting through several canvases, trying to decide which ones she would take with her when she visited the gallery. Just as she had made her mind up on twelve, there came a soft knock on the door.

"Come in."

Reighn opened the door as Ocean looked up. Seeing him there, when she had expected Birdy, took her breath away. He filled the doorway as his presence reached out and surrounded her. "Have you come for your ten dollars?"

Reighn's lips twitched. "Ahh no, not really. Although while I am here, I will collect it."

Standing with a painting in her hands, Ocean's mind went blank she could see no reason for the Dragon Lord to be here in her home. Then the thought crossed her mind. Did he want his home back?

As if he read her mind, he said softly. "No, I do not want the house back. It is yours. Ocean. May I enter?"

"Oh... oh of course, sorry, rude of me."

He walked in with his hands in his pockets, a tall imposing figure of a male. "I see you have been mixing with Frankie."

"How do you know?"

"Rudeness is not to be tolerated. Frankie's rule."

Ocean grinned at the exasperated tone he affected. "She does seem to be a stickler for it."

Reign looked around at the canvases stacked against the walls. He eyed the twelve she had lined up. "Who do all these belong to?"

"How do you know they are not mine?"

"You take photos, amazing photos of people who tell a story."

"Oh!" Once again she was taken aback. "I did not know you knew that?"

Reighn looked at her and smiled. "I have several of your works in my home."

Pleased beyond belief that the most powerful and important Dragon Lord liked her work. Ocean smiled. "Really, thank you, I was going to ask if I could take photos here."

"Of course you may and if it would not be an imposition, I would love for you to do some of my young and shadow."

"Oh, I would love to and you and your dragon?"

Reighn's dragons swamped him with pleasure. Smiling, he told her. "He likes that idea."

He picked up a painting from the ones she had placed in a line and looked at it. Ocean saw it was one of the ones she was debating taking, he asked. "Who is this?"

It was a painting of a tall dark haired male and a little girl with light purple hair around three or four, her hand tucked securely in his. The bottom of their pants rolled up as they walked along the sand. Ocean flicked her eyes at the painting and away as her voice took on the neutral tones she used when discussing her mother. "I have no idea, someone she painted I guess."

Reighn took it to the window and looked at it in the light. "The hair is the same color as yours except there are red steaks whereas yours are blue."

"Really." Ocean moved closer. "So it is, well that is not me, I never had a dad or male to take me to a beach."

Reighn wondered if she heard the pain and anger in her voice as he looked at the painting he realized this was probably Ciana and her grandfather. "Did your mother know Ciana and her grandparents?"

Ocean looked at the painting, then Reighn, then out the window. He could see emotions whirling in her eyes, yet she did not speak them, only shrugged, saying neutrally. "I do not know what or who my mother knew."

She gently took the painting from him and placed it with a stack of others. Then lifted another of a house and placed it where that one had been. "So why are you here, if not for your ten dollars?"

Reighn saw pleasantries were apparently over. "Ocean did you open a portal yesterday?"

"Yeah, to get all these from my storage unit." She told him as she crouched down to look at another canvas.

"Ocean?" Reighn's voice took on a questioning tone.

She looked up. "Yes Reighn."

"How were you able too?"

Ocean stood up and cocked her head to the side as she looked at the male. He looked mildly inquisitive, but more he seemed confused, as though he was unsure who he was talking to. "Was I not meant to?"

"No, I have placed a ban on Dragon's Gap. I am the only one who is able to open a portal, unless I give my permission for someone else to do so."

"Oh well, okay. I am sorry, I did not know that?"

"So I ask again. How did you?"

Ocean frowned. "I don't understand, I opened a portal. I won't do it again."

Reighn ran a hand around the back of his neck. "Ocean it is not that you did so. It is you are not meant to be able to do so. I banned it."

Ocean stood looking at him for a moment, processing his words, then said. "Oh, I see... Reighn I don't know how." She shrugged. "I just did it."

"Can you do it again?"

She raised her eyebrows. "Well okay... I suppose." With that, she reopened the portal within the storage unit. Reighn nodded. "Thank you, close it please."

Ocean dismissed the portal. "So what did you learn?"

Reighn smiled. "I assume you are looking at taking these to Edith's gallery?" He nodded to the paintings leaning against the wall in a line. Accepting the change of topic, she agreed. "Yes, she called last night. I take it you told her."

"Actually I did not, she told me who your mother was, are you taking anything of yours?"

"Yes." She sighed. "She was most insistent."

Reighn laughed. "That is our Edee. Now are these the ones needing to be taken downstairs?"

"I see, you think there is a need for tea and coffee for this conversation?"

Reighn sighed. "Yes, I feel it will need that at least."

"Okay." She pointed out the paintings leaning against the wall. "All those."

Between them they carried the twelve from the room to the

foyer where she had placed several framed photos earlier. They met Adam and Ian as they finished placing the paintings against the wall.

"My Lord, Lady Ocean."

Ocean smiled at the dragons, Reighn nodded. "Good morning, gentlemen."

Adam asked. "Lady Ocean may we help?"

"Yes, are you going into town?"

"We are about to, yes."

"Great, could you take these to the gallery? Lady Edith is waiting for them.

"We will do so."

With utmost care, the males picked up the canvases and framed photos and took them to their truck. Birdy walked out from the kitchen. "I am off to get the rest of my things. The guys finished our place already. Tea and coffee are on the table, as is my famous chocolate cake."

"Thanks Birdy."

Birdy greeted Reighn. "My Lord, good morning."

"And to you, Birdy. You are happy to work here?"

She smiled. "Immensely, My Lord."

After they were alone, and before she took him to the kitchen. Ocean offered to show him around. "We have been busy in only two days. They have done so much. Would you like a tour?"

Reighn smiled at the gracious offer, and he knew it was heartfelt. This was a very different female than the one who had entered his office a few nights ago. Or the female who had punched her knuckles until they had been broken and raw. He wondered if it was Conor or her young or maybe the magic of Dragon's Gap that had given her some peace as Claire predicted.

Gently, he said. "I can see that. You know if I could, may I bring Sage, so together we can see everything?" At her enquiring look, he said. "Otherwise, I will have to give her a blow by blow account of every room, and you and I know. I will miss something about the rooms design or furniture or color."

Laughing Ocean held her hand up. "I see your dilemma, I

think waiting will be wise."

"I thank you." He sounded relieved.

"It probably will be for the best, apparently Adam and Ian as well as Ivan and George will all be finished by the end of next week." She looked at him and issued an invitation for him and his family.

"You know, come for dinner on Friday next. We will grill, apparently Conor is an expert in grilling. That way you can bring your little ones and we can tour the whole place, the girls will love to entertain your girls."

"I will advise Sage; she will be pleased." As they walked into the modern kitchen, Reighn sighed. "This is delightful, see I would never be able to describe all this." He admired the black granite counters with the stainless steel appliances. He especially loved the way they had not hidden the stone away. Ocean smiled as she looked around.

"The basic design is ours, but once we met Adam and Ian, we let them at it. They are true artists. This is nothing compared to the bathrooms."

Reighn sighed again, this time with delight. "My great grandfather commissioned this home for my great grandmother on my Dam's side of the family. My Sire says he was a pretentious male. Well, he uses another word, but I am being polite."

Ocean grinned. "I see and was he?"

Reighn shrugged. "I do not know." At the sly look he gave her, she knew he remembered the golden room, and she was proved right when he stated. "I think the great room answers that question. What do you think?"

Ocean laughed out loud. "So, that was not you?"

Reighn looked affronted. "Hell no, how could you think that?"

"Well..."

He held his hand up. "Do not answer that. No, that room remains as it was the day they decided on it."

"It is rather..." Ocean gave up, she could think of nothing but disparaging descriptions.

Reighn grinned. "Yes... yes it is."

"So as you may have guessed it is being redone and I have photos of how it was, because I don't think words do it justice. Something like that should never... ever be forgotten."

Reighn's grin widened. "I agree with you, and seriously no one without proof would believe us."

"There is that!" Ocean laughingly agreed as she took her seat at the table while Reighn took his own. She poured him tea, and he cut a slice of cake. They remained in companionable silence until they both heard a tremendous roar from outside. Ocean's eyes widened as Reighn grunted while he took another slice of cake. When another roar sounded closer, she asked.

"What was that?"

"That would be your shadow." Reighn calmly told her. "He knows you are alone here with another male. Lions are territorial, especially with their mates."

Ocean blinked at him. "But it is you?"

Reighn raised a black eyebrow. "I am unsure whether to be flattered or insulted."

Ocean waved her hand, "You know what I mean?" But before he could answer a shadow covered the bay window, Ocean looked at Reighn. "You see like I do, how huge he is, right?"

"I do."

"Umm! I have not met his lion yet."

"Well, he is here. I would advise letting him in, unless you wish them to renew the door."

Ocean jumped up and opened the large back door. "Huh, now I understand why they made it so big."

Reighn helped himself to more tea and cake. It was really good cake, Ocean moved back into the room as a humongous lion padded into her home. He was fully maned, with bright amber eyes in a head that... Ocean's thought processes stopped working as more of the gigantic lion entered.

She gauged him to be as big as a full-grown grizzly bear she had photographed once. "Oh my Conor, you are so handsome." She whispered as she sat in her chair, and he moved to her. She ran her hands over his fur and then hugged him around the neck or tried to. Her arms could not go all the way around, she asked because she could think of nothing else to say. "You are massive, so do you want tea?"

He replied with a grunt. "Well change, so you can have some, although we need to try my idea of the bed later."

At Reighn's choked laugh, she hurriedly explained. "I wanted to know if all of us and Conor in his lion skin, could fit on our bed."

Reighn smiled. "I forgot about that bed, if I remember it is huge."

"It is enormous," Ocean told him, "See the reason for the curiosity?"

He nodded. "I do."

She told Conor. "Reighn has come to find out why I can open portals."

The lions head swung to Reighn, as his eyes narrowed and his growl vibrated deep in his chest which sounded to Ocean's amusement like a small engine idling.

Reighn nodded. "I did, you have not explained the dangers of doing so to her. Which is understandable, as I did not know of her ability to do so either? So we find ourselves in the position of having to explain the situation to her earlier than you wished too. Plus, this cake is divine."

He took another huge bite to empathize his point. Conor snarled, which shook the windows and made Ocean tighten her hands on his mane which she had been stroking.

Reighn grinned unrepentantly at the lion. "No use being annoyed, she has a right to know, how can she be prepared if she is in the dark."

At another snarl, he said. "Oh, do you mean the cake, first in first served, you know my brothers?

Conor, the lion sniffed loudly and then with a shower of sparkles, Conor appeared and growled at Reighn as he hugged Ocean. "Why are you eating my cake?"

"I told you first in, first to eat cake."

Conor grunted as he turned from the cake scarfing dragon and looked down into the happy face of his mate. He kissed her and growled. "Why did you give him my cake?"

"Cause I did not know you would be coming home, otherwise I would have hid it. I swear." She solemnly told him.

He grinned and looked at Reighn. "It would have made no difference. He would have found it."

"True, I would have." Reighn told her as he took another bite. "It is really good cake. I see why Birdy called it her famous chocolate cake."

Conor snorted as his phone rang, he excused himself and left the kitchen but not before admonishing Reighn to leave him some cake, making Ocean giggle as she murmured. "That is one huge lion."

Reighn agreed. "He sure is, I have never seen another one bigger."

"Do you think Paige will be that big?" Ocean asked him with a worried frown creasing her face.

"What does Conor say?"

"That each, first is unique, so we will not know until she is mature."

"Well, I agree with him. We wait and see."

"But Reighn, that is big."

He laughed with her, which is how Conor, returning from his call found them. He sat and took the cup Ocean passed him and sliced himself a large piece of the remaining cake.

"Thanks for leaving me some." He muttered to Reighn, who grinned. "No problem."

Conor gave him a look that spoke of retribution then asked. "So what has happened?"

"We are not going to discuss the arrival of the lion?" Ocean asked.

Conor looked at her. "No, you have a male here. My lion is very territorial. He did what he will always do, when that happens."

"Oh okay. Then one question?"

"Yes my mate."

"How did he know?"

"We are the Leo, every bit of dirt, stone, basically everything he places or has placed his paws on, we know and we can find out who is where."

"Wow... that is territorial." She looked at Reighn. "How does that work with you?"

"Extremely well, we have an understanding. I am the Dragon Lord, he is a First. It works."

Ocean could see that was all she was going to get from either male and sighed. "Okay, so the portal?"

"Yes, let us address that first." Reighn filled Conor in on what had taken place. After that they together explained to Ocean what they knew about the lock and key and what was expected of her and Ciana. And why there was a ban on portals opening. When they finished, Conor reverted back to the topic of the portal she had opened as Ocean sat deep in thought about all they had told her. "How was it possible she could do so?"

Reighn shrugged. "I have a theory. Ocean have you shifted?"

"No, can I?"

"Maybe, will you try?"

"Sure."

Conor asked. "Wait... what if she gets stuck like Ciana did?"

"Ciana got stuck?" Ocean screeched causing the males shoulders to go up around their ears.

"Ocean calm, not forever and that was because of the Goddess." Conor told her,

Ocean looked at him as though he was speaking in a foreign language. "Explain please?"

"Of course." Reighn explained in a few sentences, what had taken place once he was through, Ocean took a deep breath in and said. "Okay, let's see if I can?"

"Just see if you can partially shift your arm and hand." Reighn asked her.

With her nod, she placed her arm on the table and Reighn said quietly. "Now visualize your arm having scales and a claw, like this." His arm and hand morphed into a scaled limb with claws.

Ocean eyes widened all over again. "Wow, you are red?"

"I am a fire dragon, so red."

"Okay, what color was Ciana?"

"Silver." Conor told her. Ocean nodded, then concentrated and realized she did not have to put that much effort into it, her dragon said. *You do it like this?*

Instantly her arm to her elbow was covered in golden scales, and her hand became clawed. *Thank you.*

"That is great, gold a beautiful color." Both Reighn and Conor murmured.

"My dragon helped."

Reighn asked. "You are talking to her?"

"Sort of, mostly she comes and goes, sometimes she is here for a little while then not for a while."

"Ahh I see, she is still emerging, she will remain with you longer as she grows stronger. When she helps you as she has today, she will need time to recover. It is a great time when our dragon reaches out for us, she and you will grow closer as time moves on."

"Oh okay. So we are alright then?"

"Yes." Reighn smiled. "It truly is, so you are the golden dragon and Ciana the silver dragon that we have always been told about, but have never seen."

"What does it mean?" Conor asked as he ran his fingers over her scales and claws, fascinated as much as Ocean was with her transformed arm.

"It means as Keeper and Olinda predicted Ciana and Ocean are the key and lock who will release the hold over our females, and they will fly."

Ocean sucked in a worried breath. But she did not let either male know she was concerned that maybe she could not get pass her anger and resentment. To make the prophecy happen. She asked Reighn. "How do I make it go back to human?"

"Do in reverse what you did to transform it."

"Oh yeah, that makes sense." She thought about what she and her dragon did and smiled when she felt her dragon take over. It felt sluggish, like she was trying to make it happen without the power she had before. When her arm was human again, she told her. *Sleep now. We will talk later.*

She heard a mumbled reply, but it was so soft she could not make out the words. Then she knew her dragon was no longer there. Reighn's. "Good." Seemed relieved when her arm returned and made her smile.

"I think Ocean. You are more powerful than an average dragon. In fact I would place you eventually with training on a par with my abilities and if you wanted, you could become a Dragon Lord."

Ocean was quick to assure him. "No thank you, I think you do a fine job. You cannot get rid of the mantle that easy."

Reighn feigned sorrow. "I was so close."

They laughed as Ocean took hold of Conor's hand. "Sorry cousin, you are it. I am who I want to be, a shadow, mother and photographer. Believe me when I tell you I have never ever been so happy."

He believed her; she shone with happiness. "You will need training, specialized training."

"Alright, from you?"

"Yes from me." He looked at the silent Conor as he asked. "Are we going to have a problem with that? Because other than Papa and myself, there are none other to help her."

Conor closed his eyes as he said. "I hope not, we will cross that bridge when we come to it."

Ocean smoothed her hand over his. "We will be okay, things like this make relationships stronger, if both people in it want that. We will work to make it so."

He gave a sharp nod, hoping she was right, but she did not know his beast as he did. Reighn changed the topic again. "Now, as I am here, I will tell you Conor, you and Paige need to meet and work with Patrycc Maythom."

"Who?" Ocean asked as she looked at Reighn, then Conor.

Reighn answered. "He is my mother's brother.

"Why would we need to do that?" Conor asked as he looked at the worried Ocean.

"Because Patrycc Maythom is a Redeemer." Reighn then went on to explain what and who that was.

"So why do Paige and Conor need him?" Ocean asked as Reighn looked out the window on the sunlit day, amused to see several lionesses stalking through the long grass. He dragged a memory that was passed down to all Dragon Lords to the forefront of his mind.

"In the beginning when there were many differing types of, first ones. I should be able to tell you whose memory this is, unfortunately it is not known. All Dragon Lords are born with this knowledge." He looked at Ocean "I am sure your dragon will know of this as well."

"Oh, like an imprinted memory?"

Reighn smiled at her simplistic explanation. "Maybe something like that. I am sure all Firsts have similar memories, if not the same."

Conor shrugged. "It is possible none come to mind."

Reighn realized Conor would not speak of it. Maybe he did not have this memory or did not want to know of it. "Anyway, in the beginning the first of many species were created and unfortunately they were not ethical or well loved. They ruled with an iron hand. The first ones created life without regard to the care of their young, they indiscriminately killed the ones they were sworn to care and protect. Nothing was saved from their attention, the land, the animals, everything was for their pleasure and nothing else. It was a sad time of fear and inhumanity, for use of a better word. Atrocities were the norm, not the abnormal. Eventually, it was finally noticed by the Divine or Creators of the worlds, whoever they may be. It is said they took one look at what the Firsts had accomplished, which was nothing good and wiped them and the world from existence."

He sighed and shook his head as he stared at the wide-eyed Ocean and the somber Conor. "Because of the horror of what those firsts had done. They, the divine or whoever, were unwilling to create another world. It took many millions upon millions of years before they would try again. And when they did, they created Earth and placed here. Dragons, fae, and many differing species, and of course the Redeemers, who were created to be the moral compasses for the Firsts. The Redeemers were imbued with the powers of the creators or Divine to guide ethical behavior of the Firsts and place ethics into the memories of all beings."

Ocean and Conor stared at Reighn, Ocean said. "That is amazing, history at school was never like that?"

Reighn smiled, "No, this is magical history."

Conor asked. "Your uncle is a Redeemer?"

"Yes and willing to work with you and Paige."

"I knew one was in the world but have been unable to find him."

Reighn shrugged. "A gift, to hide among others."

Ocean frowned and asked, "Don't you find that strange, that he is here now. Unless he has been around forever?"

Reighn shook his head. "No, he has not been around forever. Like all dragons, he is long lived and yes. We always wondered why he was here now and there was never a Redeemer before. I suppose we have our answer now."

Conor asked him. "Did you request him to come home?"

Reighn nodded. "Yes and not because I thought you were unethical. You are the most moral person I know. It is because there was always the possibility there would be more Firsts and I worried they may not all be like you."

Ocean nodded and said. "Seriously, why would he not be here, you are, and now Paige? Seems smart to me, guess that is why you are the Dragon Lord?"

She smiled at Reighn, who dryly agreed. "I think so."

CHAPTER FOURTEEN:

Frankie stared at her friend Ciana until she wiggled in discomfort and then demanded. "What do you mean, you are not going to talk to her?"

Ciana stared straight back and said. "She said I was unwelcomed in her home."

Frankie threw her hands up in the air. "Of course she did, she is hurt and angry."

"Frankie, maybe we should not interfere. This is about family." Johner tried telling her as he sat with Andre` who held a baby and drank his tea as he watched his daughter fidget under Frankie's stare.

Johner and Frankie had arrived at Andre`s apartment where Thorn and Ciana were staying until their estate was renovated to accommodate their family as well as the other elves who had arrived the night before. Frankie had insisted early this morning that they needed to go to Andre`s, after they learned the previous night that Ciana had contacted Ocean who had shot Ciana down. This had made Frankie annoyed, which meant he was here under protest to fix this family, apparently?

He listened now as his shadow said in her annoyed do not piss me off voice. "Of course it is family, my family, and we have a fracture that needs fixing."

Thorn bravely said. "Perhaps Ciana and this sister are uninterested in meeting, or perhaps they have no interest in fixing this?"

Frankie gave him a sweet smile as she paced the room. Thorn thought that in no way was that a nice smile from her, and he just stopped himself from wiggling in his chair as Ciana had. "I see, so we should just let it all lie idle and it will fix itself, is that what you are saying?"

Not giving him a chance to answer which he decided he would not have, as her voice lost some of the sweet tones when she said. "In the meantime two sisters who are hurting remain estranged, and a father is without both his daughters and his granddaughters. Who, I should tell you, those same granddaughters are planning to sneak around to meet him without their mom knowing. Which in essence is lying and so not healthy for a happy family?"

Andre` just stopped himself from smiling at the thought of his granddaughters who he had not met yet, sneaking to meet him. It warmed his and his dragon's hearts.

Thorn agreed. "Ahh, I see your point."

"I thought you might." She looked seriously at Ciana, and intentionally, or maybe it was not. Johner was unsure. All he knew was it was happening more and more lately. She enthused her voice with power as she told Ciana and her father.

"I have called an intervention for this morning."

Ciana frowned and crossed her arms, anger spiking as she pursed her lips. Frankie said before she could say no. "This is so much bigger than you and Ocean, this involves every dragon female here and their ability to know their other half. Unless you forgot, you and your sister as well as your daughters are dragons too. Maybe for you being righteous is more important than dragon females ever knowing the sensation of flight, but I hope not." She looked at the shamed faced Ciana. "I will tell you the same thing I told Ocean before I came here. How dear you both be so very selfish as to withhold that from dragon females."

Softly, Ciana said. "I am sorry, if it seems like that. Where is it to be?"

Frankie relented a little, still obviously annoyed she told them. "Olinda has offered a conference room at the library at ten o'clock. I thought neutral ground may be warranted."

"We will be there." Andre` assured her, then he smiled at

Frankie and winked at Johner. "Frankie?"

"Yes?" She looked up at him as he came to her and took her hand in his, kissing her cheek. "Thank you sweet lady."

"Oh... oh okay." She shimmered with happiness as Johner swept her from the apartment. When the door closed behind the couple, Ciana said. "Well...

Thorn cut her off. "No, my radiance, you must go."

"I know but why?" She whined, "She hates me."

"No." Andre ` said, "She does not, she is frightened and a little jealous of you."

"What?

"My dear, look at your life and how you were raised, then tell me you would not be jealous if you were her. Apparently from what I gleaned from Rene ` she was raised by an uncaring, neglectful female. One that spent her life regretting having a child and whatever else was going on with her. She obviously did not want Ocean. Think about it, she made a deal with a Goddess and maybe she ended her days regretting that."

"We don't know that she did make a deal, do we?"

"Ciana!" Andre ` said sternly. "You know she must have. I and my dragon have no knowledge of either of your mothers; the Goddess removed that from me."

Ciana thought about that for a moment, then said quietly. "Okay, well, we better get ready then."

She was still unhappy about going and in truth she was nervous, she had only spoken to Ocean on the phone and that had not gone well. To actually meet her sister in person was a little scary, but for the sake of dragon kind and for Andre ` she would do it. Smirking she thought, if it was needed she would beat her sister into making sense, now that she could do. Her smirk became a smile, thinking she sounded like a sister and wondered who was older.

Ocean paced her suite as Conor lounged in the chair before the cleaned fireplace, watching her. She moved with grace and elegance, not wasting a movement. He thought she would make a great lioness. "What has you so upset my mate?"

He grinned as she whirled around, outrage on her face until she saw his smile. Her expression turned to a grimace.

"Oh, you were being funny."

"I was trying."

Ocean growled as she crossed her arms, looking like Ciana at that moment as she asked him. "Do I really need to go to this... this intervention, which is really a stupid name? I am not sure I want to meet my father and sister."

"You know you do, and you also know we must go."

"We?" She asked with raised eyebrows.

Conor grinned as he told her. "Yes, your family as is our right; this concerns us all. Your daughters have a right to meet their grandfather and aunt unless you want them to follow through on their plans to sneak out and see him?"

"Well..."

Conor's voice hardened a little in warning. "Ocean."

Hearing the tone, she shrugged. "Yeah... yeah, I know still..."

"Ocean, it is as Frankie said, this is far bigger than all of you, and it concerns the dragon females. I told you how distraught Verity was."

"Yes, I know and am still unhappy about that."

"As I was, but you do understand?" He rose from his seat and took her in his arms, "You know she is beside herself with worry."

"I know and so am I." She looked up into his face, which was quickly becoming dear to her and let him see her fear. "What if I am unable to do this, what if we are not the ones needed to unlock this wonderful gift?"

"I have no doubt that when everything is resolved, flight will be granted to all female dragons. Now my sweet, that means you may take me for a flight above the clouds."

Ocean laughed. "Really fly a lion atop a dragon?"

"Yes." He kissed her, "I will allow you to carry upon your back my magnificent body."

Ocean laughed again at his boastful tone and thought about his body, because it was as he said a magnificent one, she could attest to that. “In fact…” He whispered between kisses as he swooped her up in his arms. “Let me give you a refresher course in how magnificent it is.”

Giggling, she wound her arms around his neck and peppered his face with kisses as she said. “Okay, let’s do that. I think I missed something last night.”

“Shame on you. Pay better attention.” He growled softly as he kicked the door closed to their bedroom, knowing they would not be disturbed. Having established the rules with the girls, the first night in their new home.

CHAPTER FIFTEEN:

Ocean entered the library with Parker in her carrier ahead of her family. Olinda met her at the door. "Good morning, Olinda."

"Oh... oh, good morning Ocean. Look umm..."

"Yes Olinda?"

Olinda rubbed her face. "This was not my idea, and I did try to persuade her to leave, but well..."

"Olinda, is there someone here to see me?"

"Yes, the Moon Goddess, she just arrived."

Ocean's eyebrows rose. "Really, isn't that a little presumptuous?"

"That's what I said... sort of."

"It is okay, Olinda. Where is she?"

Olinda blew a breath out. "Third door on your left. Would you like me to come with you?"

"Thank you no. If you could hold my family off, for a little while."

Olinda grimaced. "I will try, don't break my library."

Ocean smiled. "I will try not to."

She then walked into the room Olinda had directed her too, as Olinda walked to where Ocean's family were just entering saying. "There will just be a short delay."

Conor asked. "Why?"

"Umm... the Goddess has asked to talk to Ocean."

Frankie drew in a breath. "Well, that may not be wise."

"That's an understatement." Olinda murmured.

Conor agreed. "Not wise at all."

Ocean pushed the door to the conference room open and came face to face with the Goddess and stopped. She was tall, beautiful and of undetermined age, with long silver hair that fell around her like a cloak. She wore a gown of moonlight, giving her an ethereal quality. The power that came from the Goddess was almost overwhelming.

Ocean placed the baby carrier on the table and stood with her hand on the handle. "Good morning."

The Goddess's silver eyes flashed as she gave a small nod.

"Good morning Ocean."

She glided closer to the table and looked down at Parker. "A sweet baby girl with much potential."

"Yes. Why are you here?"

The silver eyes of the Goddess stared at Ocean as she asked. "You are angry still?"

Ocean laughed, a bitter sound that grated against the beauty of the figure before her. "What gives you any idea I would be anything other than angry?"

The Goddess's face tightened. "I am here because you refused to speak to Ciana last night. I wish to know why?"

"I also refused to speak to Andre`."

"Yes."

Ocean smirked. "But that does not concern you, does it?"

She seemed to ignore Ocean's words. "I have looked after Ciana her entire life. It is a very hard responsibility to let go of; she has pined for you since she became aware that you existed, it has hurt my heart."

Ocean snorted in disbelief and looked out the glass door to see Andre` walking toward the room and Olinda stepping in front of him, the Goddess asked. "You find that amusing?"

"No, I find it amazing, that you think you have a heart."

"Take care, little dragon. I am not to be trifled with!"

Ocean growled low in her throat as golden scales covered her face and arms, her eyes elongated and her voice deepened. "You dare to reprimand me. You left me alone, unguarded, at the mercy of a narcissistic woman who hated me."

The Goddess threw her head back. “Why is this my fault? I made it so you could have a life. I do not believe your life was so different from Ciana’s.”

Ocean hissed. “You believe... You know nothing. Did Ciana have a mother that ignored her daughter for days on end because she needed to paint? To create because it was her divine right.” Ocean’s voice deepened even more as she said. “My earliest memory is being locked in my room for days until she finished creating her latest masterpiece. Then she had to sleep, finally coming to see to me only when she was forced too. This happened time and again until I was old enough to feed myself and when she was not ignoring me. She was berating me for stifling her life, her creativity. How she was unloved, abandoned... all my fault. Tell me, Goddess, was that Ciana’s life?”

The shocked look on the perfect face of the Goddess said it all. “No... No, it was not.”

“So I ask, why did you allow it?”

“I... I cannot answer that. It was not my intention.”

Ocean crossed her arms as the scales and the appearance of her dragon subsided. She leaned back against the table, her tone hard and as unyielding as her face, which was set in a hard, unforgiving expression as she stared at the Goddess. “Oh really? Let us talk about that. You stole us from our father, a grieving male that would have found comfort from two daughters. You made him betray the memory of his wife and you made it so he and his dragon never knew he had impregnated anyone. Then you... you took us from him, so we never knew we had a father who would have loved us, cared for us, kept us safe. Tell me Goddess, what does that make you?” Ocean felt the door open behind her, then heard Andre ` ask. “Yes Goddess, what does that make you?”

The Goddess drew a cloak that appeared around herself, as though it was armor and stated. “I am a Goddess.”

Ocean scoffed. “This does not excuse your behavior you had no regard for me Ciana or Andre `, your whole focus was on what you wanted. You screwed with our lives for your own agenda.

Tell me Goddess how has that worked out for you. I am the lock, Ciana the key, and yet the females do not change or fly. Why is that your holiness?"

"You mock me. I told you to take care. You have no idea what my sister and I gave up for you?"

"I DON'T CARE!" Ocean stated her voice was filled with the power of her dragon causing the building to rock and the Goddess to gasp, as Andre` stumbled back against the wall.

Ocean drew in a breath and let it out slowly, settling her temper. At the same time her body and eyes returned to normal, her voice was once more her own as she said. "Because you and your sister were disappointed in the dragons, you had a petty temper tantrum that condemned all the females to a horrendous existence. While you sat in your Ivory tower or on your moon and island, thinking righteous thoughts. You both were wrong to do so then, and you are wrong now. No matter what you two Goddesses tell yourselves, you cannot right a wrong by willing it to happen. All the pieces of the whole are here and yet the females do not fly, why is that Goddess? You are the great creator of events, explain why?"

"I cannot!"

Andre` asked. "Or will not?"

"No, I cannot!"

With those words, she disappeared. Ocean turned to Andre` and looked up at the beautiful dragon and said. "She answered nothing and yet I feel like it is finished."

Andre` shook his head as he stared down into eyes so much like his own and let his eyes rove over the beautiful face of his daughter. "They played so many games to correct something they should have been above in the first place."

Ocean grinned. "Yes well, as that was the first and only time, I wish to be in the presence of a Goddess. I think it went well."

Andre` just stopped himself from telling her how proud of her he was. She had stood up to an Entity that most people revered and feared, but he knew it was too early for him to say such. He felt she would be suspicious of his praise. Instead, he nodded and said. "Yes, let us put this behind us, we have family matters to talk about."

His dragon told him. *She is much like we were in our youth.*

Andre` agreed. *Before we learned discretion.*

Maybe or we became old!

I am not old. I am discerning.

Or a chicken.

See this again, is why I end up in trouble.

His dragon's response was to laugh.

Ocean turned fully to look at Andre`. "I suppose I should tell them, it is all clear in here?"

Andre moved further into the room. "I asked for some time alone before the others join us."

"Oh, okay. This is Parker." She turned the carrier so he could see the tiny baby. Andre`s face softened as he looked at the sweet baby with silky blonde hair. "How old is she?"

"Less than a week." Ocean leaned against the table as he placed a hand on the baby. "So very little, a whole lifetime to grow and seek the pleasure and sorrows of the world around her." He looked at Ocean. "I saw the photo of your mother. I am sorry but as with Ciana's mother, I do not recognize her and before you ask as Ciana did. I remember or more precisely my dragon and I remember every female we have laid with."

At her raised eyebrows, he growled. "You and your sister have the same cynicism. As I told her, there have not been that many."

"Well okay." Ocean hid her grin. It seemed like Ciana and she had a lot more in common than she thought possible, mainly annoying their father. Andre` said. "I believe the Goddesses have occluded the female from us and as I look at you and your sister I find I do not care."

She told him. "Just so you know, we know you had no choice in that. So let that rest. We cannot go back and change it. I am sorry the Goddess left you alone, it was cruel of her, for you and us."

Andre` eyes teared as he heard the sincerity behind her

words, he knew she believed what she said. Sighing, he softly told her. "Thankfully, we have time now to become a family. I will do everything in my power to make that happen."

With that short sentence, something wonderful happened. Ocean's eyes lingered on Andre`s face and she smiled and right then and there she realized her anger at him and Ciana was gone. "Oh… that is amazing."

Andre` quickly reassured her. "What… What I swear I will do whatever…"

Ocean waved her hand in apology. "I am sorry, I believe you. I have been so angry at you and Ciana, since I got here and just realized it is all gone. All the anger and the jealousy just gone." She looked at him, really looked, and saw a well-preserved male around fifty who had long blond hair with purple streaks and lavender eyes with silver specks in their depths. This was her father, deep in her heart and soul it was as though her dragon called to his.

Her dragon whispered. *I do, he is our Sire. Why would you doubt it?*

I think I did not want to be disappointed again. Ocean shrugged as she blurted out. "My life with my mother was difficult, she barely tolerated me and I never knew what I had done wrong. I don't know why she despised me, but she did."

Andre` nodded, not daring to speak in case he said the wrong thing, causing her to stop confiding in him. Ocean sighed and looked at her baby girl. "I grew up alone and angry for many years it was my default emotion and I really thought I'd conquered the feeling until I got here. It was like I was back there, living in that house with her. I am sorry if I have caused you upset. I should not have done that. Sadly, anger for me, is an easy emotion to cope with. I find other emotions complicated, but I am willing to learn."

When she stopped talking and stood looking at him, he smiled softly. "I understand, as you know I lost my wife. We were together for many years. She was not my shadow, but I loved her with everything I had in me. When she was gone, my grief turned to anger. I was banished from my home for many years." He laughed at her astonished look. "Mainly you understand to keep people from killing me, as much as stopping me killing them."

"Oh wow, so I come by it naturally?" Ocean asked, startling a laugh from Andre`.

"Probably. So why has your anger gone? Please don't get me wrong, I am grateful, but why now?"

Ocean looked at him then the sleeping Parker and then let her gaze travel over the people waiting, her family. "I think confronting the Goddess is one reason. That, for me, was cathartic." She smiled with a glint in her eyes that Andre` read as pride. "But really it is this place. Conor, my children, and truthfully you and Ciana. All the people I have met so far, Dragon's Gap makes me feel secure. So why hold on to the past. I have so much here today, and in the future to look forward too." She took a breath and asked. "Can I ask you a question? I know you don't lie, Frankie told me that."

Andre` bowed his head a little in acknowledgment. "I do not, what is the point. We live so long we would forget a lie spoken. It is better to tell the truth or say nothing."

"Yeah, I get that."

"Ask your question."

"Do you think one day we will know each other well enough for you to love me? I have to tell you I am a hard nut to crack or at least, that is what Conor told me."

Andre` drew her into his arms slowly, allowing her time to pull away if she so desired. It appeared to his relief she did not, as she came easily to him. "My dear daughter, they never told me you existed and then they kept you from me. It will take me a very long time come to terms with their audacity. There is nothing in this world and beyond that will keep me from loving you, not you or any Goddess. For the rest of my life, you are mine, as is your sister. Together we will forge a new relationship in a new time and place. Let us make that here and now."

"I would really like that." Ocean sucked back the sob trying to work its way up from her chest and asked for reassurance from a father she had never known but instinctively trusted. "What if I can't do what they assume I can?"

He shrugged. "They can go to hell. You are not here to just fulfil some prophecy. You are here for your sister and me and these delightful girls of yours."

"Conor too."

Andre` grimace. "We will see."

"Oh Andre` he is a lion. A very big lion."

"I am a dragon."

"Well yeah, but he is mine. I sort of promised to stay with him." Andre` sighed magnanimously, causing Ocean to grin as she said. "Alright."

Andre sighed again. "Seriously, I just find you and your sister and these males come and snatch you both from me."

Ocean agreed with a mock frown. "I understand, but in our defense we brought you granddaughters. I imagine you will have fun scaring the males that come sniffing around them."

Andre`s face went from woebegone to predatory. "Now that is truly poetic." He pulled her to him and hugged her tightly. "My dragon and I welcome you home my daughter."

"Thank you, now may I call you dad?"

"I would enjoy that although I think I am more a Papa."

"Oh, you are probably right. What does Ciana call you?"

"Andre`." He told her blandly, and she knew he was hurt by it. She sort of understood Ciana's decision. "Well, that needs to change. So is it okay then?"

"Yes... yes most definitely."

"My girls told me that to belong, we have to be a family, they call us, mom and dad." She looked up at him as she heard the door start to open. "Regardless of how we got into this, you are my father for now and always."

"As you are my daughter forever." He kissed her forehead and held her as he closed his eyes on the relief he felt. Conor had been right in his advice to approach her first, before she put her defenses up, he owed his new son-in-law.

Ciana walked in and around the table until she stood directly behind Ocean, who turned with tears in her eyes as she looked at her mirror image. "Holy shit, we are alike, no wonder people kept calling me Ciana."

Wide-eyed, Ciana nodded. "Yep, wow, it is freaky, right?"

"So right." Ocean agreed. They circled each other, checking each other out. Ocean made a face, "Although, got to say you are not as chunky as me."

Ciana snorted. "Huh, that is only because I have not stayed home long enough to eat like I normally do. Hope you like the gym?"

"I box against a bag." At her and Andre`s confused look, she explained. "The girls told me I have to tell people that, otherwise they may think I beat people up."

Ciana said. "Ohh! I might like that, will you teach me and do you lose weight doing that?"

Ocean grinned. "If you do it right and often. Whenever you are ready, I will show you."

"Cool." Ciana held her arms open and growled. "Sis, why the hell did you shoot me down last night?"

Ocean walked into her waiting arms and instantly felt at home. "Ciana, I am sorry, nerves, I swear... just plain nerves."

"Me too." Ciana held tightly to Ocean as she did to her, they stayed like that for few minutes then Ciana pulled a little away and said as she stared at her father and sister. "I am so angry for what they did, they had no right."

"They thought they did." Frankie told them as she entered. "Are we good here?"

"Yes." Ciana and Ocean said together.

"Why?" Andre` asked.

"We are moving to your place for snacks and baby cuddles, plus the girls want to get to know their grandfather and aunt and uncle and cousins."

"Well, that is enough of a reason." He scooped the carrier with Parker off the table and walked out with Frankie. Ciana asked Ocean. "You okay?"

"Yep, you know I really am, now I have you in my life."

"Okay, me too." Ciana smiled as she felt her life balance.

Ocean said. "It is like all the pieces came together, huh?"

"Exactly."

"Now why do you not call Andre` Papa, it hurts him that you don't?"

Ciana stood with her mouth opened. Ocean nodded. "I see, you did not realize. Well, let's go, and you can think about it?"

Ciana snapped her mouth closed, then said. "I did not know it did?"

Ocean grinned as she pushed the door open. "I thought so. This is why you have me, the older sister, to explain these things."

Ciana retorted as she followed behind her. "You are so not the older sister."

Andre` smiled all the way to his place, even more so when Joy ran up puffing. "Hey guys."

Kadee squealed when she saw her, which caused Joy to squeal in return, as the males all groaned. Paige moaned to Ocean. "Seriously, they only just saw each other."

Frankie asked. "Joy sweetie is your mom home yet?"

"Yep, just now."

Frankie turned to Johner. "I have to go see Harper."

He smoothed her hair. "About what my heart?"

She whispered. "This stuff, that keeps happening, plus I told you what Ocean said, right?"

He nodded and whispered back. "You did, would you like me to go with you?"

"No thank you." She hugged him. "I will be okay."

Johner kissed her, then said. "Well then, if I am not wanted. I will return to work."

Ocean murmured to Conor. "About the Goddess?"

He looked down at her and smiled as he brushed a hand down her hair. "Let's talk about that when we are alone. You do not look unhappy, so why spoil this great day with your father and sister. We have plenty of time to discuss all this later."

She smiled as she hugged him, he leaned down and whispered in her ear. “Although I assume you will not be unhappy if I do not stay?”

She shook her head and laughingly replied. “Escape while you can.”

Conor gave her a quick kiss, then said loudly. “Sorry, I have to leave, work commitments.”

Andre` did not think the male sounded sorry at all. And when Thorn, on hearing this, also hurriedly made excuses to return to work. Andre` scowled and snarled, of course you do as he watched the disappearing backs of his son-in-law’s.

Then smiled as he said to his daughters and granddaughters. “My ladies let us go have tea and coffee.” As they all moved into his apartment, he quickly messaged Verity and Grace to come with reinforcements.

CHAPTER SIXTEEN:

Frankie opened the door to Harper and Ace's apartment slowly, getting an eyeful of her friends bare asses once was enough for any lifetime. Although Ace naked was something to behold. Seeing it was clear, she strode in and yelled. "Harper, why did you not call to say you were home?"

"In the kitchen and who needs too, when we have a Joy."

Grinning, Frankie pushed the door open. "True, that girl sure can gossip."

Harper scowled as she asked. "I wonder where she gets that from."

Frankie shrugged innocently. "No idea. I need to talk to you."

Harper was sitting at the table, a cup of coffee in front of her. She nodded. "Take a seat and do it."

"Harper, it is about my parents."

With the cup halfway to her mouth, she lowered it gently to the surface; this was the last thing she expected. "What brought this on?"

"Stuff." Frankie did not mention Ocean. She knew Harper had a problem with her, so she said looking uncomfortable. "Stuff keeps happening. Johner is getting worried."

Harper drummed her fingers on the table as she sipped her coffee, placing the cup down again she asked. "Frankie. Have you ever wondered why I cannot find out who or what you are?"

"Sure Harper, but we decided it was not meant to be."

"Yes, we did, but we have powerful people, like Edee, Claire, Reighn, and the Keepers and yet no one knows what you are? Doesn't that seem strange to you?"

"Well sure, now you say that, it does."

"Your power is growing every day. I can see it. You can see it, does it frighten you?"

Frankie did the lip thing as she thought, and finally she shook her head? "Nope, don't care."

"Frankie, it should worry you, as it does us."

Frankie replied stubbornly. "No, I don't want it too!"

Harper rubbed her eyes. "Why?"

"Because if it is something horrible I will have to leave, and that is not happening."

The walls shook, and the floor rolled beneath their feet. Harper grimaced as she grabbed her cup. "Frankie like that, you know you did that right?"

Frankie looked out the window and wanted to be gone from this conversation. She wondered why she had decided now was the time to talk about this stuff; she hated all this. If she was honest with herself, it scared her. She should have just left it alone. Now there was a ball of something moving in her chest, and she was scared. She could taste the fear in the back of her throat. "Frankie!" Harper touched her hand and pleaded. "Frankie look at me, come on sister look at me."

Slowly, as though she was swimming in molasses, Frankie moved her head up to look at Harper. It was so hard to do and seemed like ages before she could focus on her. When she finally managed to, Harper looked like she was a long way away. "Harper, you are fading. Where are you going?"

"Frankie!" Harper jumped from her chair. "Frankie, you are the one fading. Shit... Stay with me... Frankie, stay with me."

"I want too, can't. Got to find out."

Harper yelled as Frankie disappeared. Panicking, she stretched her hands across the table in a fruitless attempt to stop her leaving. "Oh my Goddess, Frankie please wait." She slumped in her chair, muttering. "He will kill me. They will kill me." She slowly picked her phone up and touched a number. Johner answered on the second ring. "Harper what's up? How's my lady?"

"Johner…." She choked out. "Come, I am sorry… so sorry…" She dropped her phone as she heard running feet and yelling.

Frankie stretched, then frowned. *Weird, I thought I was with Harper? Now why am I lying down? Strange… very strange.*

Then like a coiled spring she jumped from what she assumed was a bed but was a layer of white fog or cloud to a standing position. "What the hell?" She looked around, "I am definitely not home. Where am I?"

"Frankie Spring. I have waited a long time for you." A voice that sounded to Frankie like he was under water stated.

She sat again on the cloud thing and thought about what the voice had said. "Huh, who are you and my name, is Frankie Kingsley?"

"It is I, your giver of life."

"Shut up… giver of life, so funny."

When the voice did not talk again, she asked. "Oh, you were serious." She used her respectful voice. "Do you mean you are my father?"

The voice returned, but it sounded annoyed now. "No, I am your giver of life."

"Oh my mother, funny you don't sound female."

"Impossible… No, listen. I am your giver of life."

Frankie stood up from the soft fluffy bed or cloud or whatever it was and slammed her hands onto her hips. "Listen, giver of life. I have no idea what that means, and you never told me where I am. I don't appreciate the attitude. You were not just yanked from one realm to another, if that is actually where I am, now were you?"

"She has a point." A light voice spoke that could have been male or female.

The first voice asked. "Really, how does that help me?"

Frankie's lips twitched, trying not to smile at the indignant tone. The lighter voice took on a condescending tone. "Well, I was only trying to help. You are making quite a mess of it. Giver of life, where did you find that term?"

"It is a divine term, it means…"

"Oh, I know what it means but really!"

Frankie interrupted what to her seemed like a long argument in the making. "Listen you two. I don't know what it means. Would one of you explain where and what I am doing here?"

"Oh quite right, so sorry little one." The light voice said as the first voice grumbled. "I was trying too."

"And doing a very poor job of it." Mocked the light voice.

"Enough!" A new voice that sounded like Reighn's deep bass tones but had more depth and seemed to make Frankie's body vibrate stated. "How could you two not do this? It was a simple task I set you, contact the new one and explain who she is."

The first voice wheezed. "Well, we did try, she is uncooperative."

"Oh, that is harsh. I found her charming." The light voice crooned.

"I second that." Frankie stated. "You said nothing, explained nothing."

"Again enough. Child of light."

Frankie's skin pebbled with sensation as she whispered. "Who?"

The light voice said soothingly. "He means you dear, listen…"

"Oh… oh okay, sorry."

Then the bass voice began talking. "Frankie Kingsley, you are the product of light. Your mother was of the light, who sacrificed much to bring you into the world."

Frankie felt her heart race. "Oh, so she is dead then?"

"Yes dear one, she is." The lighter voice told her. "On your arrival to the world. Her only reason for existence was to birth you."

"Okay." Frankie felt the sadness like an old friend, well up in her heart as she asked. "My father?"

The voice of authority answered. "There was no father; your mother willed you into existence."

Frankie frowned. "She was a brownie. How could she do that?"

"She was not a brownie." The first voice said. "She was of the Elements."

"What... I don't understand?"

The voice of authority said. "Listen and you will understand. Your mother, who birthed you, willed you into existence. You were not born as the children of flesh are."

Frankie sat again and hung her head as she whispered. "Then I have no mother or father. I am just here..."

"The universe is your mother and father. You are an Elemental of the Earth and the Universe, the first of your kind." Stated the voice of authority.

Frankie lifted her head as she asked. "Do you mean like the four hooded guys?"

"Yes, they are the Elementals of natural magic. They came back to Earth to set it on its correct course once more. When the time is right, you and others like you will take over as stewards."

Frankie nodded. "Well, I do not know what to say to that, so I will say nothing."

The bass voice seemed to have a smile when it told her. "Good, you are capable of learning."

Frankie rolled her eyes but did not comment. Then the voice said. "You Frankie Kingsley along with more of your kind as well as the Firsts and the dragons, will together herald the next evolutionary stage of Earth."

"Wait... wait, let me get this straight. Myself and Conor and Paige as well as some others and the dragons are going to lead the world into the next magical phase of Earth. Is that what you are saying?"

Softly, the deep voice said. "Yes little one that is so."

"Oh, I am not old enough. I don't know enough to do that." Frankie could feel herself panic as her heart sped up and her breaths came in short pants.

"Calm sweet one, calm Frankie, child of light, all is well." The light voice soothed, making her heart settle and her breathing calm.

The first voice said. "At least I never made her panic."

The bass voice growled. "Excuse me, would you like Saturn detail for the next million years?"

"No divine creator. I would not."

"Then give me silence!"

Frankie felt better. The sniping at each other made her feel centered. "Sorry, I panicked there for a minute."

The light voice said. "We find that understandable."

The deep voice told her. "Do not concern yourself with what you will do, you are far too young. You have many years ahead of you before you and the Firsts are ready to lead the world into its next stage."

"Thank goodness. So why am I here?"

"Your power has exponentially developed. It necessitated us meeting earlier than we had expected. We needed to explain who and what you are and allow you to think about controlling your powers."

"I don't understand?"

The light voice told her. "You, little one are the only one who can control your powers, to lessen the impact on the world from your emotions."

"What? I have to become emotionless now?"

There was laughter, and then the light voice told her. "Frankie, that would be impossible for you, sweet child, you are all emotion. No... no, you just need to look inside yourself and find the place your power comes from and cage it, until you wish to explore its potential. Here I will show you."

With that Frankie was looking inside herself and was directed by a beam of silver light to a ball of blue and red slowly spinning. *Oh my, is that me?*

No, it is where your power resides.

It is pretty.

Laughter followed this statement. *It is, as you grow, so will your control and power. For now, place a cage like this around it.* A silver box appeared around the colored ball, then it disappeared. Frankie's lips twisted as she thought. Then she made a box with yellow sides and gently placed the ball inside.

Why yellow?

It is cheerful.

Which earned her a giggle and two grunts. She came back to herself and blinked rapidly as she asked. "Now what?"

The voice of authority told her. "Now you know how to care for the well of power. The Elementals will take over your education in the future. For now, that was a very good first lesson. You are very quick and willing. You and your world will remain safe."

Frankie smiled at the compliment. "Thank you. May I ask who you are?"

"We are they, who came before you." The voice intoned.

"We who allow the universes to exist." The first voice told her.

"Like gods?"

"Something like that." The light voice murmured.

"Wow! Can you be much more evasive?"

Then Frankie found herself in medical, surrounded by Johner, Sharm, Harper and Reighn, she smiled then said. "Hey, you look worried?"

Johner pulled her into his arms. "I am,"

"Sorry, I am alright. I swear." She soothed him as he shook with her clasped to his chest. She reached out and took Harper's hand. "Sorry, not your fault."

Harper nodded, her throat too tight to speak, she had spent the last fifteen minutes with a frightened, angry Johner and a disturbed Dragon Lord. It was not her finest moment.

Johner managed to mumble into Frankie's hair. "I thought I had lost you."

"Well, me too. I am sorry, my love. What happened?"

Harper managed finally to say. "One minute you were there, then you weren't, then you were, then you weren't?"

Frankie grinned. "Oh okay, got it."

Harper nodded. "Good... okay, need to sit down now."

Reighn helped her to a seat, then shoved her head between

her knees. "In case you feel faint." He told her as she growled at him.

Frankie almost laughed at the smug look on his face. Sharm tapped her nose. "Okay young lady, spill, what happened?"

She spent the next few minutes talking and for her it was without her normal rambling explanation. This was far too important to dither about with. When she mentioned Ocean, Harper's head came up and her lips clamped together.

Johner, Sharm and Reighn asked her questions until they felt they had the full story and Sharm finally ordered Johner to take her home. Which he did and kept her with him for the remainder of the day. Even going so far as growling when she tried getting out of bed.

CHAPTER SEVENTEEN:

Harper rubbed her face and yawned as she walked into her kitchen the following morning.

"Good morning Joy, how are you?" She asked as she spotted the cheerful girl munching on her cereal.

"I am great, it is Friday."

Harper assumed that meant something to the teenager but having discovered that often as not it was just a statement. She gave the customary grunt as her only comment. It never seemed to upset Joy, who normally carried on her conversations as though Harper used words.

She helped herself to the coffee and cereal, then sat at the table where Joy was and poured juice into both their glasses.

"Did you have a nice time last night with Frankie and Uncle Johner?"

"We did thank you." She mentally grinned the young ones all called Johner uncle but never called Frankie auntie it made Harper laugh, she sighed as she remembered they had spent the evening discussing Frankie's revelations. Even this morning she was having a hard time getting her head around the fact that her Frankie was an Elemental or would be in the future. To stop her mind circling those thoughts, Harper asked. "What are you doing today?"

"I am going to go to Kadee's place."

"Whose?"

"Harper." Joy sighed, forgetting Harper had been away on a mission for Reighn with Charlie trying to track down the male faerie, Definiao. So far he had eluded all attempts to capture him. It was as though he knew they were coming giving credence to the fact, there was an informer at Dragon's Gap.

Harper grinned. "I was away remember?"

"Oh yeah, sorry. So Kadee and Paige Walker, the new girls I told you about, when I messaged you."

"How do you know where they live?"

"Me and Frankie were there when they moved into their new house and I stayed the night it was fun. We had pizza and everything. Also, Kadee's mom is mated to Conor. Eww! So now Kadee's last name is Towers."

"Wait… wait you had a sleepover and Conor Towers… Our Conor Towers?"

"Yes, Harper really, everyone knows that."

"I didn't and watch your tone Missy."

"Sorry. Harper, can I ask you something?"

"Sure what?" She answered absently, her mind still reeling from finding out Joy had a sleepover and Conor was mated.

"Can I call you mom and Ace dad, Kadee and Paige are only just claimed by Ocean and Conor and they call them mom and dad already?" Joy looked down at the table, too scared to look at Harper, in case she saw rejection.

Harper's whole body softened as she heard the plea behind the words. Her voice became quiet, like it did when she was moved. "If that is what you want, I would love that and I know Ace will be proud to be your dad, as I will be to be your mom."

Clint stumbled in, rubbing his eyes and yawning he had spent a night out with his brother. Harper knew he and Hayden had not returned until two o'clock this morning. He was on duty at the medical center at ten o'clock. She hoped he would stay awake long enough to finish his shift. Ace and Hayden were showering after their early morning training session, which they had gotten in the habit of doing since Hayden had moved in with them. So far neither of the brothers had talked of moving out, so Harper left it alone. As long as they stayed here, she was happy.

"So can I go to Kadee and Paige's place with Frankie this

morning?" Joy asked as Harper finished her cereal.

"I don't think so."

Joys eyes widened, "Why, is Frankie sick?"

"No, she is okay, but she is coming here. We are to go to the gallery to see some art for Edee, and I do not know this lady, so no."

Joy's face became militant as she said. "That is just dumb, dad let me sleepover there and Conor is her mate. Saul will come and get me, what is the big deal?"

"Well, I have said no. So you don't get to go, and if you go on much more, it will be a grounding for a week. Look you have family day Sunday and school stuff to get ready for Monday."

Joy stood up fast and looked at Harper, tears filling her eyes. "She is my best friend."

Harper's eyebrows rose in fascination at the normally happy Joy, who was so not at the moment. Clint stood eating a bowl of cereal as he listened and watched Joy and Harper go at it.

Harper asked. "Who is your best friend?"

Joy stamped her foot. "You don't listen ever. Kadee is my best friend."

"Pffft! Please... how can she be? You have only just met."

Joy remained standing her arms crossed, her face showing her anger as Ace followed by a smiling Hayden walked in. Harper asked Ace. "Did you know about Conor and this female?"

"Ocean Walker, yes." Ace nodded as he looked between the annoyed Harper and an obviously angry Joy, carefully he told her. "They are good together. Joy stayed the night there."

"Conor is a really nice guy and she, Ocean, is very intense." Hayden told her as he reached up and pulled two cups down from the shelf for coffee.

Ace asked. "Why?"

Joy turned to him and said. "Mom says I cannot go to see Kadee. Even though she is my best friend in the whole world and I have not seen her for two days now. She says she can't be my best ever friend, because I have not known her long enough and she does not know Ocean yet. She knows Conor, and you let me stay the night there. Dad tell her she is wrong. That I can go, you let me go before."

Ace shook his head. "Joy I cannot..."

"Why?" She stamped her foot again. "You are so mean both of you. It is not fair!" She yelled at Harper, tears running down her face now.

"Listen here, young lady. I said no, and no it is."

"Why... tell me why?"

Harper said quietly. "I do not answer to you. Now go to your room. You are grounded until I tell you otherwise."

"Fine, but I am not going to family day."

"Fine, stay here by yourself then." Harper yelled as Joy slammed from the kitchen. She stared at the three males. Ace asked. "When did I get to be dad?"

"Oh shut up." Harper stormed from the room and they heard her slam from the apartment.

"Soo... bad time to tell her I am moving out then?" Hayden asked Ace, who grinned at him. "There was never going to be a good time my friend."

CHAPTER EIGHTEEN:

Harper could feel her anger start to boil over as she entered the lift. This was all Ocean Walkers fault. Her argument with Joy. Frankie's near death experience, Ocean bloody Walker had a lot to answer for. She grumbled under her breath all the way out of the castle, so incensed she forgot she was meant to meet up with Frankie.

She stomped down the steps of the castle scattering people out of her way from just the murderous look on her face. Her temper was no better by the time she arrived at the gallery to see Edith walking in ahead of her.

Deciding she needed to get this over with, she pushed in through the glass doors and growled out a hello, ignoring the frown Edith wore as she passed her. She made her way to the back room where she knew the art would be waiting for her. And came to a complete stop when she saw the twelve canvases as well as the framed photos from Ocean.

"Oh, shit…" She moved backward until she came to the stool she knew was there and sat, her hand over her heart. All the time her eyes wandered over each piece.

"Oh Helena, you were a master." She whispered as she looked at the framed photos and sighed as her anger left her. "Helena, your daughter followed in your footsteps."
Harper felt tears enter her eyes. She had admired and respected Helena greatly, and the world was a poorer place without her.

"She was better than I was led to believe, we studied her in school." Edith told her.

Harper nodded. "As did I, Edee she was the best there was, no one was or is better. Is this all there is?"

Edith rubbed her hands together in glee, "Hell no, just a sample apparently."

"Oh good." Harper looked at her. "She has it all here?"

"If you mean her daughter Ocean... yes."

"Damn."

Edith whispered. "You don't like her?"

Harper made no comment, only shrugged. Edith told her. "Well, she is here."

"What?"

"Ocean is here."

Why did she have to be here? Harper growled to herself getting up she walked into the show room and there she was, larger than life. Harper frowned harder, *she looked good, damn female.* Helena had told her all about her angry, wayward daughter when she had studied under her, although she and Ocean had never met. On her last visit to Helena's she had just missed meeting her by days, Helena had still been upset when she had arrived. Before she could halt the words, Harper demanded harshly. "Why are you here?"

Ocean turned around. It was inevitability she thought that she would eventually run into Harper, it was only amazing she had not until now. "One could ask you the same thing?"

Harper smirked as she walked closer to Ocean, yes she knew it was a bitchy move of intimidation and was not surprised when Ocean refused to move. Edith stood behind her counter, watching the females as Harper shrugged casually saying. "As I have talent, it should be obvious, why I am here. I am asking why you are."

"Eww a burn from the great master herself. So hurt." Ocean mocked as Ciana and Frankie entered, feeling the tension immediately. Frankie asked. "What is going on?"

"Oh, your girl is being her typical obnoxious self." Ocean stated as she grinned at Harper.

She snorted and returned. "Well, it seems you have not changed, still the spoiled angry little girl."

Ocean laughed. "For the love of... Why does everyone think that?"

"Duh! Probably because you do nothing to change anyone's opinion."

"You know Harper, I never asked you here. Please feel free to leave. Like now."

"Wow, bitchy too."

"No, just pissed at stupidity."

Harper smirked again. "You know Ocean, if this has to do with your mother, she sought me out. Not the other way around. She wanted a real artist as a daughter. Someone to talk to that did not demand all her attention. It is not my fault you were not capable of being that kind of person for her and she had to go looking elsewhere."

Ocean jerked her head as though she had been slapped, losing the color in her face, as she said quietly. "Didn't take you long to tell me what a lousy daughter I was, did it?"

Harper pointed an angry, laced with guilt finger at Ocean. "I have no idea what kind of daughter you were, she never spoke about you. In fact, I never knew she had a daughter until years later when I visited her. You had just been there, some of your photos were there. That was when she told me she had a daughter."

The silence in the room after she had stopped talking impinged on her. And as she looked around at the expressions of disbelief on her friends faces. She went back over everything she had said. Shaking her head at her own callousness, she looked regretfully at the pale faces of Frankie and Ciana.

Ocean raised her eyebrows and in a voice devoid of expression said. "That would be about right. I am amazed she had not thrown them out." She turned and walked from the gallery. Ciana went to go after her, stopping only long enough to demand. "How could you, Harper? That was just cruel."

She found Ocean down the street, she took one look at Ciana's face and sighed, "It's okay Ciana, let's go to my place. I want to show you something."

"Sure, I am sorry Ocean."

"Oh Ciana, it was what it was. I have you now. She cannot hurt me anymore. Nor can a female who knows nothing. Come on."

Edith stood, arms crossed, looking at a stunned Harper, whose eyes rose to hers and she stammered out. "I... I... I am sorry; that was mean, it sort of slipped out."

Edith shook his head and looked behind her to where Frankie stood in the doorway to the back room. "Frankie!" Harper said and came to a stop as Frankie pointed a finger at her. "I am ashamed of you. Harper, that was cruel, you hurt her on purpose."

Harper cringed, embarrassed and ashamed so she hit back. "Oh yeah, take her side. You don't know what she was like. Her mother told me she was a nightmare. She was never home. That was the first time in ten years she had been to visit her. Helena liked me, really liked me. We talked and laughed, painted together. She said I was the daughter she wished she had. I was angry at Ocean. I wanted to track her down and bring her back to her mother, but Helena begged me not to."

"Because you would have found out she was a not the saint, you painted her to be. She was a horrible, nasty, neglectful mother that hated her own daughter." Stated Frankie.

Harper said weakly. "You don't know that Frankie?"

"Yeah, I do, so does Ocean and worse of all, so do you." Frankie looked at her and for once it was not with affection. She was cold as she said. "If you don't believe me, read this." She placed a notebook on the counter. "It is all there, her hatred and contempt for Ocean and her talent. Her anger at being impregnated by Andre`. The Goddesses. Everything. Your precious Helena was a cruel, spiteful, bitter female. Her daughter, that horrible daughter you despise, wore the brunt of her mother's anger and hatred for years. Yet when Helena fell ill, Ocean cancelled her world photo tour and rushed to her mother's home and nursed her for two long, arduous, thankless years. Where were you, Harper?"

Harper looked at the journal and shook her head. “She was not that female to me.”

“Lucky you.” Claire said as she entered. “Why have you not sought the truth? That is what your gift is for, and yet you persist in painting Ocean as the bad person, the one who hated. Are you so afraid to be proved wrong, that your judgement was wrong? You should ask yourself why you never looked beyond the surface to what kind of female Helena Walker was.”

Harper looked at Claire. “It is not like that?”

But she could tell Claire did not believe her. Frankie sniffed. “Well, it seems whatever Helena Walker was like with her daughter. She would not be like that with you. I am leaving with Claire. See you later, Edee.”

“Frankie… Claire…”

“No Harper… I am angry with you, stay away from me for a few days. Maybe you should practice your gifts. They seem to be letting you down or are you not willing to see the truth of who Ocean and her mother were as Claire said.”

With a nod to Edith, Frankie and Claire left to go find Ocean and Ciana and try to make some sense of what just happened. Harper looked at the book and shook her head, leaving as she had come, except her anger had turned to sadness. She sought her barn and her art.

Edith picked up the old book and flipped the pages open to see nothing. No writing, no words on the lined sheets and smiled. Crafty Frankie, she knew Harper would not read it and had called her bluff. Although one had to wonder how Frankie knew all that about two people she had not long known.

CHAPTER NINETEEN:

When Ocean and Ciana reached her house, they found Birdy with Sparrow and Loa, who was cuddling Parker.

"Hello Lady Ocean. I would like to introduce my friends Sparrow. Commander of Queen Scarlett's guards and Loa her captain. They came over for a visit. I hope that is okay?"

"Good morning Birdy, this is your home, your friends are always welcomed." Ocean said. "I am happy to meet you both. Do you know my sister, Ciana?"

They all said yes and hello to Ciana. Ocean took Parker from Loa and asked. "Where are the girls?"

Birdy looked at her two friends, then grimaced. "In their rooms, they have been fighting."

"Again." Sighed Ocean.

Birdy nodded. "Sorry but yes."

"Seriously, they need to go to school. Okay, so I have to show Ciana something. May we have morning tea when we get back?"

"Sure, I will make it now."

Ocean nodded her thanks to Birdy. "Ladies stay and visit as long as you like."

Ocean took Ciana upstairs by way of the lift. "I wanted to give you a painting from my mother."

Ciana was a little stunned. "Really why? Not that I don't want one, but they are yours?"

Ocean shrugged. "You will see why in a minute."

They moved along the hall and entered a small room, and Ciana's jaw dropped. "Wow! There are heaps. Your mother was prolific."

"That she was."

Ciana asked. "Will you sell them?"

"Maybe or I will show them with Edith then keep them for my children." She picked up the same canvas Reighn had the day before and handed it to Ciana, who looked at it and cried out. "Oh my Goddess, that is my grandfather and me. I remember this place. It was Pink beach in Indonesia. I was four. It was one of my first digs with them." She looked at Ocean. "She was there?"

"Yes, I think so."

"Why do you think she was there?"

Ocean shrugged. "I have no idea maybe she knew them. Well, she would have to have, really. She gave birth to you as well."

Ciana shook her head, "Why did she give me away. I wonder about that, since I found out. I wonder, was there something wrong with me?"

Ocean moved Parker in her arms, and took Ciana's hand, leading her from the room. Softly, she said. "Ciana do not go down that rabbit hole. It is a nasty, horrible place, and it takes far too long to come back from. Believe me, I have been there."

Ciana thought about what Ocean said, looked at the painting in her hand, then sighed. "Okay, thanks."

Together they walked down the stairs, half-way down they heard the angry arguing coming from Paige and Kadee.

"That sounds bad." Ciana murmured to Ocean, who grunted. "I think it is to do with coming off the pills. I hope." She muttered.

"So when will they shift?"

"Any day now." Conor assures me. "Can't be soon enough for me, then they may cease to be brats."

As they reached the bottom of the stairs, Ciana smiled in sympathy as a particularly loud scream was heard from above. Claire and Frankie walked in, and Claire asked. "Who is killing who?"

Ciana laughed. "The girls are annoyed with each other, it

seems."

"That is putting it mildly." Ocean told Claire.

"How long have they been like that?" Claire asked Ocean as she passed Parker to her.

"For a day or two now."

Frankie hugged Ocean. "I am sorry about before with Harper."

"Look you two, I will tell you what I told Ciana, my mother was who she was. Harper is who she is, and I believe she will figure it out."

"You are very charitable." Claire said, knowing the anger Ocean carried or had.

"Maybe or maybe, I have my family and friends and I am trying very hard to make a new life for her." She pointed to Parker in Claire's arms and as they heard a thump from upstairs. "As well as those two."

Frankie said. "Okay, so we are here for morning tea and to take the girls shopping or I am."

"Well, Sparrow and Loa are here so let's go." Ciana told them and started for the kitchen.

"I will go get the girls." Frankie told them as she raced upstairs.

"Good luck with that." Ocean muttered as she followed the other two. "Please let there be cake."

CHAPTER TWENTY:

Early Saturday morning after a quiet or not so quiet night, depending on if you were a parent or child. The girls had argued on and off all evening. Their shopping excursion with Frankie had only increased the irritation they felt with each other. Kadee was positive Paige hogged all the attention from Frankie. While Paige called Kadee a spoiled baby. Variations of these themes were discussed or yelled at each other until they went to bed.

Ocean was positive this anger was related to losing Joy's happy presence, mixed in with their grief. Conor was positive it would all be sorted out when they finally shifted. Regardless, Ocean was thankful when she could shut herself in her bedroom for the night.

Early the following morning, just as the sun was deciding about getting up for the day, she heard Parker snuffle through the monitor and what sounded like several growls. She turned over, Conor was flat on his back in his normal pose of sleep. Again she was thankful for the massive bed.

Smiling she nudged him, his eyes sprang open instantly, it was something she was getting used to. Apparently it was a Leo thing. He would be deeply asleep one minute, then awake the next, unlike Ocean, who took a while to wake completely. "What is it?"

Ocean smiled and kissed him. "I heard some growls from Parker's room I am fairly sure a baby a week old cannot do that."

"What kind of growls?"

"Like whiny growls."

"Huh, you think the girls have shifted?" He got up, and she sighed, admiring his physique. The male was built just fine with muscles and lightly tanned skin, even the few scars he had could not distract from the perfection of him.

"Maybe." Ocean said as she got up and pulled her dressing gown on. Conor cocked an eyebrow at her, noticing the look of desire in her eyes. "We don't have time for that?"

"Are you sure?" She pouted as he grinned.

"Sadly yes, I have an early meeting with Reighn this morning."

"What?" She clutched a hand over her heart as she asked. "Why?"

"About you know who."

Wide-eyed, she asked, or whined, she did not care what it sounded like. "You are leaving me with them?" Her voice rose at the end. Conor just stopped himself from laughing at her horrified face, "They are your daughters."

"No, they are not. They are possessed teenagers."

Conor could no longer hold it in, he laughed and headed to Parker's room as Ocean followed. He pushed open the door to the nursery to be greeted by two obviously young lionesses.

"Oh my." Ocean said as she peeked around his arm, "You were right." He smiled as Ocean said. "I thought they would be like full-grown lions?"

Conor crouched down as the girls both slowly came to him. "No, if they were just wild lions, they would be fully mature and able to hunt and look after themselves." He looked up at her, "And have their own cubs."

Ocean frowned. "What?"

He laughed out loud, then said. "But as shifters we develop slower so while they are human teenagers, as lionesses they are just coming out of being cubs. So between a year and two years old. Sharm thinks the drugs have held their maturity back some."

"Oh, so they still have years before they are mature?"

"Very much so, which is why we are long lived by human

standards, not so much by dragons."

"Well, who is?" She quipped back.

By this time the two young lionesses had reached Conor where they started to rub against him as he petted them. He pulled Ocean down next to him, saying. "They need to mark you. It is an instinctive reaction, so they know who you are from others and who you belong to."

"Ahh, so that explains you?"

Conor smirked. "No, that is me just wanting you, marking you is a by-product."

Ocean grinned. "Good to know."

She looked into the face of the lioness when she came to her and realized she knew who this was, "Paige, hello sweetheart, you are beautiful."

Paige mewed, which sounded like a purr. Ocean asked Conor. "Do lions purr?"

Conor cocked an eyebrow at her. "Remind me to show you tonight."

Ocean laughed at him as Paige rubbed against her. Kadee having finished with Conor came to Ocean and snarled at Paige. She cuffed her with a paw and growled low in her chest, causing Kadee to cower on the floor. "Dominance." Conor told her as they both watched the young lionesses. "They are working out rank. It is okay, I won't let it get out of hand, but it is what they would have figured out as cubs in a litter."

"Oh." Ocean whispered as Paige went to Conor, he made a sound in his throat and she dropped to the floor. He smiled at Ocean's concerned look. "I am Leo they need to know even as young as they are that I out rank them all."

"What about me, do I have a rank?"

"Yes, we will teach them that."

"Okay." She petted Kadee and looked into her pretty amber eyes. "Kadee sweetheart, you make a very pretty lioness."

Both cubs had golden fur with amber eyes, and they had little tuffs of fur at the end of their ears. They were both muscled, although she could see it was under-developed. Some training and running in their lion skin would strengthen that.

Conor stood and helped her to her feet. "Well, I will take them for a run. They need to learn some lessons that cubs would know by their age."

"What about your meeting?"

He shrugged, "I will be back in time." He grinned. "You will have a peaceful morning; they should sleep when we return. Learning to be a lion is exhausting."

"Oh, goodie but you still owe me?"

"What do you want?" He asked, eyeing her with trepidation.

"An hour to shoot some photos when you get back later."

"Done." He agreed as he kissed her and left followed by the young lionesses who both brushed by her in goodbye. Ocean smiled at the thought of having a camera in her hands again. She picked up by now a grumbling Parker and looked out the window and saw Conor as his lion, with the two young lionesses following sedately behind him.

"Now that would make a great photo." She murmured to herself and sighed. "Next time."

She was surprised when Conor powered into a run, as it seemed the two cubs were, suddenly they took off like rockets after him. Ocean laughed as she changed Parker, telling her she too would be able to run like her sisters one day. She wondered what it would be like to fly the skies, to soar among the clouds, the views would be amazing. She spent some time thinking how she could photograph as a dragon. Smiling, she fed Parker her bottle and once she was settled in her bassinet, went to shower. Thinking pancakes sounded good for breakfast as it was Birdy's day off, so she was nominated as cook.

After a happy breakfast where both girls did not once snipe at each other. They were too full of excitement about finally shifting and running with their dad, the Leo. Conor had to leave for his meeting after sending both girls to bed for a nap, which they happily complied with. As they scampered up the stairs, he kissed Ocean and assured her the girls would not shift again today. Their other halves were in need of rest as much as the girls would be, which pleased her, thinking of a peaceful morning.

Sadly, an hour later she would gladly have taken two snarling lionesses than the arguing teenagers that he had left her with. Only the promise of an hour to herself, when he returned, stopped her from finding a dungeon and locking them in. She settled for bitching to Ciana on the phone, figuring that was what sisters were for.

When Conor arrived at Reighn's conference room, he was surprised to see Storm and three other people with him. He scented a cheetah and tigers. "Good morning."

"Morning Conor." Storm greeted him as Fin walked in with Queen Scarlett, King Elijah and their guards, he greeted each one of them as well. Then Storm introduced the three people with him. "This is Joseph Ian Michael, known as Mitch and his lovely mate Sara. I know you all have heard Sage mention both Mitch and Sara. We found them and Mr Harris here, on our way home last night."

Conor grinned as he shook hands with the couple. "I actually know Sara. We met many months ago. How are you?"

She grinned and bowed her head in response to his smile.

"Fine and glad to be home Leo."

To Mitch, he said. "I have heard of your exploits, welcome both of you to Dragon's Gap."

Mitch too bowed his head in respect to the Leo as he said. "Thank you Leo, as with Sara it is great to be home."

While Storm introduced the couple to the Queen and King. Conor turned to the older male, waiting patiently. "I know of you, Warren Harris. We do not have many cheetah's here."

"Leo." He said softly and bowed his head. Conor waited while Storm introduced Reighn, Sage and Charlie to Mitch and Sara, as the three of them entered from Reighn's office.

Conor asked. "Why cheetah Harris, did you not find your way to Dragon's Gap when you heard I was here. I would have helped you?"

"I cannot say Leo. I think I was so confused by then, all I

wanted to do was keep on running."

"To what?" Sage asked the male who was still handsome for his age in the way of shifters. He had light blond, almost white hair with black streaks. He had dark brown eyes that were shuttered and his body was lanky and wiry like a cheetah's she supposed. He looked beaten down, like life had been unkind to him and yet she knew from Reighn, he had a wonderful mate waiting for him.

His answer was unexpected and left her a little stunned as how to answer him. "To sanity, Lady Sage. When one knows they can shift, yet is unable to, it becomes like a sickness and the animal side of us goes stir crazy."

"Oh, I see." Sympathy laced through her words.

Reighn said. "I have met your mate Mr Harris."

Wonder and a smile filled his eyes and face as he asked hesitantly. "She is well?"

Reighn nodded. "She is both, she is in your town helping me with the new industry there. She awaits your return."

He ducked his head and hunched his shoulders. "I am unworthy of her. I cannot believe she waited for me."

"Well no, you are not." Reighn growled. "She is a fine, honest female, and she misses you desperately. Now if the Leo says you may, and if you want to. I can make it so you can return to her."

Warren Harris looked up at Conor and begged him with his eyes. "Leo, may I?"

Conor smiled. "I insist. Later today, My Lord Reighn will open a portal for you to travel to your mate before then. Eat, shop, purchase something for your mate and some clothes. I assume you arrived with nothing?"

"That is true, Leo."

Conor grinned at the male, whose whole body looked as though a weight had been taken from him. "Maybe your mate will only make your life miserable for a few years."

Smiling, the older male bowed and made to leave, but not before Reighn asked him. "What work do you do Mr Harris?"

"I am an accountant. May I ask what industry is in the town?"

"Water, pure mineral water."

Warren Harris smiled, "I always knew it was there."

"Well, you were right." Reighn told him.

Conor slipped him a credit card. "You will need this."

With a startled thank you, the male left. Sage turned to Mitch and his mate. "Well did you find them?" Meaning Sara's brother and sister.

Mitch smiled. "Yes, Sara and I did, Lady Sage. Thank you."

"They are alive and well?"

Sara answered. "Yes both are and they are older and wiser for their experiences."

Conor asked. "What do you wish to do? Now you are home?"

Mitch shrugged. "I have no idea. For the last few years, all we have thought about is rescuing and finding Sara's family."

Reighn smiled. "I have a job for you both if you would see me later we could discuss it."

Sara asked. "My Lord does it require traveling?"

"No, you would remain in town."

Relieved, she said. "Thank you, both Mitch and I have traveled enough, we would like to settle down and start a family."

Mitch took his mates hand in his. "We would like to discuss it with you, My Lord."

Conor handed them each a credit card as well. "Go shop for your family and stay at the hotel 'Welcome.' It is a good place to stay until you know what you want to do. Tell Ken I sent you. If you need me, the sheriff's department will locate me or ask for Saul or Kai."

Mitch and Sara both thanked him and they bowed to Reighn and Sage, then left. Charlie asked Conor. "How many of those cards do you have?"

"Enough, there is always someone who needs an extra hand, so I carry cards."

"You are a very nice Leo."

He shrugged and whispered loud enough for all to hear.

"It is Reighn's money. Don't tell him."

Which made her and the others laugh. Except Reighn, who

sighed, it was not his money but now he knew about the cards, he would make sure Conor received enough money to cover them. In fact, he made a note to tell Stan to set up a specific account for Conor and issue cards to him.

"While that was nice, let's get this meeting done. I have things to do." Stated Charlie.

Reighn nodded to Sage as Loa closed the doors and Sage cast her silencing spell.

"Right where are we?" Reighn asked as they all took their seats and the guards stood against the walls around the room. Sparrow took up her customary place with Loa behind Queen Scarlett and King Elijah just as Lars and Stan walked in from Reighn's office. Sparrow smiled at Loa's snort of disgust and mumbled. "Forgot that one."

Rumoh made a signal as he went to stand in front of the now closed door. Sparrow softly said. "It happens."

Lars and Stan sat as Charlie said. "In answer to Reighn's question. We looked for the male Definiao Kiltern, but we missed him by hours at each location we searched. Harper is convinced we do have an informer and so am I. Everything points to it."

"Okay, so no luck with your teams?" Reighn asked, she shook her head no. He then asked. "Conor what about your people?"

"Whispers and murmurs, nothing concrete."

"What about you, Fin?"

"Unfortunately, the same as Conor. Our plan has not produced fruit yet, but it is early days still."

"What about you, Sage?"

"Sadly my pregnancy is interfering with my looking, so no luck either."

"Where is Andre`?" Elijah asked, suddenly noticing he was absent.

"Chasing down some information, he received this morning," Fin told them.

"Anything we should be concerned with?" Reighn inquired.

Fin shrugged. "I do not know My Lord he did not say."

"Alright." Reighn, he turned to Storm. "Brother what of your people, and how did your hunt go?"

"Other than finding Mr Harris and the Michael's?"

"Yes, I would assume you would realize that." Reighn bit out.

"Testy, you need a male's night." Storm grinned at his brother as he heard him growl under his breath. "I need something..."

"So Storm, what did you find?" Cut in Sage as Reighn started to growl.

Storm threw a large soft leather-bound book on the table. "This, it is supposedly a journal from one of Definiao Kiltern's main web masters. He ran several webs, apparently. We found him in a burned out warehouse, barely alive. Looks like Definiao is cleaning house, or he is as crazy as we suspect and is killing those he suspects of betraying him."

"Did this male betray him?" Queen Scarlett asked Storm, who smiled as he told her. "Eventually. He gave us that, it is in code."

"Damn it." Elijah picked it up and squinted as he looked at the scribbled pages. "What language is this?"

Storm shrugged. "No idea. I was hoping you knew?"

"No, sorry, nothing I have seen before. My light, what of you?" He asked Scarlett. She looked and shook her head.

"No sorry."

He closed it and placed it back on the table. Reighn drew it to him as he said. "No matter, we will have Keeper and Olinda look at it, but not today. Monday will be soon enough. Anything else, Storm?"

"Yes." He nodded to the book. "The male said, inside that was the name of our traitor."

There were several gasps as Fin asked. "Did you believe him?"

Storm's smile was predatory. "Oh yes, there was no doubt."

"Well!" Reighn frowned as he passed the book to Fin, who flipped it open and scowled. Then passed it to Conor, who glanced at the pages and then shut it. He held it up to see if anyone else wanted a look at it. None did, so he passed it back to Reighn as he said. "Okay, Monday, I will have Olinda and Keeper look at it. We are secure?"

Fin and Conor nodded as Storm said. "We are as tight as we can be."

Reighn said. "Alright, no traffic until Monday. Dragon's Gap is closed for the next two days; we re-open at midnight Monday. Let's give everyone a breath until Tuesday. Then we will convene a full meeting, and hopefully Keeper and Olinda have deciphered the journal. If not, I will contact the Elementals. How is that?"

There were no disagreements to his plan, so the meeting broke up after no new business. Conor asked Reighn. "What job are you going to offer to the Michaels?"

Reighn sat on the edge of the table as he answered. "I was thinking mayor jointly of the town I just acquired."

"Huh!" Conor looked off into the distance as he thought about that. "Yeah, it is a good idea. They would like that, they are both Alphas and she is half human, so she will relate to the humans. It will work well, they are both personable people."

"As well as very smart and honest." Sage told them. "I had them investigated when I took over the retrievers."

Reighn grinned. "I was sure you had, my dear."

"What of the brother and sister?" Sage asked Reighn.

Conor answered for him. "If they wish to remain here, let them know they can see Claire or me. We will find them a place to work and live."

"Alright, I will send Mr Harris home today with the sheriff and his wife. Now Thorn is back, it may be safer for him to not be here."

Conor nodded. "True, well I am off." He smiled as Queen Scarlett and her guards Sparrow and Loa arrived. "I promised Ocean an hour to shoot some photos."

Sage asked. "How are your girls?"

Proudly, he told her. "They shifted for the first time today."

"Oh my." Sage said with a large smile as Reighn clapped him on the back. "Congratulations, did it go alright?"

"Perfectly. They are perfect. I left them quiet and peaceful."

He smiled as he said. "No more arguing from the girls. We should have a calm, happy home."

Scarlett asked kindly. "They are arguing?"

He sighed, "So much, who knew girls could make that noise. But now they have shifted, all should be well."

Scarlett looked at Sage and raised her eyebrows, she returned the look they both knew it was not going to be that simple. Conor excused himself to return home.

Scarlett asked Sage. "What do you think?"

"We need to talk to Grace."

"Oh, good idea will you call or me?"

"I will." Sage told her, then turned to Sparrow. "Now what is this, I've heard about Hayden and you sneaking around at night."

Scarlett grinned at the disconcerted expression on Sparrows face. Loa had told her about the problems they were having in telling Harper, she and Hayden had moved out of her home and into their own place. Scarlett had spoken to Sage and here they were about to sort out her friends life. She loved being a queen.

Sparrow sighed, as she found herself the center of attention, she made eyes at the unrepentant Loa as Charlie moved to where they stood. "What is going on?"

Scarlett told her and Charlie cursed, then looking at Sparrow, she shook her head. "That sister of mine, always making life difficult."

Sparrow by now was slumped down on a chair. "He will not tell her, she is upset apparently."

"That is ridiculous." Scarlett said. "You will have too."

Sparrow's face went through about ten different expressions before settling on one that read helplessness. "How do I do that?"

"Like this?" Charlie opened her phone and when Harper answered, she said. "Hayden and Sparrow are bonded. He moved out two nights ago." She listened for a minute, then snarled into the phone. "Get over it. You whack job." She closed her phone. "See simple. All taken care of. She wishes you happiness."

Sparrow looked at her smiling face and asked. "Should I go see her?"

"Why? She is not your mother or his. She is a pouty female, and I think I will go tell her that." She hugged Sparrow. "Congratulations for you and Hayden cannot wait for the party." With a wave to the others, she left to tackle her sister literally. Reighn stood with Elijah and Storm as they watched Charlie walk determinedly from the room. He looked at Storm and asked. "Are you not going to follow her, she is your shadow?"

Storm asked. "What... am I a girl now?"

CHAPTER TWENTY-ONE:

Conor's hope of a quiet and peaceful home lasted until he opened the front door. He was met with yelling and crying and a desperate Ocean who walked into his opened arms and she begged.

"Kill me now!"

An hour later Conor wanted death, any death would do, but he preferred a quick one. After he had explained what had occurred at the meeting and Ocean told him what occurred there. He sent her out for the promised hour, to shoot photos with the assurance he could manage their daughters.

She had left, and he tried... he really did try to believe she had left with reluctance, but he knew better, she had run from there as fast as she could, and as another wail came from upstairs. He knew why, after an hour of listening to crying, yelling and so many, it's not fair, at the top of their voices.

He wanted to dig a hole and fall in face first, making sure the dirt covered him. Except he really did love his mate and... **crash...**"What was that?" He yelled, silence met his question. He sighed as he heard the large old door knocker bang several times.

"Lady Grace, Lord Patrycc. What can I help you with?" Conor asked as he opened the door, allowing the sunlight to enter along with the older couple.

Patrycc told him. "We have come to offer our services."

"I see, well please come in."

Just then they heard yelling from above. "It's mine, Paige. You can't have everything."

"Claire gave it to me. Let it go, Kadee."

"No, you let it go. She gave it to me."

"Give it back now." Screamed Paige, then there were a few thumps and bangs and a couple of oww's, then the loud crying started again. Conor looked up the stairs and said. "Boys are so much easier. Why do they have to scream and make that noise and the crying? Dear Goddess, you would think they would become dehydrated."

Patrycc asked. "When did it start?"

Conor turned back to the couple. "When they were told Joy was not allowed to come over or maybe it was before."

Grace asked. "When was that?"

Conor shrugged. "Two, maybe three days ago, it sort of all rolls into one."

"Oh my... What does Ocean say?"

Conor looked at the couple and sighed. "She says if Harper is going to be that way, there is nothing she can do."

Patrycc said. "Does she want..."

A loud crash sounded from above as Ocean walked in from the kitchen, the baby in one arm, her camera in the other. Relieved, Conor stated. "You are back, good."

"I am sorry Conor." She handed the baby to him, kissed his cheek, smiled at the couple, then ran up the stairs and before she hit the landing she was yelling. "Dear Heavens, can you please go one day without fighting and you can damn well fix this **NOW!** We have guests, and you are embarrassing your father. Now move and get dressed, brush your hair and, **DO NOT LOOK AT EACH OTHER."**

Silence reigned, and Conor said as though they asked. "And that is how she handles it." He motioned the two people in. "Come on, let's go to the kitchen, there is cake."

He closed the door behind them, sighing at the sight of all that freedom disappearing. "I heard that." Ocean said from behind him. He grunted as if he had not known she was there. She walked ahead of him to the kitchen. He shrugged at Grace and Patrycc. "Not a happy household. Bad time to visit."

"Well, this is ridiculous." Grace growled, she shoved up the sleeves of her sweater and said. "Hand me that baby." Which he did, then she marched into the kitchen and was talking before she got to the door. "Ocean Towers, what the hell is going on with your family?"

"She does know Ocean has no idea who she is?" He asked Patrycc as they moved slowly toward the door, they could hear murmuring behind. Patrycc grinned. "She knows and will handle her."

"Bet you didn't think this was what you were here for? Why are you here?"

"You know I did not, but we are here, and this is what my shadow and I do."

Conor looked at him. Patrycc told him softly. "We fix fractures. Sage called us."

Conor grunted, knowing it would have been her. "So bonded. How is that going?"

"Easier than yours. I only have four bears, two of who are male to contend with."

"Lucky you." Grumbled Conor as they made the kitchen.

Patrycc laughed as he slapped him on the back. "Hey, it could be worse."

"Can't see how?"

"There could be five of them."

Conor almost swallowed his tongue as he followed the chortling male dragon into the kitchen. Ocean stood behind the island, phone in hand. "Now what?"

"Pass me that." Grace said when the phone was answered, she said without giving Harper a chance to say more than hello.

"Harper Elliot Battle you will bring your Joy here to Ocean and Conor's home immediately." Grace listened for a minute and then said. "Do not make me get Verity... No, I did not think so. Yes, you may bring him as well. We will be having lunch. Goodbye."

CHAPTER TWENTY-TWO:

Twenty minutes later, Grace had the girls who were dressed with their hair braided. Helping her in the kitchen, preparing food for the visitors who were coming over for a discussion and lunch. Ocean had been handed a cup of coffee and told to make herself scarce. Conor was told to put Parker in her bassinet, and he and Patrycc were in his study, which apparently he had now.

She was on the patio watching her daughters, who had done nothing but argue for days, smile and talk like real people with Grace. She closed her eyes and soaked up the quiet and the sunshine. How long she would have remained like that she had no idea and would never find out, as a huge shadow crossed above her, shutting off the sunlight.

She opened her eyes to see a dragon circling above her and immediately snapped up her camera and started shooting as the large black dragon landed. A dragon was in her backyard.

The door opened, and the girls as well as Grace, Patrycc and Conor emerged, Patrycc said. "It is Andre`."

Ocean and the girls ran to him and stopped, Patrycc said as he followed behind them. "You can touch him. He is waiting for you to do so."

Instantly they all smoothed their hands over him. "Oh Granddad, you are warm." Kadee said entranced.

Paige said. "And soft, you are so soft."

Ocean looked into the eye closest to her. "You are wonderful and handsome, just wonderful Papa, thank you." She laid her head as the girls did against his hide and felt his pleasure. They stayed that way for a few minutes until Ocean sighed and said. "Come on girls your granddad needs to change and Joy will be here soon."

They all moved back to the patio as Andre` transformed from dragon to human. The girls ran to him again to be hugged. Once the girls had released him, he moved to Ocean and hugged her. She breathed in his scent and could feel his love as she said. "Welcome to our home, Papa"

"I thank you daughter for the welcome."

As they walked side by side toward the house, he asked the girls. "What smells so delightful?"

"Lunch." Both girls said at once and then hurried to tell him what each of them had prepared. He was impressed as he looked at Ocean, who said. "Don't look at me. It is all Grace and the girls."

Andre` smiled as he shook hands with Conor and Patrycc, then hugged and kissed Grace. Conor said. "We are waiting for the Battles to arrive."

Startled, Andre` asked. "What, all of them?"

Conor grinned. "No, just Ace and Harper as well as Joy."

"Ahh I see, do we have time for a drink?"

Grace nodded. "Of course."

A few minutes later as the adults sat around the kitchen table with a drink each, while the girls were making a salad. Another shadow crossed against the window. "That will be Ace." Andre` said.

"How do you know Granddad?" Paige asked with a smirk at Kadee, who had wanted to ask.

"I trained all the boys. I know his dragon."

"Oh wow! That is so cool." Kadee said as Paige frowned and hissed. "I was going to say that?"

"Well, you were too slow."

"Girls enough." Ocean warned in her, do not piss me off voice. They ducked their heads and became silent, knowing they could find themselves in their bedrooms. Andre` gave her a look to see if she was angry, she only smiled and said. "They have been like that for days."

"Ahh I see." He may have said more but a quick knock on the door and Joy burst into the kitchen. "Kadee, I am here. Paige, it is me, I am finally here." She announced dramatically as the three girls grabbed each other, squealed and hugged as though they had been apart forever.

"It's like they have been separated for years." Harper moaned to Ace as they stood in the doorway.

Conor walked around and shook Ace's hand and kissed the back of Harper's hand, which made her smile. "Welcome to our home, please come in."

As they stepped in, Grace looked at Conor. "Do you see it?"

He nodded and said. "I should have seen it before. I must be slipping."

"You have had other concerns."

He shrugged. "True."

"Well, I would like to know what you are talking about." Ocean asked as Harper said. "As would I and will it stop the sulking."

"And the fighting." Ocean grumbled. "Because I swear one more day..."

Harper laughed as she glanced at Ocean who, even though she was amused, looked like she was ready to find a hole for her girls. Andre ` smiled as Joy said hello to him.

Kadee asked. "Granddad did you know Joy was coming today?"

"No sweet girl, I heard you and Paige had your first shift and I wanted to come and tell you how proud of you I was."

Joy squealed as she hugged Kadee. "You shifted." Then she looked at her mother and said. "See what you made me miss? Kadee and Paige's very first shift. You are so mean."

Before Harper or Ace could say anything. Ocean growled. "Joy Battle. You will not talk to your mother like that. She deserves your respect at all times, even when you are mad at her, the same goes for your dad. You young lady will remember you are the child, not the parent and as a child you will mind your manners and your parents. Do I make myself clear?"

Joy's eyes widened as she nodded her head, "Yes, Ma'am."

"Good. Now I am waiting."

Joy looked at her mother as Harper snapped her mouth closed, it had dropped open at Ocean's reprimand of Joy and her defense of her. Joy moved to her mother and hugged her, saying. "I am sorry mom... I should not have been so rude to you and mean to you even..." Ocean cleared her throat.

Joy sighed. "Sorry mom."

Harper's face softened as her arms automatically wound around the girl. "Yeah, I know you are, as am I kiddo. I love you and am sorry. You are right, I don't always listen. I will try harder in the future."

Ace hugged her, then said. "Can you give us a few minutes please girls?"

When they were gone. Ace turned to Conor, "Want to tell me what is going on?"

Conor handed him a glass of whiskey and a beer for Harper as they all sat at the table. "The reason you and we, are having such a hard time with the girls, is they have made themselves into a pride?"

Harper lowered her glass and asked. "What?"

Ace said, "Paige, Kadee and our Joy?"

"As well as Kammy, Parker and I should imagine every child in the family."

Andre` asked quietly. "Do they understand what is happening?"

Conor shook his head as Grace answered. "No, they just know they need to be together."

Patrycc said. "Safety in numbers, they call to each other. Instincts."

Conor told them. "Yes, we cannot ignore it."

Ocean asked. "So what do we do?"

"Nothing, except I hope you all have enough room for sleep overs." Grace stated, they all look at her as she smiled. "They will need to be together. You have seen what happens when they are not and believe me it will only get worse as they get older."

Conor sighed. "She is right, also Joy will no doubt shift in the next day or two. Her wolf feels safe now with you and us, and her new pride."

Harper smirked as she asked. "Isn't it pack, you know cause she is a wolf and all?"

Conor looked at her and said with a raised eyebrow. "No."

Ocean leaned near her and whispered. "It's a lion thing."

Harper snickered, then said. "Oh, I get it,"

After that the rest of the lunch went great, there was laughter and plenty of food. Paige and Kadee were happy and excited about family day the following day, which would be there first.

Harper agreed for Joy to stay the night, which made them even happier, especially when Andre` offered to fly the girls so Joy could get her things. Paige and Kadee were ecstatic their first dragon flight and with their grandfather.

Ocean took Harper up to show her the paintings and as Harper stood looking at all the work Ocean had saved, she said. "I never knew she was like that. I should have. There was always a secretive side to her. I assumed it was what she saved of herself for her work, but it wasn't, she just hid the evil side of herself from me."

Ocean leaned against the wall. "I don't think she was evil. Well, I hope she wasn't. I hope she was just self-involved and bitter. No one who did work like this could be truly evil. I hope."

Harper thought maybe Ocean was trying to convince herself more than her. "Are you scared you are like her?"

Ocean shook her head. "When I was young, I worried about it, as I got older I decided I was not."

Harper smiled. "I can tell you are not."

"I know because if I was, those two girls of mine would be unable to breathe."

Harper burst out laughing, when she got herself under control she said. "See, I knew it was not just me."

"Nah! Now do you want some of her work because you should take it now? Edith is coming up here next week."

Harper looked at her with horror. "You are not letting her see all this, are you?"

"Well yeah, are you saying I shouldn't?"

"No... no, do not show her everything, only ten or so pieces at a time. Otherwise, she will nag you forever, and I mean forever."

Ocean had visions of Edith at her doorstep each morning. "Oh Goddess, thanks."

They spent the next thirty minutes finding paintings Harper wanted. Finally, Ocean said. "We can always do a loan thing. You know when you are tired of looking at them. You can bring them back and swap them over."

Harper grinned, liking that idea. "Are you selling any of them?"

"No, I will keep them for us and my young. So take what you like now and come again."

Harper grinned. "Edith will be so annoyed, can't be a better deal when that happens."

Ocean grinned as well. "Bonus then."

"Yep." Together they gathered five for Harper to take with her. She grinned all the way home and as she hung the paintings, along with the photos Ocean had given Ace when he had admired them, knowing Edith would see them and drool.

CHAPTER TWENTY-THREE:

Ocean lay watching the sun come up. It was Monday and the first day of school. She sighed as she thought over the previous day. Meeting everyone in her large extended family for family day. She had been amused to learn that this happened every Sunday. And no one missed unless dying or not at home.

The girls loved the idea, from breakfast to after dinner they were adored by all the young. Even Grace's grandsons and granddaughter, three sweet little bear cubs. Grace had told her they were in the developing pride as well. Ocean was amused to see that their parents did not seem to have any worries about it.

The adults made much of the girls and fell for Parker completely. Conor told her before they went, that dragons loved babies, he had been right. Ocean finally matched names with faces and thanks to Conor, Ciana and Andre` she felt like she knew them already. Funnily enough, she had to admit she enjoyed Claire, Harper, June and Edee the most. She thought she had more in common with them, probably because they were as snarky as she was. Charlie amused her with her dry wit, and the way she ribbed Harper. Ciana, Olinda and Frankie were similar in that they were good-hearted females and it was nice to spend time with them. Frankie was over her annoyance with Harper, especially when she saw her and Harper laughing together.

Thorn was a nice male, he and Conor seemed to get on well. Conor got on with everyone, really. The one who had more fun than everyone was Andre` he was either with the girls or had a baby in his arms. He looked slightly bemused and proud, all rolled into one.

There was only one tricky bit, and that was when Verity started to apologize about Paige. Ocean gently cut her off, telling her she understood. More so since meeting Andre`s dragon. After that, she seemed to stop avoiding her. It was a great day she thought as she yawned, but today was all about school and if she was lucky, she could persuade Birdy to look after Parker for a little while this afternoon, so she could go take some photos in town.

She finally rose and went to shower by the time she was dressed and ready. Conor had changed Parker and handed her and her bottle to Ocean as they passed on the way to his shower. Ocean grinned as she sat to feed Parker, they were like a well-oiled machine. When she made it downstairs, the girls were already at the table, Birdy had made their breakfast for their first day of school. So far, so good. She was to do the morning run to school, and Conor was to pick them up afterward. After breakfast Conor kissed them all goodbye and assured the nervous girls they would do fine and he would see them later. As promised Ocean dropped the excited and nervous girls at school, thankfully once they met up with Joy and Clint they seemed to calm down.

Later that morning when Parker grumbled, ready to wake for her bottle. Ocean decided it was as good a time as any to take a break from her computer. After returning home from school, she had helped out with housework. There were still renovations being done, and the painters were still there, which made house cleaning easier. But she and Birdy could see that Ocean's quip about needing an army was not far off. It was just as well Birdy was interviewing today for people to come in to clean; they were going to need it.

Birdy agreed to watch Parker, so Ocean was going to go into town and shoot at one o'clock. She figured she would be able to spend two hours exploring the town and taking photos before the girls arrived home, full of news about their first day. After a lunch spent with Birdy, Adam, Ian and the bears, she ended up leaving later than she wanted, so would barely get in an hour before school finished, but an hour was better than nothing.

CHAPTER TWENTY-FOUR:

Ocean walked around another corner. The town was an oasis of calm and a little confusing at first. She had taken some wonderful photos of people and dragons who seemed to enjoy being captured by her camera. She stopped and looked around, finally admitting she was lost. She had only been in town for forty minutes and knew she would have to figure out where she was and then see about returning home.

She started walking again and turned another corner, working on the principal that turning corners would eventually get her to the main street. When she turned another corner, she bumped literally into Loa. "Wow! What timing. Hello Loa, I am lost, would you believe it?"

"Oh, thank the Goddess. I have been looking all over for you." Loa said as she held onto her arms. Ocean's heart squeezed at the worry in the faerie's eyes and voice. She could barely get the words out as fear clutched her throat. "Why, has something happened?"

"Yeah, I am so sorry Lady Ocean." As she talked Loa hurried Ocean along the road. "What Loa... What has happened? Is it Parker, Conor the girls? Who is hurt?"

"No, none of them. I am sorry, Lady Ocean; it is Lord Andre`."

"Andre?" Ocean's mind spun. "What... How?"

"He had a fall!"

"Andre` fell? Dear Goddess, how... from where?"

Loa nodded. "Yeah, I am so sorry Lady Ocean."

"You keep saying that... Why are you saying that? Why are

you sorry, Loa?" Ocean asked as dread filled her heart. *Was he dead? Oh please, she thought, don't be dead Papa please.*

They turned into a darken doorway as Loa said. "I am sorry for this, well I am not really but it is what one says is it not?" She plunged a needle into Ocean's neck, instantly she dropped to the ground.

"Dammit!" Loa hissed as she lifted the small female and took her farther into the building and dumped her into an open box, taping it closed. Loa hummed as she worked, so far the plan was working. She had the box on a cart, so all she had to do was push it calmly from the building, along the street to her vehicle. Which she did, slowly walking as she pushed the cart, not drawing unnecessary attention to herself while she moved along the street. She even nodded to several people she saw on the way. Calmly she made it to her van and hefted the box inside, then she drove sedately from the town.

Loa headed toward the cabin in the mountains. It wasn't much, but it was all she needed, with careful driving it took her forty-five minutes to make it to the cabin. She drove in under the lean-to and parked. The cabin door opened as she turned the engine off.

He stood there the most hunted male in the world. Definiao Kiltern, the only person who knew who she really was. He asked as he stepped down the steps. "How did it go?"

She got out and walked to the side of the van, opening the door, "Great, as we expected."

Together they pulled the box out and took it inside. They had made some modifications to the two bedroom cabin. Not only did it have a bathroom but also running water as well as power and it boasted its very own cell. They placed Ocean on the bed provided and locked the barred door behind them as they left.

"I need coffee." Loa moaned as she walked into what was the main part of the cabin, a big open room with a small wood burner. "That was stressful."

"Did you leave the note as I told you too, so he will find it when he returns?"

She looked over at Definiao, annoyed he was questioning her. He always seemed to be doing that lately, as if she was a fool. "I said it went great."

He snorted as he paced. "Yes well, you would not be the first to have missed something, left something behind."

"Please." She waved him off as she went to the kitchen and poured her coffee. Definiao shook his head when she lifted the pot in his direction. "I left nothing. I used gloves and was careful. No one will detect my scent, and no one saw me talking to her. When I took her, it went like clockwork, so easy, now settle down. I got you here and have kept you safe, haven't I? While they have been chasing their tails out there looking for you."

Definiao nodded. "True although..."

Loa moved to the lounge chair. "What now?"

"That damn journal. If you had been able to get it, we would not have had to step up our schedule. We could have waited until the others were here."

Loa sighed as if they had not discussed this since she found out about the damn journal, again she said. "Well, we were not to know Horton would be caught, or that he had the bloody journal or even that Reighn would lock down the place. Now did we?"

"No, well, I would not know how the dragon would react. I thought you would, as you have been here supposedly studying him."

Loa bit her tongue and shrugged instead of yelling at him. "The book is gibberish I had a quick look." She had not, but refused to give him any more ammunition to take digs at her with. She hoped she was right as she told him. "No one will be able to break Horton's code; it was for him alone."

The plan called for her to return to the Grove tonight and be in place when the note was discovered, so she could direct the hunt away from here. Definiao asked as he had a hundred times already. "Are you sure? He was not the cleverest agent we had?"

Loa again waved her hand, "I recruited him for that reason

alone. I knew what he could do and no before you ask I am not surprised he cracked. The dragons are masters at breaking down their prisoners."

Definiao frowned but changed the subject, she was just saying what she had said before. "How long until she comes around?" He nodded to where Ocean lay on the bed. Loa shrugged as she too looked toward the barred door. "Who knows? Maybe never. Do you care?"

Definiao smirked as Loa snorted. "Please, you can forgo your fun. Even I will insist she be awake."

"Well true. I suppose it is more fun that way?" Definiao grinned at her.

"Seriously cousin enough. Let's start thinking about what you are going to do once you become the overlord. When that happens, you can have all the females you want."

"And what of you?"

"Do not worry. I have my eye on a few males that interest me."

"You are very sure they will capitulate." Definiao said as he watched her from sharp, mistrustful eyes.

Loa was aware of the scrutiny and countered with. "Are you not?"

"Of course I am. This is my plan, to seize the lock and hold her against the dragons, to have her back they will give me anything I ask for. Not that it will do them much good, but hope is a motivator."

They both laughed until Loa asked. "True, although what of the Elementals?"

Definiao flicked his hand as though he was swatting a fly away. "Have they intervened yet?"

"Well no."

"They will not, they serve the one in power. They will serve me."

Loa grinned. "This is going to be fun I only hope the others arrive before midnight, I have given them the codes to enter through the Queens byway."

“They will be here.”

“I hope so.” Worried Loa.

Definiao grinned as he rubbed his hands together. “It is going to be outstanding, to finally reach my true destiny. To do what our family were incapable of accomplishing. I have risen above the travesty of our family’s failure to be here at this time. To be Overlord.”

Loa frowned as she said. “We... Do not forget who helped you get here, cousin?”

“Yes... yes, of course. Were you not preparing food?”

Loa grunted as she finished her coffee. Sometimes she wondered if Del’ really thought about her like she did him. But as she passed the room with the unconscious Ocean, she shrugged. It was too late now, she and Del’s fates were fixed. Tomorrow they would rule the world, if not the universes.

CHAPTER TWENTY-FIVE:

Andre` slammed into Reighn's office, it was ten minutes past three in the afternoon. "They have targeted Ocean."

He placed the note carefully on Reighn's desk. When Andre` had found it, he had grabbed a tissue and picked the paper up, being careful not to leave his own scent. His heart may have stopped when he read the note, but his brain still worked. Evidence was important.

Reighn used the blade of his knife to turn the note around, taking his lead from how Andre` handled the paper, as Lars read over his shoulder and warned. "Conor will go crazy."

"He is not the only one." Andre` growled as his dragon rose to the surface.

Reighn stood. "Lars call Conor."

Andre` told him. "Do not bother, he is on his way. I have sent Harper to the school, and he has Kai and Saul going to his home."

Reighn asked. "Who Andre… Who has her?"

Conor walked in. "Definiao Kiltern. It can only be him."

"Here at Dragon's Gap?" Johner asked as he walked in behind him with Storm.

"Yes. Someone or many someone's have not only passed information on, they have smuggled him in and are protecting him here." Conor growled, barely keeping his lion from his voice.

Lars asked. "Who could do such a thing without being caught?"

Storm asked. "That is a good question?"

Reighn asked. "What do we know?"

Andre` answered. "Fin is searching the castle and grounds for a trace of the person who left the note."

Conor told Reighn. "Birdy said Ocean was in town photographing. She left about two and said she would be home before the girls."

Claire entered, she was pale and trembling. Lars moved to her. "My love, what do you know?"

"I saw Ocean. She was walking and then she was worried, as though something suddenly happened to upset her. Then everything went black. I am sorry Conor, I swear I just saw this. My gift is not always time sensitive."

"I understand, it is not your fault Seer."

Andre` said. "So they knocked her out somewhere."

Reighn ordered. "Johner start searching quietly, let's not cause a panic or give our hand away. They may not have counted on us learning about this so fast."

"Yes My Lord." He said as he and Stan, who had just arrived left, passing Queen Scarlett, King Elijah and Sparrow. Along with Rumoh and Dumoh, as they all entered Reighn's office. "Reighn, is it correct, that Lady Ocean has been kidnapped?"

"Yes Elijah she has."

Sage came in with Charlie, Frankie and Jacks from her office, as Birdy her arms protectively around Parker arrived with Saul and Kai as escorts. "Leo. We have brought Parker."

Conor walked to Birdy. "I thank you Birdy, will you remain with her?"

"I will Leo, none shall touch her. Any word yet?"

"No, not yet."

"Where shall we go?" She asked Conor.

Sage answered before he could. "We will go to the stone apartment."

Just then Harper walked in with Ace, Ark and Phoebe all in battle gear. She told Conor to his relief. "The girls are in the apartment." She then looked at Sage and the others. "Where you all are meant to be, all the grandparents are already there. Ash and Keeper are rounding up the others and their young. So move it along now."

Sage nodded. "Yes... yes, we are going. Scarlett, you too."

"Of course." She agreed. Birdy nodded to Conor and left with Harper, who stopped long enough to tell Conor. "She will be alright, she is no push over."

"Thank you Harper." She nodded as she shepherded her charges from the room.

"It is a good protocol you have put in place." Elijah told Reighn as he watched all the females leave. Reighn agreed as he watched the Battle brothers greet Ash. "I wish I could take credit for it, but this was Sage's idea. She and her team organized this. Harper, Phoebe and Charlie and our parents, quietly scoop up all the young and females and they all go to the stone apartment. With Thorn here now, it is even easier. His warriors help guard them, while my Shields and Hunters. As well as Conor's shifters and Olinda's unicorns, secure the town and people."

Elijah quietly said. "While we send our warriors to scout the town and territory."

Reighn nodded. "Yes, it seems to be working well so far, but as we discussed the more we train, the better prepared we will be."

"Agreed practice makes us sharper."

Fin came in. "No sign of any entry."

Reighn nodded. "Alright, are we all here?"

"Mostly." Storm agreed.

"It will do, we can fill the others in later. We are here because Ocean Towers has been kidnapped. We know this because of the note which Fin if you would please read out said so."

"Yes, My Lord. It states; by now, you will know we have the Lock. Unless you want her to die. You will hand over the world to me. You have until midnight."

Ace murmured to Conor. "You are remarkably controlled, my friend."

Conor turned darkened amber eyes on him. Ace just stopped himself from stepping away from the Lion. "Yes, although destroying the world to get my mate back, may be counterproductive."

Ace kicked up his top lip, "I can see that, you just keep on being reasonable. My giant friend."

Elijah asked Andre`. "When were you due back into your office?"

"What are you thinking?" Reighn asked as he saw the frown on his face.

Elijah shrugged as he asked. "Don't you think it is far too early for the note to be found?"

Andre` also frowning answered. "Midnight."

"What are you getting at?" Reighn asked Elijah again.

He rubbed his face as he asked. "Why give us so much time, it seems too long."

"He is right. They know us. They know we would not wait to look for her or them?" Storm said from where he leaned against the wall.

Ash put forward. "Because they are confident, we cannot find her?"

"Are they? Were we even meant to be looking for her yet?" Storm asked him.

"If you think about it, the timing seems to be wrong." Ash agreed.

Fin said. "They miscalculated somehow."

Andre` looked at Fin. "I am back early. I told everyone on Sunday I would be away until after dinner Monday night."

Reighn asked. "Why are you back so early then?"

Andre` shrugged. "My contact never showed, so I came home."

Lars asked. "Would you have gone to your office when you returned?"

"Yes, I always do, if I have been away."

Lars nodded as he murmured. "Where you would have found the note?"

"Yes, as I did."

"Hold on, how did they know no one else would have found

the note?" Kai asked Andre`.

Fin answered. "Because we lock our offices while we are away."

Saul said. "So someone knew that?"

"Yes." Fin agreed slowly. "Which narrows down the field somewhat?"

Saul nodded. "Because not everyone knows you do that?"

Saul grinned as Fin said. "Exactly."

"So they think we will not be looking for them until later tonight because no one would have known Reighn gave Uncle Andre` portals." Keeper mused as he walked in.

"Yes, we are actually ahead of them." Andre` stated, then asked. "The problems we have are threefold, as I see it. First; how do we find out who took her? Secondly; find out where she is being held. Thirdly; get to where they are without being seen or heard."

"I can solve two of those problems; the third is up to you Reighn." Conor told them as Reighn gave him a nod; they all turned to him as he spoke, he had been so quiet they had almost forgotten he was there.

Keeper said. "I did not think you had the same connection to your mate as we as dragons have?"

"I do not. What I have is a nose."

Fin said. "We detected nothing."

Conor's eyes went bright amber as he said. "You are not a First."

"Ahh... I see, of course, my apologies." Fin bowed his head to Conor, who asked Reighn. "Pass me the note please."

Reighn pushed it across the desk. Conor lifted it to his nose and sniffed, then he closed his eyes and sniffed again. Suddenly his body stilled and remained that way for minutes as they watched. Reighn was not sure he was even breathing.

Conor's forehead creased, and then he sniffed again. They heard a snarl softly rumble out of him that picked up sound until it was felt more than heard. He lifted his head and stared at Elijah. "One of yours. Loa."

"No!" Sparrow said, shocked. "No, you are wrong?"

Conor's amber eyes locked on hers. "I am never wrong."

"Well, you are now." She snarled at him. "Loa is loyal to her Queen, to the people of Dragon's Gap."

"I am never wrong." Conor stated simply as he placed the note down again.

Sparrow turned to Elijah. "My King, he is wrong."

"If he is, where is she? We called our guards to us. Where is she, Sparrow?" Elijah asked softly, anger riding his tone. Sparrow's voice filled with desperation along with a touch of despair as she told him. "She went into town to shop."

Johner came in, he gave Elijah and his guards a quick look, then said to Reighn. "My Lord, Captain Loa was seen talking to Lady Ocean, and then Captain Loa was seen pushing a large box on a flatbed cart and then loading it into a green van. Which she was reported seen driving up into the mountains."

"Thank you Johner, remain here please." He turned to Elijah. "Do you require any more proof?"

Elijah shook his head. "No, there is enough proof, Commander Sparrow?"

Sparrow's eyes were filled with bewildered rage as she asked anger and hurt in her voice. "How could she do this? Why would she? Her life was not hard."

"Because she is a traitor to us, to our home." Stated Elijah.

"I will kill her!" Sparrow vowed. No one doubted her words. Elijah placed a hand on her arm. "No Commander, you will do your duty and bring her to justice. She will confess her crimes and tell us everything she knows. Then she dies."

"As you will, my King." Sparrow agreed as her eyes hardened with determination.

Reighn asked. "Conor, can you find her?"

He smiled without humor as he looked at Elijah, then Reighn. "My Lord, where my paws have touched. I know who is on the land."

Andre ` commanded. "So find her."

He nodded. "I will, although My Lord, you know she is not

alone?"

Reighn eyes gleamed as he agreed. "Yes, he will be there."

There was a stunned silence as everyone assimilated what they were both saying. Then Fin suggested. "It could be a feint?"

Lars agreed. "We rush around chasing ghosts and he steals in and scoops up someone else."

Reighn told them. "No, I think he has who he wants."

"What makes you think that?" Johner asked.

"The note." Reighn said, "He calls her the Lock, he knows, we will move the world for her."

"That seems definite then." Lars growled as he said. "He is here, Definiao Kiltern. Which means Loa has been hiding and protecting him."

"I will kill her." Kai stated as he glared around him.

"Me first." Sparrow hissed.

Conor nodded to Saul and Kai. "Let's go."

Reighn called. "Wait Conor please, Johner I leave you the castle, secure it protocol one."

"As you will, My Lord."

"Brother remain alive."

Johner smiled at Reighn and Storm, then looked around at all the males there. "I will, and I beg you, stay alive your shadows terrify me."

There was muffled laughter, then Reighn ordered. "Storm, Ace, gather units to accompany us." He looked at Conor. "Find me where they are Leo, and I will open a portal."

Conor nodded as he and Saul with Kai walked outside but stopped as Rumoh told Reighn. "They will know My Lord. Definiao will feel it, as we do when you open a portal."

Reighn smiled. "No, he will not. I am the Dragon Lord, you only feel what I allow you too. Conor?"

"On my way."

He along with Saul and Kai hurried from the room. They slipped through the castle until they reached the back meadow, where he nodded to the unicorn stallion, who stood back waiting. Seconds later, he shifted. "Leo, we will protect the castle."

"I thank you my friend."

Conor shifted to his Lion, he shook his massive frame, then snuffled and snorted and walked farther away from the castle and placed his large dinner sized paws on the green blades of grass and closed his eyes, becoming silent and as still as a statue. Elijah asked. "What is he doing?"

"Searching." Saul said. "He has covered this whole place from corner to corner. East to West, North to South. Not one bit of ground has he not placed his paws on."

Storm raised surprised eyebrows as he asked Saul. "When did he do this?"

Saul grimaced. "When we first arrived, I was exhausted."

Reighn laughed along with the others. "It was very good he has done so."

"So you say. Your paws were not aching for a month afterwards."

Reighn smiled as all his teams assembled. When he was sure they were all there, he told them. "I will open a portal where the Leo indicates. For those of you who are dragon, remain human. Shifters shift and faeries the same. You will be our scouts. Do not engage, just find them and report back."

Hayden slipped in beside Sparrow. She took his hand, her eyes hard chips of ice. He squeezed her hand in comfort. She nodded but did not look at him again.

Conor shifted to human. "I have them."

Reighn moved to him as Conor leaned his head near him. It looked like he was telling him where to open the portal, but in actuality, Conor slipped along the mental pathway they had established months earlier. *Reighn I have them, they are here.*

He showed him the ground, trees and the cabin.

I have it, Conor.

When they were finished, Reighn turned and looked at the Battle brothers saying. "They are using the Tomas's old cabin."

All three brothers jerked at the use of the name belonging to their father. Ace said. "I thought that place was torn down."

"Apparently not." Ash muttered as Ark suggested. "We could

do it now with the rats in it."

Reighn grinned. "I like that idea. I know the coordinates. We will arrive a click away, scouts will go through first."

Instantly Elijah, his guards, Kai and Sparrow with a squeeze of Hayden's hand shrunk. Saul and several wolves shifted. When Reighn opened the portal, they ran through and disappeared. Conor, who had not shifted, stepped through with Andre` who asked him. "You did not shift."

Conor shook his head. "My beast would kill whoever was there or near her, you included, if I let him out. So best not to tempt him."

"You have much restraint." Andre` told him with admiration coloring his voice.

Conor grimaced. "It is hard won, but for my beast's sanity and my mate, who would not be pleased to learn he had killed on her behalf. Especially her new family. I will not release him. Although if she is not alive, all restraints are gone."

Andre` nodded. "For my family, I thank you, also know this, if they have taken her life, I will unleash the wrath of my dragon. We have just found her, to lose her now is not worth thinking about."

"I agree." Conor growled. "We will keep each other sane and human for now."

"For now." Andre` stated, both knowing death would follow in their wake if she was dead.

Within a short time the scouts returned, Elijah reported as he landed and grew. "We found them."

Sparrow said. "They have set traps for your kind and mine."

Storm asked. "Could you make out what they were?"

Elijah crouched down and drew a circle. "They have encased the cabin twenty feet out, with a wire it is set in the ground."

"With what?" Storm asked.

"They have adapted those damn sticks that have electricity, and there are wires around the doors and windows, from what I could see." Kai told them. While every one of the dragons and faeries frowned in worry, the shifters along with Saul and Conor were smiling.

"Why is this amusing?" Ace asked Conor.

Bringing the others attention to him and the shifters. Saul drawled. "Isn't that amazing, fancy them using that nasty old electricity?"

"Doesn't seem fair somehow." A tall lean male, who was obviously a wolf with blue grinning eyes stated.

Ark said. "Why are you grinning, it is not fair? We cannot beat that?"

"See, this is the problem with only magic uses." Saul said to Conor as Ace snarled to Storm. "Can I beat him?"

Kai growled. "No, that is my job. Get on with it, Saul, stop playing. What have we missed?"

The shifters laughed at Saul's affronted look as Conor told them. "It is not their fault. They do not really live and understand the outside world."

"But you would think the great, Definiao Kiltern would know?" Saul said with disdain.

Conor smiled. "Well yes, although a great male like he probably never even thought about it, which would be Loa's job."

"What are you talking about?" Storm growled starting to get annoyed now with all the references to magic and not knowing something the others seemed too.

"Electricity has to have an off switch."

"I thought only the one who turned it on could turn it off." Ark stated as several of the others nodded in agreement with his assumption. Conor told them. "No, anyone can, I will make sure you are all instructed on how electricity can be used later."

There were several smiles and nods as Conor said to Saul and the wolves. "Go find the generator."

They shifted and were gone, only to return minutes later with a location of the generator. "We have it." Saul told them, "It's under cover, they camouflage it with brush."

"Now what?" Andre` asked Reighn, who grinned without humor and said. "We go and talk to the happy couple."

Someone asked. "Will they come out?"

Conor nodded, "Yes."

Fin asked Reighn. "What about Ocean? Will they bring her out with them?"

"He will have to, to prove he is superior, that he has her life in his hands."

"And then we cut the electrical supply and rescue my Ocean." Conor growled.

"That easy?" Someone asked Conor, who nodded.

Reighn said. "Yes that easy, he wants an audience we will give him one. Plus we will have the element of surprise, remember they are not expecting us. I am sure we would have been contacted later and told where to meet, when Loa was back at the Grove."

"Acting all innocent." Sparrow muttered, seeing the whole scene in her mind's eye. There were a few grunts and snarls at Sparrow's comment.

"So we have that going for us, the surprise of being confronted by all of us. They, of course, will feel safe as well behind this wall of electricity."

"What of Loa?" Elijah asked Reighn, who shrugged. "We will leave that to you, bring her down so she can stand trial."

Conor waved two wolves over, "Shut it down at the Dragon Lords command."

"Very well Leo."

Reighn called out, "We move out, surround the cabin, take down any who try to escape, non-lethal, we want them to answer for their betrayal." When he finished speaking, they all moved out at a run with the scouts leading the way.

Within a short time, the cabin was surrounded. Reighn saw the two wolves split off and go to a small covered shed. One came back out and waved his arms. Signaling they had the generator secure and ready to be shutdown.

Conor stood with Reighn on one side and Andre` on the other. Saul and Kai were to the right side of the cabin he could see the faeries and members of his pride standing between the dragons. There was twenty feet between the cabin and the ring of warriors.

Storm stood on Reighn's other side, Lars and Stan beside him. He watched a dragon signal, letting Storm know everyone was in position. He nodded to Reighn, who called out.

"Come out Definiao Kiltern and Loa Karten. Wanted traitors. Come out and show yourselves!"

Loa fell from her chair as Definiao dropped to the floor. He hissed at her. "You were followed."

"The fuck I was." She snarled back as she crab crawled toward the window.

"Then explain how they found us and why now?"

"I don't know, they were not meant to."

"But they have, you fucking whore of an idiot female." Definiao snarled at her with contempt spilling from his mouth.

"Shut the hell up Del'. You crazy bastard, I told you this was a stupid plan to begin with. But no you had to play the big…"

"Come out Definiao Kiltern and Loa Karten there is nowhere for you to go!"

Definiao screamed out. **"Never, I will kill her first."**

Loa hissed as she sat up under the window. "Like hell you will kill her; we need her. She is our only way out of here."

"Do not tell me what to do. You fool, I know that, but they do not."

Loa took a breath and looked out the window. "Thank the Goddess they are behind the wall of electricity, it worked." She laughed. "I told you they would be foiled by that and halted at the line."

She started to get up when Definiao snarled. "Bullets can still pass through it, can they not?"

Loa slumped down against the wall. "Yeah right, and do not call me an idiot cousin, we are from the same blood remember."

"Come out Definiao Kiltern and Loa Karten."

Definiao called back. "We don't want to die."

"You will not die today."

"What assurances do I have?"

"My word as the Dragon Lord that is all you will get."

"I don't believe you."

Loa's eyebrows rose at the back-and-forth conversation. "What are you doing Del, are we going to give ourselves up?"

"Wait, Loa... Wait."

Loa slumped back watching her cousin, he was up to something.

Reighn called back. "I do not care if you do or not this is my final warning, come out or you will both die."

"She will die too, your precious Lock."

"That is a risk I am willing to take. Are you?"

Loa looked at her cousin. "Well?"

"We have no choice, if we stay here we will die eventually, whether she lives or dies they will kill us."

"So what do we do, die later... either way we are dead?" Loa stated.

"I have a plan."

Loa prayed. "Dear Goddess, another one?"

Definiao's face twisted in rage as he snarled. "Shut up, this one is fool proof. Even you should be able to follow it without trouble."

"You know Del' I could kill you and be a hero if I played it right. Tell me why I need you."

Suddenly his rage morphed into smiles and a beguiling tone entered his voice. "Loa my dear cousin. You know I value you, and this will work. It is simple and we will both survive. Because we are the last of our line, we owe each other to live our lives as the rulers of this world and beyond, remember this is our dream. No one can take it from us. We have worked too hard to fail now at the finish line."

Loa looked away and sighed he was right but still. "Fine but we rule fifty-fifty?"

Definiao smiled. "Of course... of course, would I cheat my only living blood relation?"

Loa muttered so he could not hear. "In a heartbeat." She smiled as they shook hands. "So what's the plan?"

When they did not hear anything or see any movements for a

while Storm said. "Looks like he didn't believe you?"

"He will." Reighn said. "He wants an audience to his greatness."

Conor commented. "You seem sure of that."

"I know him. He needs to tell me how he is better than me. That I am not anything more than a lowly lizard."

Just then the door to the cabin opened. Loa shouted as she walked out with her hands in the air. **"Don't shoot, we are coming out."**

Behind her was Definiao who was holding Ocean in front of him. She was unconscious and tied around her neck and waist to Definiao. Conor drew in a breath as Reighn said. "Steady, do not react, it is what he wants. Give him nothing, do not weaken our position."

Conor gripped Andre`s arm. "That means you too."

Andre`s dragon snarled deep in his chest as Reighn called out. "Does she live?"

"She lives." Loa smirked. "She is asleep sort of."

They walked halfway to the line of warriors, Loa in the front and Definiao with Ocean tied to him behind her.

Reighn said. "Well, let's get this done. What do you want Definiao?"

"I want an assurance we will have our day in court. We demand a trial to be attended by the world. I like how you conducted the trial of the dragons minus the Elementals. We demand that."

"I see and for that I get what?"

Definiao laughed. "Freedom as will I, together we will see if the people of the world worship you or me, as they should, as they will."

"No. That serves you, not me."

"I will give you my network."

Loa hissed. "What are you doing?"

Definiao grinned at her. "I will not need it, will I, when I am overlord?"

Reighn said. "A tempting offer, but why will the people of the world want you as their leader?"

"They will, you fool of a dragon. What do you think I have done all of this for, waged this war for. To over throw you from the position, you are unworthy to hold...

He remained speaking as Storm asked Reighn. *Do we have to listen to this much longer? He is a raving lunatic and is hurting my ears. Can I just shoot him?*

Reighn sighed. *Charlie's solutions are not always the right way of doing things.*

Storm sighed as well. He looked at the male spewing forth his achievements and how clever he was compared to Reighn. At least he thought that was what he was saying. He decided not to listen to the fool as he answered Reighn. "And yet in its simplicity it works."

Reighn agreed. "You are right, let's end this."

Storm brought his hand to his inside coat pocket, as Reighn hurriedly said. "Without gunfire."

He was positive he heard Storm sigh before he called out. **"Enough!"** The male stopped talking, Reighn said. "I am sick and tired of listening to an arrogant self-indulgent asshole that thinks the world revolves around him and only him. We are not here to dance to your tune. We never were, you are a speck on the horizon of my consciousness, when and only when I allow myself to think of you."

"How dare you?" Definiao raged. "I am the only true divine being. I have lived lifetimes waiting for the day to take my rightful place as a First' and Overlord of the world and beyond, then amongst the Gods and Goddesses, you will not thwart my divine right to do so."

Reighn looked at him. "And to do that, you have to kill and sacrifice my people?"

"No, you fool, not just dragons, all the peoples of the universes, it is the will of the divine that all Firsts rid the worlds of their abominations."

"To achieve what?" Conor asked as he took a step closer to the ring of wire.

“Watch out.” Loa hissed to Definiao, “He is going to charge it.”

Definiao snorted as he mumbled. “And if he does, he dies. I win still.”

Loa looked at him from the corner of her eye as she said. “That is not the plan cousin.”

Conor called out. “You think history will remember you as someone of worth?”

Definiao called back. “I am someone of worth and will prove it.”

Conor laughed a harsh sound of contempt. “I have news for you that is never going to happen. I am a First as many before me and many after me will be, but you are not and never will be. Nothing you ever do will make you so.”

“You lie I am a First, I am divine.” He screamed as his face twisted into a caricature of hatred.

“I do not lie.” Conor stated. “Ask those that stand behind me and see if what I say is a lie.”

From behind Conor rose ghostly forms. Males and females from all races and universes. Every one of them a First who originated a new species drifted to stand directly behind Conor.

“Dear Goddess, he is divine.” Said a stunned Lars as his eyes like everyone else’s beheld the ghosts of the past.

Reighn asked. “What did you think a First was?”

“Not this.”

Dragon Lord Kato Kingslayer and his shadow, moved forward they stood next to Conor as Kato Kingslayer raised his hand and between one blink of an eye and another. Ocean was taken from Definiao her lax body filled Conor’s arms as he cradled her next to his heart. “I thank you My Lord.”

Conor bowed his head to the Dragon as the Dragon Lord returned the gesture. “As we the First of all species thank you and your daughter for what you are to do.”

Then he and his shadow turned to Reighn and bowed deeply. All the dragons, Reighn included returned the salute and as suddenly as they arrived, they were gone.

Before Definiao and Loa recovered their wits and at a signal from Reighn, the generator stopped working. Sparrow flew faster than an eye could follow across the space dividing her from her target. She grew and hit Loa hard dropping her to the ground. Saul rose up behind Definiao knocking him unconscious, instantly there was someone to gag and cuff the male and female faeries.

Reighn opened a portal to the medical unit under the castle, Conor walked through with Ocean in his arms. Reighn looked around and told Fin and the Battle brothers. "Find what you can, then burn it to the ground. Commander Ace portals are yours."

"Thank you My Lord."

He and Andre` stepped through the glowing doorway, to join their family in a vigil for one of their own.

CHAPTER TWENTY-SIX:

Minutes after Conor walked through the glowing doorway and placed Ocean on the bed. Paige and Kadee came running in, only to halt when they saw their mother unconscious, pale and with marks around her neck.

"Mom." Paige cried.

Kadee screamed. "No, mommy... no."

Paige turned to Conor. "Daddy what happened?"

He scooped them to him, Kadee sobbing as Paige held tears in her frightened eyes. "Hush now my girls, your mom is getting the best care. Uncle Sharm and Auntie Ella will look after her now."

Conor could barely look at his pale, barely breathing mate. His heart ached for her as his beast snarled out his rage at the male who had done this.

"But why won't she wake?" Paige asked him as he hugged her.

"She was drugged." Sharm told them. "We will heal her, I have called for more healers." He told Conor, who nodded as Ciana and Sage walked in. "Granddad!" The girls called as they threw themselves into Andre`s opened arms.

Ciana went to Conor and hugged him. "Conor, she will be alright."

"Will she?" He whispered, aware the girls were close to them. "She has not woken."

Ciana held back her tears as she assured him. "She is a fighter, don't forget she just found us. She will not want to leave us now."

"Okay." His eyes went back to his mate as the room filled with their family. He found himself pushed into a chair and a cup of coffee in his hand. Frankie kneeled in front of him.

"It is okay, Conor. I will go get her."

"What Frankie... What do you mean?"

She gave his shoulder a pat. "I will go get her."

She moved to a seat across from him and closed her eyes. Conor shook his head as he frowned. Sometimes Frankie made no sense. Nothing made sense; he had to go.

"Conor..." Andre ` said urgently as Conor stood and made to leave. He would kill the male, and then his beast would stop roaring for blood. He was the Leo it was his right.

"Daddy no, don't go." Paige called to him, she could see the decision he had made in his eyes. Kadee hugged him around his legs. "Daddy no, stay with us, daddy please."

Paige pleaded. "Daddy no, please... Don't leave us."

Conor was in two minds. He and his beast wanted to go and claw and rip the male who dared to touch his mate. To kill him as his beast demanded, but as he looked at his frightened daughters who clung to him as though he was the last person in the world. He and his beast remembered a time he too had begged his father to stay with him. He shook his head as memories of that night swamped him.

Of a time when his father, the Leo of his pride had walked out to fight another pride, for an imagined slight to his honor. He saw himself again as a cub with Saul hugging their father's legs, begging him to stay home. He lost everything that night, his father, his brother, the female he called mother, when his father and those he was responsible for never returned.

Conor sat as the girls piled on his lap and looked up to find Patrycc standing by the door. "You needed to remember why you are who you are, and what you have to lose."

Conor, barely able to speak, managed to say. "Thank you."

A few minutes later when they knew he was not going to leave them. The girls calmed and slipped onto chairs next to him as everyone else did the same.

Sharm and Ella stood over Ocean in a healing trance. Prudence and Elijah with Scarlett flew in the window and grew, immediately they entered the healing trance. As though her body had a mind of its own, Kadee moved to her mother and placed her hands on her toes and cried out. “She is not there, she won’t come back.”

Conor removed her hand and lifted her into his arms as tears streamed down her face, he whispered to her. “Yes, she will, baby girl. She loves us; she will return.”

Kadee sobbed. “We are not enough.”

“Yes, we are, you must have faith.” Andre` told her. “We are more than enough, wait and see.”

He prayed he was right; he could not lose her. He feared to fall into the well of grief he had sunk into once before. His Ocean would live, she must for him, for her young and dragon kind, but mostly for a lion who he feared could and would destroy the world.

CHAPTER TWENTY- SEVEN:

Ocean looked around, the view from this room was spectacular. She could see the sun rising over the landscape, it was beautiful.

"What are you doing here?" Demanded a harsh voice she thought she would never hear again.

"Mother!"

"You are not meant to be here. Go away, this is my sanctuary."

"Well, it is hardly my fault. One moment I was walking around in town, the next I am here. Why are you here?"

"It was created for me after I left."

Ocean looked around at the beautiful room. "Is it a tower?"

"Yes, my tower. I live here."

It was amazing the walls were plastered smooth and painted a burnt orange. There was a curved bed on one wall and in the middle of the room was a daybed with a small table next to it. With a filled glass of wine and a bowl of fruit. The floor was warm and the wall her mother stood in front of with her easel was just a huge wide opened window.

"Wow, this whole place is amazing. Who sent you here?"

Helena shrugged. "How would I know, like you, one moment I was asleep the next I woke up here?"

Ocean bit back the retort hovering on her lips and asked instead. "You are painting?"

Helena sniffed as though the question was stupid, a normal reaction Ocean remembered to anything she asked her. "Of course, why would I not?"

Ocean could feel the resentments of the past clog in her chest as she looked at her mother. "No reason, just asked. Well, I will leave you to it."

Helena cursed her tongue, her daughter stood before her and she could find nothing more than sharp words and unwanted feelings to say to her.

"Why is that?" Frankie asked as she strode around her. "Your daughter is here, for months you have supposedly pined for the right to make amends for the wrongs of the past. Begging for a way to show her you loved her and are proud of her. Not only the artist she has become but the person she is, despite all the obstacles you placed in her way, she shines. That is what you pray for each night and yet when you are given the opportunity you ask for, to redeem yourself. All you can do is bark at her. **Look at her!"**

Frankie demanded as Helena stood staring out the window at the view. She turned and stared at her daughter, who appeared frozen.

Ocean stared back. Did her mother really want all that, it seemed improbable? Helena's voice was hard and unforgiving as she said. "I am held here, she holds me here, her anger and her resentment of my talent. She will never be as good as me, and yet she has the power to hold me here. Not allowing me to move on."

"Huh, I thought as much." Ocean smirked as she told Frankie. "Never could see the loving, sorrowful mother happening."

Frankie circled the female again. "As I did not, but I had to give her the opportunity to try." She said to Helena. "This is not about you, Helena. This is about your daughter Ocean."

"No!" Helena screamed. "It is about me, always about me. My life, my art, my passion."

"I was never your passion was I mother?"

Helena mocked as she looked at Ocean with hate. "You… Passion, how could you be when I was wronged."

Frankie scoffed at her words. "You were not wronged, you were selfish. You believed you were better than your sister. A sister you were jealous of. Tell your daughter who your sister is?"

Helena turned away as Frankie hissed. "Tell her."

"My sister was the one I gave the baby too, her sister alright?"

Ocean asked with disbelief. "Wait... wait. Ciana's mother is my actual aunt, your sister?"

Frankie nodded. "Yes, she was the rightful vessel for the Goddesses, but that night when she was to meet the dragon. Helena drugged Luna, then met the dragon in her place and became impregnated. You never told your sister what you did, for months you watched Luna suffer, she was heartbroken thinking she had betrayed her Goddess. Only when she was at her lowest, did you whisper to her, how you had taken her place and when she cried out in despair, you laughed. Then you somehow hid from everyone, even the Goddesses."

Helena smirked as she said proudly. "The power of my art protected me from their prying eyes."

Frankie nodded. "Oh, I see, magic... magic allowed you to hide. The gift of concealment, as long as you painted, you hid from those hunting you, clever. No wonder Ciana and Ocean are gifted, a mother with abilities and a dragon for a father, a magical combination."

Ocean stood amazed as she listened to Frankie, so much made sense now. Frankie circled the female once more, as she said. "Then when you had the baby, you were shocked to find out it was twins. What to do... you did not want one baby, but two would really screw your life up."

"I had to paint." Helena said defensively.

"One of the babies was small, weaker. So a plan came to mind you were never going to tell Luna about the child, but suddenly you had an idea to punish her..."

Words burst from Helena. "She stole him from me he was mine. Tony was to be my husband, but she took him from me."

Frankie clarified. "He dated you once and when he met Luna, he fell in love, it was fated, they married and you never forgave him."

"No, why should I, he was mine."

Frankie snorted as she continued. "So after you had the babies, you did what any narcissistic person would do, you paid someone to drop off the sickly baby to Luna. Not because you were worried about her. No, it was more dastardly than that. You were hoping she would die, and could show Luna how you once again, triumphed over her with the healthy baby and Tony would come back to you."

"Yes… Yes!" Screamed Helena.

Frankie laughed. "But you forgot about whose creation she was. The Goddess stepped in and saved her. I know she never told Luna, Ciana was a twin; what good would it have done? They could not find you or Ocean; you hid yourself and her so well from prying eyes?"

Helena moaned. "I was wronged again, the baby did not die, and I was left with her." She pointed at the immovable Ocean. "A freak, a girl that had no talent, she could not even give me that. I could have nurtured her, made her famous."

"To prove again to Luna and Tony that you were a better parent."

"Yes much better than them and that thing they raised, but would she even try to paint, no never?"

Ocean snarled. "Why did you not just give me to Luna and my sister?"

"Hah! She would have liked that. She had everything already, Tony and a healthy beautiful intelligent daughter. No… never."

Frankie told Ocean. "She did finally tell Luna and Tony of you. And every year on your birthday, she would send her a picture of you, until you were twelve. Just to torture her."

Helena laughed. "Some years, I would call her or find out where they were and go to her without you of course."

Faintly, Ocean said. "Of course."

Helen grinned. "No, she could never see you, I would show her a photo. Then she would beg and cry for you. She offered me money, a home, anything to have you. She even gave me a letter for you once, telling you about Dragon's Gap and where to find information about your father."

Frankie stated. "But you hid it away and denied Ocean as well as Luna. Then when Tony died, you never contacted her again, you left her wondering if Ocean was alive or dead."

"Of course I did. She had no right. She cheated me and killed the only man I loved." Helena smirked. "She lost, I won."

Ocean curled her fingers into fists and shook with anger. "Why was it so important to keep me; you could have given me to someone else?"

Helena turned from her and said nothing. Frankie said sharply. "Tell her or I will?"

When Helena still said nothing, Frankie told her. "Because of the deal."

"What deal?" Ocean asked as she looked at Frankie with bewilderment, then at her mother. Frankie replied. "The original deal the Goddess made with Luna. Helena realized the loop hole and took advantage of it, as is her nature. The deal went like this. She who gave birth to the prophecy will, as long as the child remains alive and within the home of the life giver. Hold the look of youth as hers."

Ocean thought over the words, then drew in a breath. "Oh, I see."

Frankie nodded as she asked. "Did you not wonder why she hid away from the public and stopped going to her shows, when you were a teenager? Why she never aged?"

Ocean eyes widened. "No, I guess I never thought about it. So that is why her sister was Ciana's grandmother, not mother?"

"Yes, even then she was older."

"I needed to paint and create. To give myself to the world."

"So you could be adored." Frankie stated.

"I supposed the Goddess assumed at some point the baby would mature and find her way to Dragon's Gap." Ocean murmured as she looked at Helena. "But there were two loop holes, one for Helena to take advantage of and one for the Goddess." Ocean said slowly thinking again about what Frankie had said.

Frankie agreed. "Yes, the Goddesses thought they made sure the baby would be cared for. And the mother would only have the appearance of youth, she would not remain young. Helena was devastated to learn that eventually her body betrayed her."

Ocean said thoughtfully. "They never counted on two babies?"

"No." Frankie sadly said. "They did not, originally Ciana was to carry both lock and key."

"But when there were twins, the key and lock became separated."

Frankie sighed as Ocean looked at her, she told Ocean. "Goddesses should not meddle in lives."

"I was wronged again." Helena moaned, bringing their attention back to her.

"She's crazy." Ocean said to Frankie, who shook her head. "No, she wants you to believe that, so you will feel sorry for her. But you are not crazy, are you Helena? You are just angry you ended up not winning in the end."

Helena snarled and flung herself from the window, screaming as she fell. Ocean rushed to the opening, Frankie sighed. "Don't worry, she is unhurt. It is just a temper tantrum. She is alright."

"What are you doing here, Frankie?"

"I think what you really mean, is how can you be here, Frankie?"

Ocean grinned. "Yeah… okay."

Frankie walked around as she said. "I am able to be here, because I am an Elemental in training."

"Oh, I see."

Frankie looked at her and smiled. "Well, you would know right?"

"Yeah, I know, my camera never lies."

"Because…"

Ocean laughed. "My Parker is also like you."

Frankie laughed, then asked. "Was that so hard? Parker will be alright, she has you and her dad, sisters and me, all our family. We won't let her lose herself. I didn't."

"Well, that is true. So Frankie is my anger holding her here?"

Frankie shrugged. "There is some truth to that, but what holds her here, is herself. Her belief she is right, keeps her in this place. The day she recognizes who and what she is, she will be released, until then she will remain here painting."

Ocean snorted. "Not a hardship, she loves to paint."

Frankie snapped her fingers and told her. "Depends on what she paints."

Ocean's eyebrows rose as she looked out at the beautiful scenery, then at Frankie, who pointed around the room. Ocean was amazed as canvas after canvas appeared one at a time lining the walls. Each painting was Ocean in differing poses and ages.

Frankie told her. "This is what she paints, every day, every time she lifts a brush. Portraits and scenes of you, images she combs from her memory, canvas after canvas."

"Does she know she is painting these?"

Frankie snorted. "Of course, what would be the point, if she does not see them?"

Ocean shook her head. "This must be hell for her... Oh my!" She reached for one that was the duplicate of the one she gave Ciana, except this girl had blue streaks in her hair, not red. Frankie looked at it and said, "Guilt, this should have been you with him."

"Hell... This is her hell!"

"Perhaps, but you have to remember, it is what she considers hell. She creates this each minute she is here. What she sees or dreams, what she eats, what she paints. It is all from her."

Ocean shook her head in sadness, feeling the anger and resentment leave her soul. "Will my not hating her. My anger at her help her leave?"

"Well, it won't hurt." Frankie wrapped an arm around Ocean and drew her to the window. "This is not your burden. It never was. You know that saying, we are our own worst enemy?"

"Yes."

"Well look around you, this is what it means." Frankie then took both of Ocean's hands in hers and said. "You have a choice now, stay with her and fight every day to be someone you will never be to her. A person and a daughter loved by her or realize she is incapable of love for you, her sister or the man she says she loved. She loves only one person, and that is herself. Do not accept that truth and stay. Alternatively, you can accept that truth and leave. Return to those that do love you and truly know who and what you are. You are better than this." Frankie lifted Ocean's hands, so she could see them as they were last time she had boxed. Broken, bleeding, swollen, a shattered mess.

"So much better than this. So I ask, which way is it to be my friend."

Ocean took a breath and relaxed her hands held in Frankie's and smiled as she realized all the anger, the hate was gone. Sadness was present and would be for a while, grief she knew would run its course, but there was nothing here for her. Guilt at not being enough for her mother vanished, making her lightheaded. "Home... home to my shadow and children. Home to you and my family."

Frankie's. "Good choice." Faded as she came back to lights above her and quiet crying, she turned her head and looked pass Sharm to her family, all of them. Sharm eyes found hers and he frowned, quietly he said, "Welcome back cousin, you had me worried for a minute."

She touched his cheek with soft fingers. "I am sorry. I love you Sharm, is Frankie alright?"

Surprised but delighted, he kissed her cheek and whispered. "I love you too cousin and yes she seems well. Your family awaits you, dear one."

"Conor!"

CHAPTER TWENTY-EIGHT:

The morning after an uncomfortable night in a cell beneath the castle. Loa was led in silence into the interrogation room by Sparrow and Daru.

In the observation room were Reighn, Sage, Scarlett and Elijah. Reighn had agreed when Conor asked for the interviews to be made available for any to see. He had been petitioned by members of his own family wanting to witness the interrogations. Some were viewing from the stone apartment, and others were in Reighn's conference room with a large screen set up. "We should have popcorn." Frankie suggested.

Andre` grinned as he agreed. "I like that, Jenny luv, remember that for the theater we are installing."

She laughed as she asked. "Are we installing a room with a big screen?"

Andre nodded. "Yes, an entertainment theater. It is my contribution to the castle."

Ethan said. "Maybe we could get one of those machines that make popcorn?"

June told him. "I can get those and will get us a soda machine as well. Popcorn makes you thirsty."

"Ohh! Yeah, good idea as well as ice creams we need ice creams for the movies." Frankie agreed as Harper hushed them. "Quiet, we will miss the opening line."

"It is not a movie." Charlie growled.

"Well, it sort of is." Frankie argued.

"Quiet again." Andre` quelled the argument he could see brewing with those two spoken words.

In the interview room, Conor sat at the table with Fin as Daru chained Loa's hands to the bolt on the table top. Sparrow chained her feet to the one on the floor. Then they retreated to stand either side of the door. Sparrow's face was expressionless unless you looked in her eyes and saw the rage and hurt there.

"Should she be in there?" Sage asked Scarlett, hurting for the Commander.

Scarlett nodded as Rumoh who was Commander of Elijah's guards said. "She wanted to, as is her right."

He, along with his second Dumoh, stood behind Elijah and Scarlett, their faces inscrutable as only seasoned warriors could be. Reighn commented. "Still hard on her."

"Yes." Replied Scarlett.

Conor looked at Loa and felt his beast stir. His anger was a palpable feeling in the small windowless room. Only with great control did he avoid unleashing it on the faerie who sat opposite him. When he spoke, his voice was laden with his beast in every syllable as he read out the words written in the report. "Your name is Loa Kiltern, not Kartern as you have led everyone to believe. You had it changed so you could climb the ranks of the High Queens guards and not be associated with your traitorous family or cousin."

There was no reaction from Loa, in fact she looked bored. Conor carried on reading. "You are almost nine hundred years old and not the five hundred you have also told everyone you were. You and your cousin Definiao Kiltern are the only ones left of your line. Due to the fact every one of your family, males, females and young were put to death by the ones they betrayed. You and Definiao were left alive, a mistake perhaps or just a lucky break for you both?"

Loa shrugged and sounded amused as she finally responded. "Who's to say, maybe they were not very good at their job."

Fin smiled like a shark. "That could have been it. You and Definiao were taken to your Grove. Where the Queen arranged adoptions to willing families, I have to wonder if she told them of your family's reputation."

Loa shrugged again, but offered no comment this time. "Regardless, Definiao's family eventually were relocated to the High Queen's Grove. You remained at your small Grove until your cousin found you again, whereby you started out on your campaign to take over the world."

Loa yawned, then adopted a small smile but refused to speak. Fin smiled as well, then said. "We know your cousin assigned you to worm your way into the graces of Queen Scarlett. It must have seemed like divine intervention when she was chosen to replace the High Queen's chosen..."

A little jerk of Loa's head was enough for Fin to stop talking, he raised an eyebrow. If he had not been watching for something, a tell-tale sign, he would have missed the involuntary twitch.

Conor smiled as Fin said. "Oh, I see, it was not an accident that killed the Queens light. You or Definiao killed him, so Queen Scarlett and King Elijah would be given Dragon's Grove, because you knew she was next in line for the position. Well done, quite clever." He applauded.

Loa could not help it, her smile grew a little more.

"Wow! That was some long game; they were playing." Edith murmured from her seat next to Sharm.

"Sleeper agent." Ash agreed, he grinned at their surprised expressions. "Olinda likes spy movies and books."

Conor asked Loa. "Nothing to say?"

Loa shrugged one shoulder carelessly and did not answer. His voice turned menacing as he snarled. "As the mate to the one, you and your cousin almost killed. I want so very much to take your life. In fact I want to make you bleed so much it is taking everything I own not too."

Loa's eyes widened as she lowered her head so she did not have to look into the burning amber eyes of Conor's, beast, because she believed him. She could feel the sweat slip down her back as Conor said. "Instead, I will make a deal with you?"

Loa's head came up and her eyes narrowed. She found it hard to believe the Leo would make a deal with her or be allowed too. After all, it was as he said, his mate she had lured into a trap. But a niggling sliver of hope still remained in her heart. That she would survive this, so she asked. "What deal?"

"Tell us everyone in Definiao's employ and his complete network structure as well as where all his funds are."

She laughed. "And for that, even if I knew that information, what would I get in return? A nice retirement plan or a nice safe cell, or no... no, let me guess a safe house somewhere hidden away with guards." She looked at Sparrow as she said the last. Sparrow returned her look without expression.

Conor leaned back in his chair as Fin smiled and said. "No Loa, none of the above."

She looked back at the two males sitting opposite her and smirked. "I thought not."

Fin carried on as though she had not spoken. "What you will get is to choose how you die."

This approach and decision had been agreed upon by the dragons, shifters, and faeries. As she had betrayed so many of the people, it was deemed a necessity, especially when so many wanted to end her life. This, as they expected it would, captured her attention. What was not expected by those watching on screens, was what she said next. "What if I call for Combaal?"

Clint asked the others in the room. "What is that?"

"Trial by combat." Birdy who entered with Joy, Paige and Kadee answered.

Andre` looked at the girls as Rene` asked. "Are you allowed to be here?"

Harper answered. "Joy is."

"Paige?" Ciana asked.

"Mom said if you say it is okay, we can stay and watch."

"Alright."

Harper asked. "How is she?"

Paige sighed as she said. "She is okay, her throat is better, but she has the shakes still."

"Cuddling dad makes her feel better." Kadee told them as she moved to Andre` therefore missing the smothered laughs.

"Granddad, will you come visit after this?"

He kissed Kadee's forehead. "We all will."

She sighed in relief. "Good."

"Do you want to be here?" Verity asked Paige, who nodded. "Yes, Lady Verity."

"Alright, well if at any time you wish to leave, let me know."

Kadee wiggled in beside Andre` as she asked him. "Is it okay if I hold your hand?"

He took her hand in his. "Of course my dear."

Paige sat on the floor between his feet and looked up. "Is this okay?"

Andre` grinned softly. "Of course."

His eyes found Rene`s as Ace and Harper made room for Joy. Rene` smiled warmly back at him. *You are as blessed as I am.*

Yes, I am so very fortunate. Andre` replied, then he asked. Paige. "Where is your mom now?"

"With Parker in the stone apartment with Uncle Saul and hundreds of shifter warriors and elven warriors as well as the dragon warriors. Grandma Grace and Grandpa Patrycc are with her. They are watching this on a screen with tea and coffee. We wanted to be here with you, and Birdy said she would come with us."

Andre` brushed her hair. "That is good."

Birdy took a seat next to Clint. "So what have we missed so far?"

He filled them in as she looked at Hayden when Clint was finished. Birdy told him. "She will need you after this."

He asked her. "You think Loa will choose Sparrow for this Combaal?"

"The rules state the one that calls for Combaal, cannot then name their opponent."

Joy asked. "Why do you have that rule?"

"So a Queen or King can have a proxy fight for them."

"A what?"

Ace explained. "It means a Queen or King may have someone else fight for them in combat."

"Oh, is that not cheating?" Kadee asked him.

Birdy answered for him. "No, in our rules it is allowed."

Clint asked Birdy. "So Loa will try to goad Queen Scarlett into calling for this Combaal?"

"She has to really." Birdy stated. "She would love to fight Sparrow, if the Queen calls for it. She, Loa will nominate Sparrow. Because Loa thinks she is far superior in her skills."

"You don't think she is?" Charlie asked Birdy, who shook her head. "I do not know. I can only guess that Sparrow is far better than she has ever shown."

"She could choose me. I would fight her." Harper said.

Birdy laughed as she told her. "That will never happen, Sparrow would never allow it."

Silence descended as they heard Fin ask Loa. "Are you calling for Combaal?"

Loa smirked, knowing there was no one strong enough that would go up against her. Time and again in training and in battle she had shown she was merciless. She was in a class of her own, she and Definiao trained for years, hard, unforgiving training to prove just that. Even Sparrow had never been brave enough to challenge her.

She would have been surprised to learn how many warriors had wanted to be her opponent. When Queen Scarlett had advised them of the very archaic custom of death, by combat that was probably going to be called for.

Loa smirked as she said. "I will have to, there is none here courageous enough to do so, even our dear sweet Queen will not." She swung her head toward Sparrow. "Or am I mistaken, Commander Sparrow, are you brave enough to call for Combaal? I am sure you know what it is." She laughed when Sparrow did not move or speak. "Oh dear, did little Queenie tell the good little Commander, she is not allowed to challenge me? Is that in case you get hurt and prove, once and for all how absolutely useless a Commander you are for your precious Queen?"

When neither Scarlett appeared nor Sparrow responded, Loa laughed harshly and stated. "So be it." She nodded her head to

Fin, after another look at the impassive Sparrow. She was positive she saw a flicker of fear in her eyes, which bolstered her decision to demand Combaal.

Conor said. "We need the words."

At her sharp eyed look, he smiled. "For the records, you understand?"

Loa drew in a breath and stated in a voice devoid of humor or warmth. "I Loa Kartern, demand as is my right, Combaal."

Fin stated just after her. "Let the record show Loa Kartern, formerly Kiltern demands the archaic form of trial known as Combaal."

Loa laughed, then sobered quickly, saying. "Good luck with that. You know if anyone is stupid enough to go up against me and I win, which I will. I walk free and clear and there is not a thing anyone can do about it. That is the beauty of trial by combat. It is a perfect trial for the strong and righteous."

"As far as the Faerie Nation is concerned, you are right." Conor told her. "Sad for you, you harmed dragons and shifters. So the trial is open for all. Do not forget that as you dream of your freedom."

Which managed to wipe the smile off her face as Queen Scarlett and King Elijah walked in. Scarlett without looking at Loa stated. "Combaal is granted, only after information is given and verified." Scarlett looked at Sparrow. "Commander select the opponent tonight if everything is satisfied. We set the time at dawn the day after tomorrow."

"Yes my Queen." Sparrow answered as she left the room.

Conor nodded to Dumoh and Daru who dragged the faerie from her seat and between them, escorted her from the room, her expression one of defiance.

Once she was gone. Fin called for the screens to be turned off. Conor asked Scarlett. "Who will you nominate?"

"Sparrow, she will not allow anyone else to fight."

"She could die." He stated worriedly, he liked the Commander. Scarlett looked at him and smiled, then laughed softly and with a nod to Rumoh, who quietly told Conor and Fin. "Before Sparrow became Commander of Queen Scarlett's guard, she was the former High Queens favoured champion. I think this will be her thirtieth Combaal."

Fin asked him. "Does Loa know this?"

He shook his head. "No one other than the High Queen, Queen Scarlett, King Elijah and myself knew until today."

Sage asked. "How can you keep something like that a secret?"

Rumoh shrugged. "If you are fully covered and masked, it is easy."

"Well that is understandable as to why you did not put up an objection." Conor said as he gathered up the single folder.

Scarlett agreed. "Yes, now how do we find out quickly if what she tells us is the truth?"

"You are forgetting Charlie, my light." Elijah told her softly.

Scarlett nodded as ravaged eyes stared at him. "I did."

He gathered her into his arms as he asked Reighn. "When will you interrogate Definiao?"

"Now, I want this done with."

"Who will you get to do so?"

Reighn smiled. "Ace and my brother."

"Storm, is that a good choice."

"No not Storm, it will be Keeper."

Elijah looked at Rumoh, who shook his head, he did not understand why either. Elijah asked. "May I ask why?"

"Keeper is the most terrifying interrogator we have ever had."

"Really! I am surprised, he does not look like he would be."

"That is my secret weapon." Keeper said as he and Ace walked in. "Now if we may have the room, he is on his way."

"Of course, we will leave you to it." Elijah told him as he moved with Scarlett from the room.

"Are the screens shut off?" Keeper asked Reighn who nodded, "Yes, this is just us."

After the screens had gone dark. Frankie had left the conference room. Charlie turned to Storm and said. "I hate this, how could Loa have done this to her, to us."

Storm's voice rumbled out. "Family is very strong, blood is loyal to blood. Her first allegiance was and will always be to Definiao. You heard Conor, there is only the two of them left."

Andre`s calm voice filled the room. "This is what happens when a race is long lived. It is a malaise we fight against all the time, especially with the nobles."

"Why don't I understand that?" Charlie asked, looking bewildered.

Andre` explained. "Sometimes the only ones to place your trust in is family because they live as long as you do. So if you have a... a..." He searched for a word that would not offend his granddaughters. "Rotten... yes, a rotten family like those two, it is hard to see anything else or trust anyone else. Family is family."

Conor walked in and both girls jumped up and ran to him. He hugged them tightly and sighed. "This is why the shifters are facing evolution, they trusted in blood, pure blood only."

"You say that like you are not a shifter." Charlie grinned as she teased him.

Conor inclined his head as he replied. "I am not. I have never been a shifter, just like my daughter Paige is not."

Bewildered as much as the others were, except for Andre`, Rene`, Verity and the girls. Charlie asked. "What are you then?"

"We are Firsts!"

"First what?" Harper asked as Joy giggled with Kadee. "We know."

Harper's top lip kicked up. "I am sure you do. You are so nosy, but I want to find out from an adult."

Conor smiled as he looked around the room; he could feel Paige trembling slightly, he hugged her to him as he reassured her. "It is alright, Paige."

She nodded but kept her eyes down until Andre` said. "Granddaughter, it is nothing to be ashamed of. Stand proud like your father as we do for you."

Paige's head came up rapidly. "I am not ashamed. I am proud to be what my dad is. I just don't want people to think I am weird."

Kadee laughed. "Too late, you are weird but we love you, anyway."

June grinned. "Kiddo, you just joined a family that are all weird."

Conor let out a breath as he felt the overwhelming warmth and love from the people in the room, who had come to mean so much to him and his family, flow out and surround them both. "We, Paige and I are the first of a new species."

Charlie's mouth dropped open as she looked at an equally stunned Harper who asked. "What the hell, does Ocean know?"

Conor and Paige both nodded yes to her question.

"What does it mean?" Charlie asked.

Edith answered for them. "That shifters are changing, becoming another species, better, greater, more of who and what they are now."

Conor told them. "Which is what the new species will be called. Changelings."

"That will manifest how?" Olinda asked, curious as always. "Do you know?"

Conor place his hand on the table and his hand shifted to a paw with claws while his body remained human. "Oh my, so you can partially shift. I have never seen that before." Verity stated, she looked at her shadow. "Have you?"

Rene ` shook his head. "I have not. I am going to say that apart from Conor, no one has."

Conor nodded as he said. "And until changelings evolve, you will not see it in anyone else."

Harper asked, fascinated with all that was being revealed. "What else can you do?"

Conor smiled. "Now Harper, you don't expect me to answer that, do you?"

"Well, I was hopeful." She answered wishfully.

CHAPTER TWENTY-NINE:

Definiao Kiltern was led in with Frankie by his side as well as King Elijah's guards, Rumoh and Dumoh, followed by Johner.

Definiao like Loa was also chained to the bolts on the table and floor. Frankie with Johner moved to the observation room where she was greeted by Reighn and Sage. Elijah and Scarlett having left earlier. "How are you?" Reighn asked her.

Frankie sighed. "Good, not as tired as I was last time I did this. He is very powerful but knowing who I am, has helped me squash his abilities."

"Good." Reighn hugged her, then Sage hugged her, saying. "Almost over now."

Reighn nodded as he looked at the three males seated at the table. "For today. The next few days will not be happy, he will call for Combaal."

Sage agreed. "Especially when he hears Loa has."

"Well, he would." Johner agreed. "He considers himself far more intelligent and stronger than his cousin."

"And it is his plan, he believes he will win and walk out of here a free man." Reighn told them.

Sage asked. "What about Loa?"

Reighn told her. "Scarlett said Loa believes she will also win and be free."

Sage mused. "I wonder if Definiao really considers her part of his plan."

Frankie stated. "This is why bad people always lose, because they are just dumb."

"And this is why we need a party." Sage told them all.

Frankie grinned as she danced in place. "Yes, we do. We need a big, happy, fun family Dragon's Gap party."

Definiao looked around as he waited for the two males to do whatever they had decided needed doing. He sat smugly, knowing his shields were impregnable. He had spent the better part of five hundred years learning how to shield himself from others, especially the so-called dragon Keepers.

What Definiao had no idea about was that while he had been rendered unconscious by Saul's attack. Keeper had slipped pass his shield and into his mind. It was an ability, not many, knew about or had. Keeper's gift allowed him, once inside a person's mind to disguise his presence by using the persons own thought patterns to hide within while he searched for information. Just like he was able to use their own shields against them, so while they thought they were keeping him out, they were in fact keeping him in.

While Ace would ask Definiao questions and they listened to the males answers. Keeper knew with the right question asked, Delfiniao's mind would search for the answer. In essence all answers were derived from memories, be that words, actions, or an actual event, and when those memories came to the surface of Definiao's mind. Keeper could search and find other memories of accomplices. Hidden bank accounts, and other people who had been turned into sleepers awaiting activation. What he wanted was the details to his actual plan. As well as anything that pertained to the plot against the dragon nation. He would search for information leading to someone other than Definiao being the mastermind. Reighn felt he would not find anyone, but it was better to be safe rather than sorry.

Definiao sat comfortably he knew it was only a matter of time before his people broke him out of here. If they had actually arrived as they were supposed to. He just had to bide his time, as long as he kept his temper and was patient he would not have long to wait. It was a shame he would lose Loa, but there were always casualties in war, she was just one of them and could be replaced. He had many followers, sadly not as devoted or as deadly as her, but acceptable and with training could be turned into weapons. He would miss her devotion, though.

Ace leaned back in his seat as he got comfortable, the male was, he supposed, handsome. He thought Harper calling him a pretty boy was accurate. He carried himself well, and it was easy to see he had training, he had callouses that denoted use of a sword, so not a wallflower as Charlie had muttered on seeing him.

He smiled and said. "So let us begin, I will not insult you or ourselves by pretending you do not know who we are. After all, Loa would have briefed you fully."

"She did. Where is the Dragon Lord?"

"Not here."

Definiao smirked. "Was he too afraid to face me?"

Both Keeper and Ace laughed, causing Definiao to scowl at their mirth. Ace told him. "Our Dragon Lord has more pressing matters to attend too. Contrary to what you believe or what you want to believe, you hardly register on his radar."

Definiao affected a bored look as he fumed. *How dear that dragon ignore me. I am the instrument of his demise; death is too good for the lizard.* Casually so as not to alert these imbeciles to his anger, he smiled and stated. "You lie! He is too afraid to face me, knowing I am the better male, the stronger leader. Is he hiding in his castle or behind the skirts of his witch? If he was a strong, discerning leader like I am. He would demand to face the one instrumental in the near death of his brother and his brother's shadow. As well as the death and destruction of his people."

His laugh was high pitched with a trace of madness in it. Then he suddenly stopped and eyed both males as he told them.

"If you think what happened at the High Queens court was a random act. You are wrong, that was all of my choosing. In fact I have waged war against the Faerie council, and your so-called Dragon Lord and his precious territories before he was even the Dragon Lord." Definiao could not help boasting, so perfect was his accomplishments he had sown the seeds of discontent and mistrust throughout the Dragons kingdom. Like all seeds he knew they would grow and finally he would take his rightful place as Overlord of the world as was his destiny.

Keeper relayed the male's thoughts to Reighn and Ace, along with. *The male is delusional.*

Ace nodded, letting Keeper know he heard before he told Definiao in a bored voice. "Our Lord knew, he just did not care."

Definiao laughed with disbelief, Ace thought he detected a little more crazy in the sound. He watched the male closely, even though he knew Keeper would let him know if he was pushing him too far.

Definiao repeated himself. "You lie, the Dragon Lord knew nothing. He is not that clever, my plans have been long in the making and are complex. A mere dragon could never decipher them."

Keeper told Ace and Reighn. *He is hoping if he stalls us long enough, he will be rescued.*

Reighn asked. *Does he say who he is waiting for?*

No, just that his people will come for him or he hopes they will, he is unsure if they are here.

Thank you. Reighn opened his phone and connected to Conor. "My Lord what can I do for you?"

"We may have a breach. Definiao seems to think he will be rescued.

"Our people are out patrolling. They have detained no one so far."

"Good, remain on patrol until further notice."

"Done, we will set up schedules. If Johner is there, we will need him."

"Good work. I will send him. Keep everyone safe, Leo." Reighn shut down his phone and looked at his brother. "Johner, you are needed."

"I assumed so." With a kiss to Frankie and an admonishment to remain with Reighn, he departed rapidly from the room.

Ace asked Definiao. "What is it you wanted to do Definiao,

why this long range war, what did you hope to accomplish?"

Definiao leaned on the table, his hands clasped together. "The people of this world need guidance, they are going to be inundated with other beings that have no right to grace our lands. Especially without rules, and this Dragon Lord you all protect will just allow them to return here. Before we know it, we will be overrun with them. Their wants and needs will strip the world once again of magic. Look what happened last time this happened. Your females were the ones to suffer and still do to this day. What or who will be next, maybe it will be the shifters ability to shift or yours that will be taken away. I can change all of that."

Keeper asked. "You think you can give that back to the females and keep the world from becoming a magical waste land again?"

"I do not think it. I know it. I believe I was chosen to do so. I am the only remaining survivor of my family. Why, because I was chosen to succeed where they failed. I alone can save the people of earth and the magic."

"What of Loa?" Ace asked. "Is she not of your line?"

"Loa?" Definiao gave a laugh filled with derision. "She could not even form two sentences until I found her hidden away. Everything she is today is because of me. It was I who taught her to fight, who taught her to climb the ranks. Without me, she would never be where she is now."

Ace asked. "In a cell calling for Combaal."

Definiao smiled. "Such a clever puppet. None can best her; I taught her well."

"It would seem you did." Ace agreed as he rubbed his chin, "She is very brave, not many would call for combat by trial. She must be very secure in her abilities to do so."

Definiao beamed with pride. "Of course she is. Loa is a merciless adversary."

"And you say you taught her?"

"I did, I excelled at her training."

"So you will call for Combaal?" Keeper asked off hand as

though the question meant nothing.

Definiao narrowed his eyes at the question. He thought about the implications and saw nothing to worry about. “Why would I not, my cousin is half the warrior I am?”

“Oh sure… sure you are fairly fit and look in shape but Loa trains every day.” Ace agreed with him, or so it seemed. “No, better for you to go to trial. I mean, if you called for Combaal it would force Elijah to have to accept the challenge and… well…” Ace shrugged. “You know?”

Keeper stifled a smile when he told Ace. *You have him.*

Ace silently laughed. *Really, it seems too easy?*

Keeper replied. *That is what he is thinking, he knows the laws well. He knows if he bests Elijah in combat he will be free, but remember he is convinced his people will release him long before that. Ahh! I see this is not part of his plan. He secretly wishes to humiliate Elijah. It seems Definiao is desirous of Scarlett and he believes there are none that can beat him, least of all Elijah. He has convinced himself when he wins. Scarlett will rule with him. Okay, see right there that proves the male is twisted.*

Ace agreed. *So twisted, needs to die for that alone.*

Definiao again ran through all the logistics of calling for Combaal. He had told Loa to do so, while he would be spirited away by his rescuers, leaving her behind but now as he thought about it. He realized there was not a faerie who could beat him. Certainly not that flop of a pixie Elijah. Then he would have his deepest desire, the one secret he had kept hidden since the day he had first seen her, Scarlett his Queen. Finally, he would be able to claim her as his. When that fool pixie was dead at her feet and he was shown to be the better warrior. He knew Ace was right. Elijah would never allow anyone but himself to have the reward of combat with him. Pride was all the King thought of. Elijah would have to show Scarlett she had chosen well, when she took him a pixie as her Light. How else to do that but to defeat Definiao in combat?

He stated with a smirk, knowing Elijah would be informed immediately. “I call for Combaal.”

Keeper said. "We need you to formally ask, it is for the records."

Definiao sneered at him. "Yes, I am sure you do, as will your precious Dragon Lord and Faerie court."

When they did not comment, he sighed and said. "Very well. I Definiao Kiltern demand as is my right. Combaal."

Keeper, as Fin had done with Loa, stated. "Let the record show Definiao Kiltern demands the archaic form of trial known as Combaal."

Reighn walked in, without addressing Definiao he stated. "The request has been granted."

Then before Definiao could say anything he walked from the room. When Definiao looked at the two males who were getting to their feet, he roared. **"HE WAS HERE ALL THE TIME?"**

Ace nodded and said with a smirk of his own. "Of course. He is the Dragon Lord. You trespassed against his family and people."

With that, they nodded to the two guards to come forward and unlocked the stunned faerie. Who was starting to realize he had been played? And as he watched the two male's leave the room, he knew there would be no rescue. He would be required to fight. In that instance Definiao added a little more to his reality, as pleasure swamped his senses and he smiled. If they thought they had bested him, these lizards should worry. For when he walked free from here, the carnage he will reap on them after this humiliation would leave them with nothing. He will take everything from them. Before now, he would have been willing for the Dragon Lord and his family to be banished only. Now they would die, slowly and painfully all of them when he became Overlord.

CHAPTER THIRTY:

Later that evening, Sparrow arrived at the cells beneath the castle where Loa was kept. Rumoh stepped out from the first room as she entered the corridor.

"Commander what do you need here?"

"Just a few words with the prisoner Loa."

"Granted."

"Rumoh has she fulfilled her part of the bargain?"

"Yes, she gave her statement to Lord Rene` and King Elijah, with Lady Charlie observing. They spent most of the day with her. She gave up everything she knew without a qualm. It was as though she was relieved to spill her guts."

"I have found cowards often are." Sparrow muttered as she stood looking down the corridor. "I never believed it would be one of ours, did you?"

"I did not. I had it pegged as a shifter."

Sparrow snorted. "As did I, what does that say about us?"

Rumoh grimaced. "That we are as not as enlightened as we think we are?"

Sparrow sighed and ran her hand through her hair. She looked at him and asked. "Did you hear I found my Light?"

Rumoh smiled, he, like most people liked and admired Sparrow and was glad for her. "I had not heard. Do I know him?"

She nodded. "Hayden Sorren, dragon."

Rumoh stilled as he quickly shifted through his memories of the dragons and his smile grew. "Yeah, that makes sense."

She asked with a frown. "Why does that make sense?"

"Only a dragon could hope to match you."

With a grin of her own, she nodded. "Well okay, I see that."

Rumoh asked. "What does he think of all this?"

Sparrow shrugged. "Justice is justice. Dragons are simple that way."

"That is true. Congratulations Sparrow, whenever any of us find our Light, it is a cause for celebration. Are you having a bonding party?"

She sighed as she looked at the mischievous twinkle in his eyes. "What do you think? Queen Scarlett and Lady Sage could not arrange it fast enough. After all this is done with, Hayden and I, Conor and Ocean, Ciana and Thorn as well as Lady Grace and Lord Patrycc have been informed a party will take place this Saturday. As there are four couples, it is billed as the largest Gap party ever, with games."

"There are always games." He said happily.

Sparrow snorted again. "Not like the old ones. Edee has the young girls helping to devise new ones."

"Oh!"

Sparrow smiled. "That is what I said. Well, that is for later, this is for now. See you when I am finished."

"I will be watching." Rumoh told her, letting her know she would be on screen.

Sparrow nodded, then with hands in the pockets of her trousers she continued her walk toward the cell. While Rumoh went back into the room, he was sharing with Dumoh, who lifted his head as he entered. "Great news about her and Hayden."

"Do you know him?" Rumoh asked as he retook his seat in front of the screen that showed Sparrow slowly walking along the empty corridor.

"Yes, I have trained with him and Ace in the mornings. He is a nice guy, a good fighter."

Rumoh's eyebrows rose, Dumoh never gave out idle praise, he would have to go to a training session and match skills with this male. Dumoh told him. "He has taken over from Fin at Broadswords."

Rumoh was surprised and showed it. "Fin, will not go back,

now we have caught everyone?"

Dumoh shook his head as his eyes also followed Sparrow on the small screen. "No, he is to take over the investigative unit. The Dragon Lord has decided it is needed."

"What will happen to Lord Andre`?"

"I don't know, we will see I am sure."

"True." They stopped talking as Sparrow reached the barred cell where Loa sat on her bunk watching her approach.

"Why?" Sparrow asked in a neutral voice. She had spent time since the interrogation deciding how she would approach Loa. Her first instinct was to just beat an answer from her, but she soon discarded that idea, mainly because she promised Queen Scarlett she would not and unlike Loa she did not break her promises. So she decided she would go with disinterest, knowing Loa's pride would dictate her answers.

Loa looked into the face of a female she had befriended. Granted it was for her own agenda and not because she particularly liked Sparrow. Although she admired her leadership abilities. She was, as her cousin Definiao had told her, a means to an end that was all. Loa shrugged as she stated. "He is blood."

"And we were what, a convenience, a means to an end?"

"Yes of course." Loa got off the bunk and moved closer to the bars that separated them. "I had my duty, my mission."

Sparrow looked away and felt her throat constrict in anguish. Then she hardened her resolve she needed answers. The problem was, she was unsure what questions she wanted answers for. "Is it all so cut and dried for you? How is it you can betray your vows to the High court and your vows to Queen Scarlett, how can it be so easy?"

"Because it is easy to lie in a corrupt society and Sparrow do not fool yourself, they are corrupt, unable to move pass the old ways. We need young fresh ideas to help safeguard this world."

"This is not you talking. These are your cousin's words."

"You fool!" Loa mocked her. "Who do you think fed him those lines, it was all me?" She hit her chest with her closed fist. "I am the push behind him. He was nothing until I came into his life."

Sparrow heard the boast behind the lie and sighed. "Even now you lie." She shook her head. "I did not really know you at all, did I?"

Loa laughed and to Sparrow's ears it almost sounded manic, but she was seeing behind what Loa expressed. She was not crazy, even though she was working hard to make her believe she was. No, Loa was proud and proved it when she scathingly berated Sparrow. "You saw what I wanted you to see, what I showed you. Look at you, the mighty Commander who had her eyes blinded and her ears stuffed with her own ego and saw nothing."

"At least I saw your cousin for what he is. You know he outed you, called you a casualty of war. That there were many puppets like you for him to control." She then hummed with amusement before she pointed out. "You picked a good one to follow Loa. The Overlord of the new world. Tell me were you to be the Overlady and rule by his side?" She laughed harshly. "It was never going to happen. He had plans to replace you with Scarlett."

"You lie!"

"Whose ego killed them now?"

Loa backed away from the bars, her face contorted in despair at the ring of truth in Sparrow's words. She whispered again. "You lie."

Sparrow shrugged as she asked. "Why would I have too? I don't care enough about you to make one up."

"Who is to meet me on the battlefield?" Loa asked, desperate to think of anything else but her cousin's betrayal. Sparrow looked at her and wanted to find pity for the obviously distraught female, but could find none. "Guess?"

Then she walked away as casually as she had arrived. When she came level with the room, the guards were in, she called out. "Rumoh, Dumoh. See you later."

"You as well, Commander." They both called as they watched Loa lie back on the bunk and curl into herself, her back to the bars.

Dumoh stated. “Not harsh enough.”

Rumoh murmured. “Sparrow will kill her.”

“I know, still can’t find it in my heart to feel for her.”

“Me either.”

Hayden leaned against the cooling stone wall of the castle, as he waited for his shadow to emerge from the cells.

“You lost son?” Ace asked as he came to rest next to him.

Smiling, Hayden shook his head. “Nope. Waiting for Sparrow.”

Ace looked toward the door she would come out of and nodded. “Did she go talk to her?”

“Yep, she wanted answers.”

Ace pulled on his bottom lip. “Think she will get any?”

“Maybe, but not the ones she wants. This has shaken her.”

“You need to have Lord Patrycc talk to her.”

Hayden squinted at him. “You think he could help?”

“He helped us. Why not her?”

“Good idea. So why are you here?”

Ace rubbed the back of his neck. “Need an answer to a question?”

Hayden frowned. “From me?”

“Don’t see anyone else here?”

“You know, you and your shadow are very much alike.”

“So we have been told. Now what I need to know is. Are you planning to have Clint live with you?”

“Yes.” He saw Ace’s shoulders droop a little. “But only when he wants to. Which seems to be one or two weekends a month.”

“Great!” Ace smiled light-hearted once again, “Harper, and I were worried you would be taking him from us. Not that you cannot, he is your family but…”

Hayden looked over at the mountains as he said. “His place is with you and Harper. He loves you both and I cannot take that from him, he is happy. Probably for the first time in years, he feels safe and most of all…” He turned to Ace and said. “He sleeps deeply now, he told me he had not done that since I went away.

So for that, I thank you and Harper."

Ace tried to keep the smile from his voice as he said. "Thank you. He is ours as much as Joy is."

Hayden cocked an eyebrow up. "He told me he wanted to remain with you at least until he moved into his own place."

"Which will never happen." Ace told him. "Harper will never allow it."

Hayden grinned. "I did try warning him about that. His answer was he is hopeful you two will breed a parcel of hatchlings and he won't be missed."

Ace laughed as he said. "Again, I say it will never happen."

Harper arrived and stood three feet away watching the laughing males, good she would not have to threaten death. She called out. "Did you ask him?"

Ace nodded. "I did, and he said he was staying with us."

Harper grinned and ran to Hayden; she hugged him, then hugged Ace. "Thank you, I would really miss him."

Hayden admitted. "I did ask him to stay with us at least a couple of times a month."

"Oh sure, he is your brother. I don't want that to change. He loves you."

Hayden smiled at the happy female. "Thank you for keeping him safe."

"Aww, Hayden, it was easy."

Arm in arm Ace and Harper said their goodbyes and left happy, animated and pleased their family was to remain intact.

"That was nice, you could have made it harder for them all." Sparrow told him as she stepped up next to him.

Hayden nodded as he turned his head toward her. "I could have, but we would have all lost in the end. Did you get your answers?"

She shrugged and started to walk with him. "Yes and no. I decided it did not matter anymore."

"Can you still follow through with the combat?"

"Yes, she betrayed us, almost got my friends killed. Allowed Definiao to enter the Gap. She would have killed Ocean without a thought and condemned the females. She has no remorse for what she has done and is proud of fooling us all. She needs to face trial."

"She does, for those reasons alone. Justice should be served. I am asking, is there no one else that can do it?"

Sparrow stopped. "Hayden, do you not think I am capable?"

He took her in his arms and nuzzled her neck below her ear. Then he spoke against her skin, causing little shivers of delight to skate over her. "My shadow, I worry what this will do to you?"

"Oh, I see!" She gasped as he nipped at a tender spot, then moved closer to his body, so he could kiss her better, when they heard a voice call out. "Get a room, seriously there are young about."

Fast as lightening, they broke apart to see Edith's smiling face as she and Sharm walked toward the lake. Sparrow called back. "Really, Edee!"

Hayden pulled her toward the car he had parked, waiting to take them to their home, and laughed at the blush that was stealing over her face.

CHAPTER THIRTY-ONE:

Dawn on the day of the trials found the arena filled with spectators who were there to witness a trial by combat.

Every person there knew what was to happen, this was not a day for winners and losers. Today justice was demanded and would be given; there would be no reprieve. Sparrow walked in from the opened gates, dressed for combat in a leather vest and trousers without her usual weapons, as was tradition. She looked resolved and every inch the Commander she was.

Ocean walked between Birdy and Ciana, her hand in hers, since her kidnapping she had not been alone, Conor, the girls or Andre` as well as Ciana and Birdy had stayed with her. No matter that she told them she was well, she had come to the conclusion it was for their comfort, more than hers. She knew as time passed they would relax and life would become as it had been, at least she hoped so.

"Ciana, Ocean, Birdy, good morning. I did not think you would be here?" Edith greeted them as they made their seats.

"Conor is to fight." She replied softly. "And I, like everyone else, need to see justice done. Otherwise, I will always wonder."

"We get that." Claire moved toward her and hugged her. "Hey, my friend, how are you?"

"Hey, is not a greeting." Ocean told her the same thing she always said to Kadee, which made Claire laugh. "Ocean you are a pistol."

Ocean grinned. "Good morning Claire, and thank you, I am much better, no more shakes."

“Good, Kammy is demanding we come to visit, will later today be alright?”

“You know you are always welcomed, please never wait for an invitation. We are back home after this. So all of you who want to come visit. The girls are to go back to school soon, so it is just us. Well Conor, Andre` Kai and Saul as well as Ian and Adam and Birdy and Ciana and Thorn but other than that, it’s just us, right Ciana, Birdy.”

Laughing, they agreed. Ciana whispered to Claire and Edith. “Her shakes were more from the drugs they used, rather than from residue fright. She says she doesn’t remember anything, so how could she be scared.”

Edith asked. “Do you believe her?”

Ciana looked away, then back at them. “Yes, I think it is what happened afterward with Frankie that upset her.”

Edith said. “Yes, we have to talk about that.”

Claire agreed. “Frankie has been withholding secrets.”

Harper leaned over and told them. “She plans to share with everyone on Sunday family day.”

Claire nodded. “Just as well, as there are some wild rumors floating around.”

Harper laughed. “I know, I started most of them, so funny.”

Edith shook her head. “You have a very strange sense of humor.”

Harper sniffed. “So says you.”

Changing the topic, Edith asked Birdy. “Birdy, why are you not with the other faeries?”

“That was not going to happen. The High Queen and King are here. So no.”

“Chicken.” Olinda said. “I like them.”

“Good for you.” Birdy grumbled. “She is not your relation. Kai got stuck being there. He is not pleased.” She could not help the smile spreading across her face.

They laughed as Phoebe arrived. “Hello.”

Ciana asked. “Phoebe, I thought you were with Sage?”

Phoebe grinned. “She was required to be present with the

Queens. She is not thrilled, but that is what happens when you are royal."

Ciana, trying not to laugh, asked. "Did you tell her that?"

Phoebe gave her an amused look and asked. "Was I not meant to?"

There were several grins and scattered laughter. Ocean asked. "Anyone seen Frankie?"

Harper shook her head. "She is here, she loves the High Queen and King, who love her. So she and Johner are with them."

Edith sighed. "I will be glad when today is over."

"As will we." Charlie said for everyone else.

Ciana asked. "Where are all your males?"

"With Conor or guarding." Charlie answered, then asked her. "Where is Thorn?"

Ciana pointed to where the royals were. Olinda squinted as she looked across the arena. "How come you are not there?"

Ciana put a fake expression on her face as she said. "Sadly, I have to be with my sister."

In a shocked voice, Harper asked. "Oh my Goddess, you used your sister?"

Ciana looked at her appalled face and back to Ocean. "Don't get it, do you?"

Ocean frowned as she thought, then said. "No, that is what sisters are for, isn't it?"

Charlie grinned. "Only in your world, in Harper's, there are whole other reasons for sisters."

Harper growled. "And you all have daughters."

Olinda asked Charlie. "What do you think?"

"Oh, I dump on Harper all the time."

Harper yelped. "You do?"

"Of course what are sisters for?"

"Speaking of sisters, where are your girls?" Edith asked Ocean and Harper.

Ocean said. "With the young ones and their nannies and a hundred pride members, elves and unicorns in the stone apartment."

"They did not want to come?" Claire asked, knowing the three girls, and expecting them to be here.

"Of course they did, but there is time for them to see this kind of justice." Harper told her. "Ocean and I said no, they bitched. Then their fathers said no, they bitched. When their grandparents said no, there was no arguing or bitching."

Claire laughed at the look on Harper's face. Obviously having to call in the grandparents was not something she liked doing, but she could detect a small amount of smugness from both mothers.

Edith murmured. "I agree with you and if we are lucky, we will never need to see it again either."

"Good morning Ladies." Grace and Patrycc greeted them all as they arrived.

"Good morning." They all returned.

Olinda asked. "Where is Lady Verity and Lord Rene`?"

Grace smirked as she told them. "With the royals."

"Oh okay." Ciana smiled. "Is Papa there too?"

Patrycc smiled. "He is not pleased."

Ocean asked. "How did you two miss out?"

"We are faster than them." Patrycc stated with a twinkle in his eyes. "We were missing when Reighn suggested people for the royal seats."

There were a few snickers of laughter at his smug expression. Harper saw Clint and Hayden, who were seated with the other dragons. Hayden looked passive, but she knew he was not pleased. He worried at the effect this would have on his shadow. Funnily enough, she mused, he was not worried she would lose, he was very confident in her abilities, it was more the after effects this would have. She asked Patrycc. "Lord Patrycc, will you be speaking to Sparrow later?"

With a smile, he inclined his head. "Yes as well as Conor."

There were several sighs of relief as Patrycc told them. "Ladies don't worry, they will be well cared for."

Then there was no more time for pleasantries or thoughts as the gate was opened and Loa was escorted in with five guards surrounding her. They halted four feet away from the relaxed, waiting Sparrow.

"What stops them just shrinking and flying away?" Asked the curious Olinda.

"Oh yeah, good point." Edith said, as they all looked at Birdy, who smiled and pointed to the royal seats. "The High Queen, she can suppress any faeries ability to use their wings or reduce in size. That is why she is the High Queen."

Ciana said. "And here today."

"Yes." Birdy agreed.

They stopped talking when Sparrow turned to the royal seats and bowed as Loa remained standing. She did not move from her position, nor did she acknowledge the Queens and Kings seated watching her. When Sparrow rose from her bow, she asked. "My Queen, do you still sanction Combaal?"

Queen Scarlett as the reigning Queen of Dragon's Grove stood. She inclined her head, her eyes on Loa, who refused to meet her eyes. "I do. There is no reprieve granted."

With that, the guards left the arena and Sparrow turned to face Loa, who smirked at her. "So it was you after all?"

Sparrow shrugged. "I did tell you?"

"No, you said guess."

"I am shocked that you, the great Loa, could not work that out? I mean, the clue was fairly obvious. Maybe I should have spelled it out for you?"

"You cannot beat me, Sparrow. I am fitter, faster and way stronger than you."

Sparrow shrugged. "And yet I will kill you and you will be lost to history as a failed traitor, just like your family. You will be another line in a history book; no one will care about. Sad for you."

Loa screamed her rage and slammed into Sparrow, who was waiting for just that move. Having studied Loa at training as any good Commander would have. She knew her moves, knew her tactics. Loa was not wrong when she said she was stronger than Sparrow and she was definitely faster, but she was also just so predictable.

Sparrow absorbed the impact and as Loa wrapped her arms around her, they fell back against the wall. While Loa was struggling to contain Sparrow, she was slipping her arms from Loa's grasp. And then with a well-practiced move she broke Loa's hold and punched with her feet as she bounced from the ground causing Loa to be thrown backward.

Loa landed in the dirt and skidded for a few feet. She flipped over and growled as she stared at Sparrow, who stood with her eyebrows raised and her hands on her hips. Spitting dirt and blood from her bleeding tongue, she snarled loudly.

"I hate you!"

Sparrow shrugged. "I know and do not care. Get up Loa so I can end this, then shower off your stench."

Loa leaped to her feet and slowly paced closer to Sparrow when she was within reach. She threw a direct punch toward Sparrows chest, who swiftly turned side on, receiving only some of the impact of Loa's fist. Not enough to throw her backward or incapacitate her, but enough to have her instantly retaliating. For a few minutes they spent time trading blows. Loa coming off worse for the encounter than Sparrow.

As hard as she tried, Loa could not seem to find a way through Sparrows defenses. It appeared to the warriors present as if Sparrow was toying with the faerie, maybe she was trying to increase her anger or wear her out. As they watched Loa, her punches became more wild and uncoordinated. Several seconds later Loa screamed in frustration as she threw several quick jabs toward Sparrows solar plexus, which she easily blocked.

Loa followed these up in quick succession with hits to Sparrows face which again she easily blocked, then she tried sweeping Sparrow legs from under her, which she also blocked. This must have been too much for Sparrow or she became bored because within a blink of an eye she dropped to the ground and flipped Loa over her head and was thrown a distance away.

Loa rolled as she landed then snapped to her feet and swiftly charged Sparrow, who stepped to the side at the last minute, unable to halt her momentum Loa ran straight into Sparrow's outstretched arm. Causing her larynx to be crushed by the force of her throat hitting Sparrow's immovable arm.

Loa collapsed on the ground, hands clasping her throat as she struggled to breathe. Sparrow crouched down next to her and brushed the hair from her eyes. "You were my friend, my captain. I trusted you and you betrayed me, and for that I want so much to make this last. To watch you struggle for every breath until the final one. To make you regret your decisions and believe me Loa I could so easily do that."

She looked up into the stands and found Hayden's eyes on her. "But I will not, my light expects much more from me and I find I want to live up to those expectations." She looked down into eyes haunted with the knowledge that death had found her. "I do not want you to go to the afterlife wondering how this happened. So I will tell you, freedom was never going to happen for you. You never had a chance, this is my thirty-first Combaal."

With that Sparrow hit her with a short hard punch to her heart, splitting it in half. Killing her immediately. She then stood and bowed to the royal seats, then walked slowly, accompanied by silence from the arena.

Justice had been delivered.

In a dim cold room, used for changing uniforms by the trainees. Dumoh turned to Definiao who awaited his trial.

"You are, it seems, the last of your line. Loa has been delivered justice. I would wish you luck but seriously for you the well of luck has run dry."

Definiao snarled and rattled his chains. "You know nothing. You think your King can best me, a full-blood faerie."

"Don't care how you die. Just that you die."

"Fool."

"Yeah... yeah." Dumoh said as the signal came to get the male ready to meet his fate.

CHAPTER THIRTY-TWO:

It was the first time, most of the people of Dragon's Gap had seen Definiao Kiltern, the mastermind behind the attacks against the royal family and peoples of their world. He stood surrounded by guards led by Dumoh as they entered the arena.

Scarlett looked at him, then Sage, who sighed and mouthed, *what a waste!*

Scarlett shrugged, maybe it was but evil was evil no matter what the package looked like. In saying that, there was no denying the male was beautiful, even for a faerie. Especially as he was reportedly around twelve hundred years old. Definiao was over six feet tall with shoulder-length blond hair and beguiling blue eyes. Scarlett thought one had to admire how he stood unbent under the weight of his crimes.

As with Loa, Definiao had called for Combaal and as with Loa, they who called for combat, did not get to name their opponent, hence Sparrow fought Loa. Definiao's opponent was not named yet, which Scarlett saw did not seem to daunt the male any.

He stood relaxed, stripped to the waist, oiled and defiant, knowing there was not one faerie who could best him, male or female. Definiao was not really surprised to find himself here. His chances of being rescued had been slim to remote and a foolish hope of a desperate male. But as he stood here in this arena, in front of this audience and what passed for royalty and his secret love who was held prisoner to their beliefs.

He Definiao Kiltern, the last male of his line, was prepared for his finest performance. Before he took up the mantle of the Overlord of the universe. As the gates to the training arena opened, Definiao was unsurprised to see Rumoh enter with Elijah. What did surprise him was the male that walked with them?

"What is the meaning of this, he is not a faerie?" Demanded Definiao of the High Queen, who ignored him. As the males came to within four feet of him, the three males stopped and turned, bowing to the royals.

Elijah then rose and spoke to the audience. "As you have seen today, this is faerie justice as asked for by the prisoners. Definiao Kiltern asked for Combaal, as is his right. Just as it is my right as King of Dragon's Grove to take up the challenge. Or in this instance, to nominate a proxy to fight in my stead. Conor Towers, Leo of Dragon's Gap pride, will fight as my champion."

Definiao screamed at Elijah. "No, this is not right, you cannot do that?"

"I believe I can, and furthermore I just did!" Elijah bowed his head to Conor. "Fight well my friend."

He and Rumoh turned about and walked at the same pace they had walked in, leaving a stunned Definiao and an amused Conor behind.

As with Sparrow and Loa's bout, there was no official, no rules. Just death. Together the two males waited for the king and his guard to leave the grounds. Although Conor suspected the male, as stunned as he seemed, was actually trying to figure a way out of the mess he found himself in. Rather than waiting for Elijah to leave.

He was right when Definiao said quietly. "I will give you a hundred million dollars to throw this fight."

Conor kicked up his top lip as he stared at the male with bright amber eyes. "To do that, I would be dead and what use would the money be to me then?"

"You are right. I will give you two hundred million dollars to walk away. Just turn around and walk away."

Conor's lip went up again. "Tempting, very tempting."

Definiao knew he was right; everyone had a price. Sadly, he should have studied shifters better, and especially Firsts, because bright amber eyes denoted how close to the surface Conor's lion was. Definiao started to relax and plan his freedom, when the giant of a male said. "However, my mate, which was the female you and your cousin kidnapped and almost killed with your drugs."

Definiao's face fell and his hopes plummeted as Conor told him. "Now my mate would be really pissed, and she can growl, plus my lion likes how she scratches in all the right places. So I will decline the offer."

Desperate Definiao hissed. "Three hundred million."

Conor frowned as he asked. "Just out of curiosity, where are you going to get that kind of money from? We seized all your accounts?"

"Impossible!" Definiao scoffed. "There is no way you have them all."

"And yet we do. Loa was so very helpful. I bet you would be surprised at how much she knew and the records she kept." Conor looked passed him to Keeper, who signaled they had found and seized the last of Definiao's hidden accounts.

Within days Conor knew they would have all the money and have found all the people he had used or wanted to use. Thankfully, they were sure once Definiao died, his control over these people would cease. In the last twenty-four hours, all the information Loa had given them had been checked and double checked for validity. She may have been a traitor to her race and friends, but she kept her word. For her, it was a point of honor. Conor was unsure Sparrow or any of the faeries saw it that way. He did not, as far as he was concerned, she was a murderer and a traitor.

Definiao, thinking Conor was distracted, suddenly moved and started circling him. Conor turned slowly, keeping him in his line of sight. He would not put it pass Definiao to try something devious. Seconds later he was proved right when Definiao grinned and asked. "Did your little mate tell you of the fun we had, while we waited for you to arrive?"

Conor remained expressionless as Definiao laughed. "Ahh, I see she did not. I am sure she also did not tell you. She was not always drugged. Should I tell you how I so enjoyed the little, sweet noises she made as I took her over and over again?"

Conor said nothing and kept his face devoid of the rage he and his beast were feeling. Definiao laughed. "Would you like to hear great lion, how she begged for more, how she told me I was the only one to satisfy her? Your little mate could not get enough of me. I call her my little sweet plum, all sweet and juicy."

Conor could feel his lion stir. *Do not let him see he is getting to you. You know he did not touch her.*

Maybe mate is too scared to tell us. Growled his lion.

Conor laughed. *No, you know better, she would tell us. Do not forget, Sharm assured us she was untouched.* Conor then asked his beast. *Have we dallied enough?*

Yes, kill him and let us wash this day from our body and mind.

Agreed!

With that Conor took one step into Definiao's body and clamped his large hands around the males head. Definiao started to scream and struggle, punching wildly at Conor's ribs as he screamed. "No... no... noooo." Conor twisted and snapped the male's neck, almost twisting his head off his body.

Beast.

Sorry, he annoyed me more than I thought he had.

Understandable.

Conor dropped the body, then bowed to the royal seats. Turned again and looked directly into Ocean's eyes, placing his hand over his heart. She stood and placed her hand over hers as tears ran freely down her cheeks. He then started the silent walk from the arena. This was not a time for rejoicing as with Sparrow, silence was their applause. It was a gruesome and archaic form of justice that no one wanted to be involved with or to witness. Conor was not the only one who was pleased this day would not be repeated.

CHAPTER THIRTY-THREE:

Conor stayed in the shower way longer than was necessary. He knew his family and friends were in his home; he was just not able to face them yet. He wondered if Sparrow was having the same feelings of guilt and anger he was. He stood with his hands braced on the shower wall and his head lowered, eyes closed as he allowed the water to pour over his back.

Suddenly small cool hands slid around his wet torso; he felt her body press against his back and her lips caress his skin.

"Why are you in here?"

"I needed time; this seemed like the right place."

"I see. Are you hiding from them, yourself or me?"

He hung his head lower as he finally said what had been in his heart since she had been kidnapped. "He took you."

Ocean kissed the smooth skin again and felt his shiver as she whispered. "Yes, they did."

"I did not protect you; I failed." His voice rumbled out, filled with his lion.

Ocean smiled against his warm skin. "No, you saved me, always you save me from being alone, from being like her. You give me freedom to be me, and you have saved me from being unloved. He did none of those things he said he did, he never touched me... you know this?"

Conor turned and looked down at her. "How do you know what he said?"

Ocean rolled her eyes. "Oh please, a male like that, against you. He had to say something and the viler, more disgusting it was, the bigger the chance you would lose your temper." She hugged him. "He had no idea who he was messing with." She took his face between her hands. "I know this is wrong. People died today, but thank you. I will not fear walking in town or being on my own. I will not fear for our girls, because you and Sparrow made it safe for us. You protected us. I love you."

Conor kissed her, then said. "I love you, my mate."

Ocean smiled as she told him. "Do not become swallowed by what-if's. I have learned that the what-ifs are just that, and they serve no purpose. Now as I am wet and you are wet, and we are both naked, you should show me once more how much you adore my body." She grinned at him and blinked, in what she hoped was a sultry fashion, until Conor cocked an eyebrow and asked. "Do you have water in your eyes?"

Pouting Ocean snarled. "No you..." The rest was lost under his kiss.

"Maybe they fell over or something." Kadee worried as she looked up the stairs. Joy frowned as she too looked where Kadee did. "Maybe your dad fell asleep."

"Well, he could have. I know he and mom have not slept for the last two nights."

"Oh, because they were at the stone apartment?"

"I guess, the bed must have been uncomfortable."

"Why?" Joy asked as she bit into a red apple while she handed one to Kadee who answered.

"Because there were a lot of noises from their bedroom, like they were trying to find a comfortable part of the mattress. I think mom fell out once too."

Joy shrugged. "I do that sometimes, when I roll over too much."

They jumped when Andre asked. "What are you two doing here?"

"Granddad!" Both girls yelled with fright. "We were going to see where mom and dad are, but thought they may be asleep." Kadee told him as Joy grinned.

Andre` smiled at the innocence of the two girls. "I think

your mom and dad just need a few minutes together."

"Oh, they are cuddling. Lions need lots of cuddles." Kadee told Joy. "I read that and told mom."

Joy nodded wisely, then asked Andre\`. "Were you looking for us, Granddad?"

"I was, because I wondered if you wanted to help me with the grill, seeing as you are not in school. I thought we could cook out. I have never done it before. Paige said you helped your grandpa often."

Kadee smiled as she said. "I did, it is easy I will help you. Joy, do you know how to grill food?"

"Yep."

"Well, let's go then." Andre\` said, before the girls ran to the kitchen Kadee stopped and asked Andre\`. "Granddad, can you tell us all about when you were a Pirate."

He raised his eyebrows in surprise. "I suppose I could do that."

Joy asked. "Were you really a pirate Granddad?"

"Yes, I really was."

"Wow!" Both girls had wide round eyes as they stared at him. Growling worthy of a pirate, he said. "Go, we need to grill and I will explain how it is was I traveled the high seas."

"Yippee!" They both cheered as they ran for the backyard.

Claire looped her arm through his. "Nicely done, Granddad."

Andre\` looked down at her. "Thank you, was that young Sparrow and her shadow Hayden, I saw walking in."

"It was, they came for family, and a grill apparently."

Andre\` grinned. "Well they are in the right place for both."

CHAPTER THIRTY-FOUR:

Saturday morning, the day of the big party dawned with clear skies and the promise of warm weather. Due to the amount of little ones and teenagers now living at Dragon's Gap. Lady Sage had decreed that the party would start at midday and go until it finished, or when people passed out from exhaustion.

Kadee was so excited it was her first Dragon's Gap party. Even though it was really a bonding party for her mom and dad. And Auntie Ciana and Uncle Thorn, Granddad Pat, and Grandma Grace. As well as Sparrow and Hayden. They did not want to be called auntie and uncle because they were too young. Which Kadee thought was wrong. Paige said they were really old, like older than her mom. It made no sense to her.

She sighed, then smiled, she was glad this week was over; it had been a bad week. People died, her mom nearly died. Her dad was sad, people had been angry and Loa had been a bad person which was really sad. Because Birdy had liked her, and she thought Loa was nice. But there had been some good things, too. Like she and mom, Paige and Parker had a new last name now. It was their dad's name, Towers. She really liked it; Kadee Towers lioness, healer. Yep, it was a good name.

And today was the day she would have her first class in healing with Uncle Sharm. He told her, after she had been tested, that she was exceptional and it was party day. Then tomorrow was family Sunday.

"Dear Goddess, shut up. I can hear you thinking from over here." Paige groaned as she placed a pillow over her head.

Kadee grinned. “Can’t help it. I am so happy. Party day and healing class.”

“Well, try to think softer. Please.”

Kadee giggled. “Sorry, not going to happen, I am too happy.”

“Hate you so much.” Paige grumbled as she dragged herself out of bed. Wrapping her blanket around her, she walked pass Kadee, who grinned at her and was still snuggled down in her bed next to Joy, who was still asleep.

It had not been an easy night for Paige. First Joy had cried in her sleep for hours, and then she had vivid dreams that kept intruding on her own dreams. And now Kadee with her loud thoughts. It all made trying to sleep in here impossible. She debated smothering her sister… or slamming the door, but did neither. Sighing, she knew her mom and dad loved Kadee, and slamming her Auntie Harper’s door this early in the morning was not a good idea, ever.

Usually sleepovers at Joy’s home was fun. Especially with Uncle Ace, who loved the same kind of games she did. And watching Auntie Harper trying to figure out what Kadee and Joy were laughing about was just plain funny. She padded soft footed to the balcony. She could have used the other bedroom, but she liked the balcony off the lounge. It probably had something to do with her being a lioness. She reached the lounger and snuggle down and scowled at the lightening sky. The sun was not even up properly yet. If she was tired for the party, she vowed, she would sit on both Joy and Kadee.

Harper stood looking at the scowling teenager and smiled as she asked. “Bad night?” She moved quietly onto the balcony and made Paige scoot over and threw her rug over them both.

“Yeah!” Paige sighed as she laid her head on Harper’s shoulder. She loved her Aunt Harper, secretly more than her other aunts. She found Auntie Harper comfortable to be with.

Harper asked now. “Want to tell me about it?”

“You can’t help and might get mad.”

Harper smiled. “Nah, its Saturday, party day.”

Paige growled. “Yeah, so I heard. That is all Kadee can think about."

"So what... you don't want to go to the party. After all the work you girls and all the other kids have put into it. With the new games as well as the Ferris wheel and merry-go-round and that dunking tank?"

"Yeah, I do, but Joy doesn't. She misses Axl, she cried in her sleep last night and then she dreamed of him. It was annoying."

"What? The crying or the dream?"

"Both, but the dream was worse. Will Axl really read her poetry, does Uncle Ace read you poetry?"

Harper laughed, then said. "Dear Goddess, no. Okay, I will fix this. You know they are bonded, right?"

"Yeah, it must be hard for them?"

Harper sighed, feeling sad for Axl and Joy. "Yeah, it is, but they will manage. Time moves on and dragons and wolves are long lived. They have plenty of time in the future."

"Although isn't it a bit weird she is bonded to her dads brother?" Paige stared up at Harper from where she had slumped beside her.

"Eww! Seriously, why do you say things like that? Do you girls have a competition to see who can make me crazy first?" Harper demanded of the teenager.

Paige did not want to tell her that Frankie had thought up the competition to see who could make Harper cry in horror. So she shook her head and apologized quickly. "Sorry, didn't think."

Harper grumbled but said no more, although now the thought about Ace and Axl was in her mind, she would not be able to shake it easily, *damn girl.*

Paige said. "I don't think we can kill him or her."

"Thought about it, did you?" Harper asked with a smile in her voice.

Paige grinned in return, this was why she loved her aunt she got her instantly. "A tiny bit."

"So what else?"

"Auntie Harper, I am scared."

"Of what. Is it that boy who was hanging around yesterday?

Because I can talk to him?"

Paige laughed. "No… not him, of this thing inside me."

"What your lion?"

"No, the other thing."

"Oh I see." Harper looked out at the lightening sky. "Well sweetie, it is not really a thing is it? It is you. I think you need to see your granddad Pat and talk to your dad. You are not meant to be afraid of yourself."

"Yeah, I know. Maybe I should take up a sport or something?"

A little baffled at the change of topic. Harper asked. "Well, what do you want to do?"

"I don't know, I could box, like mom does."

"That does not sound like you like that idea?"

"Nah, not really." She looked at Harper. "I do like blades a lot."

Harper grinned. "Well, I will see what I can do, maybe classes."

"Ooh yeah."

"You know Paige you are not meant to be hearing everyone, right?"

"I don't, only Joy and Kadee, Kelsey and Parker. Not that she thinks much, just about food and wet diapers. Funny, really. Of course there is Molly and Kammy." She looked at Harper. "Oh, I see, okay who do I see about that?"

"You see your Uncle Rene` he will help you shield your mind, to stop the dreams and other people's thoughts. Then you will not hear how happy Kadee is."

Paige eyes widened. "You heard that too?"

"The whole world heard her." Harper groaned. "Why else am I up already. If I am tired today, I will make that girl do the dunk tank. It will serve her right if the water is cold."

Paige laughed as she snuggled down next to her favorite aunt and talked about the parties at Dragon's Gap.

Around the time Paige was having her heart to heart with Harper. Ocean was having a somewhat surreal discussion with an Elemental.

Why dragon Ocean, mate to the Leo, have you called me here to your dreamscape?

"I wish to ask you two questions."

I see and these questions could not be better answered by your Goddesses?

"Maybe, but I do not trust them."

You do not trust the Goddesses?

"No, they have given me no reason to."

I see, well ask your two questions and then I will ask two of my own.

"Agreed." Ocean was not sure, but she thought she heard a laugh from under the hood of the robed male. "First question; I am going to assume you know who and what my daughter is. So my question is why?"

A hard question to answer. She, who you have named Parker, was born from necessity. One; to help someone redeem her honor. Two; to give her to you and the Leo, to enrich this environment and add to Earths magic. Three; an Elemental born from magic, is a bridge for what is to come.

Ocean thought about that for a moment, then nodded. "Okay, second question. If Ciana and I are the lock and key and the sun and moon dragons are here. Why have the females not transformed yet?"

Belief holds them to a shape. Cause just one to believe, and all will.

Ocean smiled. "I thank you."

Now my question. One. If he cannot do it, will you?

"No."

Two. Why?

"He will do it. He has the strength and fortitude."

We hope your faith in the Dragon Lord is justified.

"It is."

Ocean rolled over and snuggled down into Conor's warmth.

"Mate, don't ask males into your head, without prior warning; it irritates my beast." He rumbled in his early morning voice that sent shivers down her spine.

"Sorry." She mumbled. "I did not think it would work. Calling them to talk to me."

"Reighn told you that you had the potential of a Dragon Lord."

"Guess, I believe him now."

"So no more early morning visitors."

"Okay, let's go back to sleep. We have another hour before we have to get up?"

"Or we could cuddle. You know I am a lion and as a lion. I need lots of cuddles."

"Oh good, I like our cuddles."

"As do I."

CHAPTER THIRTY-FIVE:

Ocean sighed as Kadee once again yelled at her to hurry. "It's time... It's time. Mom hurry, it's time. We will be late."

Ever since she had returned from her morning healing class, she was trying to get them all to hurry. Ocean yelled. "Kadee we cannot be late to a party that goes on all day."

"That is what is so great about a Gap party, you can never be late." Saul announced as he came in from the kitchen.

"Oh, are you sure Uncle Saul?"

"Yes, I am sure, are you really going like that?"

"Like what?"

He looked down at her feet where she had no shoes on. "Oh no, I forgot." She wailed as she raced up the stairs.

Paige waited until she was sure she was in her bedroom before yelling. "We are leaving."

They heard her scream and a thump. Paige laughed. "She fell off the bed trying to put on her shoes. So funny."

Conor told her. "You have a warped sense of humor, just like your Auntie Harper."

Paige growled. "She woke me up early this morning."

Conor yawned. "I know the feeling."

Many hours later, the party was in full swing. People had come out in droves to wish the couples well and to unite against the horrendous week that Dragon's Gap had just experienced. The elves were seen enjoying the atmosphere of their first ever Dragon's Gap party. The new rides and games were big hits. The dunking tank was a very big hit with all the older family members taking a turn as well as several of the younger males. Ace and Storm had come in for a turn each and been dunked by their shadows, much to the young ones delight.

When the sun was leaning toward setting, Edith found Verity sitting alone at a table. Despair filled her soul, Verity's heart was broken, and she did not know what to do about it.

"What can I do to help; I hate seeing you this way."

"I do not understand why we have not transformed into our dragons. We have everything right. The sun and moon dragons are here. Both Ocean and Ciana are here, sane and unencumbered by emotions. Edee, what have we not done?"

"I… I don't know Verity. I just don't know?" Edith said as she shook her head in sorrow. "I don't understand it either."

"Is it because I have not been a good enough dragon? Maybe I did not do everything I was meant to?"

"Or maybe…" Ocean said as she and Ciana each took a hand and drew Verity from her chair.

"Maybe you have been too good a dragon." Ciana said as they walked through the party leading a compliant Verity. People parted to allow them to pass while leaving in their wake silence as they realized something momentous was about to happen. They arrived at the open area which had been set aside for the landing and take-off of dragons.

Verity finally pulled to a stop and cried again. "I don't understand?"

"We know." Ciana told her. "But you will."

Ocean looked into Verity's confused and hurt eyes and said. "You are such a good dragon and have been a loyal, dedicated Dragon Lady. You held your females together since your Rene` took office and then afterwards when Reighn became Dragon Lord. You held them through it all. Showed them how they could rise above heartache. Believing and accepting who you were, never trusting that there could be more. So I, Ocean Towers as the Lock."

"And I, Ciana Moonwalker as the Key."

Ciana said. "We ask you to believe in what is meant to be. Believe in the possibility of flight. Believe you are good enough!"

Ocean told her. "Your belief holds you human, let go. Believe in your dragon. Listen to her. She will lead you to the skies. If you will only believe."

Ciana and Ocean both kissed her cheek and then stepped away. Verity closed her eyes as she wondered. *Was it really that simple? Could it be?*

You will never know dear one unless you believe.

Oh my dear dragon, I do want to believe.

Then do so, do not hold to the ground any longer, let us soar among the clouds.

Within a blink of an eye, Verity the human became Verity the dragon.

Ocean laughed as she said. "He was right. If one believes all will believe."

Rene` moved slowly, with tears in his eyes, toward the dragon who was his shadow. "Oh my dear, I always knew you would be a delightfully beautiful dragon and now I am proved right."

Verity stood in all her forty foot glory, a beautiful bronze dragon with golden eye ridges and golden bands around her legs. Edith called out to her. "Oh wow, Mama Verity you are a gorgeous, she dragon."

"You should take her for a flight." Reighn told his father as he and all his brothers came to see their mother for the first time as dragon.

"Mama you are beautiful." Each one of her sons told her as they caressed her hide. Ocean nudged Rene` "Don't you think she needs to fly?"

Sage agreed. "Papa take her flying."

Rene `grinned. "What a wonderful idea. I know the perfect place for your first flight. Come, my dear."

Instantly Rene` transformed into his emerald green dragon and with a thought he gently lifted from the ground. Verity cocked her large head and watched him. Then she too lifted and reached for the skies.

Within seconds they were but a speck on the horizon as Reighn looked around him with a quietly weeping shadow in his arms. He watched as female after female transformed into their dragon and with wonder and awe left the Earth for their very first flight. "Look!" Someone called, and they all lifted their eyes to the sky as Keeper hovered nearby with a small, thirty foot female next to him.

"Ella!" Charlie called out. "You are beautiful."

There was no denying Charlie's statement; the female dragon was indeed delightful. She was gray with bronze rings around her legs and tail. Reighn inclined his head toward her, and within seconds she and her shadow were gone. Reighn looked down into his shadows tearful eyes. "Why do you cry, my love? We are witnessing a prophecy come to life."

"Happy tears, my shadow. Our young, if they are female, can look forward to transforming now. These are happy tears."

He looked at the softly crying Ocean as she was held in her mate's arms, as Ciana was held in Thorns while she shed tears.

"I thank you, cousins. All of dragon kind, thank you. Without you, this could never have happened. You have every dragons' eternal gratitude." He bowed his head to them both.

Ciana wiped her eyes and replied. "We thank you cousin, but in truth we did nothing more than be here."

"Will you not shift?" Conor asked Ocean and Ciana. They looked at each other and shook their heads no. Ciana said quietly. "Another time for us. Maybe tomorrow, this is more than enough for now."

They stayed looking skywards for what seemed like hours but was no more than thirty minutes as dragons male and female flew the skies in victory. Eventually, Edith, wiping the tears from her eyes, walked to Reighn, and smiling told him respectfully. "It is time My Lord."

It was as if those very words were echoed around the world, within minutes every dragon flying landed and stood with their shadows encased within their embraces. Reighn looked around and saw all his brothers and uncle, his friends and their shadows, faeries, elves, shifters and their loved ones, held in loving arms. His father and mother, Keeper and a glowing Ella, returned and were swarmed by children. Happiness surrounded him as he moved to stand within the circle of his family.

"Time for what?" Sage asked as she clutched his jacket. Reighn kissed her and put her from him. "Wait my shadow."

Mystified, she stood with Grace and Patrycc, who stood arms clasping Molly and Ava. For once neither of them reached for their father as he walked to the middle of the field while everyone became quiet.

For the first time since he had received the mantel of the Dragon Lord, he felt complete. Standing tall and strong with the power of the Dragon Lord wrapping around him, he called the mantle forward as his dragon surfaced. His eyes elongated, and a covering of red scales replaced skin. He kept his human form, and on his shoulders a short cloak of seven colors appeared. For the first time in history, gold and silver were included. Not since the time of Kato Kingslayer had the complete mantel been seen.

Reighn spoke with his dragon in his voice as the ancients sang from the stones.

I, Dragon Lord Reighn Kingsley.

Holder of the mantel for Dragon kind.

Holder of the mantle for the world.

Release Dragon's Gap from behind the veil of my illusion.

From this day forward we are part of the world, as the world is a part of us.

Welcome to our future!

THE END

Here ends the series of Dragon's Gap. I hope you enjoyed reading each adventure as much as I did writing the series. It will be hard to say goodbye to all the characters but I must as so many others clamour for their stories to be told.

So for now we wish the people of Dragon's Gap happiness.

Goodbye and let love enter your days...

"A Christmas Surprise." Will follow.

L.M. Lacee

Visit my website at www. LMLacee.com and sign up for information, FREEBIES (Love's Catalyst, Lars and Claire's Story), and updates.

Printed in Great Britain
by Amazon